LOVE'S TENDER TREATY

"I love you," he said quietly. The night was rapidly drawing away the last of the daylight, but he could still see the glow of submission in her dark blue gaze.

Without his mouth against hers, she felt parched and desperate for his kisses. "I love you more with each rising and setting of the sun," she whispered. After tonight, and by the time the next sun rises in the sky, my love will be even deeper. I feel as if I might burst apart with the love that grows within me."

Her lips parted to reveal an enchanted smile that could light up the darkest of nights, as her hands drew his face down against hers to resume the kisses that had turned a simmering desire into a lambent flame.

"I love you," she whispered once more.

"I love you," he replied.

APACHE TIGRESS

VERONICA BLAKE

ZEBRA BOOKS
KENSINGTON PUBLISHING CORP.

ZEBRA BOOKS

are published by

Kensington Publishing Corp.
475 Park Avenue South
New York, NY 10016

First printing: July, 1990

Printed in the United States of America

For Greg Wypych . . . a true romantic hero

Chapter One

Why wouldn't her feet move? They felt as though they were frozen to the spot. The night sky had given birth to a falling of snow that covered the desert floor with a coat of cleansing white where normally only dirt and cactus dared to dwell. The dampness seeped through the thin soles of the young girl's moccasins as the cold inched its way up her slender limbs, until the chill from the ground made her whole body shake in uncontrollable spasms. Her eyes filled with tears as the blackened smoke reached the edge of the village and spiraled up to mingle with the orange-streaked heavens of the new dawn. Still, she could not command her feet to move. Tortured screams of her dying people filled her ears before the roar of the fire overtook the permeating quiet that had ruled the land of Apachería only moments earlier. Morning Star could only stare in horror at the sight before her disbelieving eyes. Somewhere in that pandemonium of death were her parents and twin sister, yet she was helpless to save them.

She tried to scream out their names—to let them know that this side of the *ranchería* they could still run into the trees to hide. But like her unmoving feet, her voice also refused to work. The tears became oily streaks down her face as they mixed with the smoke, blinding her and making her choke, until the dark haze became so thick that she could not breathe and total blackness washed over her . . .

"Margaret? Are you awake?"

Margaret Sinclair bolted up in her bed and tried to focus her sleepy gaze on her surroundings. This was her dormitory room, not the Apache *ranchería,* and here, she was safe. Her shaky hand wiped away the perspiration which coated her brow, while she fought to control the panic in her breast. The nightmare she had just awakened from never changed, nor did it ever go away, and it was a constant reminder to Margaret that only an ironic twist of fate had spared her life on that fatal day eight years ago.

She glanced at the door with aggravation when another loud bang almost knocked it loose from the hinges. Why was Adam in such a rush? Every day, since they had arrived at this school, they had walked to class together, and not once in all those years had Margaret caused them to be late.

"I'll be right there, Adam!" She pushed herself up from the bed and grabbed her thin cotton robe. She did not bother to comb her hair before flinging open the door since Adam had seen her in this disheveled state at least a hundred times. Still, a bit of vanity caused her to run her fingers through the long tangled tresses that swirled in disarray about her face. As the door swung open she started to reprimand him for his rude attitude, but the young man on the other side didn't give her a chance.

This morning Adam's usually calm and controlled manner was not apparent in his flushed face or the rush of words when he spoke. "All the Apache children have been called together for a meeting."

Margaret gave a nonchalant shrug as she tied the belt of her blue robe in a neat bow at the side of her waist. "What sort of meeting?"

Adam leaned closer and lowered his voice, even though they were the only two people in the quiet hallway. "A serious meeting. A troop of cavalrymen arrived this morning."

A chill raced through Margaret's veins, although she tried to hide the alarm which threatened to overcome her. When her eyes raised up to meet Adam's worried face the terror inside her breast ballooned. But she silently reminded herself that she was in Carlisle, Pennsylvania—not Arizona—and they were safe here.

"What do they have to do with us?" Her voice cracked, in spite of her determined attempt to act brave.

Adam's blunt features conformed into an even more serious expression, making him look much older than his fifteen years. "They have come to take us back to our homelands in Arizona."

The same type of fear which always accompanied Margaret's nightmares surged through her breast once more, but she gave her head a quick toss and shrugged again. "That's impossible!" Her chin tilted up in a defiant manner as she added, "Perhaps they have only come to give us a report of our people's progress out in the West. I'm sure that's all there is to it." She only wished her inner thoughts could be as positive as the sound of her words.

"Oh Margaret! When are you going to stop believing all their lies?" The young man reached out toward her, but Margaret pulled away and backed into her room. She did not want to be disillusioned again, especially since Adam's intuition was seldom wrong about such things. But this time he was mistaken! Margaret had to believe in the promises of the white men—if she didn't,

9

she wouldn't have a reason to go on living.

"I'll get dressed and be out soon." Her words were clipped and sharp, in the manner of the high-bred white women who brought donations from the church to the Indian school each month. For years Margaret had watched and studied the women's every movement and manner. There was a deep desire within the girl to be exactly like those ladies who wore only the finest silk dresses and the most exquisite jewelry and furs. Someday, she constantly told herself, she would dress in such a manner, and she would ride around the city in a velvet-lined coach. But now Adam was trying to tell her they were planning to send them to live on some dirty reservation after all these years of being taught how to live in the white man's world. Never!

"I'll hurry," she added as she closed the door. She tried to push away the nagging doubts that shrouded her thoughts, doubts fueled by the look of doom on Adam's face. The white men wouldn't let them down again, she told herself as she quickly dressed in a simple cotton dress that the local ministry had sent. Grabbing up her brush from the bureau, she attempted to tame her thick hair into a smooth braid at the base of her neck and then secured the strands that didn't escape with a wide green ribbon that matched her dress. Her gaze lingered on the little mirror above her bureau. Just a few days ago she had turned sixteen. She was a grown woman now. Margaret turned sideways, smoothed her calico dress down over her softly developed curves, and smiled to herself. Today, after this silly meeting was over, she planned to talk to the schoolmaster about her plans for the future, which she hoped would include a teaching position here at the Carlisle Indian School.

"Margaret!"

"I'm coming." Visions of herself standing before a

classroom of students—her own students—danced through the young woman's head as she gathered up her books. Today was going to be a turning point in her life, she could sense it, just like she sensed other things which were going to happen before they even took place. When she was a small girl the Apache shaman had told her that her visions were a great gift. However, the teachers at Carlisle had dismissed her foresight as nonsense, so Margaret tried not to acknowledge most of her feelings about impending events. And, whenever one of her visions came true, she told herself that it was just a coincidence. Today, though, it was hard to ignore the strange sensations that pulsed through her. Her hopes concerning the events to come on this day were short-lived, however, for when she swung open her door, she once again saw the gloomy look on Adam's dark face.

"You don't need those today," he said with a motion toward the stack of books in her arms.

Not wishing to disagree with him, Margaret tossed the books back on the bureau without another word to Adam. She wanted to tell him that once this meeting was finished they would just have to come back to the dormitory for their textbooks, but his anxiety was beginning to affect her and she did not like the sense of foreboding that had intruded on her dreams of the future. In silence the couple began to walk down the corridor until they reached their next destination. They always picked up Dona on their way to class each morning. The Invincible Three—that was what they called themselves, ever since they had survived the attack of their village eight years earlier. Back then, they had known a world far removed from life at the Indian School. Nothing had remained the same, even their Apache names had been changed to titles befitting

11

their new environment.

The door of Dona's room flung open even before Margaret had a chance to knock. "Did you hear?" Dona said in a breathless gasp. "They've come to take us back to our people!" In a shy manner, her ebony eyes flitted from Margaret's face to Adam's, then quickly descended to the floor.

Margaret opened her mouth to dispute the other girl, but instead she found herself at a loss for words. An intense aggravation toward Dona flooded through Margaret. Sometimes, when Dona acted insecure and timid as she was now doing, Margaret just wanted to shake her. They had been friends for all of their young lives. Why couldn't Dona look them in the face when she spoke to them? However, as usual, Margaret's annoyance with the girl was forgotten almost instantly. Instead, Margaret had the urge to fling her arms around her two friends and hold them as tightly as possible, while reaffirming their pact of always being together. But the flushed expression on Dona's dark face was proof enough that her train of thought was exactly the same as Adam's. Margaret was struck by the realization that Dona was as anxious as Adam was to return to their people.

They had talked about the possibility of being sent to the reservation when they finished school, but Margaret had never believed it would really happen. She envisioned them always living at Carlisle ... they would all become teachers and remain The Invincible Three forever. It was not possible that everything Margaret had hoped and dreamed for their future would end up dead and forsaken like the barren land of the reservations where the rest of their people now dwelled. A feeling of desertion invaded Margaret when she realized she was probably the only one who did not want to go to the reservation if it turned out that Adam

12

and Dona were correct in their assumption about the meeting.

"Let's not jump to conclusions," Margaret said in a firm voice. For just a brief second Dona's gaze raised up to meet hers, but immediately dropped again. Margaret continued to stare at the round, dark face of her lifelong friend as she became aware of how vastly different she was from the other girl. She had never permitted herself to think of their obvious differences, and she didn't want to think about them today either. But until now it had never mattered. "Let's just get this over with," she added in a hushed tone as she turned away so that neither Adam or Dona could see the moisture which had gathered in the corners of her eyes.

Before they had even reached the room which had been selected for the meeting, Margaret's feelings of imminent doom had grown into a crushing fear. Her premonition that her life was about to change drastically was stronger than ever, but not in a way that brought forth the excitement and joy she had felt earlier when she was planning to speak to the schoolmaster about her teaching career. Now Margaret's gift of foresight told her that the bright future she had envisioned for herself and her friends was about to be buried before it had even come into existence. The terror she was experiencing made her feel as though her feet had become frozen to the ground . . . just as they were in her nightmares. She clutched Adam's arm as they reached the threshold of the classroom. His steps halted for a moment when her gesture caught him unawares. His concerned gaze met her frightened eyes as he nodded his head, slowly. A sadness came over his face when he realized that his beloved Margaret finally understood what he had been trying to tell her all these years, and his young heart was breaking because he would do anything to protect her from more pain. Yet,

13

he knew that only a power greater than his own could do that.

Lieutenant Wade nervously shifted his weight from one foot to another. In the confines of the stuffy classroom his long, navy blue jacket seemed heavy and inappropriate. Undecided as to where he should put his white leather gauntlets, he finally shoved them into his belt. They bulged from the side of his hip, making him feel even more uncomfortable. With his forefinger he stretched out the high collar of his starched uniform coat, but when he released the stiff material, he felt as if he were strangling. He should have found time to take a real bath, he told himself. He felt sweaty and hot from the long trip, and the quick sponge bath he'd taken that morning hadn't helped to rid him of the grime. Perhaps a large shot of whiskey for breakfast would also have helped to disperse the gloom that had overcome him from the first moment he had been ordered to oversee this detail. However, he reminded himself, it was not his appearance that would make an impression today. For the first time in five years of active duty the lieutenant found himself regretting his decision to join the U.S. Cavalry.

With determination, he kept his eyes averted toward the window as the group of children began to file into the classroom. Inwardly, he cursed the government and the U.S. Cavalry for their continued deceit and selfishness when dealing with the Indians. If it had been his wish to destroy the lives of the Indians he would have enlisted ten years ago instead of five, while the Indian wars were still going strong. Then he could have engaged in the bloody battles which had finally led to the fall of the entire Indian nation. But because he had not agreed with the vicious tactics used against the

Indians by his own people, he had purposely waited until the last of the renegades had been subdued before joining up with the Cavalry. It wasn't fair that he had been chosen to crush one of the few remaining dreams of the Apache nation.

The anxious expressions on the young faces of those who would be affected by this latest deception did not improve his disposition when he did glance toward the children. Shock joined with dismay as he noticed that the rows of desks were only half-full. Was this handful of children all that was left? Following the surrender of the Apache warlord, Geronimo, eight years ago, over a hundred Apache children had been sent to this school. The lieutenant was aware that many had died from diseases, but until now he'd had no idea the toll had been so great. Their faces all blurred before his eyes as he tried not to focus on any of the intent stares directed at him. He felt a thin layer of perspiration form beneath the brim of his black campaign hat, making his blond hair grow wet and sticky, until his hat felt two sizes too small. Damn the government! he repeated to himself. Damn this whole society!

"Good morning, students." The tone of the school-master's voice had an odd sound, which seemed to alert the children to the seriousness of the meeting even before the announcement was presented. He cleared his throat in a nervous gesture, then with a sigh continued to speak. "This is Lieutenant Wade with the seventh division of the U.S. Cavalry, and the man beside him is Sergeant Roberts. They have been ordered by the Indian Bureau to accompany all the remaining Apache children who attend the Carlisle School to the Indian reservation in Oklahoma. Please file to your dormitory in an orderly fashion and pack the necessary things you will need for the journey." He

15

hurried on with barely a pause for breath, causing the tone of his voice to grow high and strained. "You will leave for Fort Sill immediately following the noon meal, so do not waste any time with your preparations for the trip." With his required speech completed, the man gave the officer a quick nod and then backed away from the center of the room. "Do you have anything to add, Lieutenant?" he asked.

The schoolmaster's uneasiness did not help the officer to dismiss his anger or anxieties. Almost in a trance, Lieutenant Wade stared at the teacher and then moved his head from side to side in a negative gesture. Yes, there were things he wanted to say—such as how sorry he was that these young Apaches' lives would be uprooted again, that they would be taken away from the comfort and security of the school that had been their home for so long. He wished he could tell them how much he regretted what his people were doing to them, but words eluded him.

Lieutenant Wade was reminded of the school's motto, "Kill the Indian and save the man!" It was the belief of the government officials who had laid the groundwork for the school that Indians would be able to function in their new society only if their children could be made into replicas of the white men who had stolen their lands and slaughtered their families. The lieutenant sighed as this thought passed through his mind, especially since he knew this distorted view had never been the true intention of the U.S. government. The invention of Indian schools such as Carlisle had been merely a ploy to pacify the Indian sympathizers who'd demanded justification for the hundreds of thousands of Indians who had been murdered without cause during the past century. Even those running the schools were constantly deceived into believing that their efforts would eventually lead to a better life for

16

the Indian nation.

The lieutenant's eyes traveled over to the man who was his second in command for this grim detail. Traces of a smirk were revealed between the red whiskers of the sergeant's beard and mustache. On the trip from Arizona to Pennsylvania, the lieutenant's troop had voiced their vast satisfaction over this issue many times. The Chiricahua Apaches, who had been captured when Geronimo surrendered, had spent the past eight years in swamp-infested prisons in Florida. Most of the surviving children had been sent to boarding schools such as this one in Carlisle, but now all of them, including the prisoners from Florida, were being sent to reservations to live. Over the years, the Chiricahua prisoners had begged to be returned to the deserts and mountains where their people had lived for centuries, and they had asked that their families be permitted to join them there. White humanitarians in Washington had taken up their cause, and thought they had won this minor battle for the Indians. The government, however, had struck a final blow. The Chiricahua were leaving Florida after eight years of exile—and their children were joining them. Their destination, though, was not the cherished lands of their Indian ancestors. They were being shipped to a desolate agency in Oklahoma, seven hundred miles from their native homelands in Arizona.

The lieutenant's eyes again traveled over the group of youngsters before him, his gaze taking in the mode of their dress, which was starched and proper, and no doubt originated from donations made to clear the consciences of those in the local parish. The youngsters' thick black hair was cut short, and seemed so different from the unkempt manes of the Indians who occupied the poverty-stricken reservations. The look of uncertainty and distrust, which their ebony eyes had acquired since the lieutenant's first glance, were precise replicas of the expressions of their entire race, however. Wade was struck by the thought of how odd these children of Carlisle would seem to the Indians on the reservation.

His gaze stopped its close observation of the children as it came to rest on a girl who sat at the front of the class. She was one of the oldest of the group, and though her style of dress was exactly the same as that of the rest, her appearance was drastically different. Because he couldn't help but to notice the exquisite beauty that set her apart from the other girls in the room, his eyes lingered a bit too long. For a moment he thought she must be one of the student teachers. Then he took note of the high curve of her aristocratic cheekbones, the fullness of her soft lips, the undeniable look of disbelief in her crystal blue eyes, and he instantly knew why she was here. He looked away at once. Children of mixed heritages were at the worst disadvantage, for they belonged in neither the white man's world, nor that of the Indian.

Although the schoolmaster's words were still sinking into her disbelieving mind, Margaret Sinclair's blood turned to ice when she glanced up and caught the lieutenant staring at her. As the officer quickly looked away, anger invaded Margaret's thoughts of despair. How she loathed that look. But how many times she had witnessed that exact expression and the very same reaction! Is she here by mistake or perhaps just a visitor? they wondered at first glance. But then their expressions grew tense and their eyes clouded with a look of recognition. Half-breed. Ever since she had been old enough to know its meaning, Margaret had hated that degrading label, just as her parents had despised it.

Being one of the oldest of the Apaches at the Carlisle

18

school, Margaret immediately thought of the other children who sat with her in this classroom. She purposely avoided looking at Adam and Dona, not yet wishing to admit her gullibility for believing in the useless promises of the white men. But one glance at the confused faces of the younger children made her anger at this latest deceit turn into the darkest fury. She thought of all the children who had died from the white men's diseases, and of the children from other tribes who had left the school over the years—a few at a time. Margaret had always assumed they had been sent to other schools, or perhaps had left to seek adventure in the huge cities of the white man. Now she realized they had probably all been shipped back to some remote reservation where they would know only hunger and sorrow for the rest of their lives.

Her gaze finally settled on the stern face of Adam Washington. Although he was a year younger than Margaret and Dona, it was his quiet wisdom that the rest of the children followed when faced with important matters. But, unlike Margaret, he had never allowed himself to adapt completely to the ways of the white man. He remained true to his belief that someday he would return to his beloved Apachería. Until then, however, he learned all he could about the ways of the white men—their weaknesses and strengths—so that when he was able to go back to his homeland he would know how to help his people fight against their rule.

Margaret's thoughts returned to the first day they had spent at Carlisle. The school had seemed like paradise after the long weeks they had endured on a crowded, dirty railroad car headed for Pennsylvania. A great many of the children had succumbed to illnesses on the filthy train and did not survive the trip, but the stronger ones were herded into this very same classroom and told that everything they had been

19

taught by their families and tribal members had been left behind in the lands of their ancestors, and from that day forward they were to think only in the ways of the white men. Forbidden to practice the customs of their people, the youngsters had no choice but to succumb to the new ways. In those early days they had been filled with hatred of the white men who had killed their families and had taken them away from their homelands. Through the years though, Margaret had convinced herself that, with the exception of Adam, all of the other children felt the same as she did about leaving Carlisle.

A pang of remorse shot through her when she studied the younger children. They had been so little when they had first come to Carlisle, it would be difficult for them to remember what life among their own people was like; yet it appeared that none of them were distraught over the schoolmaster's announcement. In spite of their neatly pressed white men's clothes, it was obvious to Margaret just how different they really were from the white people they had been trying so hard to imitate. Had it always been the white men's intention to send them back? And if so, why had they brought them to this school? Once they were returned to their tribes, everything they had learned at Carlisle would be useless. With fancy clothes and education, the white men had taken these once-proud Apache children and turned them into people who did not belong anywhere. This thought raced through her head as Margaret blinked back tears and made a firm vow to fight back as she rose from her seat. She fell into line with the rest of the children hurrying past the schoolteacher and the two cavalrymen without so much as a glance in their direction.

Even the familiar halls seemed to hold a feeling of estrangement as the children moved silently to their dormitory rooms to pack for the unexpected trip. There was no discussion about this latest turn of events, because they had learned long ago that whenever the white men made a decision there was no need to dispute it. Adam Washington led the group through the narrow corridor, his gait tense and quick, a strange glint in his dark eyes that Margaret had never before seen. Leaving Dona behind, she ran to catch up with him.

"Why are you in such a hurry to go back to the hunger and filth that we once knew?" she blurted out angrily as she grasped his shirt sleeve.

His raven eyes were distant when he twirled around to face her. "Do you see how they've tricked us again? Why would they send us to Oklahoma when they know our home is in Arizona?" His face contorted with rage as he added, "But I swear to you, Margaret, someday we will be back where we belong; standing on the earth where our ancestors once stood, and living under the sky that Usen created for the Teneh Chockenon."

Hearing the Apache words come from Adam's mouth caused Margaret to grow numb and speechless. It had been years since she had heard the Indian language spoken out loud. She could barely even remember how to speak in the Apache tongue, but obviously Adam had not allowed himself to forget. The reality of returning to the old ways she had so desperately wanted to escape hit Margaret with full force. Refusing to give in to the hopelessness in her heart, Margaret moved away from her friend and hurried toward her own dormitory room. She did not understand Adam's feelings about Oklahoma, nor did she care. What difference did it make which reservation they were shipping them off to? What mattered was that everything they had known for the past eight years had just been destroyed.

As she slammed her door shut, she caught a glimpse of Dona and Adam standing together, but she no longer felt a part of The Invincible Three. Being back in her room only increased Margaret's anguish over the distance she felt between herself and her closest friends. It was bad enough that in just a few hours she was going to be sent away from the home she had grown to love, and sent to some barren reservation. The last thing she needed right now was to feel she was losing Adam and Dona, too. She told herself she was being foolish, and tried to straighten out her confused mind. This wasn't one of her horrible nightmares, however. They really were being sent to Oklahoma.

Fort Sill. Even the name of that horrible place caused an icy chill to work its way down Margaret's spine. She had heard stories of the pitiful life the Indians were forced to endure on the white man's reservations. Yet she had never imagined that she would be ordered to live at one of those desolate prisons. She had believed when she finished with her schooling she would be free to live as she chose. Maybe she could still go to the schoolmaster and convince him to let her stay? But just as quickly as the thought passed through her mind, Margaret knew it would be a wasted gesture. The U.S. Government had ordered the Apache children to leave Carlisle—one schoolteacher could hardly change the rules.

With a heavy sigh, Margaret stretched her slender form out upon the mattress and closed her eyes. She could remember a time when she didn't have a real bed, only a smelly animal hide thrown on the ground to sleep upon. Even this narrow cot with its less than soft mattress was better than the primitive beds she recalled from her youth. A glance at the three empty cots that occupied the rest of the room only sent Margaret's spirits into deeper despair. Two of the girls who had once shared this room with her were dead from chicken pox, and one had run away in the middle of the night in the hope of being reunited with her family in New Mexico. At the time of the girl's escape Margaret had been shocked that anyone would want to return to the ancient ways of the Indians who still lived in the distant westerly lands. Margaret never wanted to go back to that way of life. How could they expect her to do so? Here, at Carlisle, she had been trained and groomed to be a white woman. Now they wanted her to forget everything she had worked so hard to perfect in the past eight years. Did they really expect her to leave the comfort of this world to live in the squalor of the reservation?

Bitter tears filled the girl's eyes, even as she tried to blink them away. She did not want to move from this school, or out of this room. Nor did she want to forget the ways of the white man. Eight years was not enough time to wipe away the horror of her first eight years of life among the Apaches. With a pang of guilt and sorrow she thought about her parents and twin sister. It was not memories of them that she so desperately wanted to escape. She was still running from recollections of the bloody battles she had witnessed, the starvation that had cramped her stomach into tight knots, and the horror of never knowing what new torment tomorrow would bring—if they survived the soldiers attacks that night. Yet daily, in her mind, she still returned to the faraway land of her childhood. Not a day went by when she did not remind herself to be grateful for the abundance of food at Carlisle and the clean clothes she wore each day. She was especially thankful for the feeling of security that her life in the white man's world provided. But, once again, the white men had found a way to destroy everything, even that little bit of stability she had acquired during the past

23

eight years.

Margaret squeezed her lids tighter together, and felt the hot tears drop from her eyelids. The fear which lingered from her former way of life invaded her with such intensity that she found it hard to breathe. She commanded her mind to release the terrible images of her last days in Apachería. But like filings to a magnet they clung to her thoughts, distinct pictures of the burning village that had once been her home. She rubbed at her eyes like a pouting child; still, the memories were not erased from her mind. The recollections only became more vivid, until her nostrils were filled with the putrid smell of burning flesh and dried grass from the flaming wickiups.

If she had listened to her mother on that cold wintery morning, most likely, Margaret would have been slaughtered during the ambush along with the rest of her family. But she had awakened before the others. Ignoring her mother's repeated warnings not to wander into the forest alone, she had quietly slipped from the wickiup and skipped into the forest of Palo Verde trees, which surrounded the Apache *ranchería*. During the night a light snow had fallen, and since it was such a rare occurrence in this part of the country, little girl that she was, she had been filled with a sense of excitement. She had raced through the trees, watching with delight as her moccasined feet left soft imprints in the snow, and heedless of the distance she had put between herself and the *ranchería*. Her blue eyes stared up in awe at the snow-laden boughs of the towering trees, while her ears were deafened by the overwhelming stillness of the mystical forest in the early hours of dawn. She had always believed that Usen, the Apache God, had created this time of day just for her, and that was one of the reasons why she had been given the special name of Morning Star. Engrossed by the

24

beauty of the frost-drenched trees Morning Star did not immediately hear the roar of the distant guns.

But just as clearly as if it had been only yesterday, Margaret remembered the terror which had cut through her the instant she did recognize the frightening sound. At eight years of age, Morning Star had already survived far too many attacks from the deadly guns of the white men. She did not remember her flight back through the shadowy forest, yet even now she could still recall the sinister droop of the heavy, snow-burdened branches, which no longer appeared magical and inspiring. Within seconds they had turned cold and clutching, their icy boughs hovering menacingly over the path.

At the edge of the *ranchería* she'd halted her dampened feet, and remained frozen to the spot. She tried in vain to remember all the rules her parents had taught her about escaping and surviving an attack from the hated soldiers of the white man's army. But her mind would not function properly. Nothing but disbelief and fear occupied her thoughts as her gaze scanned through the thick gray smoke to where her parents' wickiup had stood. Even at her young age she knew the brutality of the ambush, along with the heavy veil of smoke, meant that when the fires died down there would not be a hut or person left standing. Around her the soldiers claimed the victory, easily cutting down the members of the small tribe. There was little mercy shown toward the majority of the children or the elderly, because an obsession had claimed the soldiers' minds. For ten years the Chiricahua Apache, under the fierce leadership of Geronimo, had managed to evade capture. Their cunning and perseverance were constant embarrassments to the government of the United States, and the heavy burden of this disgrace was placed solely upon the U.S. Cavalry.

Living constantly on the run for the past decade had left the cluster of Indians weakened and defenseless. Most of them had given in, due to the white man's pursuit of their beloved Apachería, and with heavy hearts had moved onto isolated reservations where they lived out the rest of their lives as prisoners and slaves to the white men who now ruled the rugged vistas of the Apache ancestors. The few determined ones, such as Morning Star's family, who still ran away from the restrictions of the reservations, dealt daily with the fear of another attack by the soldiers or death from hunger and sickness. Yet, they refused to give up their dreams of freedom and their hope that someday the white men would realize the grave injustices which had been meted out to the Indians. They believed Apachería would eventually return to the peaceful ways that had been followed before the invasion of the white men, and all of the people who walked through its enchanted mountains and valleys would live in harmony and friendship with one another once again.

That chilly winter morning long ago, the young girl known as Morning Star said goodbye to everything she had ever known in her Apache way of life, and began on the rocky road that had eventually brought her to the Carlisle Indian School in Pennsylvania. As she had stood rooted to the spot and watched her entire village burn to the ground, had seen her family slaughtered before her eyes, she'd known her days of hiding and running were finally over. All she had ever known was fear and hunger, even though her parents had tried very hard to make a good life for her and her twin sister. Yet, it appeared on that bleak snowy dawn that they would all cross over into the great land of the Usen where there would be no more suffering.

Margaret choked back her sobs as she allowed her thoughts to linger on her parents for a moment longer.

Oh, they had both been so grand, even toward the end when desperate circumstances had worn their clothes to rags and their bodies were thin and weak. Her father, Nachae had been a proud man, determined to live out his days in freedom rather than on the white men's dreaded reservations. His wish had been fulfilled in that he had died in his cherished hills of Apachería. And then there was Sky Dreamer, Margaret's lovely young mother. Margaret still could not bear the thought of her beautiful mother dying the hideous death most Indian women met at the hands of the soldiers. It was a small consolation, but Margaret had one thing to be grateful for when she thought back to that awful day. She had not actually witnessed the murders of her family. By the time she had returned from the forest, most of the villagers were already burned beyond recognition. She remembered watching as soldiers speared the smoking and blackened bodies on their bayonets and flung them into a pile like a stack of broken toys. One charred body was that of another child, and Margaret had wondered if it was her twin sister, Echo. But the fear of knowing for certain had prevented her from going any closer to the charred corpse.

"Damn! She's got blue eyes." Those few words continued to echo through Margaret's mind whenever she thought about her tribe's last battle in Apachería. Blue eyes. How absurd it seemed to think it had been her blue eyes that had saved her from the long knives of the soldiers on that deadly dawn. Blue eyes. Her twin sister had had blue eyes, too, and her mother's eyes were as violet as the desert sunset. Even her father's gaze was granite gray—so different from the dark ebony eyes of the rest of the Apache clan. Why hadn't the soldiers noticed their eyes? Margaret constantly asked herself. Why couldn't the soldiers have spared the rest of her family in the same manner that they had spared her? She did not like to speculate on this thought very often, because then she would begin to grow angry with her parents. She would find herself wondering why they had chosen to put their own lives, and those of their children, in such peril, to live in squalor when they could have opted to do something vastly different.

Margaret pulled herself up from her bed and stood before the mirror hanging above her bureau. "Blue Eyes!" she repeated to herself. Her eyes were not just blue, they were a rich turquoise blue—as startling a shade of turquoise as the most precious stones that lay within the mysterious mountains of Apachería. She turned her face slightly to the side and observed her profile, while thinking of the parents who had created eyes of such an unusual hue and skin which was a deep shade of apricot. Half-Apache and half-white . . . How different everything would have turned out if they had all followed their white birthrights, rather than their Apache heritage.

Her observation of herself in the mirror grew more critical, and the terrifying memories of her youth slowly began to ebb away as she smoothed back stray tendrils of dark hair which refused to conform to the braid at the back of her head. She was still considered one of the "Indian children." How absurd! she thought to herself. At sixteen years of age she was hardly a child, and the reflection in the mirror was proof. Even more important was the type of woman it portrayed. The differences she had observed between herself and Dona earlier became even more distinct as she imagined herself no longer dressed in the simple garments provided by the Carlisle Indian School and instead wearing gowns of velvet and lace. With her hair done up properly in the latest style, and perhaps with a touch of makeup, it would be impossible to distinguish her from any white woman. At the very least, she was certain she could pass for a high-bred Spanish señorita.

The worry and fear evoked by the deception her mind was considering was evident in Margaret's dark turquoise eyes as she turned from the mirror and drew her dark brows together in deep thought. She knew she would have to carry out her plan alone because Adam and Dona would never allow her to go through with it if she confided in them. Pretending to be a white woman by denying her Apache heritage would be extremely risky, but living on some remote reservation in Oklahoma was by far the worst of Margaret's options. Although she knew the white men's hatred of the Indians had mellowed considerably, even to the point, in some instances, of compassion for the way Indians had been slaughtered by the U.S. armies, she could only judge their attitudes by what went on inside the walls of this school. However, she did recall hearing that even the dreaded and fierce, Geronimo, had become a sideshow attraction in Buffalo Bill's traveling Wild West Show. Surely that must mean that Indians were becoming a part of the white men's world.

Margaret turned back to stare at herself in the mirror, although she was no longer observing her own image. She was trying to imagine what the reservation must look like, and trying to justify the white men's decision to take away the Indians' own land and force them onto reservations to live like prisoners—but there was no justice in this deranged plan. The Indians would never be accepted in the white men's world! And because of her Apache bloodline she would not be accepted either, or else she would be living with some kindly white family, rather than here with the "Indian children." But, Margaret told herself, that is only because everyone here knows about my Apache

29

background. If I were to go somewhere where no one knew me, or was aware of my past, what could possibly stop me from carrying out my plan to live as I wish? However, if I am able to pass for a white woman and my deception is eventually discovered . . . well . . .

Margaret shook off the shiver that raced down her spine. She just would not allow that to happen!

Chapter Two

Travis Wade leaned his tall frame against the gnarled trunk of an old oak tree that stood in front of the school. His attempt to calm the nervous flutter in the pit of his stomach with a cigarette only seemed to increase the upset with each puff. Finally, in aggravation, he tossed the butt on the ground and crushed it into the dirt using an unnecessary force from his boot. Until this latest detail he had been completely happy with his decision to make a career out of the U.S. Cavalry. Patrolling the border towns between the United States and Mexico was usually a very easy task. Every so often some excitement would occur with the chase of American outlaws fleeing into Mexico, or when the comancheros who lived in Mexico became brave enough to conduct a raid on the other side of their own border. It was a life the lieutenant had grown comfortable with during the past five years. He rather liked having a bit of prestige and power. That is, until his position had commanded him to be in charge of transporting a group of scared children to some poverty-stricken reservation in Oklahoma!

His thoughts traveled back to the classroom, where

he recalled the confused faces of the small cluster of children who still resided at Carlisle. What would it have mattered to let them stay here for a while longer? he wondered in aggravation. He envisioned the girl again. Why did her face keep flashing before his eyes? Unconsciously, he shook his head and sighed. She was extraordinarily beautiful, but she was a half-breed. Once she was living on the reservation and the sun had turned her delicate-hued skin into ruddy brown and her silken tresses had become brittle and dry from the same scorching rays, she would hardly be distinguishable from the rest of the Apache women.

The lieutenant took his black hat off his head and ran his sleeve across his forehead. Beads of perspiration trickled past his eyes as rivulets dropped from the strands of blond hair plastered against his forehead. Pennsylvania was not nearly as hot as Arizona, but he had not stopped sweating since they had arrived last night. He dusted off the brim of his carefully shaped hat, taking extra time to smooth down the silver embroidered threads on the front of it that formed the emblem of two swords crisscrossed in a shimmering adornment. As he replaced the hat upon his head he glanced toward the upper dormitory level. Movement at one of the windows caught his attention and held his gaze prisoner. It was the girl—the half-breed. At first, Travis thought she was staring at him, but then he realized she was looking past him, toward the arched gateway which granted entrance to the schoolyard. Even from a distance her youthful beauty was breathtaking. Yet, there was a look of hard determination about her that worried the lieutenant. Perhaps it was just the hopelessness of her situation. Still, something else kept nagging at the back of the lieutenant's mind, although he couldn't quite pinpoint a reason for his uneasiness.

32

He continued to stare up at her still figure in the window, while his curiosity increased. His mind began to delve into her past, wondering about her parents: Which had been Indian? Which white? Where were they now? Surely she must have had white relations somewhere who could have taken her to live with them. Did the government ever look into those types of situations? Travis reminded himself that her white blood probably did not matter to the U.S. government, and since she obviously had been living with the Apaches when she was captured, she had had little choice as to where she would reside. Besides, her parents were most likely dead. If she did have any white relations, it was doubtful they would want to be saddled with a half-breed to support.

Travis Wade drew his thick brows together in an aggravated manner. Why should he care what happened to her? Although, until he deposited her in Oklahoma, she was his responsibility. Maybe he should keep a close watch on her when they traveled to Fort Sill, he told himself. With a grunt of annoyance he pushed himself away from the tree and began to stalk across the carefully landscaped grounds. The last thing he needed was an uprising of Apache children on the train, especially if they were being led by some little half-breed girl!

Margaret did not notice she had acquired an audience of one because she was too busy studying the street beyond the schoolyard. She was certain she would have a better chance of escaping from the school than she would have trying to sneak off the train somewhere between here and Oklahoma. She could probably walk right through the front gate and nobody would be the wiser. Still, she did not want to take any unnecessary risks. She remembered there was a back gate which was used only by the delivery men and the gardeners. This late in the morning, she reasoned, the deliveries should already have been made, and the gardeners were probably spread out over the vast schoolyard.

With a quick glance, she scanned the room for items she would need for her escape. Her only luggage was a tattered old carpet bag, and into this little satchel she stuffed an extra dress, which was almost identical to the calico one she was wearing; a few undergarments, and her personal grooming supplies. Actually, with the exception of a couple more calico dresses that still hung in the old wardrobe standing in the corner of the room, this bag now contained all of her belongings. When they had left for Carlisle, none of the children had been allowed to bring anything along. Margaret sighed when she looked at the meager possessions she had acquired in eight years. Well, she said inwardly, it is better to travel light. When she reached wherever it was that she was going, she would worry about obtaining a more suitable wardrobe. She thought about the church ladies again, and absently ran her hand over the smooth cotton of her dress. Someday, she determined, my garments will be made of velvet and silk . . . someday!

She had to get away from this place first, though. Her new life would begin the minute she set foot outside the wrought-iron gates of the Carlisle Indian School. The excitement of beginning this adventure caused her whole body to shake as she knelt down on her knees and slid her arm beneath the thin mattress that covered the bedsprings. The little drawstring bag she withdrew contained less than twenty dollars, but it held the sum total of her cash supply. She had earned this measly amount by doing an occasional mending

34

job for the teachers at the school. With trembling fingers, she tucked the small purse inside her bag. How far can I get with such limited funds? she wondered as she grabbed up her sole piece of baggage. At least, she did have some money. She became flooded with relief when she thought of the many times she had been tempted to spend her savings frivolously on one or another of the school outings in the city!

Her gaze flicked around the small dormitory room, which had been her home for so many years as she said a quick and final farewell to the school. She did not have time to feel regret or sorrow, because escaping was all she could think of at this moment. But once she reached the hallway and was greeted by the children who were already going down to the main entrance to await their departure for the train station, she was overcome with emotion. Margaret walked among them as casually as possible, although her knees were shaking so hard it was difficult even to move. She tried not to look at anyone's face or to listen to their young voices, because she knew this would be the last time she would see any of them. They had all grown so close that the idea of leaving them was heartbreaking, and it was impossible to ignore any of them. She blinked back a tear when a warm hand unexpectedly slipped into hers.

"We're going to be with our own people again, Margaret!" With a nervous glance, Margaret looked down at the girl who had taken her hand. She was greeted by excited black eyes looking up at her from beneath a heavy thatch of raven hair. Katherine had only been four years old when they had arrived at Carlisle—what could she possibly remember about "home"?

"But Oklahoma is not our home," Margaret reminded the younger girl in a quaking voice. She wanted to cry out to them all that Carlisle was their home, but the look on Katherine's face made her even more aware of the fact that she really was the only one who did not want to leave here. How could she have been so wrong all this time? She clutched Katherine's hand tighter, and when the girl stared up at her with a puzzled expression upon her face, Margaret forced herself to smile. At once, a wide grin broke out on Katherine's round face, her worried look disappearing.

She swung out in front of Margaret in a happy skip. "I'm going to find my father!"

Margaret nodded, although she did not answer. A lump had formed in her throat, and was slowly inching its way down into her chest. She had forgotten that Katherine's father was still presumed to be alive since he had not been at the Apache *ranchería* on the day of the final attack. She tried to conjure up some happiness over the prospect of Katherine finding her long-lost father, but all Margaret could think of was her own family, whom she would never see again. Perhaps Katherine and all of the others did have a reason to be excited about rejoining their people, after all. But this thought made Margaret feel even more distanced from the rest of them. She had no reason to return to Apachería, but in the white man's world, there was a chance that she could fulfill her own dreams.

By the time they had reached the bottom level of the building, Margaret had convinced herself that she was making the right decision. Even as she took one last, sorrowful look around at the other children, she did not have any lingering doubts. In just the short time that had elapsed since the schoolmaster's announcement, a whole transformation had taken place within the group. Around her, Margaret heard talk of the "old ways" and of Indian customs that had not been mentioned for a long time.

As she studied the faces of the children who had

gathered in the front hallway to await their departure from the school, she was reminded of the day they had all been given their new names. The teachers had tried to find names that were similar to their Indian names, but it had not been an easy task. Dona's name was simple, because she had been given the Spanish name of Doña Ana by her family. Her name had been abbreviated to the singular title of Dona, then they added a last name of Anderson, but some of the other names had not been so easily converted. The new names chosen by the schoolteachers were alien to the children's ears and most of them were long and complicated, difficult for them to learn how to pronounce. Margaret's Indian name of Morning Star was completely unacceptable to the white men, so it was changed to Margaret Sinclair. Margaret looked over at the small figure of Katherine, remembering the lyrical sound of her Apache name, Kaytee. Adam and many of the other boys were given their white names without any consideration to their Indian names, because Apache boys did not earn a real name until they reached puberty and accomplished some brave deed or proved themselves as hunters. Until that time, the young males were called such names as Boy Who Runs Fast or He Who Cries Like A Girl.

These memories were affecting Margaret in ways she did not like, and she knew she had to get away before her emotions overruled her sense. Against her better judgment, she took one more look around, hoping to catch a glimpse of Adam and Dona. But neither was in sight. She told herself it was best if she did not see them anyway. Adam was too smart; he would see through her plans to escape at once. And just seeing Dona would make it nearly impossible for Margaret to leave her behind. However, there was no other alternative.

Katherine had mingled with the crowd, and everyone was talking loudly and all at once. The disorder which reined over the entire place made it easy for Margaret to slip away unnoticed. She did not encounter anyone as she rushed to one of the back doorways and out of the school building. Outside, the late morning sun cloaked the green grass of the schoolyard with a warm glow, and its gentle rays filtered through the tops of the tall oak trees which stood majestically along the fence line. It was the month of July, and, unexpectedly, Margaret recalled how hot Apachería was at this time of the summer. She remembered going with her father to hunt for food in the scorching heat of the Superstition Mountains, and of how the soft soles on her moccasins would burn like hot coals against her tender feet as they traipsed across the fiery desert sand. On the rare occasions when they would come across an animal to kill, the meat would sometimes spoil before they could even cut it away from the dead animal's bones. Margaret shivered in spite of the warmth. She could never return to that uncertain way of life.

Pausing on the stoop, she glanced around, but could not see anyone working or moving about in the area. The quaking in her limbs did not make it easy for her to run, so she descended the few stairs slowly. Once she was standing on flat ground, however, her urge to get away from the school—and her haunting memories— overcame her fear of being caught. Her feet had never moved as fast as they did once she began to run toward the escape route she had chosen. Within seconds the gate was in sight, but to Margaret it felt as though it had taken forever to reach this point. In her panic, she began to relive all the horror of fleeing from the soldiers during ambushes on the Apache *ranchería*. The bloody images became as vivid as her recurring nightmares, until her heart threatened to explode in her breast from fear.

By the time she had reached the wrought-iron fence, she did not notice that the gate had been left wide open or that she did not even have to take time to lift the latch. Her relapse back into the terror of the past left her disoriented and too numb to continue. She paused at the threshold of the school boundary line and looked around without knowing why she had stopped or what she was looking for as she gasped, trying to catch her breath. She turned back toward the school building, half expecting to see a troop of soldiers running after her, their bloody bayonets pointed in her direction. Her eyes traced the outline of the huge brick structure, but her mind was recalling the smoke and fire of the burning *ranchería*.

She clutched her bag against her body and fought to regain control of her wild imaginings. Everything around the schoolyard was quiet and peaceful, and there still was no sign of any people in the area. Why was her mind going so crazy all of a sudden? She took several deep breaths to calm the pounding in her chest and forced herself to think rationally. Adam and Dona would be the first ones to notice she was missing, she would be long gone before anyone would go looking for her. Besides, the children had to be at the train station within the hour, so there was a good chance that no one would even take the time to go in search of her. Just one more step and she would be off the school grounds . . . Just one more step to freedom and a new life in the world of the white man.

"Halt!" Lieutenant Wade shouted as he stepped out from the clump of oaks in which he had taken refuge earlier. He'd hidden himself in the shelter of the trees in the hope of restructuring his mode of thinking before he was forced to board the train with his cargo of

Apache children. He'd kept reminding himself of his career—which had gone exceptionally well—and of his dedication to upholding the laws of his countrymen. But, so far, all he had managed to do was increase his dissatisfaction with the government and the Indian bureau. The sight of the girl trying to escape had only sent his confused thoughts into complete turmoil. He'd hollered out for her to stop without even thinking, and now that she had skidded into him, he did not know what to do next.

The officer's appearance was so sudden and unexpected that Margaret could not help but collide with him. The impact of the crash knocked the wind from her lungs, and only his tight grip on her arms kept her from collapsing to the ground. Thinking coherently was out of the question for either of them, and for several moments they stood, unmoving, while their startled gazes stared at one another.

"L-let me go," Margaret finally gasped, though she was still too weak to try to pull away from him. Her frantic eyes flew toward the gateway, which was only several feet away . . . so close, yet so out of reach now.

The lieutenant also glanced in the direction of the gate as his thoughts ran along the same lines. She had almost made it, and he didn't even know why he had bothered to stop her from escaping. He tried to sort out his thoughts in the few minutes they stood facing each other, but it was an impossible task. A part of him wanted to turn loose of her and allow her to charge through the open gate. His sensible side, though, told him she would only suffer more if permitted to flee. She did not realize it, but she was totally unprepared for life outside of this refuge. This damn school had seen to that! Book learning would do her little good from this day forth. Her only hope for survival was to stay with the other Apache children. But even as that thought firmly planted itself in his mind, he was struck by the realization that she was hardly a child anymore. Perhaps she did deserve a chance to make her own decisions, whether they were right or wrong.

His hesitation gave Margaret enough time to regain her strength. Catching him off guard, she pulled from his grasp and made another charge for the exit. She had only gone a couple of feet, however, when he reached out with little effort and yanked her back within his tight hold. Travis Wade grew even more unsure of his own actions. She would be halfway down the street by now if he hadn't grabbed her again. What had come over him? Was his dedication to his job greater than his compassion for her? he asked himself.

The brutality of his grasp, along with the sudden coldness which masked his face, warned Margaret that she would not escape from him. His green eyes flashed with aggravation as he tightened his hold on her arm. A fearful cry flew from her mouth as she ceased to fight against him. His enslaving grip gradually loosened, but not enough to grant her another attempt to flee through the gate.

"Why did you stop me?" she asked as tears began to spill from the corners of her turquoise eyes.

Lieutenant Wade could not answer her simple question. He only continued to stare at her speechlessly. She did not deserve the fate that had been forced upon her, but who was he to decide? With determination, he reminded himself once again of his position, and of the job he was required to do.

"I have orders to deliver all of the Apache children to the reservation," he said in a tone of authority. "You are included on that list."

Margaret's mouth drew into a tight line, though her bottom lip trembled slightly as she willed her tears to stop. She did not want to cry and beg him to release

41

her, because she could tell that his mind was already made up. All at once, she remembered something Adam had told her on several occasions. He'd said that in dealing with white men an Indian must always be one step ahead, or the race would be lost before it even started. Until now, she had never understood the meaning of his words.

"I . . . it was foolish of me to try to escape," she stammered, blinking back the last of her tears.

The lieutenant was taken aback by her meek retreat, although he still wondered about her sincerity. "We'll forget this ever happened, but if you try anything like this again, I will be forced to resort to drastic measures."

Though he did not tell her what types of measures he had in mind, Margaret's entire body shook at the possibilities his threat implied. She imagined herself chained to the side of the railroad car, or tied up, gagged, and left alone in some dark railroad coach for the length of the whole trip. She gulped down her fear, and gave a quick nod. She had no intention, though, of granting the lieutenant the satisfaction of knowing her inner thoughts.

The defiant tilt of her chin was not a gesture of defeat, and Lieutenant Wade wondered if she was already planning another strategy for escape. "I think you should stay close to me—just in case you get any more crazy notions of escaping."

An indignant squaring of her shoulders was the only clue Margaret gave of the anger which boiled inside her. But when his eyes met her unwavering glare, the lieutenant saw the depths of her fury in the bolts of silver that flashed through turquoise like deadly sabers. He cleared his throat, then added, "Since we'll be spending a lot of time together during the next few days, I reckon I should know what your name is?"

42

"Margaret Sinclair, but you, sir, may call me Miss Sinclair."

The lieutenant's gaze narrowed in reaction to her haughty attitude. Without realizing it, Miss Sinclair had just confirmed his suspicions about her ulterior motives. "Well, Miss Sinclair"—he accented her name, his hateful tone matching hers, "You got my name correct. Just call me, sir!"

Adam's glowering stare followed every move the couple made as they traveled to the train depot. Margaret did not have a chance to speak to him, however, so he was left to draw his own conclusions about her sudden kinship with the lieutenant. Several times Margaret caught Dona gazing at her with a worried expression, but as soon as Dona saw her friend looking in her direction, she would instantly lower her eyes. Even Katherine watched the couple constantly, a look of concern upon her young face. To all of the children it appeared that the lieutenant had taken a very special interest in Margaret Sinclair. He had not let go of her arm once since they had left the school, and since she seemed to be completely at ease, it seemed to them that a very quick friendship had developed between the two.

Adam's fierce frown increased as the minutes passed, until it was all he could do to keep from charging at the lieutenant. He could not bear the thought of Margaret being so friendly with the officer, although the expression which drew her lips into a heavy pout hinted that she was not happy to be in the company of the tall soldier. Adam did not misread the leering eyes of the other soldiers either. He tried to reason that the lieutenant was protecting Margaret by keeping her with him, but this explanation did not satisfy the young man at all. If anyone should be at Margaret's side, it should be me, Adam determined.

Adam had known since he was a young boy that Margaret Sinclair was destined to be his woman. He was just waiting for the proper time to inform her of this fact, and he didn't appreciate the lieutenant's sudden devotion to the woman he had laid claim to years ago. Even more upsetting to Adam was his belief that the only reason most white men were interested in Indian women was because they considered them to be easy targets for their lustful cravings. As the carriages rolled out of the schoolyard and headed for the station, Adam swore to himself that he would discover the real reason behind the lietuenant's attentiveness to Margaret, and if his suspicions turned out to be accurate, he intended to make sure the officer never carried out his plan.

By the time they reached the depot, the Apache boy's close observation of the couple was beginning to grate on the lieutenant's nerves. Every time he turned around, he practically stepped on the young man. The boy's infatuation with Margaret Sinclair was obvious to the lieutenant. Just as soon as he delivered them all safely to the reservation in Oklahoma, the boy was more than welcome to her, Wade told himself repeatedly on the trip from the school to the train station. She was already more trouble than he had planned on having to deal with during this detail, and he couldn't wait to hand her over to the lovesick Adam Washington. Although, as this thought passed through his mind, he began to feel a bit sorry for the young man, and decided he would try to ignore the irritation the boy's glowering stare aroused in him.

A bustling center of activity greeted the group when they reached the train station. The six soldiers who had accompanied Lieutenant Wade to Carlisle had their work cut out for them as they tried to keep the Apache children together until they boarded the train. There was a fair amount of whispering and snickering among the soldiers over their commander's dedication to the beautiful young half-breed. There had even been a couple of suggestions made that, once they departed from the train and continued the journey to the reservation on horseback, perhaps the lieutenant would be willing to share his ravishing companion with the rest of his men.

Margaret was not blind to the soldier's rude smirks, nor could she miss their devouring looks. She had noticed other men looking at her in that manner when they had gone into town for various celebrations at the church, and at times she had even caught several of the men teaching at Carlisle looking at her with that strange glint in their eyes. But since most of those men tended to be discreet in their observations, they would quickly look away when she returned their stares. The soldiers, however, leered at her without shame, making Margaret more nervous with each passing second.

"Looks like you could use some help with this one," Sergeant Roberts said, making his lurid intentions clear as he rubbed up against Margaret in an intimate manner. She recoiled and clung to the lieutenant.

The lieutenant's voice was clear and controlled, yet deadly when he spoke. "I have no problem handling my duties, Sergeant. But if you are in need of something to occupy your time, I can arrange a special detail just for you." He pursed his lips in a speculative manner, while watching the other man closely from narrowed eyes.

A cruel smirk parted the sergeant's heavy growth of whiskers as he met the lieutenant's piercing glare. He did not bother to answer as his eyes raked over Margaret Sinclair like sharp ice. His hand rose sharply to the brim of his hat when he saluted. Then he turned and stomped over to rejoin the other soldiers.

Margaret drew in a sigh of relief and stepped away from the lieutenant. She was surprised when she glanced up at him and noticed anger surface on his face. Was it possible that he was upset because the other man had made an indecent gesture toward her? Margaret's mind filled with a dozen thoughts at once. If the lieutenant was attracted to her, then maybe her dream of escaping the reservation was not so farfetched. She was already envisioning her future with the lieutenant, picturing the beautiful gowns she would wear for him, when they were interrupted by a man's rude-sounding voice.

"You've been assigned to that car back there." The pudgy train conductor pointed toward the back of the locomotive and then turned away from the lieutenant as though he did not have time to bother with any more talk.

"Hold on there," Travis Wade commanded, addressing the man's back. "That's not a passenger car."

The conductor's face bore a leering grin when he turned around again. "No, sir, it sure ain't."

Margaret felt the lieutenant stiffen as his grasp on her arm grew tighter, but the tone of his voice left little room for argument. "These are children, not animals. We will ride in the passenger compartment."

For an instant, the conductor hesitated as if he planned to contest the other man's authority. Then he shrugged his hefty shoulders in defeat. "I'll see what I can do," he mumbled as he stalked away.

The lieutenant did not bother to wait for the man to return, and under the angry stares of the other passengers, he began to load his precious cargo aboard the train. By the time the conductor returned, the children were sitting quietly in their seats. The man glared angrily at the lieutenant, but did not offer a retort. The mask of warning upon the commander's countenance did not invite argument, especially not from the cowardly conductor.

"He's going to let us stay?" Margaret said in a whisper. She looked at the lieutenant with a stunned expression. The remembrance of her first train ride briefly clouded her thoughts as she recalled being shoved into a dark car and hearing the cries and moans of the frightened children. Her own terrified cries had echoed throughout the small compartment until she had finally passed out from fear and exhaustion. Mercifully, she could not remember the rest of the journey, but for as long as she had a breath in her body, she would never forget the putrid stench of human feces and urine in the dirty cargo car where they had been held prisoners for weeks on end.

The lieutenant patted her hand in a gentle manner when the awful memory shook through her entire body and caused her to quake outwardly. Margaret's gaze traveled down to where his large hand rested on her small one; then she glanced back up at his face. He was looking out the window, presenting only his profile to her, and she wondered if he was even aware of his comforting gesture. As she studied him she became aware of the proud tilt of his chin, of the square jaw which gave a determined look to his handsome features. Pale blond strands of hair tumbled carelessly from beneath the brim of his black hat, and his jade-colored eyes were surrounded by thick brown lashes that did not blink even once during her close observation.

Margaret sighed and leaned back against the seat. She closed her eyes in contentment. All the bad memories were gone now, and had been replaced by the handsome face of the man who sat beside her. Perhaps the lieutenant did me a favor by preventing my escape, Margaret thought as a smile curved the corners of her full lips. She was more certain than ever that once they reached Oklahoma the lieutenant would be ready to save her from her most dreaded fear . . . life on the reservation!

Chapter Three

"May I go to the water closet?" Margaret's long dark lashes blinked in a precocious veiling of her jewel-toned eyes, and immediately set the lieutenant on his guard.

A crooked smile accompanied his reply when he glanced at the girl from beneath the brim of his black hat. "Can I trust you to go alone?"

"I'm not stupid enough to jump from a moving train, lieutenant! If you think . . ." at once she fell silent. She reminded herself that it was destructive to her own plan if she acted snide and defensive every time they spoke to one another. "If it will make you feel more secure to stand guard outside the door, I will understand." Her voice dripped with a sweetness which had not been present in it seconds earlier.

The lieutenant retorted with an aggravated grunt and a quick wave of his hand. Did the Indian school teach their female students to act coy and under-handed? he wondered as he rose from his seat to let her pass. Another loud huff followed when Margaret's form brushed against his as she slid past him. Since he did not know whether or not she had made such close contact on purpose, he kept silent. His thoughts, however, were running rampant. He was, after all, just a man, and in any society Margaret Sinclair's beauty could not be taken lightly. But he did not need her to add to his problems by using her obvious appeal to trick him into believing she no longer wanted to escape. When she returned he would put her in her place, nip her ploy in the bud before it went any farther. By tampering with a man's affections to win favors for herself, Miss Sinclair was playing a dangerous game.

The lieutenant's mood did not mellow as he turned so that his gaze could follow her as she walked down the narrow aisle toward the end of the coach. The motion of the train made it difficult for her to walk without grabbing onto the backs of the seats for support, and as she did so her hips swayed in a sensuous manner from side to side. Even in her simple cotton dress, which was not snug or suggestive, her gentle curves more than hinted at her womanly appeal. He couldn't help but notice the lecherous looks which appeared on the faces of the soldiers as the young woman passed by their seats. He reminded himself that it was a helluva long way from the train station in Wichita Falls, Texas, where they had to depart by horseback, to the reservation at Fort Sill, Oklahoma. Just getting this group of children there without mishap was enough for one man to deal with. Keeping the rest of his men away from Margaret Sinclair was another problem the lieutenant would rather do without, especially since Miss Sinclair did not seem to know the danger she was creating for herself by merely parading past their hungry eyes.

Once she disappeared behind the closed door at the back of the car, the officer sat down with a thud and let out another aggravated sigh. He could ask for reinforcements to help him accompany the children from the train station to the reservation, but what good would that do? He would only be increasing the male population, and he would still have to deal with Margaret Sinclair. No, he told himself with a firm resolution, he would make it his personal duty to see to it that Miss Sinclair did not cause any more trouble than she had already. Although, judging from the rude chuckles and hushed murmuring coming from the other soldiers since Margaret's trip to the back of the coach, the lieutenant was certain his worries were just beginning.

With an uneasy feeling working its way through the pit of his stomach, he turned around again and glanced over the back of his seat. Adam Washington had positioned himself outside the doorway behind which Margaret Sinclair had retreated. The boy's piercing stare was directed straight at the lieutenant when their eyes met. The officer gave him an equally stern glare and swiveled around in his seat. A jealous suitor was something else he didn't need.

"Are you crazy!"

Margaret gasped with surprise when Adam's rough hold pulled her out of the small room the instant she opened the door. "Are you?" she retorted as she attempted to pull away.

"Why are you being so friendly with that soldier?" His fury was evident from the anger that flashed like spears of lightning through the ebony of his eyes. Even his dark face carried a red flush, making him appear almost savage and out of control.

His rage caused Margaret to cringe inwardly. Adam was usually gentle and calm in most situations, but today he was acting as though he were on the verge of exploding. After her initial surge of shock subsided, Margaret straightened her shoulders and yanked her arm from Adam's grasp. The thoughts in her head were jumbled as she contemplated what—if anything—she should tell him. Would he grow even more angry with her if she told him that she had tried to escape from the school? His pride in their people would never permit him to understand why she could not return to their old way of life. She raised her eyes to look at his face, and tried to see past his anger. She loved Adam unabashedly, but not in the same manner that he loved her. He was her best friend, and, until now, there had been nothing she couldn't confide to him. Why was it that all at once he seemed like a stranger?

"Adam, I . . . I . . ." How could she even begin to explain her feelings about returning to their people? Even though he was distraught that they weren't being sent to Arizona, going back to live among their people was the goal Adam had worked toward for the past eight years. Margaret knew his feeling for her would probably turn to hatred if he were to learn that her greatest desire was to get far away from anything—and everyone—who reminded her of the Apache blood that pulsed through her veins. Even if it meant that she would never see him or any of the children again.

"The lieutenant and I are—" she glanced up at his angry face, then quickly looked away. She could not tell him she had merely taken a liking to the officer, because a deception of that nature would upset him equally as much. She silently berated herself for never taking the time to tell him how much he meant to her and how important his friendship had always been to her. To intentionally hurt him by inventing a lie about her relationship with a virtual stranger, was something she could not do.

"Doña Ana is hurt because you have chosen to sit with the soldier, instead of with her," he said quickly as though he sensed what she was about to say but did not want to hear her speak the words out loud.

Once again Margaret was caught off guard by the strangeness that had overcome all of them in such a short time. Dona had not used her second name for many years. Now, Adam called Dona by both names with as much familiarity as he had said the Apache words earlier. How could he revert to the old ways so fast, and so naturally? Even his tone of voice seemed different, deeper and with a guttural sound which had not accompanied his speech before today. She allowed her gaze to travel upward again as she studied his face with closer observation. Adam, although only a year younger than Margaret, had always seemed wise and mature for a boy of his age. Now, however, it appeared that all signs of his youth had been left behind at the Indian School, and in his place stood a man of pride and increasing strength.

He reached out and placed his hands upon her shoulders. His voice softened when he spoke again. "It is only because I care so much about you that I become angry when I see you playing games."

Margaret shrugged, innocently. "I'm not playing games." She found it difficult to face him, so she glanced toward the tiny window in the back door of the coach. The view within her sights was the front of the car attached to the one they rode in, and it did not offer her mind any escape. "I am not playing games!" she repeated in a definite tone, more to herself than to Adam.

"I love you, Margaret."

Adam's words were so unexpected that Margaret was stunned into a speechless stupor. She stared up at him, but her mind had lost all sense of coherency. Why did he have to choose this time to say such a personal thing? Didn't she already have enough to worry about without adding Adam's admission to her list? It would be even more difficult to explain her feelings to him now.

"When we reach the reservation, I want us to be married," he added in a serious tone which did not tend to tolerate any discussion on the matter.

"Ma-married?" Margaret struggled to find an answer that would not destroy him or make him feel as though she was rejecting him completely, but there was none. "You're too young," she finally retorted, knowing that was a poor excuse meant to conceal her real feelings.

Adam crossed his arms over his chest and straightened his lean form up to its full height. His short black hair fell across one of his eyes when he gave his head a proud toss. "I am old enough to provide for you."

Margaret sighed and looked out the back window again. She should have talked to him sooner about their relationship. His feelings for her had grown past the brotherly stage long ago. Now, he left her no choice but to tell him the truth. "I can't marry you," she blurted out, then quickly, before she lost all of her courage, she added, "because I will not be staying on the reservation."

Adam's arms slowly dropped down to his sides. "Not staying? I don't understand?" The look of confusion and defeat upon his young face caused Margaret's heart to twist in her breast. She hadn't expected him to understand, yet she had never intended to hurt him so deeply either.

Her voice was shaky when she began to speak. "I can't return to the old way of life, not after learning how to live in the white man's world. Forgive me, Adam. But I've decided to leave the Apaches as soon as I can find a way out. When I do get away, I'm going to pretend to be white so I can live the kind of life I want so badly." She saw the change overcome Adam's

54

countenance. In a brief instant his look of uncertainty developed into an expression filled with the blackest rage.

"Please," she added, growing panicked. "Try to see it from my point of view."

Adam's thick lips curled upward until his mouth resembled a snarl. "Oh, I can see it very clearly from your point of view. You think you're too good to live on an Indian reservation."

Margaret reached out and grabbed Adam's arm. "No, it's not like that at all. Please—"

"It's exactly like that," he interrupted. His raven eyes glistened with anger as another thought entered his enraged mind and his face assumed an expression of disgust. "The lieutenant is a part of your plan, isn't he? If you're nice enough to him, maybe he'll take you away from the reservation and buy you nice clothes and a fancy house to live in when he makes you his whore. Is that it, Margaret?"

A sharp pang of guilt shot through Margaret's breast. Although she had not planned to become the lieutenant's mistress, Adam's assumption was almost too accurate, and hearing him say it out loud felt horrible. She opened her mouth to reply, but Adam did not give her a chance to speak.

"Someday, Margaret, you will realize the terrible mistake you're making. But it won't matter by then, because you won't have another chance to go back." He pulled his arm from her grasp and started to back away. "No matter what happens to you, just remember one thing." He bent closer to her until their faces were only inches apart. Her gaze tried to focus on his eyes, but all she could see was the movement of his mouth. "No one will ever love you as much as I do," he added. He twirled around and stomped down the narrow aisle, and in an instant had disappeared behind one of the tall backs of the wooden seats.

Margaret leaned back against the wall of the moving coach, while attempting to breathe in a normal manner again. Adam would never forgive her, and once he told Dona what had happened, she would no longer be her friend. If only Adam had not confessed his love, perhaps she could have avoided telling him about her plan. Everything would have been so much simpler if she could have left without having to hurt any of them. Katherine's big, dark eyes flashed through her mind. What if Adam told all of the children how she planned to deny her Apache blood in order to live among the white men? Every one of the children would be hurt by her selfishness then. She had to make them understand or all her dreams for the future would mean nothing!

Margaret was filled with an urgent sense of desperation as she pushed away from the vibrating wall of the moving train. Oblivious to the stares and whispering among the soldiers, she swaggered between the seats. Nothing else mattered except reaching Dona and Katherine before Adam repeated the terrible things she had just told him. If only she could take it all back, but it was too late.

"Where do you think you're going?"

Margaret jumped at the sound of the officer's voice. She had not even been aware that she was bypassing her own seat. "I . . . I must talk to someone."

Lieutenant Wade eyed her closely. The large tears which had formed in the corners of her turquoise eyes were clues to her depressed state of mind. He assumed her problem had something to do with Adam Washington, because, only seconds before, the boy had stumbled down the aisle with such a look of fury upon his face, the lieutenant feared there might be more trouble brewing. Miss Sinclair, it appeared, had a talent for stirring up trouble. The lieutenant glanced

56

toward the seat the young Apache man occupied, taking note that his wrathful expression had not changed.

"Looks like you've done enough damage. Sit down," he ordered with a motion toward the empty seat beside him.

"Please, you don't know how important this is," Margaret pleaded as teardrops escaped from the cradle of her eyes and flowed down her cheeks as if released by a broken dam.

The lieutenant emitted a low grunt. He hated to see a woman cry—even if the woman was a burdensome girl like Margaret Sinclair. He began to wonder if the source of his problems with Miss Sinclair had something to do with Adam Washington. Perhaps they'd had a lover's spat back at the school, which had prompted Margaret Sinclair's wild attempt to run away. As Lieutenant Wade studied the young woman's tear-streaked face he began to feel more and more uncertain about her motives. Her sorrow appeared to be genuine, so maybe he had been wrong about her all along.

"Keep your voice low," he commanded. The relief which flooded over her face made him experience his own sense of ease. Maybe if she made up with her boyfriend, the rest of this journey would be tolerable. As he watched her rush over to the seat Adam Washington shared with the girl called Dona, he became convinced that his worries were about to come to an end.

A look of surprise was evident on Adam's face when Margaret knelt down beside his seat. But he did not allow his eyes to linger on her face for more than an instant before he turned away. The harrowing look harbored within his raven gaze caused a sharp spear of pain to cut through Margaret as she realized the extent

57

of his love for her. She closed her eyes for a second, while trying to avoid another rush of tears. When she opened them again, she met Dona's troubled look. The other girl looked downward almost immediately.

"I must talk to both of you," Margaret whispered. Her voice cracked and another rush of tears flowed down her reddened face despite her determination not to cry.

A heavy breath came from deep in Adam's chest. "There is nothing to talk about," he said through clenched teeth. His eyes did not meet Margaret's, but instead remained fixed on the back of the seat in front of him.

Dona's nervous gaze focused on his face for an instant, but as she leaned forward to talk to Margaret, her shyness once again drew her eyes toward the floor. "I do not want us to fight. We should think of today as a new beginning for all of us, and for our people, and not look to this day as a step backward."

Margaret was taken aback by Dona's wisdom. It was rare for her to state an opinion since she usually just agreed with whatever anyone else said. However, much to both Margaret's and Adam's surprise, Dona continued to speak in her quiet voice. "I have thought a lot about our return to Apachería, and I think it will be a very good thing. We can teach the others who did not have our advantages all that we have learned at the school." Her speech took on an edge of excitement, although she still did not look up. "We know how important good hygiene is to our health, so we can show the women how to sanitize the dishes they eat on, and how to clean the wickiups with strong solutions so that bugs and lice will not want to dwell in them." For the first time Dona's head rose, and her gaze fixed on Margaret's face. "And you, Margaret—the younger children love you so much. You could continue with their education so that they do not forget how to read and write."

A shy smile curved Dona's lips as she glanced quickly at Adam. "And Adam is so smart, he can teach the people how to spend their money wisely and how to make that poor reservation into a thriving community that not even the white men can take away from us!" Once again her gaze fell to the floor, but her face was shining with enthusiasm when she became silent.

Dona's uplifting speech left both of her friends quiet as they contemplated her words of inspiration. Adam had always determined that his education would serve to better his people's lot, but until that moment even he did not realize Dona's strong desire to help the Apaches on the reservation. Margaret saw the look of pride which filtered across Adam's face, and she wished some of Dona's zeal would rub off on her, too. But her urge to get away from the life they were all heading for at the reservation only increased.

In a voice shaking with emotion, Margaret spoke again. "You are very special, Dona. You and Adam, along with all the other children will change the lives of our people who live on the reservation."

Adam's face remained straight-forward, but Dona turned toward her and smiled slightly. "And you, Margaret? You will help us, too. Remember, we are The Invincible Three."

A heaviness clung to Margaret's heart when she answered her friend. "I won't be there." Dona opened her mouth to question her strange revelation, but Margaret did not allow her to speak. "Living on the reservation would kill me, Dona. Please try to understand; please don't hate me!"

"But—" Dona leaned in front of Adam as her expression grew more perplexed. "We must live on the reservation. There are no other choices."

"You're wrong, Dona. You and I don't have any options, but"—Adam's cold voice rang out in more than a whisper; his angry face turned toward Margaret as he spat out the words—"she has a choice." A chill raced through Margaret when her gaze met his look of animosity.

Dona shook her head and reached out to Margaret. "What is he saying?"

In a frantic plea for understanding, Margaret clasped Dona's hand. "Adam does not understand, but I beg of you to listen to me." Dona gave her dark head a nod as Margaret continued. "I . . . I do not plan to live on the reservation with the rest of you."

Dona shrugged with indifference, and repeated her previous statement. "But, you must. The white men will not allow Indians to live any place else."

Margaret's mouth opened in another attempt to explain her feelings more fully, but Adam spoke instead. "Margaret does not plan to live as an Apache. She is going to pretend to be a white woman, because living on a reservation is below her standards." As he finished speaking his voice grew hoarse and forced, as if the words had turned bitter on his tongue.

Dona's hand went limp in Margaret's as she met the other girl's gaze. Their eyes locked for an instant, and Margaret saw the distinct awareness of betrayal in Dona's shocked expression. "I don't expect any of you to understand why I can not go back to stay, but please try to find it in your hearts to forgive me . . . someday."

As if moving in slow motion, Dona lowered her head and withdrew her hand from Margaret's palm. She turned in her seat until she was facing directly forward, just as Adam. The silence, which hung heavy in the air seemed overwhelming, although the clanging of the railroad car appeared to grow louder and louder with each turn of the wheels. Margaret stared at the sides of their stony faces until she was convinced that neither of them planned to speak to her again.

"I forgive you," Dona suddenly blurted out, although she still did not look in Margaret's direction. The huge relief Dona's words brought barely had time to sink into Margaret's spinning mind as another small voice rose above the roar of the engine.

"And I understand, too, Margaret." Katherine could hardly speak because of the tears streaming down her round cheeks, but Margaret heard. She swung around and noticed the younger girl sitting in the seat across the aisle from Adam and Dona. Katherine had heard everything that had been said, and even at twelve years of age, she'd understood. A loud sob rattled Margaret's slender form as she swung around and threw her arms around Katherine's neck.

A light tap on Margaret's shoulder made her heart fill with thankfulness. She knew when she turned around, Adam would be waiting to tell her he would forgive her too. Instead, the tall form of the lieutenant greeted her teary gaze and robbed her of this frantic hope.

"You'd better get back to your seat now," Wade said in a low voice. He did not want to interrupt, but the poignant scene these three had been creating was beginning to cause a stir in the coach. Before long all of the children would want to join in the intense discussion which so far had involved only these four. The lieutenant had already overheard Sergeant Roberts remarking about the lack of discipline in his handling of the Apache children. Wade ignored his men's smirking faces as he helped Margaret Sinclair to her feet. He was certain her conversation with her friends would eliminate the worst of his problems.

As they moved back toward their own seats, though,

the lieutenant glanced down at Adam Washington's sober face again. The young man's expression of bitter resentment had not faded. Though the three girls had been hugging and crying like babies, Adam Washington's appearance was more disturbing than ever, which did little to lighten the unease which again struck the officer.

Chapter Four

"He's a very strong man, you know. I remember how he used to lift me high into the air with only one hand. But I'm so big now I'll bet he won't be able to do that anymore."

Margaret smiled and nodded her head in response. Katherine had spoken of nothing but her father since the beginning of the journey. At first, Margaret had tried to explain to her that it was very unlikely she would be able to find her father, even if he was still alive. Katherine, however, would not even discuss that possibility. She had already made up her mind that her father was alive and she would soon be reunited with him. Listening to her chatter about something which probably would never happen was difficult for Margaret, but it was better than sharing a seat with the lieutenant. She had nothing at all to talk about with that man, so when she was in his presence there was nothing to do but stare out the window and fret over the future, which was not very certain at this time.

On the third day of the train journey, Margaret had managed to sit next to Dona, but the other girl was ill at ease the whole time. All of the children talked constantly about their destination. Dona was no exception, but since Margaret did not plan to partake of their new life on the reservation, there was always a void in their conversation.

"Do you remember him? He was the most handsome man in all the camp." Katherine's mouth broke into a wide grin as she conjured up the face of a man she could barely remember, except in her vivid imagination.

Again, Margaret nodded her head. She could not disagree with the younger girl since she did not even recall Katherine's father. However, she knew Katherine's recollections couldn't be accurate because her own father, Nachae, had been by far the most handsome man in the tribe. With a sad longing, Margaret glanced across the aisle toward Adam and Dona. Adam was staring out the window and Dona was slumped down in the seat asleep. Feeling someone staring at him, Adam turned around. When his eyes met Margaret's, they became narrow ebony slits before he quickly looked away. With a forlorn sigh, she turned her attention to Katherine once again, while trying to resign herself to the fact that Adam probably would never talk to her again.

"What did you say, Katherine?" Margaret asked in the hope of turning her thoughts away from Adam for a minute. She had known he would be angry with her when she'd told him about her plans, but she had never expected his rejection to be so final.

Katherine tilted her head sideways, tossing her thick black hair drawn into two ponytails, one on each side. "I was telling you about what a great hunter my father is."

"Oh, yes," Margaret replied absently. Katherine's father . . . Chateo. A shiver raced down Margaret's spine for at least the tenth time . . . every time Katherine said her father's name, or whenever the thought of his faceless specter passed through Mar-

64

garet's mind. She ignored the strange sensations that caused her blood to burn through her veins like wildfire. The idea of discovering Katherine's father alive and well was next to impossible. Without thinking, she twisted around and peered over the back of her seat. Lieutenant Wade was reclining in his, but he was not sleeping. Margaret marveled once again at his good looks; he was without a doubt the most handsome man she had ever gazed upon—with the exception of her own father, of course.

The officer's compassionate nature was equally appealing to Margaret. Each time one of the other soldiers made a snide remark to an Apache child, or a passenger tried to crowd in front of one of the Indian children during meals or in the sleeping quarters, the lieutenant would immediately come to the youngster's rescue. His stern attitude toward Margaret had even relaxed considerably since the first day, although it still seemed that he watched her every movement.

"We'll be arriving at Wichita Falls in ten minutes."

Margaret jumped at the sound of the conductor's voice. Ten minutes! A hundred thoughts began to run rampant through her mind. Should she attempt to escape as soon as they departed from the train in Wichita Falls? Maybe it would be easier to get away once they were out in the open plains; she might have a horse to ride by then. But she didn't know the Texas or Oklahoma countrysides, so fleeing into strange territory probably wasn't a good idea, she decided. Perhaps she should make her break—

"I don't want you out of my sight once the train stops," Lieutenant Wade said as he rested a firm hand on Margaret's shoulder. Beneath his touch, he felt her entire body stiffen, and he knew his intuition had been correct. Margaret Sinclair had not abandoned her plan of escaping. The lieutenant remained standing at her side until the train jerked to a halt, then waited for her to rise from her seat before he clasped her arm to lead her from the coach.

A powerful rage overtook Margaret as she walked haughtily from the train. Even though her thoughts were on escape, how dare he be so presumptuous as to interfere with them again. She stood rigidly at his side while they waited for the group of children to gather in the train yard. There was a rush of activity as the soldiers herded the youngsters out of the station and toward a convoy of supply wagons and horses. Margaret was oblivious to everything except her fury at being foiled once again. There was no possible way to escape now; they had not even been given horses to ride. Instead, all of the children were being loaded into two buckboards.

Margaret glared at the lieutenant as he talked to another officer who had been waiting with the wagons at Wichita Falls. She noticed how the lieutenant's expression grew serious when the other man handed him a slip of telegraph paper. Lieutenant Wade gave the officer a quick salute, then moved among his own men, obviously relaying the message he had just received. From the sober expressions on each of the men's faces, Margaret assumed the message was not good news for any of them.

"Is there a problem?" she asked when Sergeant Roberts swung up onto the wagon seat. A foolish hope had ballooned within her that perhaps a mistake had been made, and the government had decided to send them back to Pennsylvania.

A wicked smile curved the sergeant's lips when he saw who was speaking to him, but he didn't have a chance to reply. "Keep your eyes to the front, Sergeant," Lieutenant Wade commanded as he positioned himself next to the soldier on the narrow wagon seat.

The sergeant grabbed up the reins and looked straight ahead, but the lingering effect of his suggestive smile made Margaret shiver with dread. She clutched the side of the buckboard when it jerked forward, then glanced around at the troop of soldiers who were accompanying them out of Wichita Falls. Only half a dozen men had traveled with them from Pennsylvania, but at least twice that many had joined them here in Texas. Why would it be necessary for this many soldiers to accompany a dozen children to an Indian reservation in Oklahoma?

By the time they had stopped for the night, Margaret had long since given up her plan to escape before they reached their destination. She would just wait until they arrived at Fort Sill; then, once the soldiers were all gone, she would leave to begin her new life as a white woman. It would certainly be simpler than attempting to get away while she was under the ever-watchful eye of Lieutenant Wade. Although he had not spoken to her once since they had left the Texas train station, she noticed he glanced over his shoulder every time she moved. She wanted to scream out to him each time he looked back. What did he think she was going to do— jump out of the buckboard and run out across the barren plains?

Margaret was so infuriated with him by the time they made camp on the first night that she refused to accept his help as she climbed out of the wagon. Her entire body was stiff and cramped due to the uncomfortable position she had been forced to endure throughout the long day, and all the children were groaning when their weakened limps touched solid ground. The place where they stopped was a welcome sight, since it was on a knoll beside a small waterhole. Only a scattering of sparse brush bordered the water, and there were no other trees for as far as the eye could see, but a quick dunk in the cool water was on everyone's mind.

"There will be no fires tonight," the lieutenant announced as soon as everyone was situated on the ground. At once, Margaret noticed the grave atmosphere which fell over the group again. A dry camp meant there was some sort of danger in the area. But this was 1894 for goodness sake! All of the marauding Indians had been living on reservations for years now and had long ago given up any hopes of an uprising. What kind of trouble could there possibly be way out here in the middle of nowhere?

Nonetheless, throughout a dinner of canned beans, cold biscuits, and hardtack the entire camp was somber and quiet. The children were not told why there was such a feeling of impending danger hanging in the air, so their imaginations began to work overtime. After listening to the group's wild explanations, Margaret decided to learn the answer for herself. Long after the sun had disappeared from the westerly sky, the children were still lying in the bedrolls discussing the many possible dangers they faced out here in the vast badlands of the Oklahoma and Texas border.

When, at last, the group grew too tired to converse about their doom any longer, Margaret waited until a good deal of time had passed, then made her move. She had noticed the lieutenant walking down to the waterhole a short time earlier, and since she had not seen any of the other soldiers join him, she was certain he was alone. Carefully, she pushed back her blanket, then slid from beneath the covering. When it appeared that she had not disturbed anyone, she slowly rose to her feet.

68

"Margaret? Where are you going?"

Margaret paused, her heart pounding within her breast. "I thought you were asleep, Katherine." She leaned over and touched the little girl's head lightly with her hand, while trying to sound nonchalant. "I'm just going down to the waterhole. Now you get some rest; tomorrow will be another long day."

"Don't go. It's too dangerous here," Katherine pleaded. The girl clutched Margaret's hand as if she was never going to let go.

Margaret knelt down on her knees, keeping her voice low when she spoke. "Nothing here is going to hurt me, and besides, Lieutenant Wade is at the waterhole, so he can protect me should the need arise." She pried her hand out of Katherine's and pushed the child back against her bedroll.

"Hurry back," Katherine demanded in a loud whisper. In the opaque light of the night, Margaret replied with a quick nod of her head before rushing off to find the lieutenant. As she made her way toward the waterhole in the dark, she worried that one of the soldiers, or perhaps some of the other children, had seen her leave. Oh, how she hoped Adam had been asleep. He would think she had planned a rendezvous with the officer, and he would believe his accusations were correct.

When Margaret reached the small pond she breathed a sigh of relief to find that the officer was still alone. His bare chest glistened in the darkness and Margaret could hear the sound of splashing water as he washed. A trembling started in the pit of her stomach as she watched him through the pale light. This was the first time since their meeting that she had seen him without his hat or shirt, and he was even more handsome in this casual mode. For a moment her original purpose for coming to see him was forgotten. And the only danger

69

which seemed apparent was the effect of his muscular chest upon her innocent mind.

Sensing that he was no longer alone, the lieutenant straightened up and peered into the darkness. "Who's there?" he asked as his hand instinctively slid toward his low-riding gunbelt.

"It's Margaret—Margaret Sinclair."

"Why aren't you asleep?"

Margaret crept closer, in spite of the growl in his voice. Her eyes never wavered from his bare chest. "I . . . I," she faltered over her words as she stepped within several feet of his unmoving form.

In aggravation he bent over and picked up his shirt. With his back turned toward her, he slipped the garment on without bothering to button up the front. "What do you want?" he inquired without turning around.

Margaret tried to clear her mind and act sensibly. But she was attracted to this man in a way she had never known, and this new feeling stole away all of her defenses. "I wanted to . . . to talk to you."

"About what?" the lieutenant demanded as he twirled to face her once again. In the faded glow of the moonlight his light blond hair stood out in striking contrast against his smooth tan.

Her thoughts snapped back to her reason for coming here. "The children are worried about being slaughtered by angry white people who do not want them to be here. Is that why we have to be so cautious?"

The lieutenant relaxed his tense stance as guilt washed over him. He always tended to think the worst where Margaret Sinclair was concerned. "You can tell the children that their worries are needless." He reached down and picked his hat from the branch of a nearby sage. "There have been some problems with Mexican comancheros in parts of Texas and Oklahoma recently. The added precautions are strictly because of their latest activities, although it is unlikely that we will encounter any problems between here and the reservation."

"Th-that is a relief," she stammered hoarsely. He had not moved and Margaret found that she could not seem to make herself move either. "I . . . I suppose I should go back now."

An uneasy silence shrouded the night for several moments before the lieutenant spoke again. "We should all get some sleep." He took a step forward, but Margaret had not moved, so now they were only inches apart.

She cleared her throat, still, it did not dismiss the breath that had become hung up in her lungs. What if he kissed her? she wondered in a frantic haze. Maybe he would fall in love with her, and he really would be able to save her from the reservation. Once again her thoughts filled with beautiful visions of a perfect future in the white man's world. Even more enticing was the idea of being with a man as handsome as Lieutenant Wade.

"Would you like to kiss me?" she asked, unexpectedly. Her words were just above a whisper, but her voice seemed to roar through the quiet of the night.

A heavy breath broke from the lieutenant's parted lips. "What man wouldn't want to kiss a woman who is so willing?"

Rage flowed through Margaret's veins, although she tried to remain calm. "If I wasn't an Indian you wouldn't hesitate, would you?" she spat back at him.

Travis Wade shook his head in disbelief. How could she twist morality into such a distorted frame? "Your nationality had nothing to do with my feelings. I'm an officer who has been assigned the duty of transporting a group of children to the reservation. I hardly think it's part of my orders to seduce one of my wards."

Renewed hope flooded through Margaret. If he did not hold her Apache bloodline against her, there was still a chance that he would succumb to her plans. She reached out and rested her hand against his chest. She could feel the rapid pounding of his heart beneath her trembling fingers. "Would your orders really matter if you became attracted to one of your wards?"

He glanced down at the spot where her hand touched the bare flesh revealed by his unbuttoned shirt as he tried to focus his spinning thoughts on his responsibilities. There was no doubt what she had in mind, and it would take a stronger man than himself to resist someone as tempting as Margaret Sinclair. With his head bent downward, their faces were almost touching, and their lips drawn together as though they were the controlling force of their entire beings. Her slender form melted against his hard body like molten lava, deepening the ravishment of their lips with each passing instant. In the midst of this unexpected kiss Travis Wade realized his drastic mistake. He couldn't believe that he had been overcome by her conniving tactics, not when he had known what she had in mind from the very beginning. Yet, here he was—wrapped in her arms and returning her kiss with every ounce of his energy.

With the little strength he could muster up, he pulled himself away from her embrace and stumbled backward. "That should never have happened!" he called out in a choking voice.

Margaret took a deep breath as she fought to regain her balance, although she found breathing in a normal manner was impossible. How could such a brief kiss have such a tremendous effect on her? He, too, must have felt the overwhelming power in their kiss? she reasoned. "From the first moment we met I knew this

72

would happen," she said as she took a step toward him.

He moved farther away, wishing he could somehow disappear into the darkness. If he could find the right words to say, he would say them, but his thoughts were too jumbled to discuss this madness. A kiss that had lasted no more than a few seconds could be the downfall of his whole career. His eyes sought out her face as he tried to choose his words more carefully than his actions of a short time ago. He opened his mouth to speak but never got the chance to say what was on his mind.

"Lieutenant?" a man's voice rang out. "Are you down here?"

Travis Wade's swift steps took him away from Margaret Sinclair so quickly she barely had time to realize that he was gone. "What is it?" she heard him ask the other man, but the black of the night had already swallowed them up before she could make out the rest of their conversation. She knew the lieutenant's rush to get away was because he did not want to be caught alone with her, although she was certain that he was about to confess his love to her before they had been interrupted. Not wanting to spoil the memory of this wonderful new development, Margaret decided to wait a few minutes before returning to the campsite.

She sat down at the edge of the pond and ran her hand through the cool water, remembering the feel of the lieutenant's heated flesh beneath her fingertips. The events of the past few minutes could change her whole life. Perhaps the lieutenant had been leading up to this ever since their first meeting, and that was why he was always so determined to keep her close to him. With her mind in such an enraptured state, she did not hear the man who approached her from behind, nor did she realize what was happening to her when the large hand clasped over her mouth.

"Silencio!" The Mexican word was said in a whisper, but even in such a low tone it carried a threat of death.

Margaret's body grew limp within the tight embrace of her attacker. Her only instinct was to scream, but with his hand clamped tightly over her mouth it was impossible to make a sound. Her slight form was easily overpowered and her captor lifted her up from the ground and began to drag her backward. Margaret could not make her mind function, and in the darkness she lost all sense of rationality. In a vain attempt, she tried to dig her heels into the dirt, but the man was too strong, so her efforts to stop him were useless. The sweaty smell of his hand against her mouth made her nauseous and weak, until the only thing she could do was give in to his force and allow him to pull her along.

They had only gone a short distance when Margaret became aware of men's voices. She tried to make out her surroundings, but it was too dark and the terror of being abducted had nearly rendered her senseless. At first, she was sure her captor was one of the soldiers who had been eying her since the beginning of the journey, and Sergeant Robert's leering face was most prominent in her mind. But the man had spoken in Spanish, and she could not remember any of the soldiers speaking a foreign tongue. It was not until she heard the other voices that she recalled the lieutenant's remark about the Mexican comancheros who had been causing trouble on this side of the border. The realization that she might be at the mercy of a bunch of bandits caused the last of Margaret's courage to drain from her already weakened limbs. When her kidnapper suddenly came to a halt, her knees gave out and she sank to the ground in defeat.

"What is this? You go out to see what those pigs are doing, and you bring back a woman! *Yútashchin!*"

A chill raced through Margaret at the sound of the

man's deep voice. She knew without a doubt that she was in the hands of the comancheros Lieutenant Wade had spoken of earlier. Her terror paralyzed her, but hearing the Apache word for bastard snapped her mind into action. She recalled that the Apache language contained many Spanish words, but why would Mexicans speak in the Apache tongue?

Several other voices rang out from the circle of men, and though they were kept low, Margaret could hear that the men were speaking mostly Spanish with only an occasional Apache word thrown in. Too much time had passed since she had heard either of these languages because they had not been permitted to talk in their native tongue at Carlisle, and she could not decipher their words. She was certain though, that the main focus of their discussion was about her, because their arms kept motioning in her direction. Her eyes grew strained as she attempted to make out their faces, but in the dark she was only able to see hulking forms.

Since it appeared they were arguing among themselves and not paying much attention to her, Margaret slowly rose up to her feet. Her knees were quaking so violently that it was difficult for her to remain standing. She tried to command her legs to move, but her fear prevented her from fleeing. Before she had time to gather her wits, the voices of the men grew more fierce. From their outlines, they were still in a tight huddle, and though it was almost impossible to make out their actions clearly, Margaret saw the flash of a shiny object. An instant later one of the men toppled into a heap upon the ground.

An odd silence then descended over the men, evoking in Margaret increasing terror. Even through the darkness she had been able to see that one of them had just been stabbed during the course of the disagreement in which they had all been engaged.

75

Tremendous fear stole her breath away, and grew even more rampant when one swaggering form broke away from the others. As he moved toward Margaret she tried to scream, but her mouth was so dry only a hollow gasp escaped it. Running was not even a possibility, because her whole body had turned into a quivering mass.

When the man stood only inches before her, he reached beneath his striped serape to pull something from his pants pocket. She felt on the verge of collapse from the fright that his nearness presented to her quaking being. She was certain he was going to produce a knife and slice her to ribbons. Instead, he flicked the end of the match with his fingernail, then held the light close to her face. A surprised gasp flew from his mouth when the flame crossed her face. In the flickering of the match, her turquoise eyes drew shimmering flashes of light across the rich hue of her gaze. The man's gaze moved slowly over her face until the match burned down to his fingertips. With a round of Mexican profanities he threw it to the ground and shoved his fingers into his mouth to soothe the hurt.

His close presence made Margaret afraid even to breathe. All she could think of was that he was most likely the man who had just knifed his comrade. Now he was standing here, trying to look her over as though he had just won some sort of grand prize. Another icy shard of terror cut through Margaret when she realized she was undoubtedly the bounty the men had just fought to claim. His voice suddenly broke through the deathly silence, and caused Margaret to recoil in horror.

"One of our men went out to find out what the soldiers were doing here, and he returns with you." His speech was heavily accented, and his breath was lightly scented with liquor. "Now that you know we are here,

76

what do you suppose we should do with you?"

His question was not spoken in a hateful tone, yet Margaret knew his exact meaning. How could he permit her to return to the camp once she was aware of their presence? "I-I won't tell anyone you're here," she stammered. Her voice sounded small and foolish, even to her own ears.

A crude chuckle came from beneath the large sombrero which covered his head and hid his face from view. "No, you will never tell—this much even I know." His hand cupped her chin, drawing her face upward as he leaned closer. The brim of his huge hat rested on the top of her head and the slight pressure felt as though it was crushing her into the ground. "Why are those soldiers here?" he asked through clenched teeth.

Margaret's thoughts were shattered into a hundred fragments, and thinking rationally was no longer possible. Sharp prickly spears of pain began to shoot through her chin from his rough hold, and her voice did not seem to be able to cooperate when she opened her mouth to speak. "Wha-what do you mean?" she managed to gasp.

His hand squeezed her face tighter, until Margaret cried out in pain. "Don't play dumb with me. I want to know why that battalion of soldiers is in this area, and I'd better get an answer real soon 'cause I'm not a very patient man!"

A quivering sigh came from deep within Margaret's chest when she opened her mouth again. "They're going to the Indian agency at Fort Sill." With his hand clasped so brutally around her chin her words were jumbled, but her brief explanation seemed to satisfy him. He turned her loose and drew in a heavy breath, then looked over his shoulder and said something to the other men in a rush of Mexican words. His announcement caused a round of relieved sighs to echo through the stillness of the dark night.

"Why are you traveling with them? Do you belong to one of the soldiers?" he asked when he turned back around.

She could sense that some of his tension had eased up, so she began to breathe in a calmer manner. Her mind also started to react coherently for the first time since her capture. She carefully mulled over the man's question before replying. His inquiry made it apparent that he did not think she was an Indian, but would it be wise for her to begin her masquerade as a white woman at this time? She took a deep breath and leveled her gaze at the shadowed face of the man who waited for her reply.

"I am only traveling with the soldiers until we reach the next town. I don't belong to anyone," she said rapidly before losing her courage. Heaven help her if the man asked what town she was going to, because she had absolutely no idea where they were at this moment.

"Are the soldiers carrying any money with them?"

His question stunned Margaret since she had been expecting him to ask more details about herself. "No!" she retorted in an indignant tone. "Only defenseless Apache children!"

He remained silent for a long time. Then, without speaking to Margaret again, he spun around and returned to the two remaining members of his group. He spoke rapidly, briskly, causing a low grumbling among the other men. Margaret was shocked by the way they were standing over the body of the dead man as though he had not been a part of their group only minutes earlier. These men are not even human, she determined with a visible shudder. She glanced around and tried to regain her sense of direction. But she knew it would be useless to make a run for it, because she did not know which way to go. Nor did she have time to make a decision, since the man returned before she could make a move.

"I can not allow you to return to the soldiers," he stated bluntly. "I could kill you, but I would prefer not to take such drastic measures—not just yet, anyway." He smiled, and even in the darkness Margaret could see the white of his teeth when his evil grin flashed beneath the veil of his sombero. She gritted her own teeth in an attempt to keep them from banging together with fright. His insinuation could only mean one thing, and with this prospect to face, Margaret found herself regretting her wish to escape from her former situation. As she was tossed onto the back of a horse, then joined by the man wearing the large sombero, she realized the true meaning of being a prisoner. Even the dreadful idea of spending the rest of her life at Fort Sill had more appeal than the horrible visions flashing through her mind on this dark and fateful night.

"You can see where someone was dragged through the dirt," Sergeant Roberts said as he pointed at the scuff marks which scarred the rough terrain surrounding the waterhole. Rising from his crouched position, he then waited for the lieutenant to make a comment.

Travis Wade closed his eyes for an instant as he rubbed a hand across his forehead. He had never known such an overpowering sense of guilt as he was experiencing now. At first, he had been certain that Margaret Sinclair had fled of her own accord when he had left her alone the previous night. Now that the first rays of dawn revealed signs of a struggle, and his men had found a spot nearby trampled down by the hooves of several horses, the lieutenant feared his assumptions about Margaret Sinclair were dead wrong. If she had been abducted after he'd deserted her, he would never forgive himself, especially since her kidnappers were most likely the band of Indian and Mexican renegades who had gained notoriety by becoming border-hoppers —men who raided on both sides of the border, yet managed to elude capture by either country. It was the general rule that border-hoppers had very few scruples, and even less regard for human life. Some of them were reservation broncos—Indians who refused to live on the reservation—and many were Mexican desperadoes, whose own people had disowned them because of their murderous ways. The combination of these types of men was deadly to anyone who crossed their paths.

"What do you want us to do, Lieutenant?"

Wade shrugged his shoulders as his hands dropped to his sides. "We have to get the rest of these children to the agency without further mishap before we can do anything." He gave his head a determined nod and twirled on his heel. His first step was halted by the wall Adam Washington's angry form created.

"How could you permit this to happen?" the young man demanded. His arms were crossed over his chest, and his dark face wore a chiseled mask of fury. A desperate urge to fight the lieutenant raged within him, although he knew he would not stand a chance in a duel with the soldier.

Travis Wade side-stepped the boy and started to walk away, but Adam blocked his path once again. "I know you were down here with her."

The lieutenant came to a stop and leveled his gaze at the Apache. "What are you trying to accuse me of doing?"

Adam's eyes narrowed as he returned the other man's unwavering glare. "If she was abducted, it was because she was left here to fend for herself after you deserted her. But if something else happened to her . . . well, I promise you, lieutenant, I will see to it that justice is done."

Lieutenant Wade squared his jaw, while trying to control the rage that flowed through his veins. He had forfeited Margaret Sinclair's advances to avoid the very accusations which Adam Washington was now throwing in his face. But even worse, the boy was partially correct. The officer knew he shouldn't have walked away from the girl, left her alone in the dark. But last night when the soldier had called out to him he had been too worried about being caught with Margaret Sinclair to think about her safety. When she hadn't returned to the camp right away, he'd assumed she had stayed at the pond waiting for him to come back to her. Determined not to give her any further encouragement, he had deliberately wasted the time he should have used for upholding his responsibility.

"I don't deny that I talked to Miss Sinclair last night, but I will not tolerate your false insinuations." Lieutenant Wade glanced at the other soldiers who stood witness to his conversation with the young Apache. Judging from the looks on their faces, Adam Washington's charges had them thinking along ludicrous lines. The lieutenant straightened his shoulders and met the stares of his men with a deliberate green gaze. He did not feel that he owed anyone an explanation of his integrity, especially not to some lovesick Apache boy!

By late afternoon of the third day the caravan reached the Indian agency. Only the officers, however, were aware that they were already on the reservation. The terrain they had traveled over during the past few days since they had left Wichita Falls seldom changed from flat prairie land to an occasional sage-covered hillside. The land allotted for use as an Indian

81

reservation was usually the most undesirable section of ground in an area, and much of this agency was no exception to the rule. Located to the east of the Wichita Mountains, Fort Sill had originally been named Fort Wichita. For the past twenty-five years the post served as the agency headquarters for several different tribes of Indians, including the Kiowa, Comanche, Waco, and Kichai. Many of the Apaches who now resided here were prisoners of war who had ridden with Geronimo until his surrender during the last decade. After being shipped to prisons in Florida for the past eight years, the survivors had recently been sent to Fort Sill.

"I'm scared, Dona." Katherine huddled closer to Dona as the wagon bounced through the parade grounds of the Army post. They had already passed through several miles of pitifully built housing clusters where some of the Indian residents lived. Although the summer sun was scorching in the midday heat, Indians still tended to the fields that surrounded the agency. Two creek beds supplied the area with plenty of water, but most of the plains Indians that occupied this reservation did not adapt well to farming. Their meager crops did not compensate for the rations they did not receive from the U.S. Government. But, whenever money happened to fall into the Indians' hands, it was undoubtedly used to buy whiskey.

The post was well maintained, however, especially the stockades which appeared to be overflowing with Indian wrongdoers. The Indians preoccupation with alcohol led to bursts of malevolence and mayhem. They fought among themselves and with anyone else who dared to join in their drunken sprees. Maintaining a semblance of peace was a full-time job for the soldiers stationed on the reservations. The recent return of Apache prisoners of war from Florida had increased the number of men to be housed in the stockades and blockhouses, making the conditions of the filthy cells almost uninhabitable.

Dona's arm encircled the smaller girl in a comforting gesture, but still she did not answer Katherine's question. Dona was scared too, though she didn't want to increase the girl's fear by revealing her own. Although she had not imagined the reservation to be a paradise, she was not prepared for the sense of hopelessness that abounded over the entire area. Even as their wagon rambled through the middle of the post, a group of haggard Apache men scuttled past it. Their hands were held together with heavy cuffs, and their ankles were encased by wide shackles that had worn the edges of their pants to jagged peaks. Dona turned away, not wanting to see the raw flesh on the legs exposed by their torn clothes. Her dark gaze sought Adam's face for comfort, but he was too engrossed in his own observation of the prisoners to be of any help.

The wagon jerked to a halt in front of a log structure that stood amid the long column of buildings. Katherine clung tighter to Dona, even though the older girl still had not offered her any words of reassurance.

"Dismount!" Lieutenant Wade's voice rang out as the sound of hooves grew still. He remained atop his horse until the last soldier was standing on the ground, then motioning toward the backs of the buckboards, he added, "You children are to stay here. Someone will allot you each a band-tag, which you will have to place around your neck before being transferred to your living quarters." He glanced at his men, and, in the same brisk voice he had used when speaking to the children, dismissed his command.

Since Margaret Sinclair's disappearance there had

83

been a strained atmosphere between the officer and his men. His only wish at this time was to finish with this despicable detail and then return to his own territory in Arizona. Although, until he fulfilled his obligation to find Margaret Sinclair, he would not be finished with this assignment.

"What's a band-tag?" Katherine asked. Her large dark eyes fixed on Dona's face, waiting for a reply that did not come. Dona shrugged indicating her ignorance, though she sensed that a band-tag was not something they would be pleased to receive.

"They are going to tag us just like they do cattle," Adam said after a long pause. His statement was not made to anyone in particular, because his stony gaze was fixed on the building Lieutenant Wade had just entered. Although he had been hurt by Margaret's plan to live her life among the whites, his love for her had not dimmed. He would never forgive the lieutenant, nor would he ever give up on his vow to find out what had really happened to Margaret Sinclair on the dark night when she had vanished.

Chapter Five

Margaret's first glimpse of her riding companion was accompanied by the glow of the Texas sunrise. She awoke from a sleep which had afforded her little rest, and tried to stretch her aching limbs, but her position upon the back of the horse did not permit her the luxury. Her blurry eyes focused on the harsh light of the sun, while her groggy mind reminded her of the danger of her latest predicament. At once she became alert and began to survey everything around her. The first sight to greet her was the beauty of the sun's first rays slowly shedding an orange glow upon the golden mesas of the distant horizon. She knew they must have covered a great deal of distance during the night, for it appeared they were far away from the plains where she had been camped with the soldiers and the rest of the Apache children the night before.

Riding ahead were two horsemen. Though Margaret had no way of knowing, she assumed the one who had dragged her away from the waterhole on the previous night was also the one who had been murdered. Today, though, it did not matter because she knew at a glance she was in the company of a small band of comancheros. Their clothes were dirty and ragged, and the shapeless sombreros which covered their heads were coated with the dust of many trails. Even the horses they rode upon looked weary, and wore clumps of caked mud embedded on their haunches.

Margaret's stomach churned with an endless fear. Even when she had been a little girl living on the Apache *ranchería,* she had heard stories about the comancheros. Although she had not thought of them once while living at Carlisle, she could now recall every sordid tale she had ever heard. Any woman who crossed the paths of these men was treated with less regard than an animal. Aside from using females for their own lustful cravings, comancheros had gained a perverted fame for selling women into slavery. Indian women were a valuable commodity to the Mexican renegades, but white women brought the greatest reward a comanchero could command. Wealthy Mexican plantation owners would pay top dollar for a white slave. They used her for their own enjoyment, and when they grew tired of her, she was turned over to the overseers for their pleasure. When her usefulness to them wore out, the woman was retired to the fields to work out the rest of her days as a field hand.

With the realization that she was at the mercy of such ruthless men, Margaret felt her stability threatened once again. Her eyes could no longer focus on the men who rode in front of her or on the wondrous shimmering of mesas in the distance. She wanted to cry and scream for release, but her voice would not cooperate. She was overcome by an intense curiosity to see the man whose arms had held her all through the long night. The recurring chill which had plagued her, along with a sense of foreboding, during the past few weeks passed through her once again as she slowly looked over her shoulder. A gasp flew from her mouth when her eyes locked with his raven gaze.

His face was so familiar Margaret felt as though she should be able to address him by name, yet her mind was devoid of any rational recollection. Her eyes traveled over each pore of his face searching for the clue she needed, the missing piece. Beneath the swooping brim of his huge hat, sharply high cheekbones, a prominent nose, and piercing black eyes made his Apache bloodline evident. Who was he? And why did his nearness cause such a feeling of unrest to surface in Margaret?

He noticed she was looking at him, but only the slow glimmer that lit up his pitch-black eyes acknowledged her presence. He had waited all night for the light of day to grant him a clear view of her face, and in its increasing glow, he saw that his anticipation was well founded. Even with her thick dark hair entangled around her dirty face, she was a beautiful sight to behold. In the brief time they stared at each other, he memorized every inch of her face. For most of his adult life he had been riding with cutthroats and thieves, and not once during that time had he felt the emotions he was experiencing now—emotions he thought had died long ago when his Apache family had vanished in the brutal attack the white man's Army made against his village. He tried to seem unmoved by her observation, but it was difficult to hide the immense feelings that had overcome him. An eerie sensation crept under his skin, making him feel as though he should know this young woman, but that was not possible. The only women he associated with these days were the dance-hall girls in the Mexican cantinas; they did not mind sharing an hour or two of their time with an Indian.

Margaret tore her eyes away from the face of the man and turned to look ahead. The strange stirrings which shot through her had left her completely drained of energy; just hanging on to the back of the horse was almost too much effort. She did not understand the way the man affected her. Yet, on his face, she had found the same sort of puzzled expression. She wanted to speak to him, to ask him who he was and why she felt as though he was someone she should know, but her own fear prevented her from saying a word. Clamping her eyelids together, she tried to recall faces from her distant past, but none of the ones she conjured up matched that of her companion. Since it was obvious that he was much older than Margaret, she sought out memories of the warriors who had ridden with her father. Still, this man did not register in the deep passages of her mind's eye. So, who was he?

"Pare!" one of the men hollered without warning. Margaret's heart seemed to stop beating at the unexpected bellow. Even after her riding partner had stopped his horse, then pulled her down to the ground along with him, she had to take several deep breaths to regain a normal breathing rhythm.

"We are stopping to rest," he said to Margaret, although he purposely avoided looking in her direction. Along with the other two men he began to unsaddle his horse. When the necessary task was completed, he tossed a thin blanket to Margaret, then motioned toward a grassy spot beside the trail. From straddling the back of the horse throughout the night, her legs were numb and shaky. Sharp pins of pain shot through them as she took her first stumbling steps. She barely made it to the side of the trail before collapsing into an exhausted heap upon the ground. Only the memory of the uncaring manner in which these men had murdered one of their own kind, and fear of being attacked by all of them prevented her from seeking the sleep which she wanted more than anything at this time.

"Do you want to eat?" the Apache asked as he

approached her. His long woolen serape spread out around him as he sat down on the ground. His black eyes glanced in her direction while he waited for her reply. Margaret nodded her head and gratefully accepted the hard strip of jerky he held out to her. While she ate she never let her attention waver from the activities of the three men. They returned her intent glare with their own interested looks. It was not the custom of the other two to take orders from the Apache, but his rash action the night before had made his intentions crystal clear where the woman was concerned. So far, the Mexicans had not had a chance to challenge him. However, now that daylight had allowed them to get a good look at the young woman, their worry over the Indian's knife had dimmed considerably.

The knowing eyes of the Apache did not miss the lustful cravings evident in the other men's expressions when they got their first good look at the woman by morning light. But he also understood the thoughts going through their minds. Normally, his mind would be filled with the same lecherous ideas. Though he had every intention of fulfilling his needs eventually, he knew he must also discover why this young woman had triggered long-forgotten emotions and memories of his wife and young daughter, who had been slaughtered so many years ago. The two Mexicans, though, worried him considerably. With an uneasiness growing in his chest, he pulled his rifle from his saddle and positioned it across his lap. His unspoken message was loud and clear, and grumbling in Spanish, the other two men spread their blankets out on the ground and lay down.

Neither the Apache nor Margaret could rest, however. She tried to concentrate on the lieutenant, wondering what he'd thought when she disappeared. Oh, how she hoped he didn't think she had run away!

Her eyes kept shifting back to the Apache, though, and interrupting her thoughts of the lieutenant. The Indian's intent gaze had not left her face since they had stopped, and Margaret found herself growing more curious about him with every passing second. Soon, her thoughts of the lieutenant had disappeared altogether as the odd feelings of affinity she felt for this comanchero increased like water in a flooding riverbed, until she could no longer contain her inquisitiveness.

"I think I know who you are," she blurted out, drawing her dark brows together in a worried line.

The Apache's expression grew even more serious. This white girl could not know him! "Who am I?" his voice was stern and brisk. He crossed his arms over his chest, allowing his rifle to lie in his lap.

"Well?" Margaret raised her hands into the air and sighed. "I don't know your name, but I think . . . I must have met you when I was a little girl."

A smirk covered the Apache's face. "That is not likely." When she was a little girl he had been riding with the mighty Geronimo, and the only whites who crossed their path did not live long enough for introductions.

Margaret mulled over her next words carefully. If she admitted to this bandit that she was half Apache, would it make any difference to him? Or would it only make her own situation worse? She glanced at him, and once again felt icy shivers inching through her. It was imperative to her sanity to find out why this man affected her so drastically, and admitting her Apache bloodline might be the only answer.

"Both of my parents were half-Apache, and until our village was destroyed by soldiers, we lived with their Apache families." She saw shock filter into his

90

expression, and she knew he had not suspected that she was part Indian. Her dream of living among the whites flashed briefly through her mind, but she reminded herself that she had to get out of this dangerous situation first. The man was still eying her suspiciously, as though he was still trying to decide if she was lying to him, so she decided to divulge more information. "Have you ever heard of a warrior called Nachae, or of a great female shaman by the name of Sky Dreamer?" she asked, knowing immediately by his gaping mouth that her parent's names had struck a familiar chord.

"That is not possible!" His voice grew angry, and caused Margaret's tense body to jump with fright. "Everyone who lived in their *ranchería* was killed. This I know for a fact because my own wife and daughter were slaughtered on the same day that Nachae and his family were burned to death in the village."

A lump rose up in Margaret's throat. How did he know the manner in which her family had died? And who were the family members he claimed to have lost in the same tragedy? "Y-your wife and daughter?" she choked out in disbelief. "You lived with the Chiricahua Apaches?" She searched the farthest corners of her memory, but still could not recall this man's name.

The Apache looked away for an instant. His breathing had grown heavy beneath his striped serape, and a layer of perspiration broke out across his nose and upper lip. His home had been with the Chiricahua, but it was no wonder that this girl could not remember him. Even after he had taken a wife and fathered a child, he was hardly ever present in the village. He preferred to spend his time raiding farms and stealing cattle with the Mexican *bandidos* along the border, rather than seeing to his responsibilities as a father and husband. But this was not an admission he intended to voice out loud to anyone—especially not to his female captive!

His raven gaze again settled on the face of the girl as the edge of a memory floated through his mind. There had been two girls born to Nachae and Sky Dreamer— twin daughters. But he had never paid any attention to either of the children. Was it possible this girl was telling him the truth, and that she truly was the daughter of a Chiricahua Apache warrior and medicine woman?

"But there were no survivors!" he repeated firmly. Although he had been in Mexico when the attack occurred, he had received vivid accounts of the deaths of his family and tribesmen from several different sources, all of whom he believed to be accurate.

Margaret shook her head slowly. "There were survivors—mostly children. I was one of them, but the rest of my family perished in the fire. Those of us who did survive were shipped back east to the Carlisle Indian School. We received orders just last week that we were being sent to live on the Indian reservation in Oklahoma. That is where we were headed when—"

"You told me that you were traveling with the soldiers to the next town," he interrupted. "You did not tell me that you were one of the Apaches."

"I did not know who you were, and I was afraid of how you would react if I told you I was part Indian." She knew her explanation made little sense, but she didn't dare tell him she had been planning to deny her Apache bloodline altogether. "I was only eight when my ranchería was ambushed and burned. You seem familiar to me, but I can not recall who you are."

He squirmed uneasily, and wiped at his sweating brow. "I was away a lot—hunting," he added defensively.

Margaret threw her hand across her mouth to hide her gasp. Katherine's words ran through her mind. *My father was a great hunter, you know.* Was it possible? "Wh-what is your name?" She finally forced the words from her trembling lips.

The man glared at her as he hesitated. It was not a good practice for a man to relate his name to just anyone, but he would probably end up killing her or taking her back to Mexico to sell, so what would it matter if he told her his name? "I am known as Chateo!" he answered with a proud tilt of his chin.

Margaret could no longer hold in her emotions. A muffled cry escaped from behind her hand as he confirmed his identity. Katherine's father was her abductor! The man's face drew into a perplexed frown. Had his reputation as a killer and thief spread all the way to the East?

"Your daughter"—Margaret gasped as she tried to steady the trembling in her body—"she . . . she is one of the children who was traveling with me."

Chateo jumped to his feet. His sudden action caused his rifle to crash to the ground, and Margaret gave out a frightened cry. The other two men, startled from their siesta, sprang to their feet almost immediately, all eyes being directed at Margaret.

"*Qué . . . qué?*" one of the Mexican's demanded. Both had their guns drawn, ready for any unknown danger.

A slow red flush inched its way through the Apache's cheeks. His outburst surprised him as much as it did those around him. That his little daughter might still be alive was more than his spinning mind could comprehend. Through the years, guilt had eaten away at him because of the way he had ignored his small family, leaving his wife to tend to their baby daughter almost entirely on her own. When he had learned of the attack on their *ranchería,* and of his family's deaths, guilt had nearly been his undoing. For months afterward, he had taken deliberate chances during raids and robberies, but fate had taken a cruel twist. The greater the risks he took, it seemed, the more his luck held out. Among the comancheros he became known for his daring escapades. They did not know his bravery was a mask for pain and guilt, nor did the other outlaws realize that each time he rode in a raid, he was praying he would die a death so hideous that he would be set free at last from the sorrow in his guilt-ridden heart.

The two Mexicans had inched closer to the Indian, and when he realized they stood only a couple of feet away from the girl, his anger flared. *"Aco tndn-nil gon-ye?"* he demanded in a fierce tone of voice.

Both Mexicans shrugged and looked at one another. The Indian was the one who was making all the racket, yet he was asking them what was causing all the trouble? They lowered their rifles and shook their heads as they staggered back to their blankets. "All Indians are crazy," they mumbled to one another as they settled back down to sleep.

Chateo did not move until he was certain they were both asleep again. His thoughts were jumbled with faded memories of the past. He wondered if the best thing he could do was to ignore what this girl had just revealed to him, and to continue with his life as before. Most likely his daughter had forgotten about him years ago since he had rarely come to the village to see her or her mother. He would not allow this new information to disrupt his life, he told himself with firm resolution.

"She talked about you throughout the whole journey," Margaret announced to him. "It is her greatest desire to find you now that we are going back to our own people."

The tough exterior Chateo was trying to uphold began to crumble. More than anything he wanted to be reunited with his little girl, but his life of crime would never permit it. He was an outlaw on all the reservations, and even in Mexico he had to tread a thin line to avoid capture by the Mexican armies. Yet, an obsession to see his daughter again began to overcome everything else. She would be at least eleven or twelve years old now, he quickly calculated. If he were to go to the reservation to see her, would he be able to leave her again? He shook his head as the idea passed through his mind. There was no way his conscience would permit him to desert her again.

He thought of the hideout in the Mexican jungle where he spent much of his time when he was not out on raids. Although its occupants were mostly wrongdoers, many of them lived there with their families. He usually spent his time at the lawless' retreat on a drinking binge. Still, he could recall seeing children running in and out of the trees and down by the river. Compared to the life his daughter would be forced to live on the reservation, that had to be better, or at least no worse, he reasoned.

"I'm going to the reservation to get her," he stated in a tone which defied disagreement. "And you are going to help me."

Margaret opened her mouth to ask him how he expected her to do that, but he did not grant her the time to ask questions. Motioning for her to keep quiet, he carefully scooped up his rifle, then grabbed his saddle from the ground. With several nervous glances

95

at the sleeping Mexicans, Chateo pulled Margaret over to where the horses were tethered and quickly saddled his horse. He did not mount the animal, though, nor did he permit Margaret to climb onto its back. Instead, he led both her and the horse from the other horses, until they were far enough away for him to leap into the saddle and pull Margaret up with him. With one quick glance over his shoulder at the sleeping Mexicans, Chateo kicked his mount in the sides and sent the animal galloping out across the grassy plains. There was a chance the Mexicans would come after them, but he would have no problem losing them. There were very few things a Mexican could do that an Apache couldn't do better, Chateo reminded himself.

When they had gone far enough for Chateo to slow his horse down to a walk, he began to devise a plan to retrieve his daughter from the reservation. He could not go after her on his own because he was too well known at the Army posts for his thievery, but with the woman's help it would not be impossible. He glanced at the back of her head and thought of what it would be like to run his fingers through the thick mass of her long hair. It had been a very long time since he had had a woman who had not already been with every man on both sides of the border. He noticed the way her soft curves pressed against his own hard form as they bounced along on the back of his horse. For a while Chateo forgot about his daughter. His thoughts were on more sensuous things—such as how he intended to claim this young half-breed's innocence just as soon as she had fulfilled her usefulness to him. If she satisfied him enough, he would even take her to Mexico with him, so that she could help take care of Kaytee. The idea of having his little girl back, and also of possessing a woman as young and beautiful as this one, was pleasing to Chateo. All of the other comancheros would be envious when they saw the prize he had claimed during this raid. He smiled wickedly beneath his large sombrero as his eyes once more traveled down the gentle curve of Margaret's back. Luck was with him again it seemed, and this time he was going to ride its fated wings all the way.

Chapter Six

Chateo walked at a leisurely pace beside his horse. His lecherous grin consumed his face while he studied the rhythmical swaying of the young woman's hips as she walked ahead of him. She had told him she was one of the Apache children. If the white men still considered her a child, however, Chateo thought they must be blind. In his close observation of the woman's gait, he stumbled over a broken branch. He drew a relieved breath when she did not turn around to acknowledge his clumsiness. He had led them into a gully forested with cottonwood trees in order to cover their trail in case the Mexicans were attempting to follow them. It was easier to lead the horse and walk through the low-hanging branches than to ride, and Chateo was especially pleased with this view of the young woman.

Many years had passed since they had lived in the Apache *ranchería,* but he remembered Margaret's mother, Sky Dreamer, very vividly. This girl had inherited her mother's beauty. Chateo shook his head and sighed at the prospects her nearness aroused within his trail-worn body. His patience was growing thin, but he was afraid to take liberties with the girl before she had helped him get his daughter away from the reservation. Still, just being in her presence was pure torture, for Chateo was not used to denying himself anything it was within his grasp to obtain.

As the heat of the day grew scorching, he decided it was time for them to stop until the sun was not so hot. "We'll take a siesta," he commanded as he tied his horse to a nearby tree. He held out a canteen of water, which Margaret accepted eagerly. She wiped the back of her hand across her mouth when she finished drinking, then raised her eyes toward the man who was watching her with a scrutiny that suddenly made her feel shy and embarrassed.

"What is your Apache name?" he asked sharply.

Margaret tossed her thick mane of hair over her shoulder as she answered. "I was named after my grandmother, Morning Star."

"Lucero," Chateo repeated in Mexican. "I will call you"—he hesitated as he debated between the Mexican version of her name as opposed to the white man's pronouncement—"Morning Star," he announced with a definite toss of his head.

Margaret tossed her thick mane of dark hair over her shoulder. "My name is Margaret Sinclair."

Chateo snickered crudely at her uppity tone. The only other women he had heard speak so haughtily were the madams who ran the whorehouses on the American side of the Rio Grande.

With a cold glare in the Indian's direction, Margaret crossed her arms over her bosom and turned away from him. He could call her by any name he wished, she decided, because soon she would be rid of him. All she really cared about right now was seeing Lieutenant Wade again. So much had happened since their brief, but beautiful, kiss that Margaret found herself wondering if she had imagined it all. She wished this was just one more of her terrible nightmares, and soon she could wake up and discover she was still at the waterhole, within the warm embrace of the tall, blond officer. The only thing which seemed to make sense anymore was finding sanctuary in the arms of a man like Lieutenant Wade, which was exactly what she planned to do as soon as they reached the Indian agency.

Even Fort Still did not seem so dreadful when compared to what she might have endured at the mercy of the renegades. Only Chateo—and her Indian heritage—had spared her so far. It seemed uncanny that she would be grateful to admit she had Apache bloodlines after she had been so determined not to acknowledge her true origins. But soon, she repeatedly told herself, they would be back at the reservation and she could return to her original plan—to live in the white world . . . with Lieutenant Wade.

The soft smile that drifted across her lips turned to a startled gasp when she turned around to glance at Chateo again. He had removed his heavy serape and the huge sombrero that covered his head. Shamelessly, he had also taken off his tall moccasins and shirt, leaving nothing other than his tan cotton pants to cover his bronzed body. His chiseled features did not seem so harsh now that his face was surrounded by the long strands of thick black hair released from his hat. In fact, Margaret noticed with aggravation, he was rather handsome for an older man. When he looked up and caught the girl's gaping stare, he graced her with a sly grin that bordered on indecency.

Margaret's first reaction was to hurl an insult at him for being so bold, but rationality stopped her. This man was capable of doing anything he wanted to her, whenever it pleased him. The only reason he had treated her decently so far was because he needed her help when they reached the reservation, and possibly because they were both from the same tribe. However, Margaret did not doubt that it would take little to arouse his anger, and the last thing she wanted to do was make the wrong move now. When she was so close to being reunited with the lieutenant.

She turned away from the sight of the near-naked Indian and gritted her teeth in aggravation. She could remember her father and the other warriors parading around the *ranchería* in just a breechcloth, or only a pair of leggings. But, things had changed drastically since then. Nowadays, civilized men did not undress in front of a lady. But, she reminded herself, Katherine's father was not civilized—he was nothing more than a savage renegade.

"Do you want to undress, Morning Star?" he asked in his heavily accented voice. Margaret swung back around to glare at him. She forgot her vow to avoid angering him as her furious gaze raked over his bare chest.

"I will help you to find Katherine when we reach the reservation," she said between tightly drawn lips. "And I will do everything in my power to see to it that your presence is not discovered by the soldiers, because you have treated me with respect . . . up until now." She took a step forward, making her tangled hair fall in disarray over her shoulders and across her heaving bosom. "But I will never undress for you or do anything else that would suggest to you that I would be more to you than I already am. And"—she pointed a finger at him in a threatening manner, adding—"My name is Margaret Sinclair! Is that clear enough for you to understand?"

Chateo's mouth flapped open, then closed without his making a sound. Instead, his lower lip curled downward in an intense frown. He was a dangerous renegade, yet she had just spoken to him as no one ever had dared, especially a woman. So why am I not angry? he wondered with a sense of awe. Ever since he had first set eyes on her last night, he'd had no doubt that he could have this woman whenever he found it convenient, but now it had become something else . . . now it was a challenge, and he loved to face a challenge. Having sex with a woman he had taken as his captive was a simple matter his strength could easily achieve, but her assumption that she was in control of such matters had summoned up more of the strange emotions that Chateo had thought to be long dead. He had not forgotten how to make a woman come to him, and that was exactly what he had in mind for this young woman. Chateo felt elated, reborn! Since the surrender of his people to the white men, there were few challenges for men like him. That was why he liked the danger and excitement of riding with the comancheros, but this feisty lady presented him with the prospect of a new sort of adventure.

He casually removed his bedroll from his saddle and spread it out in the shade of a drooping cottonwood. He was aware that the girl watched him constantly, and he also knew she was expecting him to retaliate against her remarks by forcing her to submit to him. The panic in her shimmering turquoise eyes told him how much she feared him, in spite of her act of bravery. Chateo liked a woman who could stand up for herself. Yes, she is well worth the challenge, he told himself.

With a great deal of self-control, he stretched out upon the bedroll and pretended to ignore the presence of the girl. He even forced his eyes to close, although it was difficult to retain the smirk which hovered on his lips. He wasn't worried about his captive escaping, because she had nowhere to go. Besides, an Apache could track anyone—anywhere. If she fled, he would find her in no time. His exhaustion from the hard riding of the past few days soon overtook his senses. As sleep began to claim his tired mind, the past came back to him with disturbing clarity. He thought of the young Apache wife and the baby daughter he had deserted time and time again. Now that he knew Kaytee was still alive, he wondered if he would be able to erase some of his own guilt by trying to be a real father to her once they were together again. But his last thoughts before drifting off into the misty land of slumber were of the young woman, and of what it would be like to feel her soft skin against his own, to feel her yielding to his touch without any resistance.

Margaret did not let up her guard, even after it was apparent that Chateo had fallen asleep. His nonchalant reaction to her outburst had left her twice as worried about his intentions. Since she had been so certain he would try to force himself on her, she had been planning to tell him about her involvement with Lieutenant Wade. Even a renegade like Chateo would surely be smart enough not to mess with a woman who belonged to an officer of the U.S. Cavalry. But he hadn't given her the chance to relay this information to him. Instead he had lain down and fallen asleep as though she wasn't even appealing enough to draw his interest. Margaret told herself she must be going insane. Why else would she be angry because this savage didn't try to attack her, when she should be grateful because he hadn't done anything at all.

Margaret finally grew tired of watching Chateo while he slept peacefully, and decided to give up her intense vigil. She glanced around at the ground and frowned with dismay. The whole area was covered with branches from the cottonwood trees. The only welcoming place was where the man's bedroll lay. Margaret debated as to whether or not she would be tempting her luck if she were to lie on the edge of his blanket. She tiptoed over to it and cautiously lowered herself to the ground. Holding her breath, she slid onto her back and waited. He still made no movement and his breathing was even and heavy. Margaret exhaled and closed her eyes. Sleep claimed her tired mind at once, but it was not long before memories of her own past slowly began to intrude into the hazy passages of her mind . . .

"Morning Star, wake up!"

Margaret fought to regain consciousness, but the darkness would not release her from its evil grip. She tried to run from the edge of the burning village, but her feet had turned to clay and would not move. She could hear someone calling her name—Morning Star—but wait, wasn't her name Margaret? If they would call her by her rightful name, she could escape from this hell.

"Morning Star—I mean, Margaret!" Chateo shook her slender form with more force in the hope of tearing her from the clutches of the nightmare causing her to scream in agony. He pressed his face close to her ears and called out to her again. This time she stopped her tortured cries, and her long lashes began to tremble as though they were trying to pry apart. A cold sweat drenched her face when at last her lids fluttered open and misty turquoise eyes settled on his face. He could tell she had no idea where she was or who it was who held her. A deep compassion flooded over Chateo, another emotion that was foreign to and unwanted by his icy heart. Sometime—long, long ago—he had forgotten other people experienced suffering that was worse even than his own guilt-ridden pain.

105

A heavy veil of fog hovered over Margaret, yet something still prevented her from returning from the grasp of her dreaded land of nightmares. She felt the strong arms around her and envisioned the face of the boy who always saved her from these horrible visions of death. But it was not Adam's voice who called out to her, and her mind was thrown into a jumble of confusion again. The demons of the burning *ranchería* reached out their fiery clutches, but she withdrew into the protective arms again. Now his voice was stronger, demanding that she escape back to reality. She forced her eyes to open and remain fixed on the countenance of the man who had saved her from the demons of flames and death.

"You were having a nightmare," Chateo said as a relieved sigh escaped from his throat. He began to wonder if she was completely losing her grip on reality and would not be able to wake up. Even now, she seemed distant and confused. "It was only a nightmare," he repeated.

Margaret tried to nod her head and attempted to speak, but her tongue felt thick and seemed glued to the roof of her mouth. This was the worst nightmare she had ever experienced, and it had stripped her of all her energy. In the past, it had always been Adam who had come to her rescue whenever one of the terrible nightmares had claimed her in slumber. She felt lost and alone because he was not with her now. The loss of his friendship was something she would never learn to live with, and she felt the deep void it left in her more than ever at that moment.

Chateo continued to hold her in his arms, unsure of what else he should do. Whatever was causing such terror in her sleep had also invaded his soul. Living in Mexico among the comancheros had erased most of the legends he had learned from the wise old shamans of his tribe. But now every evil and wicked superstition he could recall from his Apache teachings flashed through his mind and caused a chill to trickle along his spine.

"I'm all right," Margaret ran a shaky hand over her drenched brow and tried to sit up. "I always have these nightmares."

Chateo gave her a worried frown. "Always? What are they about?"

She glanced away from him, suddenly embarrassed that he was holding her so close against his bare chest. "About the day my family died."

"Oh," Chateo said in a hoarse whisper. He was not accustomed to extending words of sympathy to anyone, and he could not think of the proper thing to say to her, so he fell silent. He cleared his throat after an uncomfortable pause. "If you're up to it, we'll be on our way. I want to reach the reservation by nightfall."

Unintentionally, his words sounded gruff and without emotion. Margaret's feeling of despair expanded throughout her entire being until she wished her nightmare had just swallowed her up so that she could have joined her family within its black depths. She nodded her head weakly and permitted Chateo to help her to her feet. As he quickly dressed and saddled the horse so they could be on their way again, Margaret leaned against the base of a cottonwood tree and waited. She wondered if her life would ever turn out the way she dreamed, or if she was destined to live with the uncertainty of never knowing what would happen from one minute to the next.

When Chateo motioned for her to join him on his horse, she complied without resistance. As she settled into the uncomfortable position upon the saddle, she became aware of the drastic change in them. Chateo also sensed the difference, though neither of them could understand the strange emotions that ran amuck in their beings. It was as if the past had somehow become intertwined with the future, and the two of them had become trapped in the gap which bridged it all together.

Not even the idea of seeing Katherine and Dona, or especially Adam, could dismiss the cold foreboding which overcame Margaret when she gazed at the dim lights of Fort Sill. Arriving at the reservation was the nightmare that plagued her waking hours with visions almost as disturbing as the ones she experienced in her sleep. In Margaret's mind the reservation represented loss of freedom and entrance into a life of pure hell.

"How will I ever find Katherine in there?" she asked with a trembling voice.

Chateo tipped his head back and looked out from beneath the brim of his sombrero. "They should've arrived late this afternoon. By the time they were tagged and counted it would have been almost dark, so they'll probably be spending the night on the post. They won't assign them to a family until tomorrow."

"Tagged and counted?" Margaret repeated as another shiver shook her with visible force. She felt sick at the thought of the children being treated as though they were not human. Her determination to remain free grew stronger than ever, even if it meant giving up the friendship she had known all of her life.

Chateo slid from his saddle, then pulled Margaret down next to him. He tied the horse's reins around a clump of sagebrush and walked to the ridge of the incline where they had stopped. The material of his

108

shapeless serape waved back and forth in the gentle breeze as he reached forward and pointed his finger through the last of the fading twilight. "See that log building at the end of the barracks? That's where they'll be sleeping." He continued to survey the area from the hillside, then sighed and sat down in the deep prairie grass which grew thick upon the ground. He motioned for Margaret to join him, adding, "We will rest here tonight. It will be easier to sneak onto the agency tomorrow."

"In the daytime?" Margaret asked. She found it hard to believe that he actually thought they would be able to walk onto the reservation in the broad daylight without being caught. However, considering the way he was reclining upon the ground, he didn't act too worried about the prospect.

"They will send them out into the fields to work. We will find her then." He reached into his pocket and produced a piece of hardtack. Margaret shook her head when he offered it to her. With a shrug of his shoulders, he shoved the jerky back to its hiding place. He removed his sombrero and tossed it on the ground beside him, then leaned back and placed his hands behind his head for a makeshift pillow. Pretending to close his eyes, through narrow slits he watched the woman. Every minute which passed with her in his presence caused him more turmoil. He had not practiced restraint with a woman since his youth, when he had first pursued his wife. Being with Margaret Sinclair had caused all those ancient memories to resurface and, with them, a fear so powerful that it made Chateo's soul quake in response.

Once, many years ago, he had asked the Apache god, Usen, to help him to overcome his wicked ways, and to teach him how to be a better father to his tiny daughter, a dependable husband to his young wife. In reply, Usen had taken Chateo's family away from him altogether, or so Chateo had believed for all of these years. Now he wondered if his daughter's return was Usen's way of testing him. But he felt so undeserving of a second opportunity. He was a murderer and a renegade—wanted on both sides of the Rio Grande. What kind of a life could he offer a little girl?

A twinkling light broke through the black velvet of the night sky and caught Chateo's attention. As he watched the dark heavens fill with millions of tiny glistening stars an odd sense of destiny overcame him. The comancheros he rode with hardly ever came this far north to conduct their raids, but for some reason they had wandered all through Texas and found themselves on the land bordering the Oklahoma territory. Chateo hated Oklahoma and all of its inhabitants. This ugly land was not the homelands of his people, and no Apache deserved to be sent to such a foreign place to dwell. Fort Sill was worse than a prison; it was the death of the true Apache way of life.

Only yesterday, when they realized they had almost traveled across the Texas line, Chateo had told the other men that he did not want to go any farther. Just knowing they were in the vicinity of the reservation had made him feel uneasy. The Mexicans had just decided to return to Sonora with him when they had encountered the soldier's camp. Normally, such a small band of outlaws would have avoided any contact with the cavalry. But this time they had been unusually careless and had decided to see if the soldiers were transporting any valuable cargo. What they had encountered instead was Margaret Sinclair . . . and her knowledge of Chateo's daughter.

Chateo's gaze remained fixed toward the sky, which had grown into a speckled mass of shining stars. A man's imagination could draw a million pictures out of that endless maze of lights. But tonight Chateo's thoughts were on the strange irony of all that had happened recently. Maybe Usen had finally determined that Chateo did deserve one final chance. If that was the case, though, Chateo wondered, how did Margaret Sinclair fit into this plan?

Chapter Seven

Fort Sill, beneath the warm rays of the morning sun, did not appear to be the tower of evil Margaret had imagined it when they had arrived the night before. Today, even Chateo's idea of entering the agency in the light of day did not seem so farfetched. From the brush-covered hillside on which Margaret and Chateo observed the Army headquarters, they could even see exactly where the children had been sent after leaving the post. A group of thatched huts, along with several newly built log cabins stood a short distance from the fort. Chateo explained to Margaret that the reservation covered a great deal of the Oklahoma territory, but the most dangerous Indians—such as the Apaches who were prisoners of war—were forced to live under close supervision. Other tribes lived farther away from the post and only came to the main agency to receive their weekly rations and supplies.

"The children will work in the fields until the midday meal, then they will attend school throughout the afternoon." Chateo smoothed back his bluntly cut hair with the palm of his hand, then placed his sombrero atop of his head. His raven brows drew into a thoughtful line. "We will have to find Kaytee this morning and be off the reservation before the children are called for school." He tossed a thin, ragged blanket at Margaret. "Here, drape this over your head and rub dirt on your face."

The look of disgust which Margaret cast in Chateo's direction did little to improve his tense spirits. The night had granted him little rest, and the disturbing thoughts which had plagued him throughout the long night were still haunting him. He grunted from aggravation and turned away when she had donned the blanket and patted a layering of dust upon her cheeks. Even in this guise, she did not look anything like the women who worked in the fields on the reservation.

Margaret grew indignant when she heard his rude grumblings. "It is the best I can do. Besides, this is a stupid plan!"

Chateo swung around, anger growing on his dark face like a brewing storm when he looked at her again. "Everything I do must seem stupid to an educated squaw like you."

Margaret cringed outwardly at the sound of his insult. She was not a squaw, but he was correct about her education. She had studied hard, had spent every hour of her time perfecting the ways of the white women at the school, and she hadn't done all that so she could rub dirt on her face and follow the orders of some Apache renegade. In a moment of irrational exasperation, she yanked the blanket from her head and tossed it at Chateo's feet.

"I'm smart enough to know that this will never work!" She stepped back when Chateo moved toward her, but he reached her in only one long step. He grabbed her by the forearm and pulled her close to him.

"You're not in a position to make decisions. You are my captive."

Margaret pulled away from him as far as possible,

114

but his tight grip would not allow her to escape. "What makes you think I won't get down there and start yelling for help?"

Chateo yanked her closer again. "Because you don't want to spend the rest of your life with a dirty blanket hanging over your head and grime smeared across that pretty face. You need me as much as I need you."

"You couldn't be more wrong," Margaret retorted. "I don't need you to escape life on the reservation." She tossed her head back defiantly before continuing, "Why, right now, there is a lieutenant waiting at Fort Sill for me to return to him."

Chateo released her abruptly as the sting of her insinuation sank into his mind. He dropped his hand from her arm as if she were poison. "I was wrong." His eyes narrowed and his breathing became short gasps. "You are not very smart if you believe such foolishness."

Unexpected tears sprang into Margaret's eyes. "He is waiting for me. He kissed me and—"

Rage left Chateo a man without control, overpowered his senses. Once again he grabbed Margaret and yanked her toward him until their bodies were crushed up against one another. "Of course he kissed you, and he probably did a lot more once he learned you were willing to do anything to receive extra attention. But are you so ignorant you would really believe that a white soldier would still want a half-breed squaw once he has returned to his own kind?" A low, grating chuckle rang from deep in his throat. "I thought you were innocent and untouched." He gave her a brutal shove, knocking her back into the deep grass. "I was stupid, too!"

The violent fall knocked the wind from Margaret for an instant. She tried to regain her breath, along with her spinning senses as she struggled to get back up to

115

her feet. Chateo was wrong! Lieutenant Wade was not using her, and she would prove it. "He only kissed me," she said in breathless gasps. Another crude chortle broke from Chateo when she added, "And I know he cared for me. I'll show you when we get to the fort."

"Don't bother." He kicked at the ground with the curled-up toe of his tall moccasin, flinging grass and dirt into the air. "Just get out of my sight—go back to your white soldier boy." His face twisted into a hardened expression that sent shivers down Margaret's spine.

A tightness worked its way through her chest as she balanced herself on her quaking limbs. His cruel words had reached her in a tortured way she could not ignore. What proof did she have that the lieutenant did not feel the way Chateo predicted? She shuddered at the realization that the only relationship she had with the lieutenant was in her own dreams and hopes. Their brief encounter at the waterhole might have meant nothing to him. What if she did go into the reservation to find him, only to learn that the officer had hoped to seduce her because he figured an Indian girl would be an easy target? Was that why he had kissed her so impulsively when she had come to see him at the waterhole? Margaret would not permit herself to believe the lieutenant capable of behaving in such a low fashion, so she forced those terrible thoughts from her mind.

"I want to help you to find Katherine—I mean Kaytee." Her voice trembled, but not with the fear of being caught when she entered the agency. Her greatest fear was that she would have no choice but to stay on the reservation if the lieutenant did not want her to be with him.

Chateo did not answer her for several minutes. His rage surprised him. Why should he care if this woman wanted to be some soldier's whore. He'd had more than one opportunity to have her in the past couple of days, but now he was glad he hadn't laid with her. He never had preferred white women to his own kind, and it was apparent that Margaret Sinclair's white blood had strangled the Apache blood that had pulsed through her veins at birth. Chateo shook his head in an attempt to think of something other than his fury at this traitor. He did need her help to find his daughter, though. He did not even know what Kaytee looked like after all these years. For now, he told himself, he would have to put his feelings aside.

"You'd better hurry, before the sun is up all the way."

Margaret stumbled forward and grabbed the blanket from the ground. "What should I do once I'm there?"

"Blend in with the others." He glanced at her, but the heated flush of his anger had not left his face. "Don't let that blanket fall off your head." He blinked, then turned away as if it hurt his eyes to gaze upon her face. "When you find Kaytee, explain to her that she is to pretend to be sick. Take her to the shade of those trees that border the far side of the cornfield."

Margaret swallowed the heavy lump in her throat. "Then what?"

He forced his cold raven gaze to remain leveled on her face. "When you are sure no one is paying attention, tell Kaytee to run through the trees—to the other side, where I will be waiting for her."

A strange feeling of desertion overcame Margaret when she realized that Chateo had said he would be waiting for only Kaytee to emerge from the trees. He was right though, she reminded herself. Once she found Lieutenant Wade, she would be able to prove to herself—and to Chateo—that the lieutenant's attraction to her was honorable.

The sun was already resting the curve of its fiery ball upon the distant horizon by the time Margaret had skirted the fort and made her way to the side of the agency where sprawling fields of corn and pumpkins claimed the open spaces. She felt as though she had not taken a breath since she had left Chateo at the top of the hillside. She'd practically had to crawl down the slope on hands and knees to keep hidden in the deep grasses. The long calico skirt of her dress and petticoat had kept twisting and wrapping itself around her legs, until she'd wished she could disregard the garment altogether. After skidding halfway down the slope on her knees, however, most of the material was shredded beyond repair and hung in long grass-stained tatters about her legs.

Scattered clumps of brush and sage provided sparse cover as Margaret slouched down and ran from one bush to another, until she had reached the back side of the first barracks. She was still holding her breath as she inched her way along from building to building. Reaching the opposite side of the post almost seemed too easy, and to Margaret's surprise, she did not encounter any soldiers along the way. The fort was still quiet at this early hour, but the Apaches were already making their way out into the fields to work. Once Margaret stood at the edge of the cornfields she took a deep breath and nearly choked as air rushed through her empty lungs. Knowing she was past the danger of being caught on the post did not ease her mind, however, because she was just as terrified now as she had been when she first started on this dangerous mission.

How will I ever find Katherine out there? she wondered as she watched the Indians move slowly through the rows of tall cornstalks. From Margaret's viewpoint everyone looked virtually the same. The women and girls all wore long skirts with leather leggings or high moccasins. Their heads were covered with serapes or scarves, and nobody's face was visible unless one got close enough to look through the narrow gap of material hanging in front of it. All of the men wore identical clothing, too. Their outfits consisted of cotton trousers and long tunics, which were topped by loose breechcloths that hung past their knees. Strips of material had been twisted and wound around their head to create colorful turbans to keep their hair away from their faces while they worked.

Margaret felt a sense of remorse as she watched their wearisome progress through the rows of cornstalks. Everyone walked with shoulders hunched, without speaking. They seemed a pitiful lot, and it broke her heart to remember the pride the people in her *ranchería* had once had. Life on the reservation seemed to have stripped the Apaches of everything, except the meager thread they clung to for survival. She recalled Dona's brave words about making this such a wonderful place for their people. But when Dona had spoken those gallant words, she'd had no idea of the bleak situation they would be encountering.

Margaret reminded herself of the reason she was here, and her tear-filled gaze searched over the forlorn shapes scattered along the rows of stalks.

She realized the only way she was going to find Katherine was to walk down each row of cornstalks, but just thinking about being so close to the other Indians was horrifying. What if she ended up spending the rest of her days clawing and digging in this field like a slave? Even her feet seemed reluctant to move as she made her way along the rows of chest-high stalks. Several elderly women tried to force her to kneel down beside them, pointing toward the scraggly weeds that grew abundantly around the stalks. Margaret shook her head frantically and ran down the row in a panic. Beneath the blanket, she could feel beads of sweat popping out upon her cheeks and forehead, and her nerves were so shaken she wished she could flee from the field, get as far away from this awful place as possible.

Locating Katherine in this hellhole did not seem possible, yet Margaret knew that the girl had to be here somewhere. She took long strides as she made her way up and down the rows, trying to make it seem she was on an important errand and could not be bothered. She was ignored by most of those she passed. There were little girls working in the field, but so far none was Katherine. When Margaret spotted a couple of children from Carlisle, she pulled the blanket over her face and hurried past. She did not want her presence to be known until that was absolutely necessary. Once she found Katherine and sent her off to be with her father, she would throw off this wretched blanket and wipe the dirt from her face so that she could go in search of the lieutenant.

Margaret's footsteps slowed as she approached a small girl sitting among the corn rows in a motionless heap. Though Katherine had her head covered, Margaret recognized her at once, but the tear-stained face peeking out from the gray shawl that protected the child from dust, bugs, and scorching sun broke through all of Margaret's defenses. She fell down next to the younger girl and gently touched her cheek where the tears had made muddy trails.

"Please don't cry, Katherine."

"Margaret? Is it really you?" Katherine's onslaught of tears stopped at once. The trace of a smile cut through the heavy smudges on her round face. "We were so afraid the comancheros had taken you away forever."

Margaret almost laughed, in spite of their predicament. The comancheros had taken her away, and then one of them had brought her back. "Listen to me, Katherine. This is very important." She glanced around, all at once feeling as though someone was watching them. "Pretend to be working," she ordered as she bent over and started yanking the spidery weeds from the dry ground.

Katherine followed her lead, but whispered in a frantic voice, "It's awful here. They are going to make us live with families we do not know and . . . look!" She sat up straight and pulled out a silver chain, which had a square tag attached to it. "I don't even have a name anymore. They call me L24." Her lower lip trembled as another rush of tears flowed down her cheeks.

Margaret felt a quivering in her chest, but she fought against the urge to cry. "I have a surprise for you, but you must do exactly as I say." She waited for the girl to nod in agreement before continuing to speak in a low tone of voice. "I want you to act as though you feel faint and weak. I will pretend to help you over to the grove of trees at the far end of the field. When we get there, I'll tell you what to do next." Katherine's worried expression did not inspire bravery in Margaret, but the young girl did not ask any questions as she took a deep breath and rose to her feet.

Margaret stood up next to her, wondering if her shaky legs would be strong enough to support her own weight. Without prodding, Katherine staggered forward in a pretend stupor. She clutched at Margaret as she slumped against her and acted as though she could not stand without help. Margaret's mind was spinning with a hundred visions of being caught in this charade, but she slid her arms around Katherine's slender waist and began to walk down the narrow row without looking to either side. She heard low murmurings from several women, but no one offered to help.

121

In no time at all they were at the end of the field. Margaret kept reminding herself not to run, although both of them were taking rather large steps, considering that Katherine was supposed to be ill. Margaret glanced around to locate the grove of trees, and to see if anyone was observing them. It did not look as if they were being watched, so she motioned to Katherine to head for the trees. Their hurried strides had only taken them about halfway when a woman's voice rang out from one of the corn rows.

"Katherine! What's wrong?" Dona rushed toward them, wiping grimy hands on her full skirt. She stopped several feet away from the pair and gasped when she recognized who was holding up the slumping form of the young girl. "Margaret!"

Margaret's whole body was invaded with panic when Dona called out her name. Her mouth flapped open, but terror left her speechless.

"Lower your voice," Katherine hissed at Dona. "And help Margaret to get me over to those trees."

Katherine's calm and mature grip on the situation snapped Margaret back to her senses. She gave Dona a look of determined resolution, which immediately made Dona's gaze fall downward. Without glancing up again, Dona stepped up to Katherine. She held one of the girl's arms as they walked along the edge of the field without saying another word. But when they reached the grove of trees she ferociously turned on Margaret.

"What are you up to, and why have you involved Katherine in your madness?" Dona's dark face was flushed, and her eyes flashed with an anger Margaret had never before witnessed in her friend. "Where have you been hiding the past few days?" Dona demanded before Margaret had a chance to reply to her first questions.

122

Katherine slumped down to the ground in a mock faint. The other two girls stared down at her in confusion. Dona's attack had almost caused Margaret to forget their plan. She fell to her knees next to the little girl and pretended to feel her forehead with the back of her hand.

With a concerned gasp, Dona joined them on the ground. "Are you really ill, Katherine?"

Margaret's mind finally began to work in a rational manner again, making her realize the urgency of getting Katherine away before it was too late. The three of them huddled under the trees, instead of working in the field, were bound to catch someone's attention soon. "I don't have time to explain everything to either of you. But please believe I am only trying to do what is best for everyone." Dona opened her mouth to dispute her, but Margaret did not have time to listen to her arguments. "On the other side of those trees is Katherine's father, Chateo."

Katherine gasped and threw her hand over her mouth to keep from crying out in joy and surprise. But Dona's face filled with a look of distrust.

"I know this to be true," Margaret said determinedly as she glanced at Dona. She looked back toward the younger girl and rushed on, her tone of voice revealing panic. "You must run through the trees, and don't stop for any reason. Your father is waiting for you on the other side of that grove."

Dona continued to shake her head in disbelief. "But, how . . . where—"

Katherine, however, did not hesitate to make her move. All that mattered as she jumped to her feet was that her father was alive and waiting for her on the other side of the clump of trees. She smiled at her two friends, but did not speak as she charged beneath the low-hanging branches of the piñon trees. Margaret and Dona both rose up and glanced around with apprehension. Katherine's departure was not very discreet, still, it did not seem to draw anyone's attention. In unison the two older girls sighed and turned back to watch Katherine disappear from view; then Dona swung around to face Margaret once again.

"It was foolish of you to send her off like that. How do you know what kind of a life she will have with a father she has not seen for eight years?"

"I know it will be an improvement over this life," Margaret said defensively as she motioned toward the rows of cornstalks. "But I don't have time to talk to you about that now, Dona. I must find Lieutenant Wade."

Dona's eyes narrowed as she pushed the shawl from her head. "Why?"

Margaret raised her hands and clasped them together, "Please, I beg of you, I have to find him."

"Well, he's gone. He went back to his own post in Arizona yesterday—just as soon as he dumped us here." Dona seemed to find satisfaction in informing Margaret that the lieutenant had not waited for her return.

All hope drained from Margaret at this smug announcement. Her worst fears were realized. She had nowhere to turn now—and she would rather die than stay on this reservation. Her eyes traveled toward the dusty fields, then back to Dona's accusing face. "Where's Adam?"

"He's going to be the new schoolteacher for the younger children who are still attending classes. You had been assigned that job, but since you conveniently disappeared, they gave the position to Adam."

Margaret could tell there was no way she could convince Dona that she had not run away, and at any minute their parley was sure to be discovered by one of the field workers or by a passing soldier. Right now Margaret had to make a choice . . . the hardest choice of her young life. And it would have to be made within the next few minutes.

"I'm going with Katherine and her father," she said sharply, surprising even herself with the unexpected decision. "Please come with us?" she added in a pleading tone.

Dona's gaze turned toward the fields as if she were considering the offer; then her eyes fell back to the ground. "No, Margaret. Someday we will make a difference here. Besides, we are not going to stay here for long. The soldiers told us last night that eventually we might be sent to the reservation at San Carlos. That's in Arizona," Dona added as her voice rose with excitement.

Margaret shook her head in a forlorn manner. If they ever were permitted to go to San Carlos, they would be back in Arizona but not back home. None of them had a home anymore, because Apachería no longer existed. All they had to look forward to was the long days spent working in the fields, and lonely nights filled with dreams that would never come true. The Apache way of life was dead, and as Margaret gazed at the barren land that surrounded the agency, she wondered if they all would not be better off dead.

Her jumbled thoughts snapped back to Chateo and Katherine. In alarm she turned in the direction in which Katherine had fled. There was still a slim chance of finding a life outside of the white man's reservations, but time was racing like wildfire. She could not hesitate a moment longer. Without warning, Margaret reached out and hugged Dona. "I hope someday you will understand why I must do this, but remember that I love you, my friend," she whispered.

When she turned loose of Dona's limp form, she

did not wait for a reply. Her feet moved as though they didn't have time to touch the ground, and her heart thudded like dynamite exploding within her breast. The open meadow beyond the clump of trees loomed ahead of her like a giant web waiting to entangle her in its clutches. What if she had waited too long? Chateo and Kaytee might already have gone? She would not even know what direction to take to search for them —she would be trapped here!

In blind panic she charged out from the shelter of the trees. Not knowing which way to look or what she should do, she twirled around in a mindless circle. Katherine's cry stopped her crazy turmoil. Margaret did not waste any more precious time, but began to run the short distance to where Chateo had stopped his horse. She was breathless when she reached them, but Chateo did not offer her a ride. Instead, he slid down to the ground beside her, leaving Katherine alone in the saddle. His eyes met with the deep turquoise of Margaret's worried gaze for an instant, yet she could not decipher the strange expression which masked his sharp features. He began to lead his horse by the reins, still, he did not speak or give her any clue as to his feelings.

Margaret glanced up at Katherine, but the girl only shrugged and motioned for her to follow. She stumbled along behind the horse as she gathered up the shredded hem of her dress and petticoat to keep from tripping on them. Chateo had not told her that she could not come with them, she reasoned, and even his silent treatment was better than what she had just escaped on the reservation. As she fell into step behind Chateo's horse, she tried to put her deranged life into perspective. She never wanted to live on the reservation, that much she'd determined the instant she had decided to run after Katherine and Chateo. But by accompanying them into Mexico, she would also be giving up her goal to live in the white man's world. Oh, why did everything in her life have to be so unfair? Without invitation, the handsome face of Lieutenant Wade passed through her mind, yet he hadn't even had the decency to wait at the reservation long enough to see if she would be found. She glanced at the muscular form of Chateo as he walked beside his horse, but her thoughts were on the lieutenant. The predicament she was in was all his fault, she told herself in a moment of outrage. If she ever encountered him again, he would wish he had never met Margaret Sinclair!

Chapter Eight

The two riders made their way along the steep embankment in a slow procession. Behind them loped a cavalcade of pack mules. The *aparejos*—fully equipped packsaddles—the mules bore were empty for this portion of the journey. But soon they would be loaded high with beans, flour, and bolts of cloth.

The couple had traveled this route dozens of times, but they never grew careless or impatient with the creeping pace. To the west of the steep trail was the Nacozari Canyon, yet rarely did they gaze at its awesome beauty. A person could become dizzy just from glancing down its steep walls. On the eastern slope of the path, a golden ridge built a natural stairway to the tree-infested forests of the Sierra Madre where glistening white snow capped the high mountain ranges. Pine trees and junipers blended with majestic oaks and sycamores, all carpeting the ground with an array of different shapes and colors.

When the riders reached a lush plateau, which created a less threatening trail, they rode their horses abreast. Pools of clear, cool water dozed silently in the warm rays of the sun, while farther along the trail miniature waterfalls cascaded over rocks coated with deep green moss to end in a gentle stream of water that meandered beside the pathway. A smile drifted across the man's tanned face when his eyes met the contented gaze of his companion. He knew how much she loved this journey through Cima-silkq, or as the white men called it, the Sierra Madre. Whenever it was necessary to leave their beloved Pa-Gotzin-Kay, to go into the valley below for supplies, he always asked her to ride along with him. Today they were going into Bisbee, Arizona for medicinal purposes. Last night they had drunk the last of their whiskey, and without the precious brew, the entire *rancheria* thought they would surely die.

"Look! An Ista," the girl said excitedly, pointing up toward the azure sky where an eagle floated on the wings of the gentle breeze. Its body motionless, the bird seemed suspended by invisible threads from the flawless heavens above.

Nachae glanced up at the eagle with a sigh of contentment. It was rare to see an eagle or a hawk these days. The advance of civilization was rapidly chasing away the most fragile of Usen's creations. It was only in their beautiful Pa-Gotzin-Kay, their Stronghold Mountain of Paradise, that such wonders still existed. The tall Apache chief looked away from the giant bird and turned to observe his daughter once again. He did not want to miss anything she beheld in her gentle perspective. To view life through her eyes was a rare and wondrous gift too precious to waste.

Her lyrical laughter rang out as she noticed two *itseskosi* chasing one another around the base of a tall juniper pine. The squirrels did not acknowledge their audience as they scurried up the base of the tree and disappeared from view. Echo's dark blue eyes glistened with excitement as her head turned from side to side so she could be sure of seeing everything she possibly could as she passed each tree and meadow. How I love this land, she told herself for at least the millionth time. Once she had thought they would never again live in a place as beautiful as their cherished mountains and deserts of Apachería. But the white men had claimed all of those lands in Arizona for their own.

Echo did not like to think of the past; it was too painful to remember all that they had lost. Now, though, they were blessed with good health and plenty of food. The wickiups they lived in were built of the strongest branches and did not permit the cold winds of *chawn-chissy*—the chill of winter—to blow through their interiors. A soft smile curved Echo's mouth when she thought of their home high in the mountains of Sonora. The red shelf of earth, which was secluded from all intruders, was truly a paradise to the small band of Apaches who called it their home.

For over a half a decade they had dwelled in peace and harmony, because the white men did not know they were there. In fact, the white men did not even know of the Indians' existence. The Mexicans who lived in the towns at the base of the Sierra Madre were aware that the Apaches had built a *ranchería* some-where in the high mountain peaks, but since the Indians had not caused any problems, they did not bother to look for the hidden village.

"What do you want me to buy especially for you in Bisbee?" Echo asked her father. "Some tobacco perhaps?" Her head tilted to the side as she glanced at Nachae, a beaming smile upon her face. The deep hue of her blue eyes sparkled with shimmering bolts of silver as the morning sunlight bathed her in its rays. Rebellious strands of her long hair had come loose from the thick braid that hung to her waist, and they created an ebony frame of tousled disarray around her radiant countenance.

131

A warm glow spread throughout Nachae. It did not seem possible that they could be so happy after all the sorrows they had endured in the past. He had a beautiful wife and a daughter equally as lovely. Only one dark cloud hovered over their enchanted lives; yet they would always retain cherished memories of Echo's twin sister, Morning Star, who had been killed by the hated *soldados* at their old home in Arizona.

"I don't need any tobacco," Nachae replied. "But your mother would like a new scarf."

Echo shook her head in agreement. Her mother had developed an addiction to the colorful scarves the Mexican women dyed in vibrant shades of red, yellow, and blue. Echo would also buy a pouch of tobacco for her father while she was shopping at the store. A rush of excitement shot through her as they continued toward Bisbee. They normally did not travel this far north for whiskey and supplies, but the saloon across the border carried a better variety of whiskey than the Mexican cantinas, and the Phelps-Dodge Mercantile stocked a few more luxuries than the small stores on the Mexican side of the border. Already, Echo's mouth was watering for a piece of black licorice and a drink of the sweet-tasting soda which she knew the store owner kept in stock.

"I want you to be out of the town by sundown," Nachae repeated as he always did whenever Echo went into town alone. Because her appearance was not a dead giveaway of her Indian bloodline, it was easy for her to walk the streets of the American town without arousing suspicion. The Apaches valued their tranquil life too much to intentionally alert their Mexican or American neighbors to their whereabouts.

"I can spend our money faster than you can blink an eye. Long before the sun sets in the sky I will be broke and headed out of town." A mischievous grin lit up her face, and melted her father's heart with an overpowering sense of love.

"If there's any trou—"

"I know," she interrupted. "I will hightail it out of town if I see any *soldados,* or men who look like they could be comancheros . . . or if there are any people at all walking around on the streets," she glanced to the side and laughed when she noticed her father shaking his head firmly in agreement. He was protective beyond reason, but she adored him unabashedly.

Nachae pretended not to notice her jest, and gave his head another proud toss. In his love for his family, he knew no shame, and if his constant warnings could prevent his daughter from taking any unnecessary chances then he would tolerate her innocent chides.

The four-day ride from the *ranchería* to the border town of Bisbee was a delightful trip for the couple. The days were hot but tolerable, and the nights were warm and pleasant. And there was always an endless array of awe-inspiring views for them to gape at as they traveled the trails of the Bavispe Barranca. On the morning of the fifth day, Echo brushed her long hair until it glistened like ebony rain; then she wrapped the thick tresses in a tight coil at the base of her neck. She covered her head with a long black lace scarf, draping it across her forehead and allowing the pointed edges to hang over her bosom. Next she donned an outfit consisting of a full-tiered skirt in multicolored layers topped by a long tunic. Her high *kabuns*—the mocassins she usually wore—were discarded for the day. Instead, she slipped her tiny feet into a pair of leather sandals like the ones the Mexican señoritas wore. In this garb she was undistinguishable from any other maiden of Spanish descent.

"Denzhone," Nachae beamed with pride when his daughter twirled around for approval of her guise.

Echo's dark golden skin flushed when her father said she was beautiful, and the smile which broke out upon her soft lips suggested that she agreed with him. The day inspired a feeling of excitement that was difficult for Echo to contain within her slender body. She sensed it would be special, and whatever was about to happen made her feel as though she were going to explode from anticipation. She tried to hide her anxiety from her father, knowing that he would misinterpret her feelings as something bad. But Echo did not sense that premonition of an evil event was causing the tremendous quaking in her stomach. On the contrary, she suspected that today would be the best day of her entire life!

Lieutenant Wade sat at a table in the corner of the dirty cantina. He was not joined by any of his men, because lately his surly attitude had not made him a pleasurable companion. He downed the shot of cheap whiskey he had purchased at the bar when he'd entered, then shoved the glass to the far end of the table. He was supposed to be on duty, he reminded himself. But the border had been quiet since he had returned from Oklahoma, so he was not too concerned about having a drink to ease the guilt he could not rid himself of since his brief encounter with the young half-breed, Margaret Sinclair.

He'd tried to find a clue to her whereabouts when he had led a detail of men out of Oklahoma and through all of Texas before returning to Arizona. Not a trace of the girl or her abductors had been found during the search, however. If she had been taken to a hideout in the Mexican jungle, there was no chance of finding her again. The idea that she had probably been sold into slavery and thoughts of the abuses she would suffer at

134

the hands of the comancheros, had caused such an overwhelming guilt to well up in the officer that he did not know how to cope with its intensity. When the search for Miss Sinclair had been abandoned, Wade had told himself that he would have to put her out of his mind and get on with his own life. That, however, was not so easy for a man with such compassion.

Over and over again, the lieutenant had tried to rationalize his feelings for Margaret Sinclair. He had not fallen in love with her, he had no doubts on that subject. And if he found her tomorrow, his feelings toward her would not change. His despair stemmed from the agonizing knowledge that his own irresponsibility had destroyed a young girl's life. He should not have kissed her when he'd known that it would mean nothing to him, nor should he have deserted her at the waterhole in an attempt to escape from his own drastic mistake. But through the years of his service in the cavalry, he had made other mistakes with his command . . . he had even killed several renegades with his own gun—so why couldn't he shake off the guilt he felt over Margaret Sinclair?

He pushed himself from the table and stomped through the small cantina without glancing at anyone in the room. His men watched his departure with interest, and after he was gone they began to speculate once again on the reason for the change in his character since he had returned from Oklahoma. Sergeant Roberts had already given the entire troop his opinion of their commanding officer's unfriendly attitude. His account of the lieutenant's sizzling affair with the luscious half-breed student had set the men's tongues wagging for hours on end.

Lieutenant Wade paused at the hitching post outside of the saloon. The gossip about his love life was disturbing, but he was more concerned about losing his men's respect. He stuffed a wad of chew into the side of his cheek, while making a determined pledge to himself once more: From this instant on, he would put Margaret Sinclair—and anything concerning her—out of his mind. He sucked the foul-tasting tobacco more rapidly, while silently repeating his resolution. I already feel better, he told himself. A bath would make him feel even better, he decided. And down the street was a nice little residence where a man could obtain a bath, shave, or whatever else he was craving. The lieutenant spat the chunk of tobacco on the ground and gave his head a firm nod . . . he needed more than a bath. A sweet little señorita would definitely improve his disposition.

The burden he had been carrying upon his back seemed to ease considerably as this thought planted itself in his head. With his mind engrossed in visions of soft dark flesh, he did not notice the small figure walking toward him, not until he had collided with her and knocked the large bundle she carried from her arms.

"I'm sorry!" He cursed inwardly at his carelessness as he crouched down and started to reach for the scattered commodities that had tumbled from the woman's arms. His hand stopped in midair, however, when he glanced at the young woman kneeling before him.

"Mar-Margaret?" he gasped. Shock spread through his unmoving form as his green eyes widened beneath his black hat. "How . . . I mean . . ." He paused, suddenly unsure and confused. The girl was staring at him with eyes that were even more startled than his own, and the hue of her frightened gaze was the basis of his confusion. Her eyes were not as vibrant a shade of turquoise as he remembered, in fact, they were dark blue—the shade of cobalt. And her mouth seemed slightly fuller, but just slightly. Her soft skin was

136

darker, bronzed by a lifetime of being beneath the heat of the desert sun. Margaret Sinclair's skin could not have obtained this rich hue in just a few weeks' time.

"Perdôneme," she said the Mexican word in a voice that was soft and deep—so very different from the stronger voice of Margaret Sinclair. Her hand moved forward to gather up her belongings, but, like the lieutenant's, it stopped and did not move for a long time. They stared at each other without speaking, both lost to the turmoil that their unexpected collision had created. Echo knew that she should not even allow the *soldado* to look at her—what if he was able to tell that she was not Mexican—yet she could not tear her eyes away from his face. In the sixteen years that she had lived, she was rarely in the presence of a white man. On the few occasions when she had associated with them, she had been nervous and guarded. What was it about this *soldado* that drew her gaze to his eyes and held her entire being a prisoner within their jade grasp? His behavior was even more unsettling to her. At first he had acted as though he knew who she was, but then he, too, had fallen into a silent stupor. The silence grew unbearable as neither of them could make their shocked minds function. It was almost as if the world had stopped at this moment so this brief time could extend into an eternity.

"Hey, Lieutenant! Ain't that—"

"No!" the lieutenant yelled more loudly than necessary when Sergeant Roberts' voice rang out from the doorway of the cantina. He shook his head in a vain attempt to regain his lost senses, then began to gather up the girl's supplies with lightning speed. The girl had only enough time to rise to her feet before he shoved the bundle at her face. He stepped between her and the entrance of the saloon, blocking the sergeant's view of her.

"Be on your way now," he commanded in a loud tone. He waved his arm in front of the startled girl's face, but did not step from her path. His unmoving form did not allow her to continue in the same direction she had been walking when he had crashed into her, and his actions left Echo no recourse but to turn and depart in the opposite direction, which she did without argument. She had been headed to the cantina to purchase whiskey, but the encounter with the *soldado* had shaken her so badly all she could think of was getting out of town as fast as her sandaled feet would carry her.

Lieutenant Wade remained in the same position until the girl had scurried down the street and around the far corner of one of the buildings. Sergeant Roberts stood behind the officer, trying to get a closer look at the girl. However, the lieutenant's towering form did not budge to permit him past, so he stood on his toes and gazed over the man's shoulder, watching the girl's retreat with a growing sense of confusion. "That was that half-breed," the sergeant finally said to his commander. "Why did you let her get away?"

"You're wrong," the lieutenant's voice was tense and hoarse. He cleared his throat, but not the tumult in his mind. "It was just some little señorita who resembled Margaret Sinclair, but it wasn't the same girl."

The sergeant looked down the street to the spot where the woman had just disappeared. "No." He rubbed his chin and scrunched his face up in a thoughtful manner. "That had to be her." He turned suspicious eyes toward the lieutenant. Why would the officer deny something so obvious?

"Well, it wasn't," Lieutenant Wade repeated in a stronger tone. He gave the sergeant a snide glance as he added, "And according to you, I should know Margaret Sinclair better than anyone. Isn't that

138

correct, Sergeant?"

A deep flush colored the areas above the sergeant's beard a scarlet shade. He didn't appreciate being reprimanded for telling things as he saw them. It was even more infuriating to him that the lieutenant still insisted the girl they had just encountered was not the half-breed from the Carlisle School. This gave the sergeant a whole new set of prospects to think on for a while.

"I'm going to take a bath," Lieutenant Wade announced as he saluted the other man and started to leave. "Inform the troop we will be returning to the fort this afternoon."

Sergeant Roberts returned the officer's gesture with a curt salute and a nod of his head. Something odd was going on here. He knew that girl was the breed, and he also knew the direction in which she had just fled. It is just a man's natural instinct to be curious, he told himself as he began walking at a fast gait toward the building around which the girl had disappeared from view.

Echo's feet flew across the hot sand as though they had wings attached. Tiny rocks found refuge in the soles of her flimsy sandals, but she did not take the time to shake them out, even though their pointed edges were cutting deep gashes in the bottoms of her tender feet. She was running from the town for fear the *soldados* would discover she was an Indian, but that was not the main source of her wild panic. The encounter with the soldier who had collided with her had left such a profound impact on her that she was filled with another tremendous fear . . . a fear of never gazing into eyes so green again, of not being able to understand why she had wished he would never look away.

With her mind in such a turmoil, she did not hear the man who ran up behind her, not until he hollered at her to stop. For an instant she thought it was the green-eyed soldier, and the joy that arose in her breast sent a shock surging through her. But her excitement was short-lived. She glanced over her shoulder and saw the soldier with the red beard closing in on her. She screamed, although she was not aware of it. The supplies she carried in her arms were scattered upon the ground as she pushed her legs to move faster. Yet, even with her arms free of their burdens, she knew her flight was futile. The man was within reach of her, and she was growing too tired to outrun him.

She screamed again when she felt his brutal grasp around her waist, and as they tumbled into the sand, she began to kick and claw with a renewed bout of energy. Horror at being taken captive gave her an added strength she did not know she possessed, though she was no match for the brawny sergeant. Within seconds, he had her subdued and pinned to the ground.

"Hold it right there, Miss Sinclair," he said, a smirk working its way through his breathless gasps. "Thought you could get away again, did ya?"

Echo tried to move, but his weight was straddling her midsection and she could barely breath. *"No entiendo,"* she cried in the hopes that he still thought she was a Mexican. But why would he call her by a white woman's name? she wondered as she was forced to yield to his rough hold. The green-eyed *soldado* had called her by a white name also—Margaret—but why? Who did they think she was?

"I knew it was you," the soldier replied with a satisfied nod of his head. "I just knew it!" His words caused Echo's confusion to expand, but she dared not speak to him as if she understood. His position atop her did not allow her any movement, so she was powerless to do anything other than wait for his next move.

"Now, how about if you and I go back to town to see your lover boy. I just can't wait to see the expression on his face when he realizes I wasn't dumb enough to fall for his lies." He clasped both her slender wrists in his hands and rose to his feet, yanking her up with him. "What was the plan, Miss Sinclair? Were you gonna live here in Bisbee, so that the lieutenant could come and visit you whenever he was in the area?"

Echo twisted away from him and fought to keep her tongue under control. She wanted to scream at him that he had her confused with someone else, and was making a terrible mistake by thinking she was this other woman whom he kept referring to; but she knew better than to try to reason with a man who was obviously so demented. Now that she was on her feet again, though, her desire to escape returned. Hoping to catch the *soldado* unawares, she raised her knee up and attempted to hit him in a vulnerable area. He was quicker than she was, however, and dodged her well-aimed knee by only inches.

"Bitch!" he spat in her face as he yanked her up against him. "If I wasn't so anxious to confront your lover boy, I would throw you down in the dirt right now and take my share of what the lieutenant's already gotten." His eyes churned with such fury that Echo was taken aback. She did not miss the meaning in his words, nor did she wish to tempt him into pursuing his despicable threat. When he tightened his grip around her wrists, she complied with him by stumbling along beside him without offering further resistance.

She attempted to glance back over her shoulder in the slim hope that she would see her father somewhere in the distance. But even as her terrified gaze glimpsed the empty horizon she knew he would not have traveled this close to town without a reason. He would not be expecting her to return for a long time yet, and he would not begin to worry about her till sunset. Until then, he would be waiting at the camp, which was at least a mile or more from Bisbee. A defeated cry lodged in Echo's throat as they rounded the corner of the building at the end of the main street. Her feeling that something wonderful was going to happen that day had turned into a nightmare of unmeasurable proportions, and there was no escape.

Chapter Nine

Taking a bath was the last thing Travis Wade could concentrate on now. Actually, he did not know what he was going to do next because his head was throbbing too hard to function properly. The girl he had just encountered was almost identical to Margaret Sinclair, except for the slight variances in their skin and eye color. Was it possible she was Margaret's sister? The lieutenant rubbed at his aching head. No . . . the girl was not simply Margaret Sinclair's sister—she had to be her twin!

He closed his eyes and reached into his memory. The children whom he had escorted from Carlisle, Pennsylvania, were Chiricahua Apaches. Their parents had ridden with Geronimo before his surrender. He squeezed his eyelids together in desperation; he knew nothing else about any of the children. It was possible that Margaret Sinclair had a twin who had escaped when the rest of her tribe had been captured, and perhaps she had been living right here in Bisbee ever since. With her mixed heritage, she could easily pass for a Mexican *señorita*. This was the only explanation that made any sense, the lieutenant decided. What should he do about her now though? Territorial law stated that no Chiricahua Apache could live anywhere in Arizona except on a reservation. But was he obligated to tell anyone that she was here?

He paused before the bath house, while contemplating this new dilemma. An error in judgment had most likely ruined Margaret Sinclair's life; he had no desire to destroy the life of another innocent girl. He would pretend that he had never run into her, except he was not sure if he could forget their unexpected meeting. There was something about the young woman that he could not shake, and it grew stronger with each passing second. This feeling was too intense to ignore; it filled him with such a sense of urgency that he felt as though his heart was going to pound through his chest. He had to see her again, no matter what the consequences!

He knew the direction she had taken when she'd fled from the front of the cantina, and he did not intend to stop looking until he found her. As he spun about, he tried to find a rational explanation for his actions, but there was none. The decision to find her again was not based on an obligation to his military status. The last thing he wanted was to see the beautiful young girl held prisoner on some remote reservation. He was going in search of her because something inside him had exploded when he had gazed into her face, and the void which still remained since she had left could only be filled by her presence.

As he started down the street, an odd sensation overcame Travis Wade. The thudding in his head and chest increased, becoming like shots from a cannon. He felt as though his fate were no longer within his grasp, and he was overcome by such a rush of panic that he could barely breathe. His need to find the girl abounded with each frantic beat of his heart. He was not prepared, however, when he turned the corner at the end of the street, to come face to face with Sergeant

Roberts and his reluctant hostage.

Beneath the covering of his red beard, an evil grin consumed the sergeant's face. "Look who I found, Lieutenant Wade. See, I was right—it was your little Carlisle squaw." He shoved Echo toward the other man and laughed in a crude manner. The stunned expression on his commander's face was not a disappointment, and it pleasured the sergeant to no end.

The lieutenant did not have time to retort to the sergeant's snide words before the girl stumbled up against him. He caught her in his arms and looked down at her frightened face. The black lace scarf had fallen from her head, and the apparent struggle she recently engaged in with the sergeant had released her hair from the bun at the back of her neck. Waist-length, it was proof enough that she could not be Margaret Sinclair, since Margaret's hair had barely reached to the middle of her back. With her hair loose and the scarf absent, the fact that they were twin sisters was even more obvious, though, and the lieutenant knew he had no recourse other than to admit this discovery to Sergeant Roberts.

Words did not come to the officer's mouth for a moment, however. As the strange emotions invaded him once again, he could not tear his eyes away from the young woman's beautiful face. She was staring at him with an identical expression of near-to-bursting suspense, and the silence that hovered around them was overpowering.

"Looks like you don't have much to say," the sergeant chortled with smug satisfaction. His smirk broadened as he watched his commander's face turn to a ghastly shade of white.

It seemed like an eternity before the lieutenant finally managed to tear his eyes away from the girl. As his sanity returned, so did his fury with the sergeant. The pale color of his face deepened to a ruddy shade of red as he leveled a piercing jade gaze at the other man. "This is not Margaret Sinclair," he repeated with authority. "Look at the length of her hair, the dark tone of her skin." He gently clasped Echo by the shoulders and turned her around to face the other man, adding, "Lord, man! Her eyes are not even the same color!"

The sergeant leaned forward and glared into his captive's face for a closer observation. "It's not possible," he retorted. He hesitated, scratching at his beard while he pondered this strange turn of events. "Well, she has to be her twin then," he added with a confident nod of his head.

Lieutenant Wade drew in a deep breath. "That is my assumption, too; but we can't rule out the possibility that this Mexican woman just bears a close resemblance to Margaret Sinclair." He did not want to take this girl as a prisoner, and he was prepared to grasp at anything that would prevent such a drastic action.

"No, sir! If the other one is an Apache, then this one is too."

A sadness filled the lieutenant's eyes as he nodded his head in slow agreement. He could not ignore his command any longer. His hands still rested on the girl's trembling shoulders as he turned her back around and gazed down at her. "What is your name?"

"No entiendo, señor?" she said in a whisper as she attempted to avoid his intense green eyes.

"She tried to pull that act on me too, but I think she understands better than she cares to admit." Sergeant Roberts' lips contorted into another belligerent grin. He felt more victorious than ever with his disclosure. It was not often they were lucky enough to locate a reservation bronco. Her discovery would undoubtedly be a point in his favor.

146

The lieutenant ignored the sergeant as he continued to hold onto the girl with a gentle grip. "You will have to go to Fort Huachuca with us when we leave here today; just until we can find out who you are. But if you are Mexican, and can somehow prove it to us now, I will not have to take you in. Can you do that?"

Echo hesitated as she tried to think coherently. She could give him a false name and tell him that she lived in a town across the border, but she had no way to prove it to him. There was not a soul in this town who knew anything about her, other than the store owner who sold her supplies. But even he did not know anything about her, so he could not verify her lie. Her thoughts flashed to her father, who was waiting outside of Bisbee for her return. His life would be in danger if he came to town and encountered the *soldados*. With a sinking heart, Echo realized that her only course was to go with them if she did not want her father to be hurt or killed. Her chin dropped down to her chest in defeat as she slowly shook her head from side to side.

The wicked laugh which came from the sergeant's grinning mouth filled Lieutenant Wade with an even greater rage. Sergeant Roberts had won this round, and he would gloat over his achievement at every opportunity. But, the lieutenant surmised, the war was just beginning, and Sergeant Roberts had no idea who he was up against if he persisted in riling him.

"Round up the rest of the men," the lieutenant said sharply. "We'll leave immediately." The soldier hesitated as his eyes uncertainly flitted from the girl to his commanding officer. "I won't let her escape, Sergeant!" Lieutenant Wade added in a loud tone. He felt the girl cringe under his touch when his voice rose so harshly, and a new sense of guilt was added to that which already consumed him.

The sergeant gave the couple one last, hateful glare

before casting the officer a quick salute and twirling on his heels. A heavy breath vibrated through the lieutenant's chest as he allowed his gaze to descend again. She was a renegade and a half-breed, yet her mere presence affected him in a way he had never experienced. Somehow he had to get his wild emotions under control before his men were witness to the immense weakness she created in him. His vast attraction to her was inconceivable, and he wondered if this crazy compulsion stemmed from the guilt he harbored for Margaret Sinclair's fate. He pulled his hands away from her and straightened his shoulders in an attempt to regain a stance of authority and—hopefully—a morsel of his own sanity.

"Do you speak English?"

Echo nodded her head in response to his question. She knew it would be foolish not to comply with his demands now that she was his prisoner.

"Am I correct in my assumption that you are a Chiricahua Apache?"

A startled shiver shook Echo's slender form. She had not fooled them at all with her disguise. A mist of tears entered her eyes and blurred her sight of the tall *soldado*. She would rather die than give up life with her family at Pa-Gotzin-Kay. In a frenzied moment she glanced at the gun which hung from the lieutenant's hip. If it were feasible she would grab the weapon and put it to her head. Death would be more desirable than being taken in as a captive.

The look of terror that crossed her face answered the lieutenant's question. She reminded him of an animal caught in a trap; it would chew off its leg rather than remain a prisoner. Reservation broncos always had that look when they were caught. He even understood the crazed thoughts that must be going through her head when he noticed how her eyes fell to his gun. A

148

hundred questions hovered on his lips, but he knew he was not going to get the answers he sought from her now.

His only certainty was that she had to be Margaret Sinclair's twin sister. He remembered her sister's determination to be free, and reconsidered his previous thoughts. If this girl's desire to escape was as desperate as Margaret Sinclair's, the lieutenant knew he would never be able to drop his guard around her. His reasons for worrying about her intentions, however, were disturbing in a different way. When he had started to go after her, it was not because he planned to take her as his prisoner. But now that she was here, he did not want her to escape. He had a desperate urge of his own. . . . However, he would never allow himself to give in to the tender thoughts filling his head with visions of holding her trembling body in his arms and kissing her full lips until every ounce of fear within her had disappeared forever.

"M-maybe you'll be ready to talk when we reach the fort." His voice was shaky and high-pitched, and did not contain the tone of authority he had hoped to project. She shrugged in response, then turned and waited for him to lead her down the street. Her one wish at this time was to leave town before her father risked his life to come into Bisbee to look for her. They only had to walk as far as the saloon hitching post where the Army horses were tied before her wish was granted.

Their arrival there was anxiously awaited by Lieutenant Wade's entire brigade. An aura of excitement encircled the troop as the men stood beside their horses and awaited the command to mount. If one Chiricahua was roaming around free, there might be others in the area. The prospect of capturing renegade Apaches was tantalizing to the soldiers whose routine

149

details had become extemely mundane and boring. The female captive created quite a stir as well, since Sergeant Roberts' description of her loveliness was understated. The lieutenant groaned inwardly when he took note of the men's lustful expressions. They were identical to the ones the soldiers had worn when they had first glimpsed Margaret Sinclair. His determination to protect Miss Sinclair from his men's lecherous yearnings was primarily due to his obligation to his command. The feelings which were running rampant within him now were strangely akin to jealousy.

Extra saddle horses were always taken along in case they were needed, and it was one of these animals Echo was told to mount. She swung into the saddle with ease, but she was not prepared for the rope that tied and bound her wrists to the saddlehorn. Nor was she expecting the second rope. Strung under the horse's belly, it held her feet tightly against the sides of the animal so that she could not try to escape. Her panic-stricken gaze settled on the lieutenant as his men secured both ropes. She sensed a compassion in the *soldado* with the green eyes, but now he could not even meet her gaze. He turned his horse away to avoid looking at her, because the sight of her bound to the horse was almost more than his tortured mind could tolerate.

"Move out," he yelled as he waved his leather gauntleted hand through the air. Echo's horse jerked forward without the prodding of its rider. The animal had been trained to follow the others, although he fell to the rear of the cavalcade and sauntered along at his own pace.

She could not remember when she had known so much pain. She wondered what horrible deed she must have committed for Usen to punish her in such a harsh manner. The heat of the scorching Arizona sun beat down unmercifully on the ropes that held her, causing them to burn deep ridges into the flesh surrounding her wrists and ankles. The cuts on the bottoms of her feet, where rocks were still embedded in the soles, throbbed and bled, but these gross discomforts could not compare to the pain in her heart. Each time the horses put down another hoof, she was taken farther away from her home and family.

She began to recall the entire sixteen years of her life, grasping in desperation at memories of joy and happiness, reliving all the sorrow and heartbreak once again as if the tragedies had happened only yesterday. But it had been over eight years since she had experienced any real loss. It had been that long ago when her twin sister had been killed during an ambush on their *ranchería*. Each day since Echo had said a special prayer to Usen for Morning Star, and at times she'd had the strongest feeling that her sister was able to hear her prayers. Echo never admitted those strange sensations to anyone, but there were instances when she felt such an overwhelming affinity with her sister that she was sure Morning Star was still alive. Of course, Echo knew this was craziness. The few who had survived the last attack on their village were all living peacefully at Pa-Gotzin-Kay.

As the long day wore itself into dusk, Echo swayed between consciousness and a lost reality. She wanted to die and tried to will herself to do so, but Usen would not cooperate. The lieutenant had even grown concerned and had fallen back to ride beside her; still, she would not respond to him when he spoke to her or offered her water and food. She kept telling herself that it would be easier to depart from this world now than to face each day on the reservation as a prisoner of the white man.

Echo had forced herself into a state of unconscious-

151

ness by the time the lieutenant had become so worried about her deteriorating condition he decided to take matters into his own hands. She was not aware of anything when he slashed the ropes from her ankles and wrists, then, carefully cradling her in his arms, rode the rest of the way to Fort Huachuca. Nor did she know how much he hurt because of her pain, or how much he hated himself and Sergeant Roberts for bringing this suffering down upon her. Right now, he didn't even care about all the whispering and the snide chuckles of his men. His only concern was for the girl, and in spite of his reluctance to admit it to himself, Travis Wade sensed that these new emotions would not go away; they would only continue to grow more powerful with each passing day.

Nachae stood motionless at the spot where he had found the scattered contents of Echo's shopping bundle. The tobacco had been dried and shriveled by the burning rays of the sun, and the bright scarf Echo had purchased for her mother had been stomped into the ground by the struggle that had taken place at this site. He fell to his knees and pulled the scarf free of the dirt that pinned it to the ground. A mournful howl escaped from deep within his chest as he clutched the silky piece of material. The heart-wrenching cry that echoed across the desert did not even begin to tell of the sorrow the chief held in his heart.

He had been gifted with two beautiful daughters, and through the years he had tried to forgive Usen for taking one away. But to steal them both from him was a grave injustice. He could not face his wife with the news of this new tragedy, because he was afraid it would be the death of her. Still, the devastating words had to come from no other lips but his own. Over and over again, as he knelt on the ground with his face buried in the colorful scarf, Nachae berated himself for allowing Echo to go into the town of Bisbee alone. Every time she had traveled into an American town he had feared for her safety. Yet, foolishly, he still permitted her to go. How could he survive this crushing guilt? If only he had come to look for her sooner, but he had not grown overly concerned until the afternoon hours grew dim. Now the fading glow of twilight had overtaken the desert, and within minutes it would be too dark to go in search of the men who had taken his innocent daughter.

This realization sent new waves of panic through Nachae's quivering insides. His keen Apache eye had already determined that only one man had fought with and subdued his daughter, and the couple's return to town was also apparent. Nachae did not waste another precious second as he quickly donned the Mexican apparel he carried in his saddlebags in case a situation arose that required such a disguise. Removing his leather leggings and breechcloth, he slipped on a loose-fitting pair of white cotton pants and a baggy white tunic like the ones the Mexican peasants wore. A striped serape topped the outfit, and a wide-brimmed black hat securely held his long raven hair from view. Since Nachae's mother had been of Spanish descent, the mixture of his bloodlines did not make his Apache heritage immediately distinguishable, and dressed as he was now it was difficult to tell him from a Mexican farmer.

The main street of Bisbee was quiet when Nachae entered the town. He realized with a feeling of hopelessness that the Phelps-Dodge Mercantile had closed long ago, so he would not be able to obtain any information from the owner of that establishment. Only the saloon was still thronged with patrons as the hours of darkness closed in on the desert town. Since Echo had planned to purchase whiskey, Nachae hoped the bartender would be a helpful source. He had to be careful, though, when he questioned the man. On this side of the border, his Apache connection was an invitation to bloodshed. His insides twisted in agony when this thought passed through his mind. What if Echo's identity had somehow been discovered? The image of his daughter's beautiful young face blurred his vision as he prayed to Usen for her safety. But as Nachae walked through the quiet street in Bisbee, he realized the odds were not in her favor on this sultry summer night.

Nachae hunched his shoulders as he entered the cantina in the hope that he would resemble one of the weary farmers who labored in the fields. Taking a stool at the far end of the bar, he sat inconspicuously among the other men scattered about the small saloon.

"What'll ya have, *señor?*"

"Whiskey," Nachae replied in his best Mexican accent. His fluency in Mexican, English, and the Athapascan language of the Apache worked to his advantage in dealing with the various nationalities in the southwestern lands of Apachería. He eyed the bartender closely from beneath his floppy-brimmed hat. The approach he used to gain information about his daughter was vital to his own survival, so he had to be careful not to draw any unnecessary attention to himself.

"Quiet today, eh, *señor?*" Nachae asked in a nonchalant voice. He downed his glass of whiskey in one gulp, then motioned for another.

The bartender nodded his head as he held the bottle to Nachae's shot glass for a refill. Without glancing down, he tilted the bottle down and let the strong brew slop over the sides of the glass and onto the counter.

"Not much happening tonight, but this morning we had a bit of excitement." He chuckled as he wiped his hands on a towel that hung from his belt.

"Oh?" Nachae was shaking so hard he could not lift his glass. He reminded himself not to act too interested. He shrugged his shoulders without speaking because he was afraid the trembling in his stomach would affect his voice.

Relating stories was a bartender's specialty, though, and the man behind the counter did not hesitate to tell the latest news. "Yep, some soldiers caught themselves a little Apache squaw. Must have escaped from the reservation." He ran his tongue over his lips, adding, "She was a real sweet looker, too."

A sweat broke out over Nachae's entire body, despite the shiver that ran down his spine. The very worst had happened; Echo had been taken captive by white *soldados*. He grew outraged and numb; then the single shot of whiskey he had just tossed down began to burn in the pit of his stomach. But outwardly his calm expression never changed. He forced himself to smile back at the bartender as though he were completely detached from anything the man had just told him. His hand reached out to pick up the whiskey glass, but when he saw the vicious tremors that caused it to shake, he quickly withdrew his hand and cleared his throat before speaking.

"I guess they'll teach her a lesson she won't forget," Nachae said, using a heavier accent than necessary to cover his shaky voice. He cleared his throat again. "It was a border patrol, eh, *señor?*"

The bartender shook his head with a casual toss. "Yep, just a routine detail out of Fort Huachuca. Bet the ride from Bisbee was a heckuva lot more fun than the ride in." He chortled in a crude manner as his eyes took on a glazed look that suggested the filthy thoughts consuming him.

Nachae attempted to laugh, but the sound caught in his throat. In an effort to contain the despair and rage that flooded over him, he grabbed his whiskey glass again and slugged down the liquor. It hit his stomach like a keg of dynamite. With relief, he glanced up and noticed the bartender had lost interest in talking to him and was meandering toward the opposite end of the counter. Nachae slid from the bar stool in a casual manner, keeping his head bent down. Only one thing could make this situation more desperate, and that would be for him to be discovered too. Then he would be of no help to his daughter, but now while there was still a breath in his body, he would go after Echo.

As he stood at the hitching post in front of the cantina and gazed down the dusty street of the border town, the past came rushing back to him in an unexpected flood. He thought of the twin daughters his beautiful Sky Dreamer had given birth to sixteen years ago. They were the product of the endless love they had given to one another, a love that had only grown stronger throughout the extreme adversity of their lives. He could not go back to the *ranchería* and face Sky Dreamer with the news of their only surviving daughter's capture, not until he had, at least, made an effort to retrieve her. He would send word to his wife that they had decided to prolong their shopping trip and would return before the *Binist ants ose*—August— the beginning of the Little Harvest.

An owl hooted, and beneath his long serape, Nachae clutched his rib cage in a vain effort to control the quaking of his entire being. He turned away from the sound of the mournful voice of the *ló-kohí-muhté,* while trying to will his ears to be deaf to it. His people harbored a deep fear of owls. They believed that ghosts of departed Apaches escaped from their graves and

156

entered into the souls of owls. If a person listened closely to the cries of the owl, he could hear the dead person speaking to him, and the living soul would be doomed. Nachae threw his hands over his ears as he walked down the dark street; his mission was too important for him to be distracted by ancient superstitions.

He had a little more than two weeks to find his daughter and return her to the *rancheria,* or else, he would be forced to face his wife with the devastating news of her loss. There was only one place he could go for help. If he had anyplace else to turn, he would do so gladly, but the few men at the *rancheria* were needed to tend to the village and protect the women and elderly from intruders. Nachae sighed reluctantly as he discarded his Mexican attire and mounted his horse. Tonight he would not rest at all, and tomorrow he would push twice as hard to reach his destination. Only the Comancheros who hid in the deep jungles of Sonora would be able to assist him on this overwhelming task. But he had done them more than one favor throughout the years without asking for anything. Now he would demand repayment!

Chapter Ten

"You have to eat," the lieutenant said as he glanced at the untouched food sitting beside the girl. She did not acknowledge his presence but continued to stare at the twisted and barren branches of the old juniper tree visible through the small spaces between the window bars of her cell. Travis Wade thought she reminded him of an injured dove that had broken a wing and could no longer soar above the treetops. Her confinement in the guardhouse infuriated him, but there wasn't anything he could do to improve her situation. The army doctor had diagnosed her condition as a state of depression over her capture, so she had been locked in this cell until she was ready to tell them where she had been living for the past eight years. Travis had no doubt in his mind that she would try to starve herself to death rather than face the future as a captive on the reservation.

The lieutenant sat down next to her on the small cot, still her eyes did not waver from the window. He had to reach her somehow, for her sake and for his own selfish reasons. "I know you must feel betrayed and scared, but you have to fight back. Refusing to eat will not help you or your people." Travis saw the corner of her mouth twitch slightly, and he wondered if he had struck a nerve. "I want to help you, and whether you believe it or not, you can trust me." He paused, hoping to see another small sign that his words were sinking into her stubborn mind, but she remained straight and unmoving. Although her suffering was painful for him to watch, the lieutenant found himself admiring the courage she portrayed under such adversity.

A frustrated sigh broke from his mouth. Since their arrival the night before, she had been questioned nonstop by the captain in charge of Fort Huachuca as to why she had been in Bisbee and whether she lived in the vicinity. But Captain Bailey had given in to Lieutenant Wade's plea to talk to their prisoner in private about Margaret Sinclair. It was imperative to the lieutenant that he be the one to ask her the questions about her sister, but first he had to show her that he was capable of being trustworthy.

"My name is Lieutenant Travis Wade," he said in an awkward manner. "And I don't suppose that it matters much, but I did not want to take you captive in Bisbee." Her face remained impassive, still he was determined to make her understand how he felt. "I was coming to look for you, though." The heavy curtain of her black lashes blinked several times in rapid succession, but she still did not speak.

"Would you care to know why I was coming after you?"

Her jaw grew taut and the lieutenant noticed that her hands drew into two tight fists. He knew she was waiting for him to tell her his reasons for going to look for her, but he realized that he had not figured them out yet. He had wanted to—no needed—to see this young woman again. Beyond that, however, he could not rationalize anything he had done recently, beginning with the day when he had first met Margaret Sinclair.

"How were you separated from your twin sister?" he blurted out, forgetting the tact he had planned to use when he posed this important question. He saw shock register on her weary face, even though she was trying hard to act as if she were ignoring him. A visible tremor shook her slim body, and she had to clutch her hands together in her lap to control their quaking. Travis knew he had hit upon something that had drawn her complete interest.

Echo had wanted to trust the green-eyed *soldado,* but she knew what his people were capable of doing to obtain the things they wanted. Until his last question, his words had seemed so sincere, and she had been recalling that his eyes held a gentleness most white men's gazes did not possess. But now she knew he was no different from any other white man. She forced herself to remain facing the window, because she was afraid if she looked into his green eyes again, she would lose all of her defenses. A large teardrop formed in the corner of one of her eyes and began to roll down her cheek. Morning Star had been dead for so long. Why was he using such a cruel tactic to gain information from her? And how had he learned that she had once had a twin sister? She had misjudged him; he was even more evil than most white men, she decided, an added sorrow filling her breast.

Her reaction confused the lieutenant more with each second that passed. Why would she be so sensitive about her twin? Travis was then struck by another idea, and he wished somebody would kick him for not having thought of it sooner. What if she didn't know she had ever had a twin—or worse—what if she thought her sister dead? He knew by the look of turmoil on her young face that she must not know anything of her sister's whereabouts. Slowly, he reached out and picked up one of the clenched hands that

161

lay on her lap. Her eyes flew to his face in fear, and he thought she would try to pull away. To his astonishment, though, she allowed him to keep holding her shaking hand.

"You didn't know that your twin sister is still alive?" Her eyes remained fixed on his face, so now Travis could clearly see the drastic way his words were hitting her stunned mind. Her blue gaze sought something in his own eyes, and he knew she was trying to judge the truth of his words by the hidden messages she could decipher in their depths. He recalled that an Indian scout had once told him the eyes never lie, so an Indian always watches a white man's eyes. But even as he finished the sentence, he reminded himself that at this time he did not know if Margaret Sinclair was alive.

Echo continued to stare into the eyes of the *soldado*. She could not see any deceit written within the jade kaleidoscope of his troubled gaze, only worry and pain. Was it possible that this white man was different? Still, Echo repeated to herself, he is a white man, and they are skilled in lying to my people. If he was telling her the truth, however, she had to find out what he knew about her sister.

"My sister was killed in the Superstition Mountains eight years ago by a troop of cavalrymen from Fort Apache."

Travis Wade was taken aback by her perfect English, and she had confirmed his suspicion that she did not know of her sister's existence during these last years. He tightened his grip on her hand, and at the same instant, they both glanced down to where their hands were intertwined. As their gazes ascended, the lieutenant felt another shiver shake her slender form, and as if it had somehow been emitted through her warm touch, a shiver also bolted through him.

He fought to calm the unsettling flutter within him,

162

but it persisted and was even more evident in his trembling voice when he spoke. "Y-your sister was not killed. Though I don't know the exact details, I do know that she had been living back east at the Carlisle Indian School for the past eight years." Echo exhaled a wispy sob, but the lieutenant felt her hand grow tense within his grasp.

"How can that be? My parents and I have thought all these years that she—" Echo stopped speaking abruptly as an expression of horror came over her face. For an instant the lieutenant did not understand her strange behavior, however, he quickly realized her blunder. She had just admitted to him that her parents were still alive. And since she was in the vicinity of Bisbee, they must be somewhere in the area.

"I meant it when I said you could trust me," he said in a low voice, although no one else was within hearing distance of the dingy cell. "Whatever you tell me will go no further—you have my word." He did not know how to stress this point in order to gain her confidence, for judging from the look on her terrified face, at this moment she only thought of him as her enemy.

"I know your sister because I recently escorted a group of Apache children from the Carlisle School in Pennsylvania to the Indian reservation at Fort Sill in the Oklahoma territory. She, along with several others were survivors from your village."

Echo suddenly withdrew her hand from his and clasped both of her hands over her mouth to prevent herself from crying out. How was such a thing possible? Her parents had searched everywhere in the *rancheria* for her sister before they had been forced to flee into the forest to hide. They had finally assumed that she had run out of the wickiup ahead of them and had become lost somewhere in the maze of fire and bullets. Later, when the few survivors had heard an account of the attack, they were told the cavalrymen had reported no survivors. For those who had run into the forest and escaped the fiery death, this news was a blessed announcement. It meant the *soldados* did not know they existed, so for the time being they were safe. But it also meant that those who had not gathered in the safety of the thick pine forest were all dead. At least, that had always been their belief until now.

Echo wanted to believe what he was telling her, yet experience told her to tread carefully. Her slipup about her parents had already told him more than she wanted him to know. She had to learn, though, whether he was just telling her things he thought she would want to hear so she would tell him what he wanted to learn or whether he spoke the truth. She searched her memory for something about her sister that would be a definite clue to her identity, then she remembered her parents used to say the only way they could tell their daughters apart was to get close enough to see the different blues in the colors of their eyes.

"Does my sister resemble me?" She watched his expression closely, but either he was accomplished at hiding his ulterior motives or he was truly concerned about the way he related this information to her.

"Your hair is much longer, and you've got a darker tan than she does."

These tidbits he spoke of were useless to her; anyone could invent those minor variations between twin sisters. But just as Echo was about to tell him that his words meant nothing, he added one more comment that stopped her breath in her lungs.

A smile that was so slight Echo almost missed it curved his lips as his gaze once again met hers. "Her eyes are an unusual shade of turquoise, but yours are the richest shade of deep blue I have ever seen."

Echo found herself locked in his enslaving gaze as

her entire soul became lost to the tender sound of his voice. It was against everything she had ever been taught about survival in the white man's world, but at this moment she trusted this green-eyed *soldado* with every fiber of her being. She became aware of the tight grasp of his hand, and a stream of fire began to work its way through her fingers and up her arm, until her body was ablaze with a rush of emotions as shocking to her as the realization that her sister was still alive.

Travis Wade saw the transformation come over her face, and as his heart pounded against his rib cage, he became aware of a startling discovery. His interest in the girl went far beyond curiosity and compassion. He wanted to know all there was to know about her, but as a man, not as a soldier. When he realized how deep his interest in this female renegade ran, an intense panic also overtook him. He was a lieutenant in the U.S. Cavalry. It was impossible for him even to think about falling in love with a girl who was not only his captive but also a half-breed Apache. He took a deep breath and let go of her hand.

"I . . . I . . . ," he could not think of anything to say. Emotions he knew he could never acknowledge were consuming him. He rose to his feet in a clumsy manner and stared down at her beautiful face. "I have to go now," he muttered in a voice that was barely audible. He did not wait for her to speak because he did not trust himself in her presence any longer. If he did not get away from her now, and learn to deny these overpowering feelings he was experiencing, it might be too late.

In a numb trance Echo watched him twirl about on his heel and depart from her tiny cell. The clanging of the door ricocheted throughout the enclosure like a gunshot that had gone wild. She heard the clicking of his heels as he left the barracks with a rapid step; then

165

she jumped when the outer door banged shut, leaving her to suffer in private. She had not been able to understand the strange expression that suddenly masked his face and misted his green eyes. But before his abrupt change, she had seen such tenderness and devotion in them, she had thought Usen had created the lieutenant just so she could gaze into his mystical green gaze for all eternity.

Now, however, she felt more foolish than she had ever thought possible. His swift exit could only mean that she had been taken in by her own desires. She grasped the rails of the window bars in a vain effort to control the shaking in her limbs. How could she have been so stupid as to have trusted any white man when all her life she had been conditioned to do the exact opposite? She had let her entire family cluster down, and if their secluded *ranchería* in Sonora was discovered because of her ignorance, she would never be able to forgive herself.

For the first time since her capture, she felt the rebirth of her lagging strength. Like her parents—and all the Apaches before them who had sought power from Usen to fight for their freedom—Echo pressed her face against the window bars and gazed up toward the hazy blue sky. She asked the Apache god for his understanding, and prayed that her family would be spared any more pain from the white man, despite the horrible error she had made today. She also requested more courage than she had ever been granted before; then she paused, growing concerned that Usen would think she was being selfish to ask for so much at one time. A rustling in the dry branches of the juniper tree outside her window startled her and caused her to jump back, but her inquisitive nature overruled her timidness, and she cautiously leaned forward to peer through the bars once again. A bushy-tailed squirrel scurried up the gnarled old trunk, but when he saw the movement in the window, he froze. After a long pause, he turned his head and returned the human's intent stare. As Echo watched the animal relax until it no longer seemed to be afraid of her, she realized that Usen was giving her a sign.

She reached over and grabbed a slice of bread from the tray of food, and began to toss small crumbs onto the branches of the tree. While the squirrel crept up to the food and began to gather the morsels into its tiny paws, Echo started to nibble on the remaining chunk of dry bread she still held in her hand. She would not give the white men the satisfaction of knowing that she had almost allowed them to win. When the many-faceted gaze of the lieutenant flashed through her mind without invitation once more, she repeated her determined resolution; she would escape from this hell-hole and return to the cherished plateau of Pa-Gotzin-Kay. And never again would she be deceived by a white man . . . especially one whose eyes were the color of jade.

"What is this?" the lieutenant asked his commander as he was handed a slip of paper.

"That just came over the wire," the captain answered. "The girl is to be sent to Fort Sill."

Lieutenant Wade tried to hide the rush of emotion that washed over him with a nonchalant shrug of his broad shoulders. "When?"

"Within the next couple of days," Captain Bailey replied. "We do not have the manpower here at Huachuca to detain any prisoners of war. They are equipped for this sort of thing at the Indian agency in Oklahoma."

The lieutenant fought to think coherently where the

girl was concerned, but as had been the case ever since he had first set eyes on her, he seemed to turn into a stuttering idiot. "Will I b-be in char—"

"You will not be leading the detail," the captain interrupted. "I'm sending a battalion with Sergeant Roberts to Oklahoma to escort the prisoner to the agency." Although the lieutenant did not speak right away, the captain could see the other man's objection written all over his face, so he quickly added, "My decision is firm, Lieutenant. I feel that you have become too involved in this situation ever since the disappearance of the first half-breed girl."

He straightened and leveled his gaze on the younger officer. "You are to return to the border with a small detail of men to see if you can find out anything about where the girl was living when you encountered her in Bisbee." He leaned forward and asked the same question he had already posed several times before. "Are you sure the girl did not tell you anything that would be useful? Even her name would be of some help."

The lieutenant felt a slow burn inch its way through his cheeks. "No, sir!" He cleared his throat loudly, then said quickly, "She would not even speak to me."

With a sigh, the captain sat down behind his large oakwood desk. "Well, she acts as though she's deaf and dumb whenever anybody tries to get her to speak, but her attitude will change when she reaches Fort Sill." He leaned back in his chair and placed his feet upon the desk. "At least we'll be rid of her."

Lieutenant Wade did not reply as he fidgeted nervously with the hat he clutched tightly. He had stayed away from the girl's cell for the past few days because he could not deal with his feelings, but absence had not dimmed the way he felt about her. In a clumsy gesture, he replaced his hat upon his head, then saluted his commanding officer. "How soon do you want me to leave, sir?"

"Today," the captain said sharply as he returned the other man's salute. He closely observed the younger man's departure from the barracks. Fort Huachuca had been too peaceful lately to let some half-breed squaw disrupt their routine. He was confident that he had made the right choice to send the lieutenant to Bisbee and the sergeant to Oklahoma—and good riddance to the whole mess!

Lieutenant Wade paused on the stoop of the officer's quarters and glanced toward the building that housed the guardhouse. The urge to go see the girl one more time nearly overpowered his common sense. He clenched his fists at his sides and forced himself to walk toward the enlisted men's barracks. As he named off the four soldiers who would accompany him to Bisbee he was hardly aware of which men he had chosen, and by the time the officer led his battalion out of Fort Huachuca and across the cactus-fringed ridges of the Arizona desert the afternoon was half gone.

As much as he tried to concentrate on his mission to Bisbee, he found that his mind would not cooperate. Over and over again, he reminded himself that he was an officer in the U.S. Cavalry, until he began to wonder if he was losing his sanity. All he could think of was that the girl would be gone when he returned to Fort Huachuca, and he had never even learned her name.

His thoughts clouded as he recalled the day he had collided with her in front of the cantina; then he remembered how lost and forlorn she had been when he had seen her sitting alone in her barren cell in the guardhouse. But worse than anything was the idea of her being at the mercy of a man like Sergeant Roberts while they traveled all the way from Arizona to Fort Sill.

"Sir?" The corporal's voice broke into the horren-

169

dous thought raging through the lieutenant's mind. Wade turned toward the soldier, his look of fury causing the man to become speechless.

"What is it?" Lieutenant Wade demanded.

The corporal gestured toward the fading daylight. "Well, sir, it's getting pretty dark. Do you plan to try to make Bisbee tonight or are we going to camp somewhere and continue on in the morning?"

Lieutenant Wade glanced around in surprise. He had been so wrapped up in his own problems that he hadn't realized how late it was getting. The sky was hanging onto the very last of the sunlight, and a hollow white moon was already settling among the purplish wisps of twilight haze. "We'll camp here," he answered. Riding into Bisbee at night would be foolish, and besides, the farther they went, the more reluctant Travis became about his decision to deny his attraction to the girl.

As he stretched out his lean body upon the hard mattress his bedroll formed on the desert ground, he was so overwhelmed by a compulsion to go back to the fort to see her that he wondered if he was strong enough to prevail. If he only knew her name! How could a man think he was falling in love with someone whose name he did not even know? Still, the image of her lovely face continued to grow clearer by the minute, and the sad look in her deep blue eyes haunted him. He could not pretend he had never met her, nor could he negate the pain she would suffer at the hands of an unscrupulous man like Sergeant Roberts.

As the campsite fell silent, with only an occasional sound of snoring or coughing coming from the sleeping soldiers, the lieutenant was already resaddling his horse. He crept over to the sleeping form of the corporal and gently shook the man until he had awakened him.

"What is it, sir?" the corporal asked as he rubbed at his sleepy eyes like a small child and struggled to sit upright.

"I have something I must attend to back at the fort," Wade whispered, hoping that no one else would hear him and he would be able to limit his lame explanation to the ears of the corporal.

"But, sir? What about our assignment in Bis—"

"You can handle the assignment, Corporal. What I have to do is too important to put off any longer. I'll explain everything to Captain Bailey." Through the faded light, the lieutenant could see the expression of concern upon the young corporal's face. He reached out and patted the soldier's arm in a gesture of reassurance, adding, "It will be all right, so don't worry."

The soldier gave his head a weak nod and remained sitting up as he strained to watch the departing form of the lieutenant. He was not worried about being in charge of such a simple detail, but he was gravely concerned about the lieutenant. He hoped whatever was so important as to draw the officer back to the fort would also seem urgent to Captain Bailey. Desertion of a command was punishable by life imprisonment or death by execution.

Lieutenant Wade gave little thought to the dire consequences of his actions on this fateful night as he pushed his horse into a gallop. The pale light of the moon was bright enough to allow him to follow the narrow road without any problems, and at the pace he was riding, he would be back at the fort long before daybreak. He had devised no plan of what to do after he reached the post. He only knew he must see the girl. He would tell her of the guilt he harbored over the

171

disappearance of her sister; then he planned to tell her of the affinity he had felt toward her ever since their first glance at one another in front of the cantina. This last bit of information probably would not mean anything to her, but he had to tell her how he felt in order to put his feelings into perspective.

After he spoke to the girl, he planned to talk to Captain Bailey about Sergeant Roberts. The captain would be angry at the lieutenant for returning to the fort and leaving his own detail under the leadership of the corporal, but Bailey was usually an understanding man. Once the lieutenant had a chance to explain about the danger the girl would be in with the sergeant, he hoped the captain would reconsider and would send someone other than Sergeant Roberts to lead the detail to Oklahoma. Perhaps it would be easier to let her go, the lieutenant told himself, if he was assured that she would reach the agency at Fort Sill in the same shape she had been in when she had left Arizona.

Lieutenant Wade called out to the night guard to warn him of his entrance into the fort, but as he began to ride through the quiet parade grounds an eerie foreboding overcame him. The feeling persisted as he led his horse to the guardhouse and dismounted. His premonition of doom increased with each step as he entered the dark structure. The young private guarding the prisoners was slumped over the desk asleep, but the sound of the door opening aroused him.

"I must see the Apache girl," the lieutenant said, barely giving the private time to awaken fully.

"But, sir—"

The lieutenant sighed with aggravation. "I'll take full responsibility, Private!"

The young soldier rose from his chair, and gave the lieutenant an uneasy shrug. "I'm not worried about that, sir. It's just that the girl isn't here."

172

The feeling of impending disaster, which had followed the lieutenant through the fort and into this room, came crashing down around him. Captain Bailey had said the girl was being sent to Fort Sill within the next few days, but Travis had thought they wouldn't leave until this morning at the very earliest. He had been so determined to ease his mind of the burdens which had plagued him recently that now he was in complete turmoil. With a quick salute to the private, he stumbled back out onto the front stoop of the guardhouse. He took a deep breath of night air in a useless attempt to clear his jumbled thoughts. The sun would not be up for another hour or so, but the lieutenant did not have that much time to waste. He had to make the most important decision of his entire life—and it must be made now.

His gaze wandered toward the dark officer's quarters where Captain Bailey was sleeping. He could go to the captain and ask for permission to join Sergeant Roberts' detail en route to Oklahoma. The captain had already stated his position on that matter, however, so Lieutenant Wade knew he would be wasting his time. If he was smart, he would just get back on his horse and hightail it back to his own command and forget about the girl once and for all! There was still a chance that his career in the military would not be destroyed if he chose this course, but the lieutenant sensed his intelligence had fled with the realization that he was falling in love with the young girl.

As he swung into his saddle and jerked the reins to turn his horse toward the front gate, he was only certain about one thing; without a doubt, he had gone completely insane. He had been devoted to his career as a cavalryman, but he would risk anything to see the girl again . . . even his life if he was branded an army deserter.

Chapter Eleven

Echo tried to achieve a more comfortable position, but the heavy band around her wrist made it nearly impossible to stretch out upon her bedroll. She grabbed the chain with her other hand and attempted to adjust the enslaving iron rope so that she could lay her arm beside her stiff body, but even that did not help her to rest any easier. She did not want to get comfortable enough to fall asleep, anyway. Her gaze sought out the unmoving form of the sergeant once again. He was a disgusting excuse for a man, and every time his lecherous glare rambled over her body, she wished she could scratch the eyes out of his head.

She knew he was just waiting for an opportunity to get her alone, but fortunately such a situation had not yet presented itself. This was only the first night they had spent away from the fort, though, and there was still at least a week's worth of territory to cover before they reached Fort Sill. When the sergeant did make his move, Echo was prepared to fight to her death, if necessary, rather than submit to the likes of him. She reminded herself that there were other types of men who were just as low as the sergeant, if only in a different manner. The lieutenant's tall blond visage came to her mind. The emotions the memory aroused were more disturbing to her than anything else, because she could not explain them or understand them.

Since his sudden departure from her cell after he had told her about her sister, he hadn't bothered to come back. When she was told she was leaving Fort Huachuca she had been certain he would at least come to say goodbye, but obviously he couldn't be concerned with her now that she had told him what he wanted to know. Along with the hurt she felt from the lieutenant's strange behavior, she also had to deal with the idea of seeing her sister when they reached the reservation. It seemed so odd to think of having a sister again after all these years of believing her dead. Echo wished she'd have a chance to learn more about her sister before they met in Oklahoma, because now she was filled with a hundred questions about the twin she had not seen for eight years. She wondered most of all about how similar they were to one another—not just in appearance but in the way they thought and acted.

She also worried constantly about her parents. The news that their other daughter had survived the last attack on their village would make them ecstatic, but Echo wondered if they would ever know? She tried not to think about the anguish they must be suffering at this time, because along with everything else which troubled her, it was almost more than her burdened heart could handle. Knowing her father as she did, she was certain he was blaming himself for her capture. She just hoped that he would not try to come after her, because the risk was too great, and her mother did not deserve the agony of losing all of them. Echo prayed daily to Usen that her father would return to the *ranchería* in the Sierra Madre and not give in to any foolish notions about coming to look for her. She wanted to remember Pa-Gotzin-Kay as it had always been, and without the strength of both of her parents, their Stronghold Mountain of Paradise would wither and die.

The sergeant rolled over in his bedroll and Echo bolted to an upright position. She held her breath until she was certain that he was still asleep; then she slowly lay back down on the hard ground. At this rate she would die from heart failure before they reached the agency in Oklahoma.

Her wary gaze ascended toward the hazy gray mist starting to streak the sky. The sun would be up soon, and they would be on their way again before the heat of the desert day became too hot to endure. They had left the fort the previous day during the late afternoon hours and had traveled late into the night because the sergeant had decided that he did not want to wait until morning to leave. His anxious attitude had worried Echo even more, and she was amazed that a whole night had passed without his causing any trouble. When he did begin to stir, his first instinct was to turn onto his side to look toward the wagon to which she was chained to prevent her from trying to escape during the night. A surprised expression covered his whiskered face when her intent stare greeted him.

"You been watching me all night long, girl?" He chuckled to himself while he kicked his blanket away from his body. As he rose to his feet, he grabbed the suspenders that hung around his hips and pulled them back up over his shoulders to secure his pants around the small paunch at his midsection. A sly smile outlined his mouth beneath the cover of his red beard and mustache as he walked to where she watched him in cold silence. With a quick glance over his shoulder to see if any of the other men were awake yet, he leaned down close to her.

177

"Well, you don't have anything to fear from me, 'cause I won't let anything bad happen to you," he chortled, and rubbed at his beard. "'Course, you gotta treat me nice too." He reached under her chin and pulled her face up toward his with his forefinger as he continued, "One thing is for certain, I won't do to you what Lieutenant Wade did to your sister." He took his finger from under her chin and continued to laugh in a snide manner as he walked to where the other men slept and began to rouse them.

His words shook Echo to the core. What did he mean by that insinuation about Lieutenant Wade and her sister? The very worst things her imagination could conjure up began to flash through her mind—visions of the lieutenant seducing her sister, then discarding her, like a used washrag, at the reservation. Was that the hidden secret she could not decipher in the lieutenant's jade gaze on the day he had come to her cell? And was that the reason he had gone to look for her in Bisbee? Did he need to have a matching set of twin sisters to achieve his own personal badge of merit? She wondered what horrible abuses her sister must have suffered during the journey from Pennsylvania to Oklahoma, and she cringed with despair as she wondered what to expect when she did finally confront her sister at the agency. Echo pictured a heartbroken shell of a girl with a face identical to her own, pining over the indignities she had been forced to endure from the green-eyed *soldado*. A renewed form of outrage flooded through her. It was no wonder the lieutenant had not been able to face her again.

She was startled once again when the sergeant approached her and bent down to unlock the iron band around her wrist. His ravenous eyes gaped at the soft swell of her bosom the entire time he was bent over her, and when he glanced up at her face he was taken aback by the venomous look which flashed from her blue gaze. Echo was prepared to lash out at him, to tell him what a filthy pig she thought he was, but she held her tongue. Mere words could not affect a man as revolting as this one, she told herself.

"For half-breed squaws, you and your sister sure do think you're something pretty special, don't you?" the sergeant said with a curl of his upper lip. He threw the chain on the ground, then spat a stream of brown tobacco juice beside her still form. "I think it's time you and me got a few things straight." He grabbed her arms and pulled her to her feet.

Echo tried to twist away from him, but he overpowered her as easily as he had when he'd first caught her outside Bisbee. This time, however, he made certain his grip was painful enough to prevent her from trying to knee him again. The heat of his foul-smelling breath hit her nostrils and almost made her gag as she held her breath and turned her head as far to the side as possible.

"I'm in charge here, got that? I can do anything I want to you, and there's nobody who can stop me." His loud voice had drawn the attention of the other five soldiers who were under his command, and they stood around the campsite with a mixed array of expressions upon their faces. The sergeant became aware of his audience and paused to think over his next action. He wanted this half-breed to be his exclusively the first time, and he didn't want the rest of his men waiting like a bunch of vultures for him to be finished with her so they could have their turns.

"Saddle up," he hollered over his shoulder. "We'll eat breakfast on down the road." Echo glimpsed the evil intent lurking within his gaze when he glanced back at her, and she almost felt defiled by that look. "Tonight!" he whispered through gritted teeth as he pushed her away and stalked off to saddle his horse.

His shove knocked Echo up against the side of the buckboard, but she was too filled with terror to notice whether it caused her any pain. His threat had plunged her entire being into the depths of hell, and his words kept echoing in her mind. He could do anything he wanted to her, and he planned to do it tonight!

This thought did not allow her a moment's peace throughout the long day, and as each hour passed, drawing the day into night, she grew more sure of the sergeant's threat. As she rode on the seat of the buckboard with a young private who drove the team of horses, she tried to avoid looking in the sergeant's direction. But he did not miss a chance to grace her with a leering grin whenever an opportunity arrived, nor did he hesitate to make his intentions known once they had stopped to make camp for the second night. The soldiers had barely unsaddled and hobbled their mounts when the sergeant began to lay the ground-work for his plan.

"I will keep watch over our prisoner tonight." His red mustache curved upward when he drew his mouth into a smirk. "The rest of you men can bed down by those bushes over there." He gestured toward a clump of sage that bordered the ridge where they had stopped. The brush was a fair distance from the wagon, and the expressions on the men's faces as they glanced toward their obscure sleeping quarters revealed their aggravation and disgust.

Visible tremors shook Echo's tired body as she watched the other soldiers walk off toward the ridge, lugging their bedrolls and knapsacks. They could not disobey their commanding officer even if they did not agree with his actions. But their frowning expressions did not reveal what they were thinking, and she did not want to beg for help if their discontent was caused by their lack of participation in the sergeant's planned activities. She told herself she would be better off alone when she faced the sergeant, although this thought did little to comfort her or add to her sense of bravery since his brute strength had already been used against her in previous encounters.

"Do you want supper first?" His raw laughter rang out through the quiet of the fading daylight. He shrugged with indifference when she retorted with another one of her defiant stares. When his glance fell upon the chain and wristband that dangled from the side of the wagon, Echo felt the last of her floundering hope disappear. Would he be so cowardly he would chain her to the wagon before fulfilling his wicked cravings?

As he took a step toward her she staggered backward. Each was close enough to sense the determination emanating from the other, and though the daylight was almost nonexistent, the sergeant did not miss the fright that overtook her soft features. Her fear of him only increased the excitement which rose in his loins as he continued to push her farther out into the open area beyond the wagon. In panic, Echo glanced around, coming to the conclusion that she had nowhere to go. She could not get past him to run toward the ridge on which the rest of the men had retired, and behind her lay the vast expanse of the flat desert. Darkness was closing in around them like a black shroud, and not even the moon had dared to venture out into the endless sky yet.

Echo paused to get her bearings, and before she was aware of what was happening, the sergeant lunged toward her and grabbed her in a crushing hold. Her horrified scream echoed through the quiet as they both thudded against the hard ground. They landed side by side, and though the man still held Echo in his brutal grasp, their position allowed Echo to make another attempt to escape. She began to kick at him with every ounce of her strength. The tiny sandals she wore worked their way from her feet and went flying somewhere out into the increasing darkness of the night. When the sergeant attempted to subdue her flailing legs, she managed to get her arms free of his grasp. With her legs and arms swinging wildly, the sergeant was confronted by the full force of her desperate urge to escape from him, and her energy surprised him for a moment.

With an infuriated growl, he made another grab for her arms as she tried to rise to her feet. With her legs concentrating for an instant on something besides kicking his unprotected groin, the sergeant was able to grasp both her arms, and as he did so he twisted them with such force she fell back down to her knees, her pain unspeakable. She tried to scream, but the sound was lost to the horrible agony of his grip, and nothing was emitted from her mouth but a weak moan. She tumbled to the ground face first, but still he persisted in cranking her arms with all his might. Her slender limbs could only take the pressure for so long before they began to give in to it, and just as her bones felt as though they were about to splinter, she heard him laugh again, the evil, breathless sound hanging like a hovering banshee in the stillness of the night.

"I told you I could make you do anything I wanted—and nobody can stop me!"

"Until now!" The low male voice cut through the air, its deadly tone making every pore in the sergeant's body pop out in an icy sweat. He was amazed that one of his men would dare to challenge his authority. But as the intruder stepped closer, the sergeant glimpsed his face and was overcome with shock.

Lieutenant Wade shoved the barrel of his rifle into

the red whiskers of the sergeant's mustache. He was furious enough to pull the trigger, but a flicker of sanity held his finger steady. "Turn the girl loose," he said in a voice just above a whisper, but his tone hinted at uncontrollable rage.

The sergeant's eyes bulged from their sockets as the gun pressed into his upper lip. The weapon left him with little recourse other than to do as the lieutenant demanded. He held in the breath he felt trembling in his chest, hoping the lieutenant's gun did not have a hair trigger. His hands felt permanently attached to the girl's arms as he tried to release her from their grasp, but one by one his fingers pried loose from their deathlike hold.

"Get up," the lieutenant commanded when he saw the sergeant free the girl. He stepped forward and steadied his rifle against the other man's face as he prepared to speed the man to his feet by using the pressure of the gun barrel under his nose as an aid.

The sergeant slowly came up with the rising gun. His fear grew in leaps and bounds once he was standing face to face with the lieutenant. Fury made the lieutenant's countenance almost unrecognizable. The hard riding he had done in the past few hours had left his face and clothes coated with a heavy layer of dust, but even the grime did not hide his animosity, and as the moon started to rise in the dark sky its opaque light illuminated him in ghoulish outline.

"A-are you crazy?" The sergeant forced the words between stiff lips.

A slow smile curled the lieutenant's mouth as he contemplated the question. "Yep," he replied earnestly, since he had recently determined he was. His eyes did not waver from the other man's face as he tried to control his urge to pull the trigger. For a time, which seemed to drag on forever, the two men stood facing one another, only the tilt of the long rifle separating their tense forms.

"Do something, damn it!" the sergeant finally said through gritted teeth. He felt the lieutenant adjust the rifle, settling it more firmly under his nose. His mind went blank for an instant as he waited for the explosion he was sure would come at any time. He wanted to close his eyes, but his lids would not cooperate and his pupils enlarged from fear. Sweat began to trickle down his face. It rolled from the tip of his nose onto the black barrel of the rifle.

The lieutenant hovered on the brink of madness and rage, but even in this state he knew he could not murder a fellow soldier. As rationality began to penetrate the turmoil in his mind, the finger he rested against the trigger inched its way to the butt of the gun. The movement was slow and almost unnoticeable, but Sergeant Roberts felt the slight adjustment.

His eyes settled back into his head, and he blinked in fast succession for several seconds to clear away the rivulets of burning sweat that had clouded his sight. Beneath the rifle barrel his lips began to curl into a twisted grin of satisfaction. He had prevailed over the lieutenant once again because the other man did not have the guts to pull the trigger. As he opened his mouth wider he felt the barrel slide up against his nose again, but the lieutenant's grip had grown lax and the gun no longer cut into his skin with its deadly weight. The sergeant's bravery returned, and he started to voice a cruel taunt. Before he could utter a sound, however, the lieutenant made a move that was so quick Roberts wasn't even aware of what hit him before he was engulfed in total blackness, his crumpling form dropping to the ground.

The lieutenant remained rooted to the spot as he waited to see if the sergeant would get up again or if the blow had done its job. His swift action had surprised even him, and he was momentarily stunned that he was able to swing the gun around and grab the butt with enough power to club the other man over the head. But he'd been determined to keep the other man quiet without resorting to bloodshed, and he had been unable to think of anything to do except knock him unconscious. When the sergeant did not move a muscle, and the lieutenant was satisfied that he had accomplished his mission, he turned toward the girl.

Echo grew stiff with fright when she saw his attention shift to her. She did not know what to expect from this man, but she distrusted him every bit as much as she did the sergeant. As she sprang to her feet, pain shot up the length of her arms from the sergeant's crude hold, but she ignored it as she tried to focus her spinning mind. In her confusion, she started to run toward the ridge, but then she remembered that the rest of the men were bedded down over there, so she spun on her bare feet and charged toward the open area where the horses were hobbled. If she could free one of the animals, she knew she could escape because she had practically been born on the back of a horse, and she was sure not a white man alive could equal her riding skills—especially this green-eyed *soldado!*

Lieutenant Wade watched her disoriented course, wondering why she was frantically trying to get away now that the sergeant was no longer a threat. He didn't realize that she feared him just as much as she did her attacker until he saw her charge for the horses. His mind snapped into action and he took out after her, but she was already to the horses before he had taken his first step. The animals did not make a sound when she approached them, but as the lieutenant came lumbering up, they began to whinny and rear up in blind panic. Shouting from the ridge alerted both Echo and the lieutenant to the threat the rest of the men posed.

Fear did not stop Echo, though, and in a matter of seconds she had loosed one large steed from the iron hobbles that kept him from straying. Before the lieutenant could stop her, she had swung onto the bare back of the animal and charged through the swirling dust. In the pandemonium created by the excited horses and the approaching men, the lieutenant could think of nothing to do but follow the girl's lead. He grabbed the mane of the nearest horse, and despite the danger of the animal's deadly hoofs, he bent down and tried to grasp the iron bands that securely held its back legs together. His hands fumbled against the band on one leg as he dodged the front hoofs of the panicked horse. His last movement had placed him in a precarious position underneath the animal, and since he had nowhere to go, he fought back his fear of being stomped to death and made another frantic grab at the animal's leg. The leg band pulled apart as the lieutenant rolled to the side and sprang to his feet to avoid the stomping hoofs once again.

He did not have time to release the hobble on the other leg of the horse, and with a rash lunge he threw himself onto the back of the animal just as the horse began to buck and rear up in terror. Only his crazed desperation to follow the girl kept Wade on the horse's back when the animal charged out from the rest of the pack and began to gallop at lightning speed across the dark countryside. The lieutenant was powerless to control the direction in which the horse fled, and his only thought was to hang on to the beast's mane for he would risk a broken neck if he fell off the animal at this speed. The horse, however, seemed to know the direction he wanted to take. He took a sharp turn, which nearly lost him his rider, and continued to race across the hard ground.

Once the lieutenant was able to regain his balance, he tried to concentrate on their direction. He sensed the horse was following the animal unfettered by the girl, but he could only hope he was correct in his assumption. With just the dim light of the moon, along with the turmoil of trying to unhobble the horse, the lieutenant had no idea what direction the girl had taken, nor did he know where this horse was headed. All he knew was that nothing had turned out as he had planned. When he had caught up to the sergeant's troop earlier that day he had decided to wait until he could use the cover of darkness to approach the girl. He'd wanted to talk to her alone while the rest of the men were sleeping, but Sergeant Roberts already had made other plans for her.

The lieutenant did not have time to dwell on this unexpected turn of events, however. He was already considered a deserter before he had reached the campsite, and his fight with the sergeant would only be added to the list of offenses the cavalry would be compiling against him. He clung to the mane of the horse, while cursing aloud his rotten luck. His own horse still remained back at the edge of the campsite, saddled and loaded with all of his gear. Even his rifle had been lost among the rush of horses's hooves; the only weapon he still possessed was the forty-five pistol that hung from his gunbelt—hardly artillery with which to face his new life as a wanted man.

Echo dug her heels into the heaving sides of her horse. The animal was tiring much too fast, and she was growing more aggravated with every lagging step he took. She remembered this old palomino as one of the horses the *soldados* used for packing their gear. Of all the animals she had to pick from, she wondered why this brute had been the one she was destined to choose. It was no wonder he had been so easy to unhobble, but that realization did her little good now.

Since the moon did not afford her enough light to see the terrain ahead of her, she knew it would not be wise to push the horse beyond his limits anyway. She glanced around and drew in a relieved breath. The campsite was far behind her, and by morning she would be able to cover all signs of her tracks, so for the time being she could just concentrate on putting as much distance between herself and the *soldados* as possible. Her thoughts, however, seemed to want to dwell on only one thing, and that was the lieutenant. He had appeared out of nowhere to save her from the demonic clutches of the sergeant, but why? She came to a hundred conclusions before the night began to wear thin and dawn seeped over the blue horizon of distant hills.

She had gone through all the wicked and bad reasons as to why the lieutenant must have come to her rescue, and now she had begun to imagine even more outlandish possibilities. What if he had followed the troop from Fort Huachuca because he had realized he could not bear to live without her? Echo became enraged when this uninvited thought entered her mind. How could she even permit herself to think of such utter nonsense? She reminded herself of the sergeant's reference to the lieutenant's association with her sister. But it was the vision of the lieutenant's deep jade gaze that flashed before her eyes as a driving instinct told her to glance back over her shoulder.

A surprised gasp flew from her mouth when she spotted the slumping form of the lieutenant atop a horse only several hundred yards behind her own animal. How long had he been following her? He could have been pursuing her all night, she realized, but she wouldn't have known it until now when the early morning light granted her a clear view in all directions. Echo could not believe her own ignorance in not sensing his presence. She swung toward the front again and glanced at the large expanse of flat ground which sprawled out before her. There was nowhere to run for cover other than the craggy hills looming far out into the distance. On this old packhorse she could never hope to lose him, especially since he was already so close.

She clenched her hands into the long mane of the large horse as she tried to sort out her thoughts. In a matter of minutes the lieutenant could be abreast of her, but something prevented her from racing on. What was it about this *soldado* that created such turbulence in her mind? Whatever it was, Echo knew she was never going to escape from it until she confronted it—and him. She reached out and patted the smooth neck of the horse.

"Whoa," she said in a commanding voice. The old steed took a few more fumbling steps before coming to a stop. Echo drew in a deep breath as she waited for the other rider to cover the short distance between them. She realized she might have just signed her own death warrant with this impulsive move, but it was a chance she had to take. As the lieutenant stopped his horse beside her animal, Echo's gaze searched his dusty, weary face for an answer to her own tempestuous thoughts. Instead, she was met by the inextinguishable look of tenderness she had glimpsed in his gaze before, and now she knew she had not imagined it. All her precautions were discarded, and she no longer cared if he was her enemy or not. If it was her intended fate to spend the rest of her life as a captive, then she would gladly submit to the enslaving power in this *soldado*'s jade green eyes.

189

Chapter Twelve

"Why did you stop?"

Echo brushed back the long tendrils of hair encircling her face as she looked directly at him. "I couldn't escape from you, could I?"

"I don't think so." He shook his head slowly, while he stared back at her as though seeing her for the first time. The morning sun seemed to create a halo of light around her head, and in its brilliance he could make out nearly obscure strands of auburn streaked in with the thick ebony cascade that hung inches below her waistline. In spite of the streaks of dirt, which she had acquired from the rough terrain, the skin that covered the soft curves of her aristocratic features was as smooth as rich dark satin. Her colorful skirt was hanging in torn shreds at the horse's sides, revealing slender, long legs and bare feet. The lieutenant drew in a heavy breath. She would never escape from him, because he would follow her through eternity.

"What do you want?" she implored, but even as she asked him that simple question, she grew fearful of his answer. What if he told her he wanted from her the same thing she suspected he had already taken from her sister?

The lieutenant's tired expression was drawn into tense lines of frustration as he imitated her previous gesture by pushing back the stray strands of hair hanging across his forehead. He became aware that he no longer had his hat on, and he wondered when he had lost it. But thinking about ridiculous things such as his lost hat would not answer her question, nor would it satisfy his own mind. Words, though, seemed to be lost to him. His own career—his whole life—was on the line because of her; yet he couldn't explain the things he wanted from her at this time.

"We'd better keep riding," he answered.

Echo stared in disbelief as his horse sauntered past her. Did he think she would just follow him back into captivity without any resistance? The route he was taking was equally as disturbing to her. He was not traveling in the direction from which they had just ridden; instead he was going the same way she'd been headed when he caught up with her. But did he realize she was headed straight for Mexico, where she planned to rally her people so they could go after her twin sister who was being held prisoner on the reservation at Fort Sill?

"Are you coming?" he shouted back over his shoulder, then added, "We can't waste any time if we're going to make it across the border before the rest of the troop catches up to us."

A perplexed frown creased Echo's face. He surely didn't think she was ignorant enough to follow him anywhere. In a rush of panic she glanced around, expecting to glimpse some sort of entrapment. She grew more unsure of her next course of action when she saw nothing but the barren countryside. Undoubtedly, the *soldados* were in pursuit of her by now, but in front of her was . . . the lieutenant. He and the terrain were enemies to her; still, much as she hated to admit it, her

192

chances were bound to be slightly better with the lieutenant. She eyed the distant hills closely. If they could get that far without encountering any other *soldados,* she knew she would have no problem losing the lieutenant. With this thought in mind, she kicked her mount in the sides, making the old packhorse jerk forward.

When they were abreast, the lieutenant acknowledged her with only a quick sideways glance. He hoped she was not planning to ask him any more questions, and, to his relief, they rode in complete silence until they had reached the gradual incline of the rolling hills that disrupted the expanse of flat ground they'd been crossing since the first light of dawn. With a nervous glance back out across the plains, the lieutenant once again surveyed the area for the cavalrymen he knew must be in pursuit of them by now. Though he didn't spot anything for as far as he could see, that did not ease his apprehension. The cavalry did not look upon desertion lightly, or the escape of one of their captives.

His obvious unrest made Echo more leery with each passing second. She had no idea what he was planning, but whatever it was, she wanted to be ready to escape from him at the first opportunity. Without hesitation, she pushed her horse up the slope. The far ridges were infested with brush and craggy clumps of trees, which would provide a barrier from their pursuers—and from him when she made her move. Before she had gone more than a few strides, Echo noticed he was only a few feet behind her again. His presence was driving her insane! What did he want from her? She kicked the old horse again in an effort to make him move faster up the hillside, but her gesture only made the horse slacken his pace. Echo determined she could probably run up this hill and be out of sight before the animal reached the peak, and her aggravation was so severe she considered doing just that. But, as this foolish thought was going through her head the lieutenant's horse came up beside hers. With a swift glance, and a new rush of fury, she noticed he had been lucky enough to pick a mount that was in much better condition than her sluggish horse. She could never hope to outrun him, so she would have to plan her strategy carefully before making her next escape.

"When we get into the cover of those trees, we'll stop to let the horses rest."

Since neither of them had spoken for most of the morning, Echo jumped at the sound of his voice. She nodded in agreement, while her mind began to turn over the possibilities of ridding herself of the lieutenant's presence. They had not slept all night, and though she was tired, she was desperate to get away. She eyed the *soldado*'s horse slyly out of the corner of her eye. This time she would make sure she fled on a better mount. Without thinking, she smiled to herself at the idea of the lieutenant trying to catch up to her on the stumbling old packhorse.

"We need to get some rest to . . ." The lieutenant paused as he glanced in her direction and caught the strange grin on her face. Most times she was so different from her sister, Margaret Sinclair. Yet, the instant the lieutenant glimpsed the conniving smirk upon her lips, he was reminded of how similar the twins often were; a realization which caused him to dismiss his idea of getting rest. As they crested the ridge and entered the thick brush, he wondered if all his training in the cavalry would be of any help to him when dealing with this one young Apache woman.

Echo tugged on her horse's mane and called out for the animal to stop. She glanced around the small clearing she had chosen, with satisfaction. The trees offered seclusion, but they could still watch the ridge of the hill without being observed. She slid down from the horse's back and, paying no notice to the lieutenant, stretched to ease the aching in her legs from straddling the horse for so long a time. With a toss of her long hair, she tilted her head to the side and eyed the lieutenant with a piercing stare. He had not dismounted, nor had he stopped gawking at her since they had stopped. Her dark gaze narrowed as she continued to imitate him by glaring back. Finally, in a rage, she placed her hands askew on the curve of her hips and squared her jaw.

"What do you want?" she demanded.

The lieutenant's mouth flapped open, then closed without offering her a reply. She must think me incapable of conversing like a normal person, he thought, since every time she asks me a question I seem to go mute. With great effort, he averted his eyes from her and swung his leg over the horse's back. The sight of her lithe form stretching so casually, her thick hair falling over the enticing curve of her backside when she tossed her head back, had left him hypnotized. He was imagining what it would be like to kiss the soft velvet of her neck and to tangle his fingers in that long mass of rich dark hair. Trying to act in a casual manner was not easy after experiencing such sweet musing.

"We'd um . . ." He blinked and rubbed his forehead, trying to think of something intelligent to say. "We'd better tether the horses and make a small corral so they don't run off while we're resting." He wondered if it was his imagination again, or if his voice sounded rather high-pitched and abnormal. When she nodded and began to search the ground for sticks or branches they might use to contain the animals, he became aware of how cooperative she was all of a sudden. In contrast to her previous attitude, she now seemed overly anxious to find them a place to rest.

195

After they had secured the horses within a loosely constructed barricade of branches, Echo wasted no time in clearing a small spot on the ground for herself. The astonished lieutenant watched as she stretched out upon the earth as though she couldn't wait to go to sleep, and since resting was the last thing she probably had on her mind, he knew he must not allow himself to doze off, not even for a minute. He joined her on the ground, but did not lie down.

"I still don't know your name."

She opened her eyes to barely more than a slit and placed her hands behind her head as a makeshift pillow. "I still do not know what you want from me?"

Travis threw his hands into the air in irritation. "I was only asking you what your name was?" He grunted with annoyance and turned around to present his back to her. The sight of her slender body stretched out upon the ground was far too tempting to a man in his disoriented state of mind.

A long silence followed; then, for no reason Echo could rationalize, she blurted out her name. Her voice was low, but the lieutenant did not miss her softly spoken word.

"Echo?" he repeated quietly as he turned around to face her. "Echo." A slow nod of his head accompanied his voice. Had a name ever been so perfect for the person who claimed it? he wondered. The lyrical name hovered on his lips again as his jade eyes met her intense blue gaze. There was an instant, as he leaned forward, when he thought he had lost all restraint, but his sanity returned. Her eyes had not moved from his face, and the lieutenant wondered what she would have done if he had proceeded to kiss her. Since he was certain she would not have been as receptive as her sister, he told himself he'd been wise to rethink that rash action. Recalling Margaret Sinclair, and the impulsive kiss they had shared by the waterhole, did not improve his disposition, however. When Echo's next question broke the strained silence, dread inched through his veins.

"What happened between you and my sister?"

"Nothing!" he answered quickly, like a child who has been caught with his hand in the candy jar. What basis would she have to ask a question such as that? He then remembered she had spent the past couple of days with Sergeant Roberts, and undoubtedly had heard the same sort of gossip the sergeant had been spouting all over the fort.

"If it was nothing, then why is your face so red?" Echo sat up and glared at him in a way that did not grant the lieutenant an easy escape. He glanced down at the ground and unconsciously began to write her name in the loose dirt. Answering her question was the only sensible thing to do, but his own guilt over Margaret Sinclair was hard to voice.

He stared at the sight of Echo's name in the dirt without looking up at her as he began to speak. "Whatever you heard about me and your sister was probably not true, but the truth is not too pleasant, either."

Echo inched forward and glanced downward to see what it was that drew the *soldado*'s attention to the ground. A strange sensation of affinity passed through her when she saw that he had written her name in the dirt. She sat back and remained silent while she tried to ignore the unwelcome feelings she kept experiencing toward the *soldado*.

"Your sister is every bit as headstrong as you are," he said as he pointed an accusing finger at her. Echo's lips drew into a deep frown, but she kept quiet. "She was a handful of trouble from the first moment I set eyes on her, and the situation got continually worse as we

197

traveled toward the reservation in Oklahoma. All she could think of was escaping."

Echo's brows rose in a speculative manner. She could not see anything wrong with her sister's goal. There had been nothing on her own mind but escape since she had encountered the *soldados*. "So what methods did you use to prevent her from escaping?" Her tone was scathing and the lieutenant could not miss the insinuation.

"I kissed her."

A cold chill raced through Echo. She had wanted him to deny that anything had happened between her sister and him, but he had just confirmed her fears. "Ju-just a kiss?" she asked without thinking, then could have hit herself for being so naive. There had to be more to it, or else the sergeant wouldn't have said anything to her.

One corner of the lieutenant's mouth twitched slightly as he pondered how to tell this girl of the foolish maneuver which had resulted in her sister's disappearance. "I kissed her—once! Then I did something much worse, something I can never forgive myself for doing to your sister."

Echo drew in a trembling breath as she waited for the rest of his confession. Oh, how she wished it wasn't true, but from the sound of it, he was about to admit to all the horrible deeds the sergeant had spoken of. Her fists clenched on the lap of her full skirt, Echo braced herself to hear the words coming from his mouth.

"After I kissed her, I-I deserted her . . . in the dark, out in the middle of nowhere, knowing that comancheros were roaming around in the area." He dropped his hands into his lap in a defeated gesture as he was filled with disgust over his own actions. He chanced a fugitive glance toward Echo, expecting to see an expression of repugnance upon her beautiful face.

198

Instead, she wore a look of expectancy as though she thought there must be more to the story.

"And then?" she asked, to confirm his suspicions.

With a heavy sigh, the lieutenant emphatically added, "She was kidnapped by the comancheros."

It took Echo several seconds to grasp what he had just told her, since her mind had been so engrossed in visions of a completely different nature. "Kidnapped? But how?"

"Because I was more concerned about upholding my reputation than defending my command." He rubbed at his forehead, wishing to disperse the pain lodged in his head. "I never should have left her alone, but all I could think of was how irresponsible I had been to kiss her, so then I ran away from her like a coward."

Echo closed her eyes for a moment to try to straighten out her jumbled thoughts. His confession was so different from what she had been expecting, it was difficult to think coherently about this new version. "I don't understand? Is she back at the reservation now?"

Another sharp pain ricocheted through the lieutenant's head as his feelings of guilt reached a new peak. "We couldn't find a trace of her."

A shocked gasp flew from Echo's mouth. "She's with the comancheros even now?" Her hands flew to her mouth as she tried to envision her twin held captive by a band of cutthroats like the outlaws who roamed throughout Sonora. When she paused to think about it, though, the idea of her sister being somewhere in Mexico did not seem completely tragic. Because their father was half-Mexican, he had many connections in Mexico. Once he knew his other daughter was still alive, he would have no trouble finding her. The pain the *soldado* felt over what had happened to her sister, however, was so apparent on his face that Echo was

199

compelled to comfort him. She scooted over the short distance to him and laid her hand on his shoulder.

"Is there more?" she asked, wondering if his vast despair was brought on by something even more traumatic that he was still refusing to tell her.

Travis Wade was surprised by her attitude. He had expected her to scream at him for being so careless with her sister's safety, but her touch was so gentle and the worry upon her beautiful young face was sincere. "No, there's nothing more except . . ."

Echo leaned forward until their faces were level. Her long hair fell over one shoulder and trailed into the dirt where the officer had written her name. "What do you want from me?"

The repeated question once again set Travis Wade back on his heels. This was a request he could no longer deny if she was going to continue to ask it over and over again. The tanned contours of his handsome face filled with emotion as he met her unwavering gaze. He had to give her the facts and let her draw her own conclusions. "I deserted my command to come after you, because . . . well . . . I think I started to fall in love with you the instant I ran into you in front of the cantina in Bisbee." There, it was out, the admission that he had not even been able to say aloud to himself.

Echo's hand limply dropped from the *soldado*'s shoulder to her lap. Her heart started to beat as though it had gone mad and was trying to crash through her breast. She had been attracted to this green-eyed *soldado* from the first moment too; yet it seemed inconceivable that he was experiencing the same sort of feelings for her. But he had deserted his command to come after her, and that must be proof of the truth in his words. She continued to stare into deep pools of mesmerizing green as a slow recognition dawned on her. All the hurt and betrayal she had been feeling had been masking the deeper emotions he had evoked in her.

"What would happen if I told you I felt the same way?" she asked in a quiet tone, while watching emotions flash through the jade hues of his expressive eyes.

"I guess this would happen." He reached out and placed the palm of his hand against the smooth silk of her cheek. His lips sought hers as if they knew exactly what was expected of them. Though she was already close enough to kiss, she was still too far away, so Travis slid his body closer until they were crushed together in an intimate contact which made his whole body vibrate with the tender urge to lose himself in this kiss, and in this young woman for this moment and forever.

Echo responded to his kiss as though she'd been deprived of something vital to her and the union of their lips was her only hope for recovering it. To deny their attractions for one another for a moment longer would have been useless, because a force more powerful than either of them had determined this outcome since the first moment they met. Yearnings which Echo could not control, or understand, were surging through her like an overflowing river, and they washed away any sensible thoughts of stopping the kiss. Instead, the feel of his lips consuming her own increased her cravings until she feared she would submit to anything he asked of her.

Their bodies pressed closer as though neither of them would ever be complete again unless they were that close. Echo's thoughts were going in a dozen directions at once, but the feel of his lips prevailed above all else. His mouth was warm and inviting, making her lips flame with a pulsating fever that was too great to be consumed within such a small area. As his tongue somehow became entwined with hers, the fire began to rage throughout her whole body. When he had first taken her into his arms they had been sitting on the hard ground; now it felt natural to lie back upon the earth so that the lengths of their bodies could meld and every inch of their beings connect.

His kisses intensified until Echo was certain she would never again be able to take a breath. Yet stopping was not possible. Her mouth was moving of its own accord, and her kisses boldly enticed him to continue this delicious assault. She felt his hand slide down along the curve of her hips and she experienced a wondrous tingling sensation in her loins. This new feeling was so overpowering she wanted to cry out in ecstasy. Her knowledge of such intimate matters was limited to what her mother had told her about a man and woman's relationship, and though her mother had been very explicit, mere words had not even begun to prepare her for this tidal wave of emotions and insatiable longings.

Eventually their lips were forced to part so they might gasp for air, and it was in this brief second that a minute portion of Echo's sanity returned. "We . . . we shouldn't, I mean . . ." She wanted to be sensible, but her mind was fighting a losing battle with her body. Apache girls were not raised to be promiscuous, and it was completely against Echo's upbringing to make love to a man who was not her husband. So, why did she feel such a great disappointment at the thought of stopping this rapturous conjunction?

Travis heard her breathless words, and a slight edge of conscience began to work its way through his passion. He wanted to make this girl a woman—his woman—in every way; still, he wanted it to be the right way. But could his impatient body take the torture? He cleared his throat, but not his whirling mind. "You're right We probably shouldn't."

His tone was so pitiful, he sounded like a little boy hoping to gain sympathy. And his tousled blond hair and pouting expression only added to his appeal. Echo wanted to pull him up against her again before the fire in her body was doused by their words, but she knew if his ravenous lips touched hers again there would be no stopping. They were both right—they shouldn't. A sigh of resignation escaped from her swollen lips as she slowly nodded her head in agreement and struggled to sit up. Her mother would be proud of her; still, Echo was sure these unsatisfied desires would be the death of her if the lieutenant touched her once again.

Now that they had both realized the extent of their passion for one another, there was a strain in the air as they separated and tried to regain some semblance of normality. Echo didn't dare meet his eyes for fear that she would do something rash, such as throw herself at him and beg him to do those wonderful things to her again. And the lieutenant's face was flushed and red as he tried to avoid glancing in her direction. Since it was obvious she was not going to say anything, he blurted out the first thing that popped into his head.

"We should get married first."

The words coming out of his mouth surprised him as much as they shocked Echo. Marriage was a drastic step to take in order to fulfill his selfish cravings, but he knew it was more than just physical attraction he felt for this young woman. He was falling in love with her, more so with each breath he took. His future was uncertain and his career in the cavalry was destroyed, but to spend the remainder of his life with this beautiful girl would be all he would ever need.

His suggestion settled upon Echo like a heavy load of wet clay. As strongly as she felt about him, she could never marry him. There were only a few Apaches living at Pa-Gotzin-Kay, and she could never desert them. She must return to the Sierra Madre, but she had to go alone. To take any outsider into their hidden stronghold was too dangerous, but to allow a white *soldado* to glimpse the location of their *ranchería* would be unthinkable.

"I could never marry a *soldado* in the white man's army," she answered, her voice full of regret.

Travis emitted a laugh devoid of humor. "I don't think I'm considered a soldier any longer. Deserter and traitor more accurately describe my new status with the Army."

In Echo's mind, his words conjured up visions of firing squads and imprisonment. "What will happen to you?"

The lieutenant shrugged and glanced through the trees toward the ridge. "Well, I reckon once I have you back to wherever it is you belong, and I know you're safe, then I'll have to go back and turn myself in to the Army. Unless, of course"—he reached out and placed a hand under her chin—"I have a reason to stay with you."

"That's blackmail," Echo whispered. His mere touch had summoned forth all the tingling sensations in her body and, with them, the fear that she could not deny him anything. She searched the depths of his green gaze for any signs of treachery, but only the radiance of his love shone back at her.

"How can I know you will never betray me or my people if I take you to my home?"

Travis' hand continued to gently fondle her chin as his gaze held hers tenderly. "I will give you my word and pledge it on my love for you. You will have to trust me enough to believe I am not a man who would do that lightly."

Echo tried to sort her thoughts out and put them into

proper perspective, but with him so near it was almost impossible. She could not answer him until she was certain she was not acting on the desirous impulses surging through her body. Her gaze traveled over his face once again and settled on his jade-colored eyes. Oh, she had been lost to the affinity of those green eyes ever since their first glance, and their appeal had only grown stronger as time passed. He was offering her only his word that he would be true to her people, and she could not forget how many times the white man's word had proven to be false in the past. How could she ever convince her family and the rest of the people at Pa-Gotzin-Kay that this blond-haired *soldado* was different from the rest of his kind?

Echo drew in a trembling breath. Her decision could destroy everything the people at her *ranchería* had worked to build through the years, and it could also mean the death of the last of the free Apaches. She wanted to ask Usen for his help, although she sensed that even Usen would be perplexed as to what path she should take this time. The hand which held her chin began to shake as the lieutenant waited for her reply.

"To accept your word will mean placing my entire village in your trust. But I have no choice, because I do not think I can deny my love for you." She grabbed onto the hand that still trembled against her chin and held on as though afraid he would try to leave. But he did not move, not even his eyes blinked as he stared into her own pleading gaze.

He would not destroy the fragile faith she was placing in him, and with every breath he took, he would work to increase her trust in him, until she no longer had any doubts. His only worry was that his time would run out before he could accomplish this staggering feat.

Chapter Thirteen

Margaret swirled the tip of her big toe around in the cool water as a sigh of boredom drifted from her lips. Kaytee—Katherine had chosen to revert back to her Indian name—was splashing around in the chilly water of the Rio Urique River as though she didn't have a care in the world. Margaret reminded herself that Kaytee didn't have anything to worry about since being reunited with her father. Chateo was making an effort to be good to his daughter in spite of the fact that he was a ruthless bandit, and though the home he had brought them to was nothing more than a thatched hut on a mountainside.

With an irritated glance in the direction of the shack, Margaret found herself wondering what Chateo was doing at this time. She could barely see the roof of the hut jutting up through the dense undergrowth of vines, dripping ferns, and *mala mujer*. The vegetation was so thick, machetes had been used to carve narrow paths through the high grasses so the occupants of the area could reach the river. Margaret returned her gaze to the young girl jumping in and out of the deep swimming hole, but her thoughts were still on Chateo. Was he resting—half-nude—on one of the grass cots as was his habit in the heat of the afternoon? Margaret closed her eyes and tried to force the vision of his glistening dark body from her mind, but the stubborn thoughts did not go away.

The sounds of footsteps approaching down the pathway jolted Margaret from her lascivious musing and nearly caused her to fall from the rock she was balanced upon. Most of the men who inhabited this outlaw den frightened her to death, especially their leader, a fat-bellied man who was called José Fernando. Margaret worried constantly that José Fernando, or one of his bandits, would become bold enough to come looking for her whenever they thought Chateo was not around. With dread inching through her thin form, she turned around. The smile which broke out across her lovely face was one of relief, but Chateo's heart took a jubilant leap within his breast. Surely she must be as glad to see him as he was to gaze upon her rare beauty, he decided as he smiled back her her.

Kaytee was momentarily forgotten as his hungry eyes devoured the young woman perched upon the rock in such an enticing position. Her dark hair was still wet from her recent swim, and the thick mass surrounded her shoulders like a veil of exquisite silk. Her white cotton blouse clung to her damp skin and outlined the pert tips of her youthful bosom. Chateo felt his knees grow weak as his gaze traveled down the length of her luscious form. Her skirt was bunched up around her knees, revealing long slender legs that dangled at the edge of the riverbank. Chateo had the ridiculous urge to run up to her and kiss her wet toes and bare legs and . . . Reality snapped him back from his dreams of seduction among the lush grasses of the riverbank.

"Father, watch me dive from the top of those high rocks." Kaytee's gleeful voice rang out from the far side of the river. The girl disappeared beneath the surface of the water, then reappeared at the base of a tower of round rocks which skirted the bank.

"Be careful," he called back with a chuckle. Without meeting Margaret's gaze, he leaned against the rock on which she was sitting. At once she pulled the hem of her skirt down to cover her legs and drew her knees up to her chest in a protective manner. Chateo wondered if she had read his thoughts. He tried to focus all his attention on his daughter's impressive feat as the young girl leaped into the water from the top of the rocks, but it was a difficult task. Margaret Sinclair's alluring presence had been tempting him throughout the trip from Oklahoma to this hideout, and with Kaytee always at Margaret's side during the journey, Chateo had been forced to contain his increasing desire. But since they had reached the outlaw den, there were times when Kaytee was not always in attendance, and Chateo was not sure how much longer he could wait for this young woman to make the first move.

Being back among his comrades made his vow to challenge Margaret Sinclair into making love to him seem stupid and childish. When these men wanted a woman they simply took her; then, when she grew mundane, they sold her to the highest bidder. Chateo had already done his fair share of fast-talking since their arrival, although he suspected most of the other comancheros did not believe his story about Margaret Sinclair being part Apache, since her skin and mannerisms were those of a white woman. This made her position in the hideout even more precarious. Chateo had to guard her day and night if he wanted to keep her to himself, and being around her constantly did not ease his ache to have her as his woman.

Both Margaret and Chateo cheered and clapped when Kaytee surfaced after her daring dive. Yet, when the girl resumed her swimming again, an uneasy silence hovered over the pair. "I need to go to Cieneguita for supplies," Chateo said in an attempt to make conversation.

A chill shot through Margaret at the thought of being left there alone. She was not blind to the protection Chateo provided whenever any of the other outlaws were leering at her. "Kaytee and I will go with you," she said in a definite tone. At the back of her mind was the idea that she might even be able to escape from him once they reached the town of Cieneguita. But then she glanced at Kaytee splashing around in the river, and her heart sank within her breast. She had never seen Kaytee as happy as she was since being reunited with her father; still, Margaret did not feel right deserting the girl in this den of outlaws. What would happen to the child when Chateo decided to go on another raid? Margaret felt trapped by an obligation to take care of Kaytee as long as Chateo insisted on keeping his daughter in this hellish abode.

"It would be safer for you to stay here." Chateo reached down into the water and scooped up a handful of the cool liquid. He splashed it on his face, then tossed his head back and ran his wet hands down his neck and bare chest. "A large group of men are going so that we can bring back enough supplies to last through the next couple of months. Just the women and a few of the men will stay behind. There is an Indian woman who belongs to one of the other men. I will ask her to stay with you and Kaytee while I'm gone." He pointed toward the canyon which loomed off in the distance. "During the late summer the rains are sometimes so heavy the barrancas fill with flood waters and we are trapped on the mountainsides until the river subsides."

Margaret's gaze followed his gesture toward the rugged opening in the rock gorge. The deep recesses

210

and canyons in the Sierra Madre were called barrancas, and their jagged walls of green and pink were an awe-inspiring sight. Envisioning these stone valleys filled with raging flood waters was frightening to Margaret, but staying here without Chateo was even more terrifying. "Take us to Cieneguita and let us stay there." She rushed on before Chateo could argue with her. "We could find a place to live, and you could come to see Kaytee whenever you wanted." She reached out and clutched his bare arm. "Oh, please, Chateo. I can't bear to stay here another minute."

Chateo's eyes dropped down to where her hand held his arm. He was fooling himself if he thought this woman would ever come to him willingly. All she wanted from him was a chance to get away. "You're the one who came running after me on the reservation, or have you forgotten?"

"I'm going to take a siesta," Kaytee broke in, unaware of the tension that hung in the air. She skipped past Margaret and Chateo without pausing to chat as she wrapped a blanket around her dripping-wet body, which was clothed only in silky pantaloons and a chemise for swimming.

As she disappeared up the trail the couple left behind were instantly aware that they were alone again. A deafening hush seemed to fill the humid air until Margaret felt as if she could not breathe. She pulled her hand away from Chateo's arm as though the feel of his skin was fire. "I haven't forgotten!" She slid from the rock and started to follow Kaytee up the path, but Chateo blocked her steps. "I'm going to take a nap with Kaytee."

"Not until we straighten a few things out!"

Margaret tossed her head back and glared up at him. By the tone of his voice, she had expected him to look angry, but the fury which cloaked his stern features shocked her. Her suggestion that she and Kaytee live in Cieneguita was not unfair, nor did she think wishing to be free was asking for too much. She opened her mouth to tell Chateo of these things, but he did not give her the chance.

"In the beginning you were my captive, but you had a chance to return to your soldier boy at Fort Sill. I still do not know why you chose to come with me and Kaytee instead, but because you came with us of your own accord, I have tried to treat you with kindness."

His words couldn't be more true; still, Margaret did not feel she had come here of her own will. Her only other choice was the reservation, and what difference was that prison from the one she was in now? "I appreciate your kindness," she replied with a downward cast of her eyes. Impulsively, she added, "I'm sure it has taken a great deal of effort for a man like you."

Chateo was overrun with rage once more. She had no idea how much effort it took for him to keep from trying to take her in his arms, and her constant jabs at him only intensified this need. His actions were not thought through as he reached out and grabbed her by the arms. Margaret gasped with surprise as she was roughly yanked against his bare chest. She tossed her head back defiantly and glared at him with all the animosity she could muster. "Why don't you just get it over with? And when your disgusting cravings are satisfied, you can let me leave this hellhole and take Kaytee to a decent place to live."

Her words so angered Chateo he almost felt capable of killing her at that moment, and when he saw the fearful expression on her face, he knew she sensed it, too. Instead of wrapping his hands around her neck, however, and watching the life ebb out of her, he was ravaged by the urge to kiss her and fulfill her suggestion that he "just get it over with"! He could not get this woman out of his mind until he satisfied his desire, so what kept him from knocking her down in the deep grass and taking what he wanted?

The terror in Margaret's face did not only stem from the look of uncontrollable rage he presented to her. A multitude of fears had washed over her, yet they were all so jumbled in her mind she could not think straight. This confusing recall of all the things that had gone wrong in her life was driving her to the brink of insanity. There was virtually no chance for her ever to live in the manner she had always dreamed of, so nothing mattered to her anymore. She thought of the beautiful gowns she had hoped to wear someday; now she wore the garments of a peasant girl. There would never be fancy coaches to transport her around the city, nor would she live in a comfortable house like those in which the white men dwelled. Her Apache bloodline had won, and this realization filled Margaret with such despair that she wished Chateo would decide to kill her and put an end to her misery.

Chateo stood in a trance, watching the transformation as defiance and then total defeat washed over the young woman's face. The compassion, which he so desperately wanted to deny, returned to him with renewed strength. He saw a teardrop slide down her smooth cheek and, without contemplating his actions, bent down and stopped it with his lips. Time was suspended for an instant as his mouth lingered against her warm skin. Even though she had not fought against his impulsive kiss on the cheek, he was afraid to pull away for fear he would again see the look of hatred in her turquoise eyes. When he did move his head back, her expression astonished him. The velvet fringes of thick lashes rested upon her cheeks like gentle ebony wings, and her lips were pursed, almost as though she was waiting for his kiss to descend on her mouth. It was an invitation Chateo would never be strong enough to deny.

Margaret had no idea of the irresistible picture her sorrow presented to the Apache bandit. But his tender kiss to halt her tears had summoned a yearning in her she could not ignore. The horrendous thoughts that had been burdening her—thoughts of ending her life—were gone the instant his lips touched her cheek. Instead, she was brimming with expectancy for something she could not explain. She had thought Chateo's touch would be revolting and nothing at all like the sweet kiss she had experienced with the lieutenant, but the brief brush of his lips against her cheek was more unsettling than anything she had ever experienced. She did not want him to stop, and when she felt his mouth crush against her lips after a breathless interlude, she returned his kiss with a hunger she did not know she possessed.

Chateo's hands, no longer clasped around her arms, encircled her small waist and drew her up against him. He kept expecting her to turn on him at any instant and start screaming for him to stop. When she responded by returning his kiss, he was stunned, but not so much that he could not continue with this unexpected turn of events. His kiss deepened as his tongue intruded into her mouth. At first, he felt her timid tongue draw away, but soon she sensed she could increase this new pleasure by allowing her tongue to caress his in the same manner. Chateo continued to tease her shy tongue as he lowered Margaret into the lush grass beside the riverbed. The vegetation was high, and it enveloped them in a tent of tall green blades once they were lying down.

To try to put a stop to this enviable event did not even cross Margaret's mind. She needed to be held like this almost as much as she needed to breathe in order to survive. The lieutenant's caress was nothing like Chateo's touch, which aroused in her a savage craving only a man as untamed as Chateo could satisfy. What does it matter if it is wrong? Margaret told herself. She knew she would never escape from this jungle prison, anyway. If Chateo's embrace offered her just a bit of escape from her awful life, then she would gladly submit. When his hand moved provocatively over her heaving bosom, Margaret felt a riveting explosion bolt through her. The tip of her breast responded at once, straining against the material of her cotton blouse in a plea for him to continue his sweet assault.

Chateo's inquisitive lips descended as his proficient hands worked the blouse over her head. He heard her moan softly when his mouth closed down upon the pert tip of one beckoning bosom. Her skin was so soft he wished his fingers could fondle her silken form for all eternity. She had entangled her hands in the long tendrils of his heavy black hair, and as his tongue taunted her anxious breasts, she held him in an enslaving grip in an attempt to keep him from stopping this passionate torture. He moved his mouth lower, reveling in the softness of her skin against his lips and hands. The waistband of her skirt was a bothersome barrier. As he sat up to fumble with the tie encircling her waist, he worried that she would take this opportunity to stop him from going any farther.

Margaret could not put a halt to this any more than she could control her own life, though. Chateo had found another void in her, but this was one that could be sated, and she was powerless to do anything other than urge him on by allowing her body to respond each time he touched her in this intimate manner. As he worked her skirt and petticoat down over her hips, Margaret felt a heated blush color her skin a deep shade of red. Without the protection of her clothes, she was even more vulnerable to this man. The look upon his face, however, dispensed with her modesty. It was not an expression of lust as she would have expected from a man of his caliber. Instead, his sharp features were soft and full of emotions Margaret suspected he rarely showed.

As his eyes traveled down over her trembling body, Margaret shivered with anticipation. She had no idea of what actually transpired between a man and woman when they made love, but she knew it was something she was ready to experience. Chateo's enthralled observation of her body increased her excitement, and made her even more anxious to learn all he was about to teach her. Her inquisitive gaze shimmered with bolts of silver light as she watched him remove his tall boots and pants. The shock of seeing a man's unclothed body for the first time was unnerving, and for an instant Margaret was not sure she wanted to continue. She suddenly remembered hearing how badly it hurt the first time, but as she opened her mouth to protest his intentions, he straddled her again and resumed his demanding kisses.

Margaret's fears of the impending pain were gone as quickly as they had appeared once she became lost to the mania of his touch. His kisses were devouring her senses and his hands, doing things to the rest of her body, were driving her to the brink of insanity. One hand was kneading her breast gently and the other had somehow managed to sneak into the soft crevice between her thighs. Margaret wanted to cry out, but not because he was hurting her. She was in tremendous pain; however, it was complete ecstasy. His fingers were skillful as they inched their way into the most intimate part of her, and she welcomed him when she felt him ease her legs apart so his own legs and hips could settle in between hers. The yearnings which ruled

216

her, her wanton desire, were the ruling factors at this time.

Chateo continued his teasing assault with his fingers in preparation for the pain he knew she would soon have to experience. He assumed she had never made love before now, and he had not been with a virgin since his wedding night with Kaytee's mother. With this young woman, he felt almost nervous as he had all those years ago. Margaret was not as timid and shy as his wife had been, and it was difficult for Chateo to remain in control much longer. The look of sheer rapture upon her beautiful countenance made him eager to claim her completely as he positioned himself for the ultimate consummation. His mouth covered hers again when he kissed her with an almost brutal force in an effort to draw her attention away from the lunge that transformed her from a girl into a woman. Her body arched upward and he felt the scream of shock well up in her throat, but his lips prevented the sound from surfacing.

For an instant Margaret grew confused and disoriented. He had hurt her when she was least expecting it, and after his prior gentleness this sudden savagery seemed like the greatest of betrayals. He did not move for a short time, he just pinned her into the deep grass with the weight of his body as his lips held her in silent agony. The pain began to subside nearly as fast as it had erupted. When Chateo hoped it had faded away, he began to move his hips up and down in a rhythmic motion which soothed rather than increased the hurt. Soon Margaret felt a natural urge to imitate his movements, and she began to recede and ascend with them. His urgent kisses continued as each penetrating thrust grew more intense.

When Margaret was sure she was about to explode from the delicious sensations awakened in her young body, Chateo took one final plunge, which sent her reeling into a new realm of rapture. She wanted to remain in this land of enchantment forever, but after his movements had ceased, reality slowly began to seep into her spinning mind. Her body was tingling and shaking in reaction to the sweet invasion as she clung to Chateo's sweating form to prolong their contact for a short time longer.

He raised up slightly and glanced down at her, a slow grin curving his mouth. *"Mi Dios!* I have unleased a tigress!" He tossed his head back in an attempt to fling back his long hair, which hung over his shoulders and dangled in an aggravating manner over her face.

His efforts were not necessary, though, because the minor annoyance of his hair brushing against her face was not noticed. Margaret was still too engulfed by her recent discovery of life's rapacious pleasures. During their moments of total abandonment she had not once thought of escape, and considering that she had thought of nothing else for so long, she wondered if she had found something which could help her cope with life's grave injustices, if only for a while.

She gave a contented sigh and drew him back down within kissing distance. Chateo offered no resistance as their mouths again took command of the situation. When their heated lips had once reignited the fire within their smoldering bodies, Chateo made love to Margaret again. This time, however, there was no need for preliminary caution, because she received him without resistance. Her body seemed to be dying of thirst, and only this comanchero's touch could quench it.

The afternoon shadows had begun to deepen the vibrant shade of the lush green grass by the time Chateo and Margaret drew their weary bodies apart. The world outside of their afternoon redezvous had ceased to exist, but eventually harsh reality had to lure them back. Margaret was drenched with perspiration, and she longed to dive into the cool water of the river. She glanced toward the darkening path, though, and thought of Kaytee. It was a miracle the little girl had not come back down to the river to look for them.

"Why don't you check on Kaytee?" she said without looking at Chateo, as a fevered blush overcame her. "I'll be up soon." Her sudden rash of embarrassmen. increased as she grabbed up her discarded clothes and hugged them against her bosom.

Chateo stared at her in disbelief. Only minutes ago, she had been an insatiable seductress. Now she was acting as shy and timid as an untouched maiden. He would gladly tolerate her demure attitude, though, if every time he took her in his arms she would respond in the same way she had a short time ago. He nodded in agreement and scooped up his pants, then noticed her longing glance toward the river. There was nothing he would like better than to join her in the refreshing water for an extension of their previous activities, but he knew Kaytee would soon be wondering where they were and what they had been doing all of this time.

"I will bring you something special from Cieneguita," he said with a mischievous smile while he hoisted up his pants. "What would you like?"

Margaret did not stop to think before answering, nor did she realize how her reply would sound to the man who listened to her impulsive words. She merely said what she had been thinking about almost constantly in the past few weeks—except for the time when Chateo had been making love to her. "I want to be free." Her tone was as wistful as the yearning in her jewel-toned gaze when her eyes glanced out toward the heavily shadowed walls of the deep barranca.

Chateo did not offer a retort, because he did not

know how to react. He wanted to be angry, yet that simple emotion eluded him. Instead, he was overcome with sadness as he turned and began to walk up the narrow trail lined by vines and *mala mujer*. He thought it ironic that his pathway was framed by the deceptive leaves of the *mala mujer* plant. Its meaning was "bad woman," and though it appeared innocent and it was lovely to gaze upon, when in contact with a person's skin it could cause a sting more vicious than that of a wasp, and the pain could last for hours. Chateo thought the plant was comparable to Margaret Sinclair; if only once a man's heart was inflicted by the touch of a woman like Margaret, it could cause him a lifetime of pain.

Chapter Fourteen

"Pare!"

Nachae watched the heavily armed man descend from the steep slope, a feeling of uneasiness washing over him. He had ridden through many of these rugged barrancas on different occasions, but he had never entered into the heart of the outlaw stronghold before now. He raised his hands high over his head as the other man approached him.

"Desmonte!" the Mexican bandit commanded with a threatening wave of his rifle.

Nachae obeyed without resistance and dropped down from his horse. Once he was on the ground, he held his hands up again to show that he was not here to cause any trouble.

The outlaw hollered toward the rocky slope, to another man who was also standing guard, then returned his attention to Nachae. "State your business," he demanded in Mexican.

Nachae quickly told the man who he was and why he had come there. Since he was dressed in his Mexican outfit, he gave the man his Mexican name of Antonio Flores, which he hoped would grant him entrance into the outlaw den. Several years ago Nachae had saved the life of José Fernando, the man who led this band of comancheros, by deflecting a rifle aimed at the desperado's back. Nachae had interfered in the feud only because the fight was unfair, not because he had any affection for the Mexican outlaw, but the man felt so indebted to Nachae he'd invited him to become a high-ranking member of his band of comancheros. Nachae had politely declined the offer, though he'd been careful not to reveal his Indian identity to Fernando. Not only did Nachae wish to hide the fact that he was part Apache, he wanted to keep his *ranchería* safe. Pa-Gotzin-Kay would be a true paradise to outlaws such as José Fernando and his comancheros because its almost inaccessible location was so secluded.

The comanchero had told Nachae if he ever needed a favor he could come to his hideout. The outlaw had even given him general directions to the stronghold. The Mexican probably would have forgotten his gratitude to Nachae if it had not been for another incident that had left Señor Fernando eternally grateful to him.

On a scouting trip last year, Nachae and his riding companions had run out of their precious alcoholic brew. As was his habit whenever he had occasion to go into town, Nachae had donned his Mexican attire and had ridden into Cieneguita for a bottle of whiskey, which the Indians valued as highly as they did the food that kept them alive. At the cantina he encountered a young man who had been accused of cheating in a card game. Though Nachae did not know if the imputation was correct, he did take note that the youth was too intoxicated to defend himself, so he intervened and persuaded the man denouncing the boy to withdraw his accusation. In an ironic twist of fate the young man disclosed to Nachae he was José Fernando's son.

Nachae gave his Mexican name of Antonio Flores to the boy, who was stunned to learn this was the same man who had once saved his father's life. As the youth sobered up, he repeatedly told Nachae he would tell his father how he had encountered their "guardian angel" again, and he declared that his father would grant him any favor he asked. It was these promises that had brought Nachae into this outlaw-infested hideout.

The man who held the rifle against Nachae's gut debated over whether or not he should believe Nachae's story. After several more questions, which Nachae answered without hesitation, he smiled and shook his head in a satisfied manner. "My boss has spoken of you and your good deeds to him and his son. I will take you to Señor Fernando myself," he added proudly. He called up to the other lookout and told him what he was about to do, then motioned for Nachae to mount his horse and follow him.

As they traveled through the barranca, Nachae glanced up nervously at the sheer embankments that towered in the distance and the thick vegetation covering the lower terrain. One wrong move to anger José Fernando and Nachae knew he would never escape from there alive. Once again he rehearsed his story, and said another feverish prayer that the outlaw leader would believe him.

Since the man who had been guarding the entrance rode beside him in a calm manner, Nachae's visit caused little notice as the pair passed the scattering of huts and shacks littering the hillsides. Perched amid low-hanging vines, José Fernando's hut was indistinguishable from the rest of the dwellings. But the man who stepped from the doorway emitted an aura of danger which could not be overlooked. His dark face bore a frown when he walked out into the afternoon sunlight. He wondered who would dare to disturb his siesta, but when he recognized the intruder his fierce expression turned to surprise.

"*Amigo!* To what do I owe this honor?"

Nachae forced a weak grin as he dismounted from his horse. The bandit leader had gained weight since Nachae had first encountered him several years earlier. His once-svelte physique was now pudgy, and his face was bloated from too much whiskey. "I have come to ask a favor, *amigo.*"

José Fernando's welcoming smile did not change, but his eyes grew cold within their dark depths. "I owe you two favors." He laughed as he motioned for Nachae to follow him into his hut.

With a quick glance around the interior, Nachae surmised that he was trapped. There was only one doorway, and the windows were too small for escape. The look, which had filtered into the bandit's black eyes a moment ago, made him uneasy, yet there was no backing out of his plan now. "My need is great enough to repay me for both debts, *señor.*" He took the glass of whiskey the Mexican offered him and sat down on one of the chairs set about a small table in the corner of the hut.

"If I can help, then we are even?" The comanchero studied the other man's face closely. He had extended an invitation to this man to come to his home in a moment of exuberance, when his thoughts were clouded with gratitude. Now he realized how unwise it had been to tell this stranger something as valuable as the location of his hideout. José Fernando had not paid much attention to this Flores when he had encountered him the first time, and his son's account of the man had still not made the impression this sudden appearance at the hideout was making on the Mexican outlaw. The man was dressed in the simple garments of a peasant, but José knew without a doubt that he was anything but a farmer. He had never met a farmer who carried himself with the deadly assurance of this man, nor had he ever met a farmer as well armed as his visitor. Why hadn't he taken the time to notice these small, yet important, things before now?

Nachae did not miss the other man's intense observation of his weapons as he prepared to say his rehearsed speech. "A terrible mistake was made by the U.S. Cavalry in Bisbee. My young daughter was taken captive by a border patrol and is being held at Fort Huachuca in Arizona."

Señor Fernando leaned forward, a questioning look on his face. "Your daughter? Why would she be taken in by American soldiers?"

This was the part of his deception Nachae hoped would sound convincing, although even in his own mind it sounded too farfetched to be believed. "They falsely accused her of being an Apache." Nachae saw the distrust increase in José Fernando's dark eyes as he quickly added, "But that is ridiculous! All the Apaches have been on reservations for years. And my daughter, she is a good *señorita* who does not deserve to be confused with one of those dogs." Nachae held his breath, while he waited for the other man's reaction. Still, he was unprepared for the bandit's next words.

"On the contrary, *señor*. Not all Apaches are on reservations. Why, I have several Apaches living right here; one of them even claims to be a Chiricahua who once rode with Geronimo. I wonder if you would know him?"

Inwardly, Nachae grew numb as he watched the other man's expression, but the Apache chief shrugged nonchalantly. "I do not know any of those pigs!"

José Fernando took a sip of his whiskey, then chuckled in a crude manner. "Maybe, maybe not. But this Apache pig has recently acquired a young woman

225

he claims is an Apache half-breed. Do you think it is coincidental that a girl who looks Mexican but is Indian would appear here at the same time that your daughter—who is Mexican but must look Indian— would disappear from Bisbee?" He paused to watch for a reaction on his visitor's face, but Nachae's expression did not waver so Señor Fernando continued. "Perhaps, you should meet them—just to be sure."

"That would be a waste of time. I only came here to ask for your help in getting my daughter back, but I can see that was also a waste of time." He rose to his feet, hoping his shaking legs could support him. His mind was being pulled in a hundred different directions at once. If he ran into this Chiricahua José Fernando spoke of, there was a good chance the man would turn out to be someone who would recognize him. Nachae was certain, however, that the young woman the outlaw had mentioned was not Echo. How could she be here with the comancheros, when she had been captured in Bisbee by cavalrymen?

The Mexican laughed again in a manner that sounded too jolly for the situation. "*No, amigo.* I am a man of my word. I owe you for my life and also for the life of my son." José Fernando pushed himself away from the table and stood up. "I will help you find your daughter if this is the repayment you seek. However"— an evil smile revealed a broken front tooth that made his puffy expression seem more sinister—"I do insist that you meet the Apache and his breed before we leave here."

Knowing he would not be able to get out of this meeting without making the outlaw more suspicious, Nachae shrugged and motioned for the Mexican to lead the way. He tried to think who the Chiricahua warrior could be, but he could not begin to imagine who, among their tribal members, had escaped life on

226

the reservation, other than the men who lived at Pa-Gotzin-Kay. His uneasiness grew as he followed José Fernando through the jagged pathways of heavy undergrowth. If the girl was Echo, he would be of no help to her once she revealed to José Fernando that he was her father. Nachae tried to think of a new course of action, but they halted at a small hut before he was able to arrive at one.

"Señor?" a young girl said as they approached the door. Her dark eyes looked inquisitively at José Fernando, since she knew he was the most important man at the hideout. She barely glanced at Nachae, though, as she waited for the other man to speak.

Nachae's heart began to pound like rushing bullets in his chest. From the girl's features he had no doubt she was an Apache, but she was not Echo and this was all that mattered. He took a deep breath to ease the tension in his tall form, but his relief was short-lived.

"Where are your father and the woman?" José asked her in English.

Nachae watched with a renewed sense of doom as the girl pointed down another path. "They are at the river. Do you want me to go get them?"

The outlaw shook his head and gestured for Nachae to continue to follow him. Each step that drew them closer to the river caused Nachae's foreboding to increase. And, when they encountered a man walking toward them, Nachae was certain he had just walked into his own doom.

Chateo smiled at José Fernando as he finished fastening up the front of his breeches. *"Hola, amigo!"*

The outlaw gave the other man a lecherous grin. "I take it that you and the woman are getting along well?" His words carried an insinuation which was immediately picked up by the other two men.

A rush of heat sprang throughout Chateo, but he

227

hoped it was not noticeable as he leaned to the side to see who was accompanying Señor Fernando. The two men recognized one another at once, although neither allowed their shock to register on their faces. Apaches are taught restraint from the moment they are born, when they are disciplined not to cry so that they will never place their families in danger by making unnecessary noise. Both Chateo and Nachae sensed it was imperative to their salvation to practice that important lesson at this time.

Chateo gave a swift nod. *"Hola!"* he said in greeting to the man before turning his gaze back toward José Fernando. "Do we have a new recruit?"

Disappointment drained the bandit leader of enthusiasm as he watched the unconcerned attitudes of the two men. He had been positive they would know one another, but it was obvious he had been wrong. "This man is looking for his daughter. Where is your woman?"

With a toss of his long hair, Chateo gestured toward the river. The quaking inside him kept him from speaking for a moment, but as the other two men started down the trail, he realized he must intervene before they reached Margaret. "My woman is half-Apache, señor. Surely, your daughter is Mexican, is she not?"

"We will see her anyway," José Fernando answered for Nachae.

Chateo raised his hands in defeat as he added, *"Sí,"* but at least let me warn her of your visit." He glanced at Nachae, then back at José Fernando, and chuckled. "When I last saw her she was not dressed to receive callers."

The pudgy rolls around José Fernando's waist bobbed up and down as he imitated Chateo's crude laugh. His tongue swiped across his upper lip as he

228

envisioned the beautiful young girl. The idea of her lying nude in the lush green grass was tempting, but José reminded himself he did have some manners still intact. And although Chateo did not seem to know this visitor, José still wanted to see Antonio Flores' reaction when he saw the girl. He glanced down the pathway and gave a quick wave. "We will give her only a moment or two."

Chateo did not waste a second of the precious time, but turned and raced back down the trail. Margaret was just about to plunge into the river when his voice reached her ears. She swung around, glaring at the intrusion, and opened her mouth to scream at him, but he never gave her the chance.

"Hurry, put your clothes on, and do not argue with me."

The urgency in his voice and etched on his face caused Margaret to fill with panic. Her nakedness was forgotten as she grabbed the clothes he tossed at her. "What is—"

"José Fernando is bringing a man to speak to you and—" The sounds of the two men approaching made Chateo's whole body jump with fear. He did not have time to explain anything else to her, so he whispered through clenched teeth, "Pretend that you do not know the man—no matter what. It is a matter of life and death!" He glanced over his shoulder, then swung back around to face Margaret. The look in his ebony eyes was so desperate, she was afraid to move. "Life and death!" he repeated as he turned to greet the men once again.

Margaret had only had enough time to slip into her skirt, so she clutched her blouse against her chest in an attempt to cover her bare bosom. She glanced at José Fernando first, and experienced her usual feeling of disgust whenever she glimpsed the outlaw leader. But when her gaze went beyond the chunky form of the bandit, her whole being was sent into a state of shock. Unconsciously, she twisted her hands into two tight fists within the material of her cotton blouse as her body began to tremble like a frail tree in a windstorm. Her father had not changed in eight years; he was still handsome and proud as the last day she had laid eyes on him. Only his lowly peasant garments made him appear any different than she remembered, but as she started to call out her joy, she recalled Chateo's dire warning.

Nachae's confusion lasted only a few seconds; then a happiness so vast washed over him, his emotions threatened to steal away his senses. His first glimpse of the girl had told his whirling mind that he had found Echo. But, almost as quickly, his keen eye had noted the minor differences between her and Morning Star. It had always been eye color that had set the twins apart, and the vibrant turquoise gaze which stared at him now made it apparent to Nachae that he was looking at the daughter he had believed dead for the past eight years. His emotions simmered like a volcano about to erupt, but when he noticed that José Fernando had turned to observe his reaction, he knew he could not allow his feelings to show. Appearing to be nonchalant, though, was one of the most difficult feats Nachae had ever attempted to achieve. He wanted to rush up to his daughter and hold her in his arms, to tell her all the things he had imagined he would say to her if a miracle such as this ever occurred, but he did not. Instead, he stood motionless, a look of disinterest upon his face.

"This half-breed is not my daughter." He wondered if anyone noticed how his voice shook when he spoke?

Margaret, however, was not as accomplished as her father at hiding her feelings, and the tears that sprang from her eyes were not intentional. She saw the look of panic wash over Chateo's face while she fought to regain control of her rampant feelings. She did not understand why her father was denying her, nor did she know why Chateo's warning had been so desperate, but she did sense her reaction would be the deciding factor in everything that happened from this moment forth. She choked back her sobs and clutched her blouse tighter against her breasts.

"How dare you intrude on a helpless woman when she is trying to take a bath!" Her use of the Apache language was not as proficient as it should be, but she recalled enough of the Indian words to get her meaning across. The anger she forced herself to summon up despite her tears was leveled at José Fernando, since she knew she could not remain composed if she looked at her father again. Silently, she prayed the outlaw would think her strange behavior was only caused by their intrusion on her privacy.

The Mexican's mouth turned into a snide grin, which caused his puffy face to be split by deep creases of dark flesh. He thought it unusual that she would be brave enough to talk to him in such a rude manner, but he was also amused by her haughty attitude. Surely she is an Apache, José decided, because only an Apache would be so confident when she is little more than a slave. He glanced at Chateo, his aggravation evident. "Perhaps you should spend less time playing in the grass with this ungrateful woman, and more time teaching her some manners."

Chateo nodded his head in agreement, then watched, frozen in place, as the outlaw leader swung around and motioned for Nachae to follow him back up the path. He had caught Nachae's quick glance of gratitude, and he was certain the man would return when it was safe. For now, however, Chateo focused his attention on Margaret.

231

Once the men were out of sight, she slowly sank to the ground, her entire body overcome by the shock of seeing the father she had believed dead. The tears she had tried to hide from José Fernando could no longer be contained, and they rushed down her cheeks in torrents. It was impossible that her father was alive; yet she had seen him with her own eyes. But, how could this be? The soldiers who'd taken her and the other children to the Carlisle School in Pennsylvania had told them there had been no other survivors. A slow burn began to fester in Margaret's stomach as she wondered if the white men had conceived the lie about the children all being orphaned in order to get them to give in to the demands of the white men without resistance.

She felt Chateo's strong arms encircle her, but his presence did not ease the tremendous despair in her heart. She had believed every single word that had come from the mouths of the white men, because she had wanted to. Their deceptions had led her to think she would be able to live among them as though there were no difference between her and every other white woman. But now she realized how stupid and naive she had been. She clung to Chateo as pain cut through her like a knife. All her dreams of living in the white man's world came crashing down like a landslide, and buried her in such a state of agony she did not know if she would ever be able to dig her way out again.

Nachae tried to concentrate on José Fernando's talk of his many escapades as an outlaw on both sides of the border, but he could think only of his daughter. He had come here to ask for help in finding Echo, but instead had encountered the daughter he had thought killed by *soldados* many years earlier. Was it feasible that fate

232

could have become so twisted? He slugged down another glass of whiskey and when the other man laughed, forced a chuckle in an attempt to act as though he were listening, paying attention to the Mexican's worthless chatter. With the help of his daughter and Chateo, Nachae felt that he had won the outlaw's trust for now, and a plan had already been devised by José Fernando to infiltrate Fort Huachuca to retrieve Antonio Flores' daughter.

The bandit leader also had another goal in mind, though, as he rattled on about the exciting life of a comanchero. A man such as Antonio Flores was someone who would be a great asset to the band of outlaws if he would agree to join up with them. Fernando's elaborate descriptions of their grand life was a determined attempt to bring this about. Nachae was attuned to the man's ploy at once, but he pretended to be enthralled by the bandit's stories as his mind busily devised a way to get back to the hut where he knew his long-lost daughter was living.

"*Amigo,* I could listen to you talk of this exciting life you lead all night, but it has been a hard ride and if we are going to leave in the morning I must get some rest."

José Fernando shrugged and gave his head an agreeable nod. "There is an empty shack farther up the hill. It is your home for the night."

Wasting no more time, Nachae said good night and retired to the abandoned shack. He knew the Mexican was not worried about his trying to leave because the stronghold was too well guarded for anyone to enter or depart without notice. Nachae was grateful that he had been permitted to sleep alone, though, or else there would have been no way for him to see his daughter again before he left in the morning.

He waited for a long time in the hope that José Fernando had drunk himself into a deep slumber, then

233

he quietly inched his way through the tangled mass of vines and trees. His eyes kept being blinded by the recollection of his young daughter standing half-naked by the riverside, and he was plagued by the insinuation of what had been going on between her and the Apache renegade, Chateo. He had a hundred questions running rampant in his mind, and a very important decision to make once he learned the answers.

Chapter Fifteen

Margaret huddled under a blanket on the narrow bed she shared with Kaytee. The cot was the only furniture in the shack besides a table and one chair. The two girls had spent the first few days after their arrival trying to clean some of the filth out of the hut, but Margaret had finally determined it was a lost cause. No amount of scrubbing would render the hovel livable.

She had finally managed to stop crying; however, sleep still eluded her. The events of the past day had left her with a mass of mixed emotions, which she did not know how to deal with yet. She wanted to go in search of her father, but Chateo had positioned himself beside the door so that she could not leave without him being aware of it. He told her that her father would find a way to come to her. But what if Chateo was wrong, and her father did not return? Nachae had, after all, said he did not know who she was when he had seen her down by the river. How could he be expected to recognize her after eight years? She glared at the sleeping Chateo in the dim light of the hut, while pondering the vast array of thoughts which kept spinning through her head. It would be his fault if she never got the chance to see her father again, because he was the one who'd told her to pretend she did not know the man with José Fernando.

Without an invitation, or a warning, her thoughts drifted to the event which had taken place just prior to her seeing her father again. However, when compared to seeing the father she had thought dead for so long, thoughts of Chateo making love to her seemed frivolous and unimportant. She told herself she would deal with her feelings for Chateo at a later date. But when she was least expecting it, a lingering ache in her loins reminded her of the outlaw's gentle caress upon her yearning body.

A soft knock on the door caused her heart to cease to beat for a moment as Chateo sprung from the chair in which he had been dozing. He motioned for her to remain still while he slowly opened the door. Margaret held her hand over her mouth as the opening was filled with the tall form of her father. She did not want to cry out and frighten Kaytee from her sleep, but a muffled sob escaped from behind her hand in spite of her attempt to remain quiet.

Nachae did not even acknowledge Chateo as he moved into the hut because his eyes did not leave the face of his daughter. "Your mother and I have grieved over your death for eight years. How is it possible that I am gazing upon you now?"

"M-my mother? You . . . you mean both of you survived the ambush and the fire at our *ranchería?*" A new bout of tears sprang from Margaret's swollen lids as she recalled her gentle mother. Faded images of her childhood at the Apache *ranchería* blinded her momentarily, and she was overcome by a sudden wish to be a little girl again, also by an urgent need to recapture all the years she had been deprived of her parent's love. Without warning, she rushed forward and threw herself into her father's waiting arms. "They lied to us!" she cried against the hardness of his chest,

236

while his arms enveloped her in a blanket of security that she had not felt for many years.

Nachae continued to hold his daughter in a tight embrace as she released the rage which also attacked him. So much time had been wasted, and so much of their energy had been put into sorrow. Yet, he knew there was no way to redo the events of the past, so he silently vowed to do everything in his power to make up for the time already lost. First, though, he had to figure out a way to get his daughter away from this place; then he must meet an even greater challenge when he went to retrieve his other daughter from the U.S. Cavalry at Fort Huachuca. He glanced at Chateo, trying to dismiss images of a man who had once been his comrade making love to his daughter at the riverbank. Nachae reminded himself to hold his anger in check until he knew all the circumstances of Morning Star's involvement with the comanchero. If she had become Chateo's woman of her own accord, then he knew he would have to accept her decision. She was no longer the child he thought he had lost on that bloody day eight years ago, but if she had been brought here against her will, and it was Chateo's plan to use her as his slave until he was ready to sell her to someone who would pay his price, then Nachae would not hesitate to kill the man before the night was through.

"There is very little time to talk because I will be leaving here with José Fernando and several of his men in the morning." Nachae stated as he stroked Morning Star's tangled mass of dark hair. It was hard for him to imagine that he was actually holding her in his arms, and he could not wait to see the joy on his wife's face when she was able to embrace her in the same way.

"Have you been living here in Mexico all of this time?" Chateo asked as his gaze traveled over Nachae's clothes. Curiosity was getting the best of him, and he was compelled to ask the questions that had been plaguing him throughout the evening. "I was told everyone had been killed. Now, suddenly, I find my daughter, Kaytee, along with your daughter. How many others survived the last attack on our village?" He shook his head in disbelief, adding before Nachae could answer him, "Then you appear out of nowhere. And am I to understand that your wife, Sky Dreamer, also is still alive? Are all of you living somewhere nearby?"

Nachae did not reply. He felt no obligation to give this man an explanation, especially since he remembered how Chateo had shirked his responsibilities to his young wife and baby. Each time Chateo disappeared to wherever it was that he went, the rest of the men in the village had to provide for Chateo's family. On this recollection of Chateo's character alone, Nachae felt he had a need to seek revenge, but he would rather wait until he knew the entire story about his daughter's involvement with the good-for-nothing outlaw. Nachae ignored Chateo as he gently eased the sobbing form of his daughter away from him so he could gaze at her young face when he spoke to her. "It seems that many of our people survived, but, sadly, we did not know of one another's existence. It is true—the white men lied to everyone."

Margaret stared up at her father as a hushed silence hovered throughout the small interior of the hut. It was difficult to believe he was really here, and that her mother was not dead either; but as she gazed at him she was struck by another thought that was even more overwhelming. A gasp flew from her mouth as the revelation washed over her. "Is it possible? Is . . . is Echo . . . ?" She could not finish for an odd sensation overcame her at the idea of being reunited with her twin.

238

"Echo is the image of her beautiful twin sister," Nachae answered in a quiet voice. "And it was because of her recent misfortune that I have found you."

Margaret could not stop the cry that tore from her mouth. Her sister had been alive, and she had been living with their parents all of this time, while Margaret had been betrayed and disillusioned by the white men. All the animosity she had once harbored for the white men returned with vengeance. The other children at Carlisle had never trusted their words, but she had never doubted them. How could she have been so foolish?

"Why did you come here?" Chateo asked as he stepped closer to the couple. Nachae's cold attitude toward him was apparent, but Chateo's lingering curiosity was getting the best of him.

Nachae tore his eyes away from the sorrowful face of his daughter for a moment to glance at Chateo. He had many questions of his own to ask this man, but they could wait until another time. "My other daughter was taken captive by a border patrol in Bisbee, Arizona. I need help to break her out of the fort where she is being held. José Fernando owes me a favor, so I came to collect."

Nachae returned his attention to his sobbing daughter. There were new decisions he had to make due to this unexpected turn of events, and they were not easy ones. "Do you want me to take you home, or"— his gray eyes narrowed slightly as he glanced in Chateo's direction—"have you made a life for yourself here?"

With a shuddering sigh, Margaret wiped away a lingering tear as her gaze traveled to Chateo. Their eyes held in silent agony as both contemplated Margaret's options. Today they had indulged in the most intimate act a man and woman could share, but had it changed

239

anything between them? She forced herself to look away, then turned to glance at Kaytee, now wide awake and staring at Margaret with a worried expression.

Chateo did not want to wait to hear her answer—he could sense what was going through her mind by the distressed expression upon her face. "We could all go . . . together?" he suggested in a hoarse tone of voice. There had been a time when this was the only life he ever cared to lead, but since he felt Usen had granted him a second chance to be a father to Kaytee, he had begun to reconsider his life as an outlaw. In a reluctant admission to himself, he knew he had to agree with Margaret—he could not raise a young girl in a dirty hut that was surrounded by murderous outlaws who rode for José Fernando. And he knew he had to include himself in that poll. But even worse was the realization that Margaret Sinclair was becoming more important to him with each passing second. If she chose to go with her father, and leave him and Kaytee behind, he was afraid it would destroy him.

Margaret remained unmoving as she contemplated Chateo's words, and the unspoken meaning in the depths of his raven eyes. If they all went together, would Chateo consider them to be committed to one another? She was not prepared to take such a drastic step. "Kaytee and I could still go with my father if you want to stay here," she retorted in an attempt to deny her own conflicting feelings.

Her words hit Chateo like a massive boulder rolling over his body. How many times would he allow this woman to walk across his heart? "Kaytee goes where I go!"

Nachae did not understand what was going on between this man and Morning Star, but he cut into their conversation. "It is not that simple. I still have to go after Echo, and I can not allow José Fernando to

240

learn of my Apache blood—or where my home is located." His face settled into a mask of deadly determination as he again glanced at Chateo. "The safety of my family depends on these secrets, and I will do anything to protect them."

Chateo did not back down as he met Nachae's piercing stare through the dim light of the hut. A few weeks ago he would have laughed in this man's face, would have told him he did not take kindly to threats, especially those made by a farmer. But in the short time since he had found Kaytee, he had come to understand the fierce responsibility a man feels toward his family. Chateo also understood why the other man would not trust him with the secret of where his family lived, since it was obvious the Apaches had lived a peaceful life there for the past eight years.

"I can only tell you that I will not betray you if you confide in me. I will take your daughter to her mother, and"—he looked at his own daughter's terrified young face—"if it is possible, I would like to take Kaytee there, too."

Nachae hesitated as he carefully studied the other man's face for any signs of deceit, but he saw only the deep concern a father feels for his child's safety. There was another sort of pain hidden in Chateo's dark countenance, but Nachae did not wish to decipher its meaning at this time, because he sensed it had to do with his daughter. He had no choice but to put his faith in this man. Usen had given him two daughters again, and both of them needed immediate help. "I will disclose the location of my *ranchería* to you so that you may take both of the girls to my wife. You will be welcome to stay for as long as you wish, but if you should ever leave, then I want your word that you will never disclose where the *ranchería* is situated—to anyone—even if you are about to take your

241

final breath!"

Nachae's words were spoken with a threatening innuendo that Chateo could not miss. If the Apache *ranchería* was ever discovered, Nachae would blame him. Since it was obvious the passing years had not softened Nachae in any manner, Chateo knew that an enemy as powerful as he was not the sort a man would care to make. He gave his head a nod and purposely met the other man's penetrating gray eyes. Perhaps the time had come for him to return to his own people—for Kaytee's sake if for nothing else.

With an imitation of Chateo's gesture, Nachae also nodded in a silent agreement. "After I leave in the morning for Fort Huachuca with José Fernando and the men who will be accompanying us, then you can work out a plan to take the girls out of here."

"I will say I'm taking them to Cieneguita to help me purchase supplies."

Nachae glanced back at his daughter again as a wistful smile curved his mouth. "It is settled then. When we all meet back at the *ranchería,* we will be a complete family again."

A trembling shiver raced through Margaret as she recalled the life they had once lived on the Apache *ranchería.* Many long years had passed since they had been together as a family. What would it be like to have a mother and father again, and, even more important, how would she relate to the twin sister who had been raised in a manner so different from the life she had known at Carlisle? Margaret managed to smile back at her father as she wondered if she would ever be able to forget her dream of living in the white man's world, and to concentrate on rebuilding a life with her family— especially with her sister, Echo.

*　　　*　　　*

242

Departing from the comanchero hideout was an easy task for Chateo and the two girls. His plan to take his daughter and his woman into the nearest town to buy supplies for the coming months did not even draw anyone's interest. Once they were out of view of the lookouts who stood guard on the outlaw stronghold, the trio merely took a turn that led them in the opposite direction from Cieneguita. It would be weeks before anyone in the hideout questioned their whereabouts. By then, they would be living quietly on the secluded plateau of the Pa-Gotzin-Kay.

Chateo found it hard to believe so many of his people had managed to escape from the white men and were now living in total seclusion from the rest of the world in the highlands of the Sierra Madre. He had even dared to wonder if his wife was among those who had survived, but Nachae had told him she had not been so fortunate. A sense of relief had filled Chateo, despite the guilt he still harbored. It was difficult enough to realize he had a daughter to care for, after all the years of remorse. To also learn he still had a wife would mean another responsibility he was ill prepared to face, and it would have added to the burdens he was tackling, those he had avoided for so long.

Besides, there was Margaret Sinclair to consider. Although, at this time, Chateo did not know what his consideration of her should be. She had hardly even glanced in his direction since they had left the hideout, but she was not being rude to him either. She chatted with Kaytee whenever the girl asked something of her; yet she seemed distant—almost forlorn. Chateo wondered how she could appear to be unhappy when she had just discovered that her entire family was alive and well. But as the day wore on and he continued to study the girl, to ponder the few things he knew about this woman-child, the answer finally began to seep into his

243

mind. Margaret Sinclair had decided to resign herself to a life that was far removed from everything she had ever dreamed of having in the white man's world in which she had grown accustomed to living during her time in Pennsylvania. Maybe she even pined for the lieutenant she had told him about on the day they had stood on the hillside overlooking Fort Sill.

Chateo rode up beside Margaret's horse and gazed at her sad, beautiful face. She acknowledged his presence with a small smile that curved the corners of her mouth but did not light up her luminous turquoise eyes. Chateo could not bring himself to smile back. He was too consumed with the ache her defeat caused to well up in his heart. By forfeiting her dreams, she had also lost her spirit, and this was a loss that Chateo could not bear to observe. He allowed his horse to fall back behind hers again so that he would not have to gaze into the emptiness of her jewel-toned eyes. A slow pain began to work its way through his being as he wondered if he had made a grave mistake by leaving the comanchero stronghold. Perhaps Margaret's constant suggestion that Kaytee would be better off with her was something he should have taken the time to consider. After all, what did a worthless bandit such as himself have to offer anyone?

Chapter Sixteen

Echo stared up at the razor-sharp edge of the cliff jutting out from the canyon wall. The blinding sphere of the setting sun had dropped from view, but a lingering array of pink and purple hues streaked the sky with vibrant colors and designs resembling those of ancient Aztec paintings. The girl smiled as she watched the misty shades of the sunset filter across the azure skyline. Her mother's eyes were the exact color of the rich violet colors that outlined the paler shades of pink. Soon she would see her mother again, and hopefully her father, too.

"Is that it?" Travis asked in a tone of awe as he stared toward the jagged edge of the high cliff.

"Yes, on top of that huge rock sits Pa-Gotzin-Kay, and as far as I know, you will be the first white man ever to walk upon its soil during the time my people have occupied this sacred land. The trail is treacherous even to those of us who know it well, and since it is getting dark, I think perhaps we should wait until morning to go the rest of the way."

Her words filled Travis with an overwhelming sense of obligation and honor. He was very aware that she was proving the extent of her love for him by allowing him to enter this secret world in which she dwelled. He stood behind her and encircled her waist with his arms as he molded her slender form against his own body. His head dropped down so that he could bury his face in the ebony cascade of her hair. She told him Pa-Gotzin-Kay meant paradise, but he had discovered paradise the moment he had found her. Traveling with her for the past few days, though, had been pure hell!

"Only one more night," he murmured, mostly to himself, but Echo heard. Her soft laughter only poured salt on Travis' festering wounds.

"Just because we will reach the *ranchería* tomorrow, does not mean that we will be married by tomorrow night. Apache marriage ceremonies last for weeks."

A tormented moan escaped from Travis' lips, his breath softly blowing the dark strands of hair that sheltered his face within their heavy cloak. "I'll die if I have to wait so long." He felt her sigh as she prepared to remind him of their vow. "I know," he said before she had a chance to speak. "We promised to wait until we were married, but"—he gently turned her around to face him as he added—"it is possible that I might die if you make me wait for one more day, let alone for weeks." His lips turned into a pouting grin. "Would you ever be able to forgive yourself if I keeled over and died because I loved you so much?"

Echo gazed up at his handsome face, in her love for him awash with devotion. He was looking at her with the innocent expression he had the habit of donning whenever he hoped to get his way. It made him look like a devilish little boy, rather than a grown man, and each time he assumed this look, Echo's reserve was whittled down a little bit more. His jade eyes twinkled with the savory thoughts which ruled his mind, and with their bodies pressed together in a tight embrace, his desire for her was making itself evident through the

246

straining material of his Army trousers. The feel of his pulsating manhood against her abdomen made Echo's entire body grow weak with the newly found longing this man aroused within her, longings only he had the power to satisfy. She wanted to toss away the strict rules that had governed her Apache upbringing, to give in to the yearnings that reached out from her awakening body; but she could not forget her teachings of moral conduct—not even when the heat of passion claimed her through these wanton temptations.

As Travis covered the length of her soft neck with wet kisses, Echo made another plea, "But it is my people's custom—"

His mouth ascended and cut her words short with a kiss that seemed to go on forever. He knew his intentions were shouting at her through the thin material of their clothing, but this knowledge only increased his determination to make love to her . . . that night. There was a mystical essence about this place—something that seemed to hold him under its passionate spell, stealing away all his senses and the rest of his waning control. The darkening dusk was filled with the sweet scent of acacia blossoms, their rich perfume making him heady and increasing his urge to make this young woman yield to their love for one another.

"It's not my people's custom," he whispered, while his hands wandered over the curve of her hip. The days and nights, which they had spent together while traveling to her *ranchería,* had given them ample time to kiss and fondle one another, but tonight that was no longer enough.

"B-but this is the land of my people now," Echo argued in a weak voice, which did not offer much of a debate. The magic of the mountain paradise was affecting her, too, but not as much as his demanding kisses on her neck and the playful way his lips kept nipping at her earlobes. An ecstatic sigh hovered on her trembling mouth as Travis claimed her lips with a kiss containing so much emotion it filled Echo's body with a desire equal to his and left her devoid of resistance. In limp defeat, she slumped down to the ground with him, oblivious to anything outside this moment in time and the feel of his fiery touch upon her fevered body.

Surprised by her sudden reversal, Travis pulled away from her to glimpse the expression on her face. The night was rapidly drawing away the last of the daylight, but he could still see the glow of submission in her dark blue gaze. He felt as though he had been living his whole life in expectation of this moment, and he hoped she would not regret what they were destined to do before this night was through. "I love you, Echo," he said quietly.

Thick veils of black lashes blinked in a shy manner over misty eyes as she moistened her lips with a dainty swipe of her tongue. Without his mouth against her, she felt parched and desperate for his kisses again. Although she knew her relentless resistance of the past few days would be in vain if she gave in to him now, she was powerless to stop him. Her own body was defying her, and in a battle with her dwindling senses, there was no way for her common sense to win. "I love you more with each rising and setting of the sun, Travis Wade. After tonight, and by the time the next sun rises in the sky, my love will have expanded even more. I feel as if I might burst apart at the seams with the love that grows within me for you." Her lips parted to reveal an enchanted smile that could light up the darkest of nights, as her hands drew Travis' face down against hers to resume the kisses that had turned a simmering desire to a lambent flame.

"Qha'n tayl-t-alu-da?"

248

The impassioned couple drew apart in a startled moment of confusion at the loud Apache demand. Travis Wade was certain he was about to be killed, and he thought it a cruel twist of fate to be done in while in this vulnerable position. Although the Apache's words sounded like a death threat to his ears, Echo did not seem to be frightened by the intrusion. She struggled to sit up and glared through the dim light with squinted eyes as she shouted back in Apache at the man who stood over them like a specter of doom. That man retaliated by pointing the barrel of his rifle at Travis Wade, but Echo did not back down and continued to speak to him in a harsh manner.

Travis managed to uncoil his six-foot frame from his compromising position, although sitting upright put the Indian's rifle within a precarious range of his head. He did not understand a word of the argument which raged between Echo and the man, but he feverishly hoped she came out the victor. Without moving anything other than his eyes, he gave an aggravated glance toward his discarded gunbelt and the handgun. The weapon was lying atop a rock several feet away. Five years of training in the U.S. Cavalry did him little good when his mind was engrossed with Echo. However, he reminded himself that he could not shoot this man even if the gun were within reach. Somewhere above his head was an entire village of Apaches, and he was the only one who was an intruder. He did not have a chance if Echo failed in her attempt to calm the fierce man who hovered over him.

As she started to rise, she reached out to Travis. He clasped her hand, and they stood up together to face the angry Apache. Echo spoke to the man again, only now her voice was not filled with the fury his intrusion had first aroused. After another exchange of conversation, she turned her attention back to Travis. Their hands were still entwined, and as she spoke she tightened her grip. "He says my father has not returned, and I fear he has gone to search for me in Arizona." Her expression filled with worry for her father's safety. "We will have to go back to the *ranchería* with this man, and when we talk to my mother we can make a decision about what should be done next."

Travis shrugged, wondering if the man planned to remove the rifle barrel aimed at his face. As this thought was going through his mind, Echo, evidently irritated, gave the man a command. The Indian grunted and lowered his gun, but fiercely glared through the fading light at Travis, seeming more angry than before.

"He does not want me to take you into our *ranchería*," Echo said. In defiance, she clutched Travis' hand tighter. "But I told him you were going to be my husband and it would be up to the council to decide whether or not you can stay." She lowered her voice and leaned closer. "His name is Hako. He is a close friend of my father, and since my father is not here, he feels it is his duty to protect me."

"Th-the council?" Travis said. He did not realize his arrival would be dealt with in such a complicated way. With a worried glance at the other man, he whispered to Echo, "What if this council decides I should be shot?"

She squeezed his hand again and gave him a reassuring smile, but the daylight had disappeared and her gesture went unnoticed by Travis. "Come, we must accompany Hako to the *ranchería* now, because he does not trust us to stay here tonight." Her voice carried a hint of embarrassment at being caught by her father's comrade while consorting passionately on the ground.

Travis stumbled along behind her. He paused by the rock where his gun had been, but the weapon had already been taken out of the holster by the Apache. He grabbed his empty gunbelt and clenched his teeth to keep from saying something that could be detrimental to his health. The sun was completely gone, and the moon had not yet appeared, so the opaque light that shadowed the towering cliffs lent an eerie feeling to the deep barranca surrounding them. He recalled Echo's words that the trail was treacherous; yet neither Echo nor the man seemed to be concerned. They left their horses behind and proceeded on foot. As he walked, Travis could feel the trail begin to slope upward, but he could not tell how high they were climbing. His thoughts were clouded with the image of the high ridge Echo had pointed to when she'd shown him the location of Pa-Gotzin-Kay. The idea that they were ascending to such a height, while engulfed in darkness, made him dizzy, and he fought the panicky feeling that he would slip and fall into the black depths his senses told him were only inches from the gravelly trail they walked upon. He remained directly behind Echo, and forced himself to concentrate on each step rather than on the gruesome possibility of losing his footing.

It seemed they had trudged up the path for hours before the faint glows of campfires could be seen in the midnight sky. Travis' uneasiness increased by leaps and bounds. He was about to enter a world where no white man had trod for nearly a decade. Here, he was not only an intruder, but also a threat to everything the Apaches had managed to rebuild after his people had almost annihilated their entire tribe. His love for Echo had blinded him as they'd traveled here, but now he realized how far removed their peoples were. It was unrealistic for him to think he could simply walk away from his previous existence as a soldier in the U.S.

Cavalry and just enter into her life.

As they crested the last ridge, Travis got his first glimpse of Pa-Gotzin-Kay. The moon was slightly less than full and had risen just enough so that it hung above the craggy treetops scattered about the flat shelf. In its glow and the flickering light from the campfires, the red soil of the fertile plateau took on a pink cast that was broken only by the shadows of the tall trees and by the patches of lush grass that surrounded the cluster of wickiups in which the Apaches lived. Running water whispered softly in the distance, and a peacefulness reigned over the entire area. Travis Wade was overwhelmed by the idea that these people had carved out such a tranquil life for themselves, but he was especially awed by the fact that none of his people knew of their existence.

"This is my home," Echo said softly as though she, too, was dazzled by its welcoming beauty. She wrapped her arm in his and turned to gaze at him through the hazy glow of the dim lights. "This will also be your home—that is, if you want it to be."

He felt as though he had just entered into another world when his gaze traveled out over the expanse of the *ranchería*. "I want to be wherever you are, but I thought it was up to the council to decide whether I stay here or not?"

A chuckle escaped from Echo, and her eyes sparkled as brilliantly as the glistening stars overhead. "Do not worry about the council. My mother is the shaman of our tribe, and she will make the final decision. Once she knows of the love we carry for one another, she will give us her blessing."

Through the filtered light, her delicate beauty was radiant, and Travis had no choice but to fall under her spell. At this moment, he would not disagree with anything she told him. He was at her command, and everyone else's who lived in this village, he reminded himself as Hako led them into the center of the *rancheria*. Their entrance caused a stir of enormous proportions as nearly everyone crowded around to watch them pass by. Travis estimated that there were at least forty or more people inhabiting this secret village. Again, he was astounded that so many Chiricahua had escaped from the Army, and from the life on the reservations, where the rest of their race was forced to reside.

The crowd halted before one of the wickiups, but since all of the huts were well built and looked as though their occupants did not suffer from poverty, Travis only assumed that they had reached the home of Echo and her parents. His questions were answered almost immediately when the heavy animal hide that served as a door was drawn aside and a woman exited from the wickiup. Travis' breath halted in his chest as he gazed at the woman; she was only an older version of Echo, but with the wisdom and confidence of a woman her age, she emitted an aura of grace and dignity that could bring a mortal man to his knees with no more than a glance from her violet-colored gaze.

Echo raised her head up proudly as she presented her mother to the man she loved, but Travis could manage no more than a weak nod of his head and a gaping of his mouth. A hundred questions filled his head about this woman who looked more white than Apache, but who obviously had won the command and admiration of all who lived in this *rancheria*.

"Welcome, Travis Wade," Sky Dreamer said in a gentle voice, much like the one in which Echo spoke. Her mouth pursed into a shape similar to that of a heart as she turned her attention to the crowd of observers who closed in around them. In a calm voice, she spoke to the group in Apache, and as Travis Wade watched in amazement, they all began to back away and return to their own huts. As the crowd dispersed only Hako remained rooted to the spot. His dark eyes leveled at the white man, he waited to speak to the shaman about the scene he had stumbled upon in the barranca.

"I wish to talk to my daughter and this man alone," Sky Dreamer stated.

Hako hesitated for a moment, then nodded and turned away. His respect for the tribal shaman did not permit him to engage in an argument with her. But, when Nachae returned, he would tell his friend of this white *soldado's* indecent advances toward his young daughter. Hako had no doubts that when the chief heard what he had to say, the invasion by the white man would cease to be a problem.

"Forgive them," Sky Dreamer said in perfect English as she faced the young couple again. "They are curious as to why my daughter would bring a *soldado* of the U.S. Cavalry into our secluded *ranchería.*" She turned her shimmering lavender gaze toward her daughter, adding, "And I must admit that I, too, am wondering the same thing."

Echo's expression did not show any fear, but as she fought to find the right words before replying, it was apparent she had an endless amount of admiration for her mother. "He is here because he is the man I have chosen to be my husband."

Sky Dreamer's face showed little surprise as she crossed her arms and took on a more casual stance. "I knew something strange was going on when I received word from your father that the two of you had decided to extend your trip until the early harvest. I had a vision that you would encounter the man who would claim your heart." She reached out and touched Echo's cheek with a show of affection, "But I never imagined that he would be a white *soldado.*"

Although her last statement was not intended to convey a hidden meaning, Travis felt the edge of her words slice through his heart. How could these people feel anything other than hatred for all whites, but especially for the men who represented the country which had taken everything away from them?

Sky Dreamer's face drew into a frown as she glanced behind the couple. "Where is your father?" Echo's heavy sigh was an answer she did not want to hear. Her shaman powers enabled her to envision or dream about certain events before they happened, but she had had no warning that tragedy had hit her beloved husband. Her arms dropped to her sides as her beautiful face filled with agony. "Where is he?" she repeated in a hoarse voice.

Upon seeing her mother's despair, Echo again was invaded by a sense of guilt over allowing herself to be caught off guard by the *soldados* across the border. A hundred times she had asked herself: what if I had been looking where I was going? What if she had seen the *soldados* before the had seen her? And what if she had never met the green-eyed *soldado* who continued to fill her with so much love she would never have been complete if she had not looked into his eyes on that hot day in Bisbee?

"I don't know," she said in reply to her mother's question. For the first time since they had begun to climb up the trail, Echo released her tight grip on Travis and threw her arms around her mother's neck. "I'm afraid he is somewhere in Arizona looking for me." She wanted to be brave, at least for her mother's sake, but she could not control the tears that glistened along the edges of her dark eyes.

Sky Dreamer wrapped her arms around her trembling daughter, and shut her eyes to try to block out the horrible images of the many dangers her husband would face on such a mission. "Your father is a smart man. It will not take him long to figure out where you are." She smiled over Echo's shoulder when her gaze caught Travis Wade's troubled look. "Everything has a way of working itself out," she added, softly.

Travis smiled back at her, feeling more confident than he had since this whole situation had begun. He knew she was not a woman who would judge him only by the color of his skin, and as that thought passed through his head he was struck by the irony of this turn of events. Here, at Pa-Gotzin-Kay, he was the minority, and despite this, these people treated him with kindness. What a change from the way it was on the other side of the border—where his people had determined that the Indians no longer belonged in their own world.

"There is more that I must tell you," Echo said, pulling away from her mother and swallowing down the hard lump in her throat.

"Let us go into the wickiup and sit down," Sky Dreamer answered calmly, though her stomach was in knots. She could not understand its meaning, but Echo's words had conjured up an image of a burning *ranchería* in Arizona, the *ranchería* where they had once lived—and where her other daughter had died.

Settled on a carpet of thick furs, the trio sat in a tight circle. "Start at the beginning, and do not spare me any of the details," Sky Dreamer said in a serious tone. She prepared herself to hear the worst, but prayed silently to Usen that her daugher's words would be the opposite.

"Morning Star is still alive," Echo blurted out, ignoring her mother's suggestion to start at the beginning.

Sky Dreamer gasped and threw her hand over her heart. "But . . . how can this be true?" She looked to

256

Echo for an answer, but the girl only shrugged. Since she had not yet seen her sister, the idea of her still being alive seemed remote and unbelievable.

"Maybe I should tell you?" Travis said in a hesitant voice.

The shaman tilted her head to the side, letting her long straight hair flow over one shoulder. In the dim light of the wickiup, it was almost impossible to tell that she was old enough to be Echo's mother. She nodded, "Then tell me, Travis Wade."

After drawing in a deep breath, Travis began to relate the details of his trip to the Carlisle Indian School. He told his story slowly, making sure that he did not leave anything out, until he came to the part about Margaret's kidnapping. He avoided looking at Echo while he talked of her sister's disappearance, and he did not tell the shaman how he had kissed her daughter prior to her capture by the comancheros. He did, however, express the deep sense of guilt he would always feel for neglecting the responsibilities of his command.

A deafening hush fell over the three people when Travis finished his story. The shaman's face carried a distant look as she thought of all the time they had been deprived of their daughter, but that was not as important as the realization that she was alive. Despite the fact that Morning Star was probably with the comancheros, there was still a chance that they could all be reunited someday. She smiled and glanced at Echo again. "Now, it is your turn to tell me what happened when you were separated from your father."

Echo's gaze moved toward Travis. Taking in his expression of love, she felt reborn. Despite all the bad things that had happened in the past few weeks, their affection continued to prosper and grow. She turned back toward her mother, and began to tell her about

257

Bisbee, Arizona; Fort Huachuca, and the trip she had begun to the reservation in Oklahoma. When she reached the part about Travis' desertion to be with her, she heard her mother exhale sharply. Her mother's father had been a captain in the U.S. Cavalry and Echo knew that her mother understood the life of the *soldados* as well as anyone.

When her daughter had told the last of her story, Sky Dreamer wiped away the thin layer of perspiration that coated her smooth skin. There were so many things for her to digest all at once. She reached out and took one of her daughter's hands, then grasped one of Travis Wade's. "The hour is late, and there are many decisions to make. We must rest so that our minds will be sharp and clear and our choices will be the best ones." Her face was weary as she forced a smile upon her lips. Tomorrow she would make the monumental decisions that would determine the outcome of many lives, but tonight she needed to be alone so no one else would see the terror and sorrow she could no longer contain within her trembling form.

Chapter Seventeen

Hako had long since given up the idea that he was dreaming, although every so often he paused to rub his eyes and shake his head just to be certain he was awake. Last night when he had returned to his lookout post on the ridge below Pa-Gotzin-Kay, where he had been when he had spotted Echo and the *soldado,* he'd assumed the rest of his watch would be uneventful. But early this morning, as he was walking through the barranca to take a final check before he returned to the *ranchería* to turn the watch over to someone else, he had stumbled upon more intruders!

The Apache stared at the backs of the three people who traveled on horseback up the narrow trail in front of him. He remembered the warrior Chateo, but he had forgotten that the man had a daughter. It was the discovery of Nachae and Sky Dreamer's other twin daughter which had left his mind reeling, though, especially since it had been only a few hours before that he delivered Echo and the white man to the *ranchería.* Rarely did so much excitement enter into the lives of the occupants of Pa-Gotzin-Kay.

Margaret clung to the saddlehorn, while trying not to glance down into the incredible sheer drop-off of the

Bavispe Barranca. She could not believe her parents had built a *ranchería* in such a perilous location. Parts of the trail were so narrow they were forced to dismount and practically drag the animals up the trail in order to get the terrified horses to continue. In other areas boulders and rock embankments left the trail barely wide enough to accommodate the animals. The riders' feet scraped against rock as they passed through the openings. The trail twisted back and forth, and in some places was not even visible. For the past couple of days, Chateo had been undecided as to how they would ascend the towering mountain, and he had even worried that they had not followed Nachae's directions and were lost in this vast array of rugged barrancas. When the Apache lookout stumbled upon them that morning, both Chateo and Margaret had been glad just to learn that they were going in the right direction. Now, they realized they probably would have spent days looking for the *ranchería* if Hako had not happened upon them and led them up the mountain.

"How much farther?" Chateo asked as he looked back over his shoulder.

"Not much," was Hako's sharp reply. He did not like the idea of so many outsiders knowing the location of their hidden *ranchería*. But, he reminded himself, if something bad happens as a result, the fault will be entirely upon the chief and his two daughters. The rest of the trip was made in complete silence, except for an occasional command from Chateo about the direction of the trail.

Pa-Gotzin-Kay came into view amid the glow of the midmorning sun, and the three newcomers could only gape at its peaceful beauty, just as those who had come before them had done when they'd come over the last of the high rimrocks. Margaret found herself wondering if she had climbed all the way to heaven just to get a glimpse of this mountain fortress. She glanced at Kaytee and, by the excited glow upon her young face, could tell the younger girl felt the same way. Chateo had been correct to bring his daughter here, Margaret decided. She only hoped he would not betray the trust her father had placed in him by revealing this secret *ranchería* to an outlaw such as José Fernando.

The village was quiet at this time of the morning since most of the inhabitants were working in the lush fields that lay at the far end of the shelf. Several barking dogs encircled the horses' feet though, and soon had the attention of those working around the wickiups. It was like going back in time for Chateo and the two girls, as distant memories from the past began to etch a way into their thoughts. Margaret was amazed by the abundance of trees surrounding the wickiups, which were in no way the shabby huts their people resided in on the reservation. These wickiups were large, built of sturdy poles, and covered with heavy leaves and stalks that would provide a strong shelter from the elements. Delicious aromas floated through the air to tantalize the senses, and there were several large piles of animal hides—the rewards of many successful hunting parties— waiting to be converted into blankets and clothes to keep the people of this mountain paradise warm when the nights grew cold.

As they neared one of the large wickiups, the commotion caused by the approaching caravan alerted the occupants of Sky Dreamer's home. Echo, along with her mother and Travis, had been discussing their situation once again, although they still had not made any definite decisions. The shaman rose from the plush hide on which she had been sitting and motioned to the young couple to follow her outside. As she pulled back the flap, the first face she encountered was the frowning countenance of Hako. But when her gaze switched to the faces of the other riders, shock rendered her numb. Her pause allowed Echo's face to appear in the opening beside her, and the sight that greeted Echo rooted her to the spot.

The reins Margaret held tightly within her grasp slid from her limp hands. Seeing her mother in the doorway had taken away her breath, but her twin sister's sudden appearance had been a shock of unmeasurable proportions. Several minutes passed before any of the three women could think coherently enough to make a move or attempt to speak. Finally, it was Sky Dreamer who moved forward with outstretched arms, the smile of joy upon her face saying all the things she was too choked up to voice.

Margaret wasted no time in dismounting and flinging herself into her mother's extended embrace. She had envisioned being held again by Sky Dreamer hundreds of times. And even now, with her mother's arms wrapped around her and Sky Dreamer's face pressed against hers, Margaret was terrified, fearing she was only dreaming this wondrous scene once again. When at last they pulled apart, Margaret met the blue gaze of her twin sister for the first time in eight years. A tender smile curved Sky Dreamer's lips as she stepped back and allowed the two girls to approach one another.

In an almost fearful mood they inched toward each other. It had been a long time. Once they had been so close they were inseparable, but the years, separation, and circumstance had made them strangers. Now each was afraid of what she would encounter when she allowed the wall between them to crumble.

"It is really you?" Echo said with an apparent quiver in her voice. Her lips also trembled as a slight smile inched its way across them and she reached out toward the other girl. Though Travis had told her that her sister was still alive, Echo had not imagined they would actually be together again. Even now, it seemed too good to be true.

Margaret did not move for an instant as her gaze moved down toward her sister's outstretched hands, then back up to her face again. With the only variation being their eye color, it was almost like looking into a mirror. But already, Margaret could sense the vast differences between them the years had wrought. She slowly reached out until her hands clasped her sister's as they drew closer together. Then the barrier seemed to break apart all at once, and instantly they were in one another's embrace, both crying and babbling about how they had thought the other was dead yet had always felt her presence in spite of that belief. It was not until they backed away from each other that Margaret caught sight of the man who had also exited from the wickiup.

A surprised gasp flew from her mouth. "Lieu-Lieutenant Wade?" Her voice was hoarse at first, but as her shock ceased to rule her thoughts, anger began to overcome her. Her eyes narrowed, her arms grew rigid at her sides, and her hands drew into two clenched fists. "You deserted me that night, and when I made it back to Fort Sill, you had taken off without so much as a second thought about what had happened to me!" Her face contorted with fury as her voice rose to the point of hysteria. She had not thought to wonder why he had turned up here, nor did she give him the chance to explain. Her outburst, though, had left everyone standing around her speechless.

"This is the man I am going to marry," Echo finally said in a small voice.

Her announcement only added fuel to the fire that raged within her sister. Margaret's smothering turquoise gaze flew back and forth between Echo and the lieutenant. "Marry! Him?" A wicked huff and a half-chuckle broke forth from the hateful curve of her mouth. She tried to sort out this unbelievable turn of events, but her rage could not allow her to think of anything except that somehow her sister had managed to steal away her dream of living among the whites, and since the lieutenant had seemed a means of fulfilling that goal, Margaret's anger was twice as intense. She twirled around, not knowing where she would go, only that she had to leave this place. But she collided with the hard wall of Chateo as he stepped forward to block her path.

Unlike the others watching Margaret's enraged explosion, Chateo saw the pain appear on Echo's face, and he also glimpsed the horror upon Sky Dreamer's when the reunion turned into a disastrous fiasco. "You owe everyone an apology," he said, his face hardening with the anger he felt toward Margaret.

She glared at him with all the animosity she could muster. She hated the whole world right now, and Chateo had made himself a direct target for her fury. She tightened up her fist, intending to pound it against his chest, but as she raised it, the fight suddenly left her. Her face filled with defeat again, and her whole body began to shake violently. It wasn't fair! She had found her family, and she should be happier than ever before. Instead, all she could think of was that she was truly trapped in the Apache world from which there was no escape. Rather than assault him with her fists, she collapsed against Chateo and gave in to the racking sobs that flooded through her slender form.

He did not feel like comforting her, but the sight of her breakdown broke through his defenses, which were always weak where she was concerned. He held her, but not tightly, as he glanced over her head toward the rest of the crowd. Kaytee stood only a couple of feet away, and her worried expression made Chateo even more angry with Margaret Sinclair. Kaytee's large raven eyes searched her father's face for reassurance, but he could not offer something he did not have or feel. He could not begin to explain everything that had transpired in the short time since their arrival. But he did know who Lieutenant Wade was, since Margaret had told him of her involvement with the lieutenant, and he was as curious as she about why the soldier had turned up at Pa-Gotzin-Kay as the future husband of Margaret's twin sister.

"I think it would be wise for everyone to spend some time apart to calm down; then perhaps we can discuss things more rationally," Sky Dreamer said, trying to disguise the unhappiness she felt. But her voice cracked and her face did not convey anything other than deep concern for the obvious gap that separated her daughters. She motioned toward her wickiup as she added, "Please take Morning Star into my home, I will join you later so that we may talk." Sky Dreamer glanced at the trembling form of Kaytee. She remembered Chateo and his family very well. As tribal shaman, it was her job to attend births, and she had helped to deliver Kaytee over twelve years ago. She also recalled that Chateo's constant absences had caused many hardships for his young family, and with this thought in mind she moved toward the girl and held out her hand. "Hello Kaytee."

The girl attempted to smile as she hesitantly placed her hand in the shaman's. "I think I remember you." Her voice sounded small, and her eyes seemed even larger than usual.

Sky Dreamer nodded as she began to lead her away from the rest of the group. "Come, we will talk about all the things you remember." She wanted to be with her daughters, but she sensed they had things to work

265

out that did not concern her, and when they were ready to ask for her help, she would be back.

All eyes were focused on the proud form of the beautiful shaman as she walked away with the girl. Chateo had always admired her, but he had forgotten how special their shaman truly was until he watched her assume the responsibility of comforting his terrified daughter. Still, he was left with a trembling young woman in his arms, and though he knew Sky Dreamer had left them so they could straighten things out, Chateo was still so furious with Margaret Sinclair, all he really wanted to do was take a switch to her hide and treat her like the spoiled child she seemed. As he dragged her into the wickiup, this was precisely what he had in mind.

With the absence of Chateo and Margaret, the shaman and Kaytee, the crowd slowly moved back to the jobs they'd been doing before all the commotion began, leaving the stunned Echo and Travis Wade to stand alone outside the wickiup. Echo had not made a move since her sister's attack on them, and Travis began to grow concerned when she continued to stare at the wickiup as though she did not know how to cope with this new situation.

"Echo?" he called out, while he reached out to take her in his arms.

She backed away from him. Her dark blue eyes became clouded with tears that she defiantly told herself she would refuse to let fall. "There had to be more between you and my sister," she said in an accusing tone. "There had to be!"

Travis dropped his arms to his sides and shrugged. After the act Margaret Sinclair had just staged, how could Echo believe anything else? "I told you exactly what happened." He stepped toward her again, but she moved farther away.

"Until I know the truth, I do not want to see you again, Travis Wade!" She twirled around, hoping he did not see the stinging tears of pain rushing down her cheeks. With no destination in mind she started to run toward the distant fields of gently blowing amber-colored wheat. She did not take the time to glance back to see if he was following her, because her eyes were blinded by the frustrating tears which would not stop, her ears were deafened by the sound of her sister's evil words. When she reached the wheat field, she collapsed in a heap among the narrow rows of stalks. The reunion with her twin should have been one of the most joyous occasions of her life, but instead it had turned out to be one of the most painful. In desperation, she threw her hands over her eyes to block out the sight of the man who had just stopped beside her.

Travis knelt down as he wiped away the heavy veil of sweat that cloaked his face. The sun had no mercy either, and he was still wearing his heavy Army trousers and shirt, which were not suited to the scorching heat of Sonora. It broke his heart to see Echo so unhappy, but if she refused to believe him, he did not know how to convince her he was not lying. Hearing the truth from Margaret Sinclair was the only thing that could validate his story, and judging from Margaret's attitude, that was very unlikely.

"Go away," Echo said from behind her shaky hands. Oh, how she hated to cry in front of him. Even worse was not believing him when she wanted to so badly.

Travis took her hands in his and easily pried them away from her face. Their eyes locked. He had not known this young woman very long, but he already loved her more than he had ever thought possible. Nothing would come between them, he decided firmly as he gazed into her teary blue eyes.

Echo wanted to look away, but once again her senses

had been stolen from her by his mere presence. He found a weakness in her when he gazed into her eyes, and she could not help but be lost within the jade pools which spoke to her of love. She cherished the memory of her sister, and she wanted to know and love her again, but in this moment of decision, Echo made another resolution: her love for Travis Wade could not be deterred by anything or anyone, especially not by her twin sister. She threw her arms around his neck and buried her face in the comforting feel of his brawny chest. "I'm sorry I doubted you, but it doesn't matter. What happened between the two of you is in the past."

The reversal in her mood stunned Travis for an instant, and caused devotion for her to wash over him. It mattered that she believed him when he told her what had happened between him and her sister in Oklahoma, but that she was willing to forgive him in spite of her doubts was beyond his expectations. He held her in a tight embrace, his entire body enveloped by love, and when they drew apart it was only natural that he would want to kiss her soft lips.

The same desire rushing through Echo, she eagerly raised her face upward as their lips were drawn together like magnets. Nothing mattered when they were together like this, and each time their wanton bodies touched, it became more and more difficult to stop the yearnings that continued to expand within them. Last night, before Hako had intruded upon them, Echo had been ready to submit without resistance. Now she was equally ready to do so, but in the broad daylight, and lying among the stalks of wheat where the entire village could be witness, this was not the time or place.

As they forced themselves to regain control and pulled away from one another, Travis coughed and drew in a choking gasp. "We can't go on like this much

268

longer. I have so much love for you, and I must release it somehow. Maybe I should go away for a while—just until everything is straightened out between you and your sister."

His suggestion filled Echo with panic. "No, I couldn't bear it if you left." She reached up and touched his cheek. Several days without shaving left his usually smooth face with a rough sprinkling of dark blond stubble. Echo thought he was devastatingly handsome no matter how he looked, and just the feel of his cheek against the palm of her hand made her whole being ache with desire for him. "If you leave, I'll follow you."

The traces of a slight grin claimed Travis' mouth. How could he ever leave her? As this thought went through his mind, however, it was accompanied by another disturbing one—something that kept plaguing him every time he tried to envision their future together. Each time this particular thought occurred, it became stronger, and his guilt increased. His love for Echo made him want to stay with her for all eternity; yet loyalty to his country and guilt over deserting his command kept eating away at him like a ravenous poison. Would it be possible for him to remain here in Pa-Gotzin-Kay with this burden weighing so heavily upon him? he wondered. Or would he never be able to lead a fulfilling life with Echo until he went back and faced up to his crime?

Margaret had cried herself into a rasping trance. She had no more tears to shed and each time she took a breath her body shook with violent tremors. Chateo's nearness did nothing to comfort her, but she was frightened of being left alone so she hesitated to tell him to leave. She felt as if she were being torn in half.

269

The knowledge that her entire family was alive was wonderful, and when she had admitted to herself that she would never live as a white woman, she had hoped she would be satisfied with just being reunited with her family. If Lieutenant Wade had not appeared at their *ranchería* as her sister's betrothed, she might have been able to live with the loss of her dreams—for a while, anyway. But the idea that her twin sister was stepping into the position she had hoped to occupy was more than her selfish heart could handle.

Chateo sat in a cross-legged position, his arms crossed defiantly over his broad chest. He refused to comfort this woman when she was acting so hateful. He was certain he knew the exact thoughts that were invading her mind, and he still could not believe she would allow them to interfere with an occasion such as seeing her mother and sister again after eight years. Like Echo, he, too, was wondering if more than just a kiss had transpired between Margaret and the lieutenant. Although, since he was certain he was the first man who had made love to Margaret, her reaction to seeing the *soldado* was all the more baffling. He was also infuriated with the way his own feelings for this young woman continued to cloud his thoughts with emotions he did not want to feel for someone so coldhearted.

"When you made love to me, it meant nothing to you, did it?" he blurted out, unable to contain his emotions any longer.

Margaret sniffed loudly and gave him a perplexed stare. How could he be thinking of something so unimportant as that at a time like this? "What does that have to do with anything?" she said in a pouty tone of voice.

He leaned close to her and grabbed her by the shoulders, pulling her close enough so that the heat of their breath touched one another's face. "It has

270

everything to do with you and me." He continued to enslave her with his grip as he watched a multitude of emotions wash over her. A faint desire still burned within him that her reply would give him just a glimmer of hope, but as the seconds turned into an unbearable silence, he knew his visions of claiming Margaret Sinclair's icy heart were all in vain. His breathing grew heavy as he released his hold upon her stiff shoulders and backed away. "You don't have to say the words out loud, I can see your answer clearly in your face." He rose to his feet and stood over her like a towering giant of stone. "It was just something that happened, because you were a curious virgin, or perhaps because you hoped to tease me with your charms so that I would eventually take you back to the white man's world." His voice remained low, but it had such a venomous tone that Margaret cringed visibly.

She slumped upon the furs in her mother's wickiup, wanting to dispute him, but knowing that his words were too close to the truth. He was an attractive man, and the intimate episode by the river in the comanchero hideout was something which had just happened. That he could see through her so easily, however, and knew her feelings of despair over not being able to live as a white woman, made her feel like a traitor to her Apache heritage. Yet, she could not deny it, so she was not able to find the words to disagree with him.

Chateo stayed until his tortured soul could not stand the pain of being so near to her while knowing her silence was an admission of all his accusations. If she would only look at him with some sort of compassion or feeling, but she merely stared down at the furs which covered the floor of the wickiup. He wanted to hate her, but he could not summon up enough rage to do so. He felt sorry for her, though—more sorry than he had ever felt for anyone. She was a sad, beautiful creature

271

who would never know the meaning of true love, because she was not capable of feeling such a tender emotion. She was too wrapped up in her own self-pity and in dreams of having something that would always be out of her grasp.

He backed toward the hide-covered doorway of the wickiup, not wanting to miss her reaction . . . just in case she decided to look up at him . . . just in case she changed her mind. She did not make a move, however, and Chateo could not stay a second longer in her presence. He ducked through the low doorway and squinted into the bright sunlight when it struck his unsuspecting gaze. He rubbed at his eyes, in an attempt to focus his blurred sight and to hide the moistness which suddenly coated his eyes with a salty substance alien to his raven gaze.

Chapter Eighteen

Sky Dreamer had rallied together Echo and her *soldado,* and along with Kaytee they attempted to carry on a conversation about things which did not require much concentration, since most of their thoughts were occupied with the happenings inside the shaman's wickiup. When Chateo and Morning Star did not exit from the wickiup for a long time, Sky Dreamer grew even more concerned about her long-lost daughter's state of mind. The women's reminiscing about the old times when they had lived in Arizona no longer seemed important, even to Kaytee, and before long it seemed that no one knew what to talk about. The shaman knew how troubled Echo was over her sister's rejection; yet, until she knew the entire story, she did not know how to help either of her daughters.

"She does not like to be called Morning Star," Kaytee said when Sky Dreamer called Echo's twin by her birth name. The young girl's pronouncement gave Sky Dreamer the first clue to a partial cause of her daughter's odd behavior.

"What does she like to be called?" she asked with a puzzled arch of her dark brows.

"Margaret, Margaret Sinclair. It is the white name

that she was given by the teachers at the Carlisle School."

A deep frown burrowed its way across the unmarred face of the Apache shaman. "But her real name is Morning Star. She was named after her grandmother, who was the first female shaman of the Chiricahua Apaches. Why would she prefer a white name over one that represents such an honorable status?"

"I think I can answer that question," Chateo cut in as he approached the group. They were sitting in the shade provided by the branches of an orange tree, and were squeezing the juice from the sweet fruit into their mouths as they spoke. Chateo's mouth watered at the refreshing sight, and before he sat down to join them, he reached up and plucked one of the succulent fruits from the nearest branch. All eyes were turned toward him in anticipation of his answer, although Travis Wade was sure he already knew what the man was about to say. As if they were both on the same train of thought, Chateo glanced at the lieutenant for a moment before he continued to speak. He was surprised to discover that he did not feel any hatred toward the white man, in spite of Margaret Sinclair. Instead, Chateo sensed the *soldado* had been used by the woman in much the same way that he had, making them closer to comrades rather than foes. So how could he be angry with such a fool?

"Your daughter," he began as he tore his gaze away from Travis Wade, and concentrated his attention on the Apache shaman, "does not want to be called by her Apache name because she does not want to acknowledge her Indian heritage. She wants to be a white woman and live among the whites as though she had never been born with a trace of Apache blood running through her veins."

274

Sky Dreamer shook her head in disagreement. "I think you are mistaken." The idea of her daughter being ashamed of her Indian bloodline was beyond the shaman's comprehension.

"No," Kaytee said in a low tone. Her dark eyes traveled back and forth between the shaman and her father as she hoped they would not be angry with her for entering into their conversation. "She told us on the train when we were traveling from Pennsylvania to the reservation at Fort Sill that she did not want to be an Apache anymore. She said she could never return to the life she had once lived among the Indians, and so she was going to find a way to live as a white woman and pretend that she was not an Indian at all." Without meaning anything by the action, Kaytee glanced at the lieutenant, and as everyone else followed her lead, a slow recognition began to dawn on the quiet group.

Kaytee's confirmation of Chateo's accusation against her daughter hit the shaman almost as hard as the sorrow she had felt eight years ago when she had believed Morning Star had been killed in the fire. She squeezed her eyes shut and tried to think coherently, but all she could focus on was that her daughter was turning against the only race of people who would accept her because she was a person, not because of her bloodline. Sky Dreamer knew this all too well, because once she had made a choice between the white world of her father's people and the world of her mother's Apache family. If only she could impart all she had learned from that decision to her daughter, but it broke her heart to know this was something the girl would have to learn on her own. Most of all, though, Sky Dreamer's thoughts were clouded by renewed fury toward the white men. During the years since they had created Pa-Gotzin-Kay, she had come to believe there

275

was nothing else the white men could steal from them. Now she realized they had found a way to take her daughter away from her a second time.

Sky Dreamer opened her eyes and glanced around at the people who were waiting and watching for her reaction. At times like this, she knew they expected her words to be wise and positive, but sometimes the real wisdom came from admitting how she really felt inside. "I have no answers that will help Morn—, I mean Margaret, solve her problems. To learn of her feelings toward her Apache heritage has saddened me more than I can say, and it will take time for me to adjust to this startling discovery. But there are other people to think of." She forced herself to straighten up and rid her shoulders of the hunch that had claimed her posture, then smiled at Kaytee and received a relieved grin from the anxious young girl. "Kaytee has not yet had a puberty ceremony, and this is imperative for an Apache girl of her age." She gestured toward Echo and Travis Wade. "And these two young people are anxious to be married and to begin their lives as man and wife. We have two celebrations to prepare for as soon as my husband returns."

She glanced around, noting that her announcement had lit a happy spark in Echo and the lieutenant, and in the youthful face of Kaytee. But when her eyes met the deep-set gaze of Chateo, she realized for the first time that he was in love with her other daughter. And as his next words were spoken, she also became aware of how deeply her daughter must have hurt this man. He swallowed hard and attempted to speak as though he had nothing on his mind other than the thoughts he voiced, but the shaman could sense the immense pain he was desperately trying to hide. Her sympathy went out to him, despite the reservations she still felt toward

276

this man due to their past association.

"I would like to go after your husband. He is riding with a band of comancheros, whose help he sought to go after Echo when he thought her still a prisoner at Fort Huachuca. If I leave immediately I should be able to catch up to them in no time." Chateo's words were rushed as he met the knowing gaze of the shaman. His need to get away from Margaret Sinclair was so great that he would have made any excuse to leave, but finding Nachae was at least an honorable one. He quickly glanced toward his daughter, adding, "When I return we will see to your puberty ceremony."

An understanding glint sparkled in the shaman's violet gaze. "I would be very relieved if you would do this for me, but"—an uneasy tremor shot through her as her gaze wandered out over Pa-Gotzin-Kay—"these comancheros you mentioned, would you be able to lure my husband away from them without—"

Chateo cut in before she could continue. "I will guard the location of this hidden *ranchería* with my life." He looked toward Kaytee again as a tender grin curved his mouth. "Usen has granted me a second chance to be a good father, and I will not allow anything to interfere with this privilege again!" His attention was averted by a rush of wind that began to howl across the flat shelf of land where the *ranchería* was situated. A gathering of dark clouds had started to edge their way across the sky, which had been clear and blue only a short time before. "Maybe I should leave before the storm hits," he said, thinking of the steep trail leading off the side of this mountain.

"No. It's too dangerous to be caught in the barranca when it's raining," Sky Dreamer said. "You can leave in the morning if the storm has blown over." With a worried glance at the darkening sky, she rose to her feet. After telling the two men where they could find empty wickiups to take cover in, she turned to Echo. "You should try to speak to your sister, now."

Echo clung to Travis Wade's arm while she nodded in agreement. It was inevitable that she had to talk to her twin, but the idea was terrifying, especially now that she knew how her sister felt about having to return to the Apache *ranchería*. Speaking to her would be like facing a stranger with whom she had nothing in common; there would be nothing for them to say to one another.

Travis rested a hand upon her arm in a reassuring gesture before he pried her hand from his arm and moved away. He wished there were some way he could comfort her, but where Margaret Sinclair was concerned, he had to deal with his own remorse and guilt. He felt as though it was his fault the twin sister's reunion had turned into an exchange of angry accusations. With great effort, he forced his reluctant feet to walk away from Echo, when all he wanted to do was take her in his arms once again, to feel the security of her love for a moment longer. But while she worked on rebuilding a relationship with her twin sister, Travis knew he must find a way to come to terms with his own feelings so he could make a fresh start with Echo, free of the past and his unrelenting remorse.

As the wind whipped around them, Sky Dreamer motioned for Echo to enter the wickiup alone while she and Kaytee waited in a neighboring hut. She felt the two sisters must face one another without interference in order to sort out their feelings for one another, and to deal with the events that had led to Margaret's outburst earlier that day.

278

Echo, however, felt as though she were about to face her own doom as she entered the dimly lit wickiup. The winds presaging the approaching summer storm were beginning to pick up, and as she dropped the heavy hide down against the door, it began to flap against the frame of the opening when the strong gusts hit it. The whole wickiup seemed to shudder with the weight of the wind, but Echo did not notice anything other than the forlorn figure of her sister sitting upon the soft elk hides.

Margaret glanced up for an instant when Echo entered, but she quickly dropped her eyes when she noticed the intruder was her sister. Ever since Chateo had departed, she had been trying to rationalize her misdirected life. She was certain everyone hated her, although she didn't blame them if they did, because she also hated herself for the way she had acted when she'd first arrived at the *ranchería*. She did not know how to rectify what she had done.

"Will you talk with me, sister?"

Margaret shrugged indifferently, even though her heart seemed to rise up into her throat. The last thing she wanted was to be the enemy of her sister. She would prefer to be close to her as she once was, but she knew it was impossible to think things could ever be the same between them. Their lives had been too different for the past eight years, and as a result they had grown into two different people.

Echo sat down opposite her sister and searched for the right words to say; it was not an easy task. "I've missed you," she said in a tone just above a hoarse whisper.

Margaret's bottom lip began to tremble slightly. "Well, I guess I've missed you too. And our mother and father," she added. She still had not looked up from her forced study of the floor, but slowly her gaze ascended until she met the tender look in her sister's blue eyes. For an instant she thought of reaching out to hug her, of telling her that she was sorry about what she'd done that day; but the thought of making such a gesture only reminded her of Lieutenant Wade, and again aroused the rage she had not yet dismissed. "He should have been mine, you know," she said in a tone which took on a hateful edge.

Echo sighed in aggravation. "I assume you mean Travis Wade?" Margaret nodded, and Echo drew in another heavy breath. If Morning Star was willing to talk to her, then perhaps this was an opportunity to hear her sister's side of the story. Still, she dreaded what her sister might say more with each passing second. "What happened between you and Travis Wade that makes you feel he belonged to you first?" This was one of the most difficult questions Echo had ever forced herself to ask. It could not be avoided; however, if Margaret told her she had been his lover, Echo was afraid she would want to kill them both.

Margaret tossed back her head and forced her gaze to remain fixed on her sister's face. Her turquoise eyes flashed with defiance as she pondered her answer. She sensed the fear in her sister by the look in Echo's dark blue eyes. For a second, Margaret began to conjure up a deception of considerable proportions. She could easily tell Echo that she and the lieutenant had engaged in a passionate love affair while they were traveling to the reservation in Oklahoma, and that was why she felt she had a prior claim on him. Margaret reasoned it would only be her word against the lieutenant's, but it would be a lie and where would it get her in the end? "He was mine, but only in my own fantasies. He never belonged to me, not really."

Relief claimed Echo's entire being as she clutched her breast and said a silent prayer of thanks to Usen. She could forgive her sister for anything now that Morning Star had affirmed Travis' account of their brief involvement in the Oklahoma territory. She scooted closer to the other girl as the sadness in her sister's admission sank into her mind. Living in a world of fantasy only made the reality of Morning Star's life seem more bitter and unjust, Echo thought as she reached out her hand through the fading light. Outside, the storm clouds had cloaked the sunlight with their cover, and the interior of the wickiup was rapidly growing dark. "Can we start over?"

Margaret stared at her for a moment, but only because emotion had rendered her too numb to move. After a long pause, she blinked, releasing a single teardrop which floated down her cheek on a lonely journey to nowhere. She wiped at the uninvited intruder with a quick swipe, not wanting to show her weakness to her sister as she slowly gave her dark head a slight nod.

"Welcome home . . . Margaret." Echo said her sister's white name carefully so she would not think it had been spoken in a degrading way. Knowing Margaret chose her white blood over her Apache heritage, Echo intended to make her sister aware of her feelings on this issue right from the start. Regardless of how or where they lived, they would always be twin sisters, and all that seemed important now was that they somehow recapture some of the closeness they had once shared.

A startled expression filtered across Margaret's face when her sister referred to her by her white name. But since it was obvious that Echo did not say it in a sarcastic way, Margaret began to sense an acceptance she had not expected from her family. A longing ache started to work its way through her until she was desperate to be close to her twin again. She flung herself across the short distance which separated them, so they could embrace once again. Unlike the first time they had hugged each other, the tenderness evoked by the gesture lingered, even after they had pulled apart.

"Would you like to see our mother now?" Echo asked as she rose from her position on the floor and wiped at her own tears, which had mingled with her sister's while they'd hugged one another.

Margaret's lips parted with a relieved smile as she nodded her head in reply. Although she did not know how long she would be able to stay at the *ranchería,* at least she did not feel as though they all despised her. She watched her sister depart from the wickiup, preparing to face her mother. Her sister had not asked her the tough questions she expected Sky Dreamer would pose about why she found it so difficult to return to the Apache way of life, and Margaret was not sure how she would answer those inquiries. She hated the white men for their constant lies; yet there was still a deep yearning in her that would never go away. She glanced around the interior of the wickiup, while outside the wind howled chillingly. The grass walls were decorated with shields and spears and a variety of cooking utensils. Against one wall was a stack of blankets, and beside them stood several baskets filled with sewing supplies, while another wall hosted an array of clothing, all of which appeared to be the cotton skirts and loose-fitting tops women in this part of the country wore daily.

With a choking sob, Margaret buried her face in the palms of her trembling hands. If only she could dispense with her dreams and learn to accept this simple life again. But her fantasies would not go away, and they kept drawing vivid pictures in her mind of grand houses, of gowns made from the finest materials. Yet, these musings only visited her during her waking hours, because at night when slumber claimed her, images of the burning *ranchería* carried her back to the land of Apachería, and reminded her that she would never be completely free of her Indian heritage.

Chapter Nineteen

Echo wasted no time in telling her mother that Margaret wanted to see her, then hurried toward the wickiup where she knew Travis would be waiting. Making up with her sister made her feel as though a thousand pounds had been lifted from her back, and even as the gusts of wind ravaged her slender form, Echo was sure the sun would shine forever in Pa-Gotzin-Kay. Her joy faded, however, when Travis held back the animal hide on the doorway so she could enter his hut. His sorrowful expression was not the one she had hoped to see when she told him how well everything had gone between her and her sister.

He took her in his arms, and gently pushed back from her face the loose strands of hair which the wind had entangled. His jade gaze harbored a sadness, and when he spoke it was conveyed in the tone of his voice. "I'm glad you and Margaret were able to work things out, because it will make my leaving a little easier."

His words invaded Echo's happiness like a brigade bent on destruction. Her body grew cold; then she was overcome with a rush of heat that caused her to break out in an icy sweat. "I-I don't understand?" Inwardly,

285

she prayed she had not heard him clearly, or that he had not meant the words he had just spoken. But the look on his face told Echo more than she wanted to know.

Travis turned his head away from her frightened gaze as he tried to remember how he had practiced this speech. "I have thought this through and"—he turned back to face her—"I cannot stay here." He opened his mouth again, but paused, leaving Echo to draw her own conclusions.

"Is it that you can't stay here, or that you don't want to?" she said in a breathless rush of words. She began to imagine every reason why he would suddenly change his mind about the future they had planned, from the possibility that he was a white man who could never accept an Apache woman as his wife to the possibility that seeing her sister again had made him doubt his love for her. With these thoughts raging through her mind, Echo tried to pull away from him, but his tight embrace would not release her.

"Listen to me, damn it!" His green eyes grew intense, flickering lights of desperation in them as he forced her to remain in his arms. "I want nothing more than to make you my wife, and to spend the rest of my life here among your people, but first I have to face up to my desertion from the Cavalry." He felt her stiff body relax slightly, giving him the courage to admit to her how deeply he felt about the gross wrong he had committed. "If I stayed here and tried to pretend it never happened, eventually I couldn't live with myself. I have to go back to Arizona and face up to my crime—accept the punishment bestowed upon me—instead of hiding out like a coward." A pleading, pained expression came into his green gaze. "Please, try to understand why I have to leave?"

She wanted to understand, but fear of never seeing him again consumed her. "They could execute you. Would it be worth it, then?"

"Could you spend the rest of your life with only half a man?"

Her gaze dropped to avoid his piercing look as she contemplated his words. She wanted to tell him it wouldn't matter to her, that she loved him all the more because of what he had given up to be with her, but she knew how unfair it would be if she told him of these feelings. When she tried to tell him that she understood why he was going to leave her, though, the words caught in her throat and all she could manage was a weak shrug of her shoulders.

"I'm going to go back with Chateo when he leaves for Arizona tomorrow."

"Tomorrow!" Echo said in panic. "Why must you go so soon?"

"The longer I wait, the worse the punishment will be." He drew her up against him as he spoke. "And once it's behind us, we can get on with our lives."

Echo allowed herself to become lost in the masculine scent of his skin as she buried her face against his neck. She knew he was correct about not waiting too long if he planned to go back to face his crime. But she could not let him leave her without first making a real commitment. "Leave me with more than just a dream of what could have been."

Her voice was trembling so badly Travis was not sure of what she meant until he saw the look upon her beautiful young face. "I can't because . . ." He hesitated to voice the thoughts going through his mind.

"I know you might not ever return," Echo said for him. "Please, at least leave me with a memory."

"Can your mother perform a wedding ceremony

without all the customary preparations?"

A smile cut through Echo's sorrowful expression. She had only hoped he would make love to her before he left, but he was willing to make her his wife in every way. Her love for him exploded within her as she began to cry, both from the ecstasy of knowing that she would truly belong to him, and from the thought that the coming night might be the last night they would ever spend together again.

Travis did not give her a chance to answer, but wrapped his arms even closer around her and lowered his face to hers. His lips and hers were drawn to each other as the ocean draws the rivers to its source, and they both became lost in their enchanted sea of love. Outside the wickiup, the storm intensified, but it was no more powerful than the tempestuous whirlwind of passion that surrounded Echo and Travis Wade as each kiss drew them farther into the web of desire.

"Let's find your mother," Travis managed to say in a barely audible voice when they were forced to halt their kisses in order to breathe, "because I intend to make love to you tonight. I would prefer to do it as your husband, but . . ." Her soft lips beckoned to him and stole away his senses as his mouth reclaimed hers with a kiss that conveyed his innermost thoughts.

It was Echo's turn to briefly snap back to reality when next they pulled apart to gasp for air. She grabbed his hand and turned her face as she laughed and tugged him along. "My mother should be in her own wickiup." As they exited from the hut and ran through the gusts of wind, a soft drizzle began to fall.

"Mother?" Echo called out when they reached the shaman's wickiup.

At once, Sky Dreamer pulled back the hide and granted them an entrance. She was alone with

288

Margaret, and it was apparent by their calm manner that they had been getting along very well. "Margaret has been telling me about the school she was sent to in Pennsylvania."

"Oh," Echo said with a shrug of her shoulders. "Will you marry us tonight?"

The blunt way she asked the question made everyone fall into a stunned silence. Although Travis knew that was the reason they had come here, even he was speechless.

"Wh-what?" the shaman stammered. Her violet gaze flew from her daughter's radiant face to the flushed countenance of the man.

Echo approached her mother with a sense of urgency. "It must be today because Travis is going to return to Arizona with Chateo tomorrow."

"Then you can be married when they return with your father."

Echo's voice crescendoed with alarm. "He might not come back with them. We must be married today!"

Sky Dreamer grew more confused as she glanced toward the lieutenant in the hope that he would be able to speak with more sense than her daughter.

"I'm going to turn myself in for desertion," he answered in reply to her questioning look. "Echo and I wish to be married in case . . ." He glanced at his betrothed, then back to her mother without finishing the rest of his statement.

The shaman did not need him to complete his sentence. She turned and gave her daughter a serious look. There were so many things she wanted to discuss with the girl before she gave in to their request, but judging by the determined looks upon the pair's young faces, her words of wisdom would go unheeded. "Are you certain this is what you want to do?"

With anxious smiles, Travis and Echo nodded agreement. "If we could just keep it as simple as possible," Echo said, "then, when Travis comes back, we could have the complete ceremony with all the customary procedures." Her voice hinted of the fear she felt about his return, but her smile did not waver as she tightly clutched his hand in hers.

With a sigh of resignation, Sky Dreamer agreed. All at once, she remembered Margaret, and how this impromptu ceremony might affect her other daughter. Her worries were not in vain when she saw the array of emotions simmering in Margaret's turquoise gaze. When Margaret caught her mother's troubled stare, she moved toward the doorway.

"I can accept this marriage, but please forgive me for not wanting to partake in it. I'll be with Kaytee." As she departed into the brewing storm outside the wickiup, Echo turned to go after her.

"No, Echo," the shaman called out. "She shouldn't have to be a witness to this wedding. Perhaps, when Travis returns and we have a big ceremony to celebrate your union as man and wife, she will be ready to rejoice with us."

Echo paused at the doorway as she contemplated her mother's words. It would mean so much to her if her sister attended her wedding, but she could understand why it would be for the best if she was not here. She returned to Travis and slid her arm into the crook of his. "Where do you want us to stand?"

The shaman raised her hands up in a gesture of confusion. She had never presided over a wedding ceremony that had not been preceded by all the proper preparations. And even then, as the tribal chief, Nachae had always helped her with the ceremony. "Well, I guess it doesn't really matter where you stand."

She glanced around the wickiup until she located her fringed rawhide bag of hoddentin, which contained cattail pollen and was an essential ingredient in all Apache ceremonies. As she approached the couple she began to sprinkle the fine powder over their heads, while speaking in a guttural Apache tongue used only by shamans. She then hung the bag of hoddentin on the belt which encircled her waist and reached out to clasp Echo's and Travis' hands. She crossed their wrists over one another as she spoke, this time in English as a gust of wind shook the wickiup.

"Neither of you will feel the wind after this moment, for you will each provide shelter for the other. The fears that plagued you are now shared and no longer as frightening, and from this day forward, you will never walk alone, no matter how many miles separate you from each other." A rolling bolt of thunder echoed through the wickiup, making its occupants jump in surprise. Sky Dreamer quickly regained her composure and finished the wedding verse. "I join you together as man and wife, and may Usen bless each day of your marriage with peace and happiness." She uncrossed their wrists and placed her daughter's smaller hand in the large palm of her new husband, a wistful smile playing upon her lips. "You are now married."

Travis Wade was too amazed to move for a moment. Making Echo his wife had been so simple. When he regained his senses, he turned and scooped his bride up in his arms, while allowing his lips to seek the sweet taste of her mouth in a kiss which sealed their union for all time.

"Take your wife to the wickiup where you stayed last night before the rain makes it impossible for you to leave and you will be forced to spend the night in this wickiup with your mother-in-law." Sky Dreamer

291

laughed when she saw the stricken look upon Travis Wade's face.

He grabbed his bride and headed toward the doorway in panic, but before he could drag Echo from her mother's hut, the girl pulled away from him and threw her arms around her mother's neck.

"I love you, Mother. And thank you."

Sky Dreamer called out that she loved her daughter, but the girl was already rushing out of the wickiup with her new husband. The shaman walked to the doorway and watched the young couple race through pelting rain to the wickiup where they would consummate their marriage. As her lavender gaze rose up to the dark, stormy sky, a shiver raced down her spine. The sun should always shine on a new bride: she remembered hearing that superstition somewhere. So, what did it mean when the heavens grew black and the sun retreated into the clouds in fear of the thunder and lightning?

Travis grabbed his bride as they reached their wickiup and halted her steps before they entered. He had no idea what the Apache customs were, but it was his people's custom for the groom to carry his new wife across the threshold of the first place where they would stay as a married couple, and he intended to abide by this custom. He swooped Echo into his arms without effort, and was surprised when she did not offer resistance. She merely snuggled into his embrace as though she belonged there, while he bent down and took her into the dark interior of the hut.

He set her down and gently wiped a streak of rain from one of her cheeks. His simple gesture made her tremble like one of the leaves that whipped across the

292

ground by the gale outside the wickiup. "Are you cold?" His voice was husky with the desirous craving her nearness had already aroused in him.

"No," she replied with a shy sideways glance of her blue eyes. She felt a heated blush come into her cheeks as she continued to wait for him to make the first move. They had been far beyond this bashfulness on many previous occasions, but now that they knew they would not have to stop for any reason, they were both suddenly hesitant.

Travis' most urgent desire at this time was to gaze upon her beautiful body and to know she was truly his woman for all time. He began to satisfy this craving by taking hold of the tie that secured Echo's skirt around her narrow waist and giving it a tug until it came loose and the garment slipped from the curve of her hips. The tiered skirt fell in a soft heap of bright colors around her tall moccasins. He then lifted the hem of her long tunic and slowly began to raise it over her hips and up past her waist. Since Apache women wore only the barest of garments in the heat of the summer, Echo had nothing under her outer garments. Once he had lifted her tunic, her firm bronzed body was completely exposed to his view.

The sight of long, lean legs extending up to where a downy patch of ebony hair drew into a soft V-shape between her trembling thighs caused Travis' knees to grow weak. The idea that he would be the first man ever to touch her in that secret area was even more unnerving. He felt his rising manhood strain against the material of his tight-fitting pants as it always did whenever they tempted fate, but now its demand for satisfaction was nearly beyond his control. He closed his eyes for a moment to regain his waning restraint, then, once he was able to continue, pulled the tunic

293

over her head and tossed it to the ground. Beneath his enraptured gaze, the tips of her youthful breasts came to pert attention of their own accord, yearning for the feel of his hard chest crushing them in intimate contact. His imaginary visions of her beauty were dimmed by the reality of the silken body shimmering in the faded light of the wickiup, and he could do no more than stand before her . . . made mute by the sight of her magnificence.

His long pause made Echo's shivering increase, due to anticipation and bashfulness. She could tell by the look on his face that he was not disappointed by her, but his intent study of her unclothed body was more than her innocent mind could tolerate. In defense, she crossed her arms over her bosom. Her action snapped him from his trance, and a slow grin burned across his mouth.

"I can't get enough of you, and I haven't even had all of you yet." He took hold of her arms and removed them from her breasts as he stepped up to her. Then he imprisoned her in his embrace. His mouth descended upon her lips and devoured them before sliding downward until it latched onto one flaming breast. His lips encircled the pleading kernel as his tongue drew it into a frenzy of longing, which suffused her whole body with an ache so great she cried out for satisfaction.

His tongue trailed a fiery path down her flat stomach as he lowered himself to his knees, then clasped his hands onto the gentle curve of her hips and pulled her down so that they were both resting upon their knees amongst the furs and blankets that covered the floor. The only barrier between them was his clothing.

"Undress me," he whispered into her ear.

Echo drew away from him. Her eyes were wide with

a mixture of passion and fear of the things she did not yet understand about this ritual. The shaking in her fingers increased when she began to undo the round brass buttons adorning his gray Army shirt. Upon reaching his waistband she stopped, but he did not allow her to quit disrobing him. He yanked his shirttail out of his pants and placed her hand against the shirt where two closed buttons still remained. While her fingers fumbled with the last of the enclosures, Echo stared directly into his eyes, mesmerized by his loving green gaze. At last, the buttons were undone, and she was able to push the garment back over his broad shoulders to reveal his bare chest. A scattering of dark blond curls beckoned her hands to caress them and to bury her fingers within their soft carpet.

He permitted her this indulgence for a short time, then led her hands down to the waistband of his pants. She pulled away the first time, but he tenderly drew her timid fingers back. Instead of pressing her hand against his belt buckle he allowed her hand to brush the bulging area where his anxious manhood throbbed for fulfillment. She gasped, but much to his surprise, her quaking hand remained, and slowly, carefully, began to rub the length of the swollen member until it was Travis' turn to cry out in ecstasy.

Her unexpected retaliation was his final undoing. Without taking any more time to engage in this enticing foreplay, he pushed her back among the furs and began to unroll the tall moccasins over her smooth calves and to slip them off her dainty feet. He then sat back and yanked his knee-high boots away from his own feet, but as he started to unbuckle his belt, she surprised him again by sitting up and doing it for him in such a sensuous way that he thought he might die of anticipation by the time her fingers were through assaulting his aching loins while doing away with his belt, unclasping the snap on his pants, and last, but certainly not least, sliding his pants down as her fingers ran in a tantalizing line down over his flaming abdomen.

Somewhere between the time they had first entered the wickiup and this sweet moment of unabashed desire, Echo's shyness had disappeared, and from her former, shy self emerged a woman who was about to discover the hidden secrets of her body and all the joys it was capable of producing. It was this woman who allowed her new husband to enter into her most private domain without fear or resistance. As she felt him lower his fevered body down upon her and position his taut hips between her legs, she braced herself—not in anticipation of the pain she knew she must experience when she first crossed the threshold of womanhood but for the absolute joy of giving herself completely to this man she loved so much she would suffer any amount of agony as long as she knew he belonged only to her.

With the tip of his enflamed organ barely touching her moist crevice, he felt her body arch upward as her natural urges took control. He kissed her again, deeply, entwining their tongues, to divert her attention from his first plunge, which he knew would cause her pain. And, when he felt her body recoil from the shock, he, too, was engulfed in hurt. There was no way to spare her this initial wound, but he had managed to demonstrate so much love beforehand, she accepted this anguish bravely.

When he felt her begin to relax slightly, Travis resumed his demanding kisses while the rest of his body fell into a gentle motion which slowly eased away the throbbing pain and began to turn it into the most thrilling experience Echo had ever known. Throughout the rest of the day, rain and wind pounded the sides of the wickiup, and for a time this mountain paradise was transformed into a land of stormy violence. But that was outside the little grass hut. Inside, the sun never ceased to shine brightly upon the blossoming love of Echo and Travis Wade.

Chapter Twenty

A chuckle rattled from Travis' mouth as he listened to his new wife explain the odd restrictions placed on the husband of an Apache woman. "You mean, if I intentionally look at your mother now that you and I are married, I might go blind?"

His laughter infuriated Echo, although she made no move to untangle herself from his intimate embrace. "Well, even if you do not go blind, it is the custom that you cannot stare at your mother-in-law and you should turn away from her whenever she passes by."

Travis thought the custom was ridiculous; but he could tell Echo was getting angry with him, so he forced himself to stop chuckling and concentrated on stroking her soft skin. Their first night as man and wife had been magical; it went beyond anything either of them could ever have imagined. They were suited to one another in every way, and throughout the night they had made love as if there would be no tomorrow; but the day was dawning in spite of their desperate attempts to make this night last forever.

"It has stopped raining," Travis said, listening for a moment to confirm his words. He remembered the ferocity of the storm that hit the mountain yesterday and lasted into the evening, but at some time during the sensuous hours of his wedding night, he had not paid it any more attention. Each second had become too precious to think about anything except the brief time he had left to spend with his bride.

Echo snuggled closer to him under the thick furs; yet she shivered anyway. She sighed when his arms tightened around her, but it was not the chill of the dawn that caused her slender body to quake. Usen had taken away the rain, despite her repeated prayers throughout the night that it would never stop. If the day was greeted by the hot sun, the barrancas would be dry within hours, and Travis Wade's departure would be imminent.

"I don't know if I'm brave enough to let you go."

Since their wedding, they had evaded any discussion of his journey, and Travis was not sure if he was ready to talk about it now. "Other than the custom of avoiding my mother-in-law, is there anything I should know now that I am part of your family?"

"Only that we can't avoid talking about it, that is, if you are still planning to leave today."

Travis knew he carried the burden of their whole lives upon his conscience as he contemplated his decision once again. "I'll be back. But until I am, I will always be with you"—his hand gently rested upon her heaving bosom, over the spot which contained her breaking heart—"in here, Echo."

She made a gallant attempt to hide her pain, closing her eyes to hold back the tears which had suddenly formed in them. She twisted onto her side and laid her head upon his chest. The blond curls on it provided a downy mattress for her cheek as she listened to the rapid pounding of his heart. "Will you always be in there with me?"

"Always and forever, even once I've returned to you."

Echo wished she could be as optimistic about his return as he pretended to be, even on the morning of his departure. But she had listened to her mother talk about their white grandfather's career in the U.S. Cavalry, and she knew the Army's disciplinary measures sometimes included punishment by death. However, Travis also knew this. Echo loved him all the more for possessing so much honor and bravery. Still, watching him leave her today would be the bravest thing she had ever done.

"How long do you think you will be gone?"

He shrugged. "Since I will be returning to the fort on my own accord, I am hoping the sentence will be light—perhaps a year."

"A year!" Echo cried. A year was too long; she would never survive a year without him. She clung to him under the cover of the furs like a frightened child, but no longer discussed his plans to leave. She tried to concentate on something else, on anything that would divert her mind from this sadness. As if they knew exactly what she needed her lips began to burn for his kiss. She raised her face up and gazed at him through the hazy morning light in the wickiup. When he glanced down and met her eyes, the dawn seemed to explode with the fire spewing from their yearning souls.

His arms pulled her up until the length of her body was stretched out upon his, while his lips drew hers into their enslaving hold. They had made love throughout most of the night, had only closed their eyes for brief periods of dozing. There would be time to sleep when they were apart. For now, nothing was more precious than being together, and loving one another again and

301

again with a ravenous hunger that would have to last until . . . maybe eternity.

While she buttoned up her husband's shirt Echo's hands were shaking as they had the past night when she had undressed him for the first time. She forced a smile upon her lips when she smoothed down his collar, then stood back to admire the handsome man she had chosen to marry. He had just returned from the river where he had indulged in a bath while Echo had gathered up the necessary supplies for his trip. His blond hair was still dark with moisture, though he had combed it back from his forehead. The stubble was no longer on his lower face since he had used a razor. Clean-shaven, he looked even younger than his twenty-five years. And when he gave his new wife the boyish grin which always melted her like ice on a sweltering day, it was all she could do to keep from falling to her knees and begging him not to leave.

"Chateo is ready to go," Sky Dreamer announced from the door of the wickiup, snapping the young couple's attention away from one another for an instant. The shaman did not linger at the doorway because she understood how important their time together was at this crucial moment.

"I guess this is—"

"Not goodbye," Echo cut in abruptly. "It's time for you to leave, but it will never be goodbye, Travis Wade."

He draped an arm around her shoulder and kissed her swollen lips one more time, then reluctantly led her from their honeymoon wickiup. The storm of the previous day had given way to a glorious sunrise, and before the morning was half over, the heat was scorching. Chateo and Travis had no reason to prolong their departure, for the barranca would be dry by afternoon. Their horses were saddled and loaded with

302

supplies, but both men lingered in the midday sunshine for a time before mounting their horses.

Kaytee stood at her father's side, while Sky Dreamer reassured Chateo that she did not mind caring for his daughter. Without actually saying it, however, the shaman also hinted that she expected him to return to his parental responsibilities after he had located her husband. Chateo tried to compensate for her fears by repeatedly telling both his daughter and the shaman that he would not be gone long. But while he spoke, his attention wavered and he looked around the *ranchería,* hoping for a glimpse of Margaret Sinclair whose absence was conspicuous.

"She refused to come out of the wickiup to say goodbye," Sky Dreamer said when she could no longer stand to watch his pained expression. "But I will give her a message from you if you wish."

Chateo hesitated as he was about to mount his horse; then, his face hardened with resolution, he swung into the saddle. His dark gaze descended to the face of the shaman as he retorted, "We have nothing to say to one another."

Sky Dreamer gave a shrug and backed away from the horse to put a comforting arm around Kaytee. She did not wish to cause this man more heartache by agreeing with him, but she knew he was correct. Last night, she had dreamed of Chateo and Margaret, and it was not the sort of musing she liked to remember in her waking hours.

The shaman glanced at Travis Wade and her other daughter. Their young faces were radiant with love but shadowed by deep worry. She wished she could see what the future held for them, but Usen had not granted her this insight yet. And in light of the *soldado*'s departure, Sky Dreamer decided she was glad not to have glimpsed their uncertain future. She smiled when she noticed how hard Travis Wade was trying to keep from looking in her direction. It was obvious Echo had told him of this ancient Apache custom, and he was doing his best to follow their rules. In spite of his attempt to be a good Apache son-in-law, Sky Dreamer approached him.

"Good luck, Travis Wade," she called out as he climbed atop his horse. Their eyes met for barely an instant as he gave a quick nod, then looked away.

Echo still held on to his hand as if she never planned to let go of him, even after he bent down and gave her one last lingering kiss which bespoke his endless love for her. "You come back soon, Travis Wade!" she said with a determined voice that trembled at the end of her statement.

With his fingertips, he tipped the large brim of the black hat she had given him that morning to shield him from the hot sun of Sonora. In the shadow of the hat, his mouth curved into the grin Echo would carry in her memory each second they were forced to remain apart. His jade eyes glistened with unshed tears, which he could not permit to fall because of his male gender. "I'll always be with you," he hoarsely replied as he pointed toward her heart.

Then, in a gale of dust and hooves, he twirled his horse around and followed Chateo toward the edge of the plateau. The three females watched them until they had become stick figures in the distance, then disappeared over the ridge and onto the steep trail below.

From the doorway of the shaman's wickiup, Margaret Sinclair also observed the men's departure. Her turquoise gaze was swollen and red from the crying she had indulged in while watching the touching scenes between Chateo and his daughter, and her sister and the lieutenant. She felt as though she did not belong anywhere or with anyone, and she wanted to blame someone: her parents who had once had a choice to live among the whites but had chosen the harsh life of the Indians, her sister for marrying the lieutenant, and that man himself for falling in love with the wrong woman! In her disoriented state, her thoughts turned to Adam Washington and her close friend Dona, even they must be to blame in some way. They had never trusted the white man's lies; yet they had allowed her to glide through life believing in a dream that would never materialize. Even Kaytee was to blame for having Chateo as her father!

Margaret Sinclair felt as though she had been betrayed by everyone, and, like a caged animal who longs to be free, her need to obtain her goal made her feel crazed and frightened. Yet, daily her desire to find an escape increased, and, like that caged wild animal, she waited for her chance to seek a solution—even if it meant biting the hand that fed her.

Less than two days had passed since the lieutenant and Chateo had passed through the barranca, but in this short time the whole area looked completely different. The deep gorges in the Sierra Madre had been created by the pounding rains that fell in this area, and the brutal elements constantly changed the face of the land. A river could appear where before a heavy rain there had been none; then the flood waters might disappear and leave a new barranca carved through the rocks amid a maze of stone cliffs.

Chateo rode in the lead, since he knew Sonora far better than the white *soldado*. Other than the barest of comments about their direction or when they should stop to water the horses and rest, the men found they were at a loss as to what to say to one another. As a result the four-day journey from the *ranchería* to the

305

American town of Bisbee was made mostly in an uneasy silence.

"You have not spoken of your plans, Lieutenant," Chateo said as he handed Wade a strip of turkey jerky from their food supply. "When we reach Fort Huachuca tomorrow, do you plan to turn yourself in right away, or are you going to wait until we have located your wife's father?"

Travis gnawed on the tough meat as he contemplated the next day. It was probable that the Apache chief was long gone from Fort Huachuca since he would not have found his daughter imprisoned there. From the fort, his trail would undoubtedly lead toward the Indian reservation in Oklahoma. But if the Apache chief and the comancheros accompanying him learned of Echo's escape en route to Fort Sill, they could be anywhere by now. Finding Nachae was a complicated matter the lieutenant did not need at this time in his troubled life.

"No use me going anywhere else. Fort Huachuca is where I was stationed when I deserted my command, and I might as well return to the scene of the crime."

Chateo was relieved to think that after tomorrow he would be rid of the *soldado*. He also understood the unlikelihood of catching up to Nachae and the comancheros, but since it was his excuse to escape from Margaret Sinclair and to learn how to deal with the pain she had inflicted upon him, he was not overly concerned with finding the Apache chief. His greatest concern was being forced to return to Pa-Gotzin-Kay and gaze upon the delicate beauty of Margaret, recalling the sweet memories of the afternoon by the river while knowing only ice surrounded her heart.

The night before Travis surrendered was torturous for him. He did not close his eyes once throughout the long hours. Several times he thought of getting back on his horse, hightailing it back to Pa-Gotzin-Kay, and giving up the notion of facing up to his crime. At the secluded *ranchería* he would never be found or heard from again. But that was too simple, and it was a coward's way out. The beautiful face of his young bride haunted him; he saw her on their wedding night, saw the way she looked when he had last gazed upon her face. It was these images which gave him the courage to ride into Fort Huachuca the next morning . . . and the hope of someday seeing her again and holding her in his arms for the rest of their lives.

"I don't believe it!"

Lieutenant Wade gave a disgusted sigh. It was just his luck to encounter Sergeant Roberts first off upon entering the fort. Their last visit had been less than friendly, and it was apparent the sergeant had not forgotten—nor forgiven—the lieutenant for cracking open his head with a rifle butt.

The sergeant drew his gun before the other man had a chance to do anything other than halt his horse in front of the officer's quarters. "Go ahead, shoot me and save me the trouble of a court-martial," the lieutenant said snidely. He had no patience for this man, and the memory of the sergeant's attempted rape of Echo made his hand itch to reach for his own gun.

"What's going on out here?" Captain Bailey asked as he exited from his office. The look on his face showed his surprise at seeing the lieutenant again.

"It's the deserter, Captain." An evil smirk twisted the sergeant's red mustache up. "Or should I say the squaw man?"

Travis Wade's body grew tense in the saddle, but he forced himself to give Roberts the satisfaction of retorting to his derogatory remark. "I've come to turn myself in for desertion, Captain."

"Put your gun away," the captain said to the sergeant with a tone of authority. "And, you, drop any weapons you have to the ground and dismount."

Lieutenant Wade complied at once, but the captain had to give Sergeant Roberts another challenging glare to impress his order upon the man. "I will handle this, and if I need your assistance, I will send for you." The commander turned away from the bristling form of the sergeant and directed his attention to the lieutenant. "I trust you understand that you are under arrest?"

"Yes, sir."

"Then it will not be necessary for me to call for the guards?"

"No, sir. I surrender willingly and without resistance."

The captain placed his hands behind his back and drew his brows into a thoughtful arch. His strong gaze leveled at the other man, he said, "You will be imprisoned in the stockade until I receive orders for your court-martial from Washington. The fact that you came back willingly will make your desertion charge much less severe. You could even get off with around six months."

The lieutenant drew in a relieved breath, but it became lodged in his throat with the captain's next words.

"Striking another cavalryman with a rifle butt, however, will possibly carry a very stiff penalty, perhaps even death by a firing squad. That is, if Sergeant Roberts decides to press charges against you."

In a stupor, Travis Wade allowed the captain to escort him to the stockade. The sergeant was still standing several feet away, since he had not followed the captain's orders, and his smirking face was filled with a deadly satisfaction. The lieutenant looked away and continued to walk, in a proud gait, beside the captain, although his entire being was numbed by the grim prospects he faced. His mind was spinning as the guards draped a chain with a twenty-five-pound weight attached around his ankle.

He had been worried about facing charges of desertion, but he had never stopped to consider the wrath he would encounter from his fight with the sergeant. Now it was too late to rethink his decision. He tried to stand on quivering legs after he was left alone in his dark cell, but the heavy weight around his ankle made walking too much trouble. He slumped back down upon the blanket on the floor, the only luxury he was allotted, and dropped his head into his hands. His thoughts returned to Pa-Gotzin-Kay and to his new bride. Had he made her certain of his vast love for her during their brief time together? Or would she spend the rest of her life alone, wondering if the loving words he had spoken to her were true? And thinking he did not keep his promise to return because he didn't want to. . . .

Chapter Twenty-One

Chateo lay flat on his stomach on the hill overlooking Fort Sill. He was in almost the exact location where he and Margaret Sinclair had observed the fort when they had come to it in search of Kaytee. As he had expected, Nachae and José Fernando's trail had grown cold. If they had traveled all the way to Oklahoma, it was apparent they were long gone from the fort by now. The activity Chateo could watch from the hillside did not hint of much excitement at this late afternoon hour.

He rolled over and stared up at the blue sky. Wispy clouds decorated its vast expanse in shades of white and light gray. They were not threatening clouds, rather they were the kind that made those who gazed at them fantasize about the pictures lurking within their depths. The soft outline of a woman's face began to take shape in one of the clouds, and Chateo immediately transformed the image into a vision of Margaret Sinclair. Her delicate beauty hovered in the heavens overhead and made him ache to know her touch once again. As he continued to study the imaginary woman, though, the cloud formations began to change, slowly merging into one another. Chateo searched them for her face, but when he thought he had found her, the edges of the gentle clouds began to turn black and stormy. He closed his eyes; he was afraid to gaze up again, knowing that by now he was bound to see the face of some sort of monster emerge from inside the beautiful image of Margaret Sinclair.

He grew angry with himself again. The main objective of his journey was to forget about that woman; yet how could he do this if he thought about her day and night? He forced her visage from his mind and turned his thoughts to his next course of action. Before he headed back to Pa-Gotzin-Kay he knew he should scout around the reservation to find out if Nachae had made it this far in his search for Echo. It would be dark soon, and he could sneak around the wickiups in the hope of overhearing something that might be useful. Until then, he would try to get some sleep, that is, if Margaret Sinclair would leave him alone for a while.

He awoke with a start, becoming confused for a time when he realized it was already growing dark. Aware that something other than the late hour had aroused him, and with a sense of impending danger, he remained as still as possible in the deep blades of grass. Close by, someone walked along the ridge of the hill. Chateo tried to remember if his horse could be seen from there, although it was too late to do anything about that anyway. The figure drew closer, but not close enough so he could see who it was. He hoped it was not a soldier from the fort because he was not a familiar figure around the reservation and his heavy collection of weapons would type him as an outlaw.

As he held his breath and waited to see where the person he'd seen was going, he heard a woman's voice call out through the dusk.

"Adam? Where are you going?"

"Just for a walk," replied the young man.

Chateo heard the youth stop as he waited for the young woman to catch up to him. He did not dare move, but if they walked much farther, they would step right on him.

"Do you mind if I join you?"

"You know I don't mind. Shall we sit here?" Adam motioned to a spot amid the gently blowing blades of grass, then waited until the girl was seated before he joined her on the ground.

Dona gazed out over the sprawling reservation. She placed her callused hands in her lap, then glanced quickly at Adam, waiting for him to speak.

He pulled a blade of grass out of the ground. As though it required his full attention, he carefully pulled away any traces of the dirt that clung to the bottom of it, then placed the blade into his mouth and began to chew on it.

"You still miss her, don't you?" Dona asked.

Adam stopped intently concentrating on the blade of grass for a moment. "Is it that apparent?" he asked himself. "I wonder whether or not she's alive, and if she is, I wonder if she's happy."

"Well, we know that she's probably with Katherine and her father." Dona sighed heavily and added, "But I doubt that she's happy. I don't think Margaret will ever be happy."

Chateo felt as though the blood that pulsed through his veins had stopped flowing as he listened to the young couple's words. Would he never be able to escape from that woman's web? Using extreme caution, he raised himself up enough to get a glimpse of the two people discussing the woman he was trying to forget. They were sitting only a few yards from him, but their backs were to him so they had not noticed his presence. Carefully, he lay back down when he heard the girl begin to speak again.

"I only hope Katherine's father will be good to both of them. Angry as I was at Margaret, I love her like a sister, and I do not want anything bad to happen to her."

Adam chomped down on the dwindling end of his blade of grass. He still loved her, too. And he was still madder than hell at her! "Do you think we'll ever see her again?" he asked, forcing his voice to remain calm.

With a shy sideways glance of her raven eyes, Dona gave her shoulders an uncertain shrug. "Maybe someday she will grow tired of running away from her Apache heritage."

Adam spit out a mangled piece of grass and tossed the remainder of the blade into the breeze. "I want to do so much good here, to help our people. As the schoolteacher, I have a good opportunity to do just that, but"—he turned to gaze at Dona—"all I can think about is Margaret." Suddenly, he felt the need to talk about her. "She'll never find anybody who loves her as much as I did and, I guess, still do." He shook his dark head in defeat and closed his eyes to block out the remembrance of Margaret's lovely turquoise gaze.

Not knowing the words to comfort her friend, Dona merely reached out and laid a comforting hand upon his shoulder. She wanted to tell him Margaret would come to her senses and realize she belonged here—with them. But, in reality, she did not think they would ever set eyes on Margaret Sinclair again. Margaret had desired freedom, and if she returned to the reservation, she would be forfeiting her dream.

"It's almost dark. Should we be heading back?" Dona asked in a quiet voice.

Adam nodded and pulled her up with him as he rose to his feet. He draped an arm around her shoulders as they began to descend the hillside. Admitting to Dona

314

that he still loved Margaret had not helped to ease the pain in his young heart, but it did help to know that she, too, still cared about Margaret. He did not want anyone to hate Margaret, in spite of the crazy things she'd said and done. Someday everyone would see the person he saw when he looked at Margaret Sinclair. Then all would know that her true beauty was inside, but even Margaret herself still had to discover this.

Chateo did not know how long he lay in the grass after the young man and woman had departed. The night had devoured the last of the twilight, though, and the glow of the moon shone through the clouds, which were still scattered across the Oklahoma skyline. The youth's words had left him dumbfounded. How many lives had Margaret Sinclair affected? Chateo wondered.

The soft whinny of his horse finally snapped him back to his senses. He no longer wanted to sneak into the fort. Besides, if Nachae and José Fernando had come this far, they would be headed back to Mexico by now. That was exactly what Chateo decided he would do as he stood up on his stiff legs. He had made an attempt to catch up to Nachae to tell him Echo was safe, but he had not been able to do so. Now he had to think of his own daughter. She was waiting for him to return so that they could conduct her puberty ceremony, and he did not plan to disappoint her again.

As he swung up on his horse's back, he reluctantly thought of Margaret Sinclair again. She was waiting at the *rancheria* too, but not for him, and it was time he accepted that fact. He felt sorry for the young Apache the girl had called Adam, because the youth had not yet learned how to deny his love for Margaret Sinclair. Chateo, however, was not going to permit himself to dwell on that woman any longer. He kicked his horse in the sides and repeated his resolution to forget about her. Maybe if he said it enough, he would be convinced

315

that he had done so by the time he returned to Pa-Gotzin-Kay.

Chateo crouched behind a large boulder and watched the activity in the gully below him. He was too far away to see the men's faces, but he had no doubt they were José Fernando and the comancheros who had been riding with him when he left the outlaw stronghold with Nachae. What worried Chateo was they were apparently headed back to their hideout, judging by the direction in which they were traveling, and Nachae's riderless horse was among the extra mounts that trailed behind the riders.

An eerie sense of foreboding filled Chateo as he scanned the shapes of the distant riders. If Nachae's horse was with them, where was he? Chateo knew these men did not hesitate to do away with anyone who got in their way. He himself had done the same for most of his life. Perhaps José Fernando had discovered Nachae's true identity and had decided the Indian's deception was the basis for murder. There were a dozen other reasons that could explain why the Apache chief was absent from his horse, but at this time Chateo could think of no good reason. Because of his feeling of uneasiness, he slumped down behind the large rock and waited until the band of comancheros and their leader had ridden the rest of the way through the canyon.

When he felt it was safe to show himself, Chateo took his horse by the reins and led it down into the base of the barranca. He glanced in the direction the outlaws had taken, then swung up onto his horse and headed in the opposite one. The bandits' trail was easy to follow because it was so fresh, and since it was early in the morning, Chateo was able to cover a great deal of territory by nightfall. Still, he found no hint of

Nachae's whereabouts. As he brewed a pot of strong coffee over a small campfire, Chateo contemplated the next day.

Every time he rounded a bend or rode over another ridge, he feared he would come across the body of the Apache chief, yet he could not give up his search, not after seeing the Indian's horse among the comancheros' extra mounts. More than anything, he did not want to have to relate any bad news to Nachae's family. As he drank the last of his coffee and reclined upon the hard ground, he decided that he would continue to look for Nachae for a couple more days, if no clues had turned up by then, he would be forced to return to the *ranchería* alone.

Chateo spent a restless night. Nightmares awakened him, then eluded him when he tried to recall them. By the time the first glow of impending dawn approached the distant ridge, he was up and ready to ride. Just as he was about to mount his horse, he thought he glimpsed something in the sky. It was not yet light enough for him to see far into the distance, but the fleeting shadow continued to plague him. He had planned to ride through the foothills today; since his attention had been distracted by whatever it was that drew his eyes toward the desert land beyond the barrancas and mountains, he decided to ride in that direction instead.

Once the sun had risen above the high ridges, Chateo was glad he had chosen this route. It was clear that there had been riders through this area recently, but as he continued to follow the trail, his happiness began to turn into apprehension. The shadow he thought he had seen earlier caught his eye once again, and now he could clearly see the ring of black buzzards that flew in a circle against the hazy blue sky. As he rode closer, the sounds of their squawking grated against his ears and caused him to shiver with dread. He could not yet see

317

what they were hovering over, but their intent was obvious. In the area below them, someone or something was either dead or about to die, and the vultures were greedily awaiting the meal they would derive from dead flesh.

The heat of the late summer day was scorching, still Chateo shivered visibly. He did not like the thoughts going through his head, and each step of his horse's hooves drew him closer to the object of the buzzards' interest, making him quake all the more. When he had ridden out of the maze of boulders and gullies, a vast expanse of white sand spread out before him, and Chateo got his first glimpse of the buzzards' next meal.

He approached the spread-eagled form, a sickening feeling inching its way through his body. From a distance the man was unrecognizable because of the dried blood that caked his face and body. A breechcloth shielded his loins, but that was his only article of clothing. At first glance, Chateo knew the man was the Chiricahua chief, and he was certain that Nachae was dead. Over the area hung an aura of death. The air felt too heavy to breathe, and the sun seemed to be hanging too low in the sky. The permeating quiet of the desert was broken only by the hollow sounds of the buzzards' wings flapping wildly against their bodies as they continued to circle the body staked to the ground. One vulture became braver than the others and took a plunge down toward the still figure. His sharp beak struck the man's chest where dried blood had grown brown and crusty, then the bird retreated. But his bravery had inspired the others to repeat his action, and all at once they charged down toward the man's body.

The buzzards' gruesome descent snapped Chateo into action. He sprang from his horse and ran out across the white sand, screaming and waving his arms madly in an attempt to detour the buzzards. His efforts worked for the time being; the birds scattered, although they did not go far. They hovered upon the ground a few yards away, watching the intruder with deadly black eyes that flashed in the bright sun like razors of death. Their mouths opened wide as they cawed and squawked in complaint at this intervention in their first meal of the day.

Chateo's sick feeling increased as he gazed down at the other man. The comancheros had staked him out as they would an animal hide left in the sun to dry out. The man had obviously been beaten and slashed with a knife before, or perhaps after, he had been tied to the stakes. Chateo squeezed his eyelids together to block out the horrifying sight. Not long ago he had practiced the comancheros method of torture and destruction without a thought of regret. But that was a part of his past.

He glanced around the area, ignoring the violent squalling of the vultures. There were no trees to make a travois on which to transport Nachae's body back to the *ranchería,* so he would have to throw the man over his horse. Without allowing himself to look at the chief's swollen and battered face, he untied the ropes, stiff with dried blood, that were binding Nachae's feet and wrists. Entering into Pa-Gotzin-Kay with the body of the dead chief was not something Chateo was looking forward to as he dragged the man toward his horse.

He was about to fling Nachae's body over the saddle, when the slightest noise rattled in the man's throat. The rattle of death, Chateo thought, a chill racing down his spine. But another sound came from the chief, a low, pain-racked moan that drew an ocean of sweat from Chateo's pores. Judging from Nachae's appearance, it did not seem possible he could be alive; yet he had made those sounds. Chateo lowered him back down to the ground and pressed his ear to the man's chest. He felt a weak vibration. Then he held his hand against Nachae's cracked, parched lips and smiled when a slight warmth met his touch.

When he'd thought the chief dead, his actions had been slow and hesitant. Now he had reason for haste, so he grabbed his canteen and attempted to give Nachae a drink of water. The chief's condition had deteriorated too much for him to be able to swallow any of it, however, and Chateo decided he needed to get him out of the merciless heat before taking the time to force water down his throat. He carefully raised the man over the back of his horse. Nachae's condition was critical, but there was a slim chance he would survive; and Chateo planned to do everything in his power to save him. He held the man's limp form on the back of his horse as he guided the animal toward the foothills with his other hand. At the base of the incline, he searched for some shelter, a place where he could tend the injured man out of the burning rays of the sun.

A rock alcove finally served his purpose. He slid the injured man down to the ground and dragged him under the overhanging rock. Nachae moaned again, and Chateo sighed with relief. He hurried back to his horse and yanked down his bedroll and the bags that hung from his saddle. As he started to rush back to the overhang, he remembered to secure his horse. On foot, he could never hope to get the injured chief back to the *ranchería*.

Using his bedroll for a cushion, he propped up Nachae's head and again tried to get him to drink water from his canteen. The chief was still unable to drink, and the water rolled from his swollen lips down the sides of his face. In another attempt, Chateo dampened the corner of a rag taken from his saddlebags and

320

squeezed the liquid through the man's bloody lips. Nachae's mouth started to open and close slightly as his constricted throat began to accept the liquid. Chateo sat back and wiped the sweat from his brow while a feeling of optimism flooded through him. The chief would probably survive the wounds inflicted by the knives and fists of the comancheros if he had not lost too much blood, but the desert heat was a demon. It would suck a man dry and mercilessly doom his soul to the pit of hell. Chateo still shuddered at the idea of Nachae being tortured by the evil-looking buzzards while still alive.

He took the rag and dampened it again, then started to wash away the sticky blood on the man's chest and arms. It seemed strange to be back in the company of one of his Apache comrades, but it also felt right. Chateo dug through his saddlebags again until he located the weathered old fringe bag he had carried since he had first become a warrior many years ago. In it was the medicine he would use on Nachae. He worked diligently over the man until he had packed all of his injuries with moxa—a compound of herbs used by the Apaches for open wounds. He then sat back against the wall of the alcove to await the results of his efforts to revive the chief.

Chateo had not intended to doze off, but he was startled back to consciousness when Nachae started to groan and try to move his injured body. He scooted over to the chief and glanced down at him. Already, the swelling in his face and lips was down, and his wounds had not bled through the packs of moxa, which was a good sign. "Try not to move around," Chateo said as he pushed Nachae back against the ground.

The chief's gray eyes were clouded with pain as he attempted to focus on the face that hovered above him. He did not know where he was, or with whom, but he knew he was grateful to be somewhere other than on the scorching desert where he had been staked out to die. His tongue felt as if it were too large for his mouth, and he was not able to talk because of the festering blisters that had formed around his lips. His spinning mind tried to recall how he had gotten out of the sun, but he was still too foggy and confused. He blinked several times and gazed up at the face of his savior. Recognition began to dawn in his throbbing mind before he fell back into the dark pit of unconsciousness again.

Chateo readjusted his bedroll behind Nachae's head and then crawled back to his own resting spot. When the chief was fully awake, they would have many things to discuss. Until that time, however, Chateo could do nothing but wait—and repeat his determined vow to forget Margaret Sinclair.

Chapter Twenty-Two

As an Apache shaman, Sky Dreamer could heal many kinds of illnesses, and she knew the proper roots and plants to use for injuries. But there was no medicine that could heal her daughters' broken hearts. The weeks which had passed since Travis Wade and Chateo had left the *rancheria* had not brought the sisters into close kinship again. The shaman tried everything she could think of to draw them back together, but though they all lived under the same roof, they just seemed to exist. There was no laughter or gossiping, no idle chatter late at night as they snuggled under the furs. The girls spoke to each other when necessary, and went through the motions of attending to the chores that had to be done. The rest of the time, however, a heavy silence hovered over the twins.

They were all worried; Echo feared she would never see her new husband again, and even Sky Dreamer had begun to doubt Nachae's return. Though Kaytee did not voice her worries, it was evident that she thought her father would not come back. Even Margaret, in her own way, worried about Chateo. She, too, hoped he would not desert Kaytee. To take her mind off her own depression, Margaret became the young girl's constant companion. Each time they went for a walk together, or Margaret went out of her way to do something nice for Kaytee, the shaman could see the pain of rejection in Echo's blue eyes.

"They have been together in the white man's world for the past eight years," Sky Dreamer said in an effort to comfort her other daughter.

Echo watched her sister and the younger girl huddle together in a fit of laughter over something which included only the two of them. She did not resent Kaytee in any way. She only wished that once in a while the pair would involve her in their activities. "I spent the first eight years with Margaret, but I guess that doesn't matter to her."

The shaman draped an arm around her daughter's shoulders. "Give her time to readjust. We always had one another, and though our homelands were taken away from us, we were still able to come here and go on with life as we had always known it. But the ones like Margaret and Kaytee thought they were alone, and nothing in their new world was the same. It's only natural they became so close."

Echo knew her mother was correct, and as she started to agree, she caught sight of two men cresting the ridge at the entrance to their *ranchería*. She gasped and pointed in the direction when she recognized them. "Father!"

Sky Dreamer swung around, overcome with emotion, but her joy faded to fear when she glimpsed the condition of her husband. Both mother and daughter raced toward the men, and within minutes they were accompanied by the rest of the villagers.

Chateo helped Nachae ease himself down to the ground, and held a supportive arm around him as he faced his wife. "I did not do such a good job of fooling those comancheros," he joked. Although it was apparent that he was in pain as he spoke, his gray eyes sparkled as he glanced from his wife to Echo. "And our brave daughter did not even need my help to escape."

Sky Dreamer forced a weak smile as she carefully placed an arm around her husband's waist, from the side opposite to Chateo, and began to ease him toward their wickiup. Before they had reached the hut, Nachae spotted Margaret standing among the crowd. As his smile broadened, he winced slightly. "We are truly a family again."

A small grin curved Margaret's lips when she met her father's gaze. Her joy at knowing he was home was genuine; yet she wondered if there would ever come a day when she would really feel part of this family again.

By the time Nachae was lowered onto the furs of his bed, his breathing was labored and his face was pale from pain, but happiness at being home was still evident upon his smiling face. His gaze lingered on his wife while she hustled around the wickiup preparing to administer the treatments known only to a shaman of her great powers. He reclined back against the soft hides when Echo approached him, a damp rag in her hand, to wipe his perspiring brow.

"I'm sorry you had to go through all of this because of my carelessness."

Nachae's brows rose slightly beneath her gentle strokes. "I understand from Chateo that I have a new son-in-law as the result of your capture and escape."

Feeling like an embarrassed child, Echo blushed a deep shade of red. "Y-yes." Her hand stopped in midair as a worried frown appeared on her forehead. "Are you upset that I chose a white *soldado* for my husband?"

The little lines starting to form around his eyes crinkled when he grinned up at his daughter. "I hear he is a good man who will not betray us, and we determine

325

a man's worth by his goodness, not his skin color." He winced again when Sky Dreamer began to rub a thick salve into his knife wounds. "Where is Morning—"

"Margaret," Sky Dreamer interrupted. "She wants to be called by her white name." A perplexed expression appeared on the chief's face as his wife continued. "I will explain it all to you later. Now I want you to rest so that you will be in fine form for the puberty ceremony of Chateo's daughter. While you were gone we made all the preparations."

Nachae remained quiet on the subject of his daughter's name, although he could tell by the tense expressions of those present that something was gravely amiss. Besides, he silently told himself, a name is not important to an Apache anyway. As he had just told Echo, it was what was inside a person that mattered.

After he had rested, the Apache chief told the others about his adventures of the past few weeks. He also told them that he had been foolish to trust the comanchero called José Fernando. The outlaw leader had been sincere enough when they had crossed the border to look for Echo, but upon their return to Sonora, he had demanded to know where Nachae's farm was located. Nachae had made up a lie about his home, but José Fernando had called him a liar and had ordered that he be staked out in the desert to die. Nachae told his enthralled audience how glad he was that he had not found Echo while he was with the bandits, or the outcome might have been much more tragic.

Echo shuddered at the possibilities, and agreed with her father that things had turned out for the best, with the exception that Travis Wade had become a deserter because of his love for his captive. Each day that passed since his absence became more difficult for Echo, especially with her sister's refusal to bridge the gap in their relationship. Echo tried to busy herself helping with Kaytee's approaching ceremony in order to take her mind off her husband and her sister, but it was in vain. Day and night she was in Margaret's company, and was forced to deal with her indifferent attitude. The relentless heartache that caused only increased her longing to be reunited with her green-eyed *soldado*.

Preparing Kaytee for the puberty ceremony meant conditioning the young girl for womanhood. Everything involved with the celebration must be done precisely and required a great deal of work. Temporary dwelling structures were erected in a large clearing not far from the *ranchería*. One wickiup was used for preparing and storing food, another for gifts and clothing. Two more wickiups were constructed, one for Kaytee, the second for the shaman. They would stay in these special wickiups for several days prior to the ceremony.

Chateo busied himself with making a cane for his daughter to use during the ceremony and later on in her old age. This was made from a straight branch; he stripped the bark before bending one end into a curve that was secured with a strip of rawhide. He then gave the cane to Sky Dreamer so that she could paint and decorate it with the various Apache symbols that represented long life and the power to protect the girl from illness. The thong of rawhide was adorned with ribbons and eagle tail feathers before the cane was given to Kaytee on the eve of the ceremony.

Along with her special cane, Kaytee was gifted with an important necklace that consisted of two long tubes tied to a chain of rawhide. From the hollow stalk of a cattail plant, the shaman cut a tube for Kaytee to drink liquids from, and a slightly longer one for her to use for scratching herself whenever she had an itch. It was the

Apache belief that if the girl scratched herself with anything other than the scratching stick, her skin would become blemished, and if she did not drink from the straw at all times during the ceremony, a dense growth of hair would erupt upon her face.

Once Kaytee was given her necklace and cane, there was no more work involved in the preparations, so a social dance commenced around a large bonfire as soon as the sun began to fade from the sky. The actual puberty ceremony would not begin until dawn; it was the only spiritual ceremony the Apaches did not begin in the nighttime.

Through the flickering lights of the fire, Chateo watched the sad face of Margaret Sinclair as she wandered aimlessly among the villagers. She had helped to prepare the festivities, but it was obvious by her woeful expression that she was not enjoying the music or activities. For one crazy instant, Chateo thought of asking her to dance. Just as quickly, however, he came to his senses. Undoubtedly she would decline, so why should he set himself up to be stepped on again?

"You and I have a lot in common where my sister is concerned."

Chateo jumped at the sound of Echo's voice. He had not heard her approach because of the music made by the drums and the singers. He turned his attention to the young woman, and marveled again at the beauty of all the women in her family. If only all three of them could be as gentle and kind as Echo and her mother. "If you mean that we are both invisible to her, then yes, I suppose we do have something in common."

Echo attempted to smile, but the gesture appeared to be more of a pained grimace. "I don't know what else to do. I care so much for her, and I only want her to be happy." She suddenly twirled around to face Chateo,

328

her expression pleading. "What can we do for her?"

The difference between the two sisters had never seemed so immense to Chateo until this minute. He tried to imagine Margaret feeling this much agony because of Echo, but he knew that selfish young woman was not capable of this much compassion where her sister was concerned. "There is nothing we can do," he answered sharply. He saw Echo's lips tremble with disappointment at his harsh tone, and he again became filled with anger at Margaret Sinclair. "Nobody can make her happy until she learns how to cope with reality."

A calmer expression came to Echo's face as his words began to make sense to her. Margaret's wish to live among the whites, as she had in Pennsylvania, was only an elusive dream. Reality was facing up to her Apache heritage, and once she accomplished this, she could learn how to be happy. Echo just needed to figure out how she was going to help her sister face reality. She glanced up at Chateo again and met his unwavering gaze as she nodded her head in agreement. The slight gesture caused her to grow dizzy, and all at once the heat from the bonfire seemed to invade her like a flaming torch. She weaved back and forth for an instant before she felt him grasp her to prevent her from falling.

"What is it?" he asked in panic. "Are you ill?"

Echo closed her eyes until the faint feeling passed. She took a deep breath and opened her eyes again, then waited until her head stopped spinning before she attempted to speak. "I-I'm fine, now." She rubbed her throbbing brow with her fingertips. "I guess I've just been overworking myself to take my mind off other things."

Chateo continued to hold her until he noticed some color begin to come back into her cheeks. He knew she was telling the truth about her busy schedule, because every time he had glimpsed her lately, she had been working like a woman possessed. "Would you like me to help you back to your wickiup? Or at least allow me to go for your mother."

"No, I'm all right." She cast her eyes downward in a moment of embarrassment over his concern, then began to back away while she forced herself to laugh as though this feeling of faintness was a common occurrence. "Maybe I just need to concentrate on having fun, instead of worrying about my sister."

Chateo allowed her to pull free of him, but he continued to watch her with concern. "Would you like to dance, then?" In the glow of the firelight, Chateo could see the blush that rose in her cheeks.

"Oh, no! I do not think it would be proper."

He huffed with aggravation over the Indian customs, which he had discarded during the years he had been away. "I only wish to dance with you because I appreciate all that you have done in preparation for my daughter's puberty ceremony. Surely, one dance would not cause us to be cast from the tribe in shame?"

Echo hesitated, then glanced around at the dancers who dominated the area around the fire. She knew she was being foolish to think a dance with this man would be harmful. "I would like to dance with you," she answered, quickly glancing in his direction.

She twirled around and walked to the ring of dancers as he followed closely behind her. He positioned himself with his back to the fire, while he faced his dancing partner. When Echo took a step forward, Chateo stepped backward, then he skipped to the front while she retreated from him. They were careful not to touch, because touching while dancing was taboo among their people. When the chanting of the song

330

ceased and the drumbeat faded out, the dancers took a break.

With a quick bow to Chateo, Echo walked at a fast stride away from the fire, and took her place at her parents' side. He followed her from the dancing arena, and paused before the chief and his wife. "Your daughter is very light upon her feet." As his gaze fell on Echo, he contemplated mentioning to the shaman that her daughter might be in need of medical attention. However, since it was obvious that Echo was now fine, he decided to remain silent on the subject.

Echo drew in a relieved breath when Chateo retreated without telling her mother anything about the dizzy spell she had experienced earlier. She did not want her mother fussing over her when it was not necessary, especially since she was certain her momentary weakness was due to nothing other than overwork, as she had told Chateo. She settled back among the pile of furs that had been arranged for her family to sit upon and glanced out toward the fire. When she saw Margaret standing in the orange glow of the flames, she was surprised. Her sister's icy glare was focused directly on her, and it was apparent that Margaret was furious at Echo for some unknown reason. Her mouth was drawn into a straight line and her hands, held at her sides, were clenched into tight fists. Even Nachae and Sky Dreamer had become aware of Margaret's brooding presence. But as Nachae started to rise to find out the source of his other daughter's obvious rage, Echo stopped him.

"Wait," she called out as she grabbed his arm. "I think I should talk to her myself." She stared back into the flickering light and met her sister's piercing glare with a look of determination.

Nachae paused as he tried to decide what he should

do; then, when he felt his wife tug gently on the bottom of his long tunic, he sat down. Margaret's fury was obviously directed at her sister, so perhaps this was one of those times when a father should not interfere, Nachae decided.

Echo suspected Margaret's anger was caused by the dance she had just shared with Chateo, but she did not understand why that should upset her. Margaret had not shown any interest in Chateo since they had come to Pa-Gotzin-Kay. The only man Margaret seemed to worry about was the lieutenant, and as far as Echo was concerned, she would not discuss her husband with her sister.

Echo closed the short distance which stood between her and her sister with several long strides, stopping when she was only a couple of feet from her. She opened her mouth to ask Margaret what was wrong, but her twin never gave her a chance to speak.

"I wonder how the lieutenant would feel if he knew his bride was dancing and having so much fun while he sits in prison because of what he did for you." Margaret's eyes flashed like turquoise jewels as she met the other girl's gaze on the same level.

Her words stunned Echo. It seemed to her that Margaret did not approve of anything she did. There had even been times in the past few days when Echo had felt Margaret was jealous of her participation in the preparation for Kaytee's ceremony. Now, though, Echo was not sure whether Margaret's anger had been brought on by feelings she still harbored for Travis Wade or whether it was due to something else—such as a jealousy of any female who associated with Chateo.

"Is there something between you and Chateo?" she asked as the thought passed through her head. After all, those two had been together before they had reached Pa-Gotzin-Kay, and maybe they had been more than just traveling companions. This had not occurred to Echo until now.

Margaret's face contorted into a mask of fury at her sister's inquiry. She stepped forward, though she was not yet certain of how she would answer Echo. Chateo answered for her, however.

"There is nothing between this woman and myself," he spit out in a hateful tone of voice as he focused a chilling glare on Margaret. They stared at one another with equal animosity for several seconds; then Chateo tossed his long black hair over his shoulder and turned to Echo. His face softened at once, though his eyes could not disguise the anger that still simmered in their depths. "I'm sorry if our dance caused you any problems."

Echo glanced at the hateful expression on her sister's countenance and felt a bolt of dread shoot through her. "It has caused me no problems." She stared at Margaret for an instant longer, then swung around, anxious to flee from the fury she could not understand.

Chateo watched her departure before once again turning his attention to Margaret Sinclair. "Surely you were not jealous because I danced with your sister." His tone was snide and did not harbor any hope that her reason for attacking Echo was what he had just insinuated.

Margaret's eyes narrowed with rage. She wanted to strike him, or at least think of something to say that would reflect how she felt; but nothing came to mind because she was not sure how she did feel. To avoid saying something stupid, she spun about and stomped away.

Her behavior confused Chateo more and more each time he was forced to be in her presence, but he decided he was not going to allow a selfish woman like Margaret to distract his attention from his daughter's puberty ceremony. When he had nothing better to think about, he would allow his thoughts to dwell on Margaret Sinclair.

The morning of Kaytee's puberty ceremony dawned clear and beautiful, without a trace of clouds in the vast Sonoran sky. Pa-Gotzin-Kay lived up to its meaning— "Mountain Paradise"—as the sun rose over the red earth and blessed it with a warmth that radiated across the land like a blanket of peacefulness. Chateo stood beside the Apache chief and his twin daughters as he watched his own daughter emerge from the wickiup in which she had been residing for the past few days.

Chateo was not alone in his admiration of the girl, for she looked beautiful in an elaborately decorated suede dress, which had been sewn for her to wear on this special day. With her cane clutched tightly in her hand, Kaytee walked to the center of the arena, where a buckskin had been spread upon the ground. She smiled proudly at her father as she began to dance upon the animal hide with light, bouncy steps. Drums began to pound, and Kaytee touched the base of her cane down upon the hide in rhythm to their beat. The long fringe of the ceremonial dress Kaytee wore swirled around her tall moccasins, and her long bluish black hair floated about her shoulders like the branches of a young willow swaying in the breeze. Chateo thought he might burst with the pride he felt for his beautiful daughter.

The puberty ceremony concerned Changing Woman, a mythological figure of great powers who never grew old. During the puberty ceremony, her invisible presence gifted the young girl with the secrets of youth and longevity. Kaytee laid her cane down and knelt upon her knees on the buckskin. This act was to symbolize the recreation of Changing Woman's first menstrual cycle. Kaytee went into a trance and began to sway from side to side as she raised her hands up toward the sun. Beside her, the shaman chanted an ancient Apache song and danced in small easy steps around the animal hide.

Kaytee then allowed the shaman to lay her down upon the soft hide, and to massage her legs and arms to give her strength. When Sky Dreamer had finished rubbing the girl's limbs, she helped Kaytee to her feet and stuck the cane upright in the dirt so that it stood unaided. The shaman then began another guttural chant as Kaytee danced around the cane. Each time Sky Dreamer finished a chant she would move the cane farther away from the buckskin and stick it into the ground. Kaytee would then repeat her dance around the cane, while the shaman resumed her chanting. After four such sequences, Kaytee had passed through the four different sections of life, which Changing Woman represented: infancy, childhood, adolescence, and adulthood.

Sky Dreamer led the girl back to the buckskin and began to sprinkle both her and her cane with hoddentin. She then bent over and picked up a colorfully woven basket filled with kernels of corn and other dried foods, which she dumped over Kaytee's head to ensure that the girl would have plenty to eat in the future. The completion of this action transformed the rest of the ceremony into a holy rite. All then crowded around the shaman and the girl so that they could sprinkle the sacred pollen upon the girl and allow themselves to be blessed as well. The Apaches each made a wish, since it was strongly believed that Changing Woman's presence during this time would grant them anything they wished for.

Echo had no problem deciding on her wish, and in this moment of joy and rebirth, she felt confident she would see her green-eyed *soldado* again. In fact, as soon as the ceremony was completed she planned to speak to her father about fulfilling her wish. She glanced around at the smiling members of her tribe and was overcome with happiness. It had been a long time since any of the females had been of the age to undergo the puberty ceremony. Echo, in fact, had been the last of the young women to have such a celebration, and her ceremony had been conducted several years ago. She realized that Margaret had missed out on this important ceremony, since the white men did not allow the Indians to follow their tribal customs at the school where she had grown up. Echo was filled with sorrow for her sister once again at realizing all the things Margaret had missed in the past eight years.

Margaret ignored her sister's sad look. Though she could feel the other girl's eyes upon her, she turned away and waited impatiently for Kaytee to finish with this nonsense. While the rest of the tribe had been making wishes, Margaret had been thinking of how stupid all these customs seemed to her now. The white men at Carlisle had been correct in their ruling that the children should forget these ridiculous ceremonies. Still, something hidden deep in Margaret could not stop her from making a frantic wish, although she knew it would never come true, regardless of Changing Woman or anybody else.

In the final phase of the puberty ceremony, Kaytee took the buckskin she had been standing upon and threw it toward the east. Sky Dreamer then handed her three more hides, which Kaytee tossed in three different directions to assure that her people would never be cold or hungry. Kaytee's young face was radiant when she turned to her father and gave him a smile that melted his heart with love. He held out his arms as she hurled herself against him. A mystical aura seemed to cloak all of Pa-Gotzin-Kay, and it seemed that nothing bad could ever happen to anyone who resided on this magical plateau of red earth.

Chapter Twenty-Three

"It's not too late to turn back if you want to change your mind."

Echo gave her father a stern frown for a reply. He had made that comment at least a dozen times since they had left Pa-Gotzin-Kay. Each time, she continued to stand by her decision to go into Arizona to find out what had happened to her husband after he'd turned himself in at Fort Huachuca. Though they had made this trip many times, neither Nachae nor Echo enjoyed this journey as they had in the past. An uneasiness prevailed over them because of what had happened the last time they had crossed the border. Their thoughts were also clouded by fear of what they would find out when they reached Fort Huachuca. This time, however, they had brought Hako and Chateo along, in case they encountered any trouble.

The Apaches knew they would have to be extremely cautious, because it had not been long since Echo had been a prisoner on the post. They had to find a way to obtain the information they sought without permitting themselves to be seen by anyone, and this was a goal they had not yet figured out how to achieve.

"We'll be outside Fort Huachuca by nightfall,"

Chateo announced. "Has anyone come up with a plan?" The rest of the group did not reply. "I think there is only one way to find out what happened to the lieutenant, and that is to go directly to the guardhouse and see if he's there." He still did not receive an answer from anyone else, since his suggestion sounded like a death sentence for the one who walked up to the guardhouse. Chateo did not bother to elaborate on his idea when no one granted him any acknowledgment. However, since no one else had thought of a plan, he figured his was the best so far.

They made a dry camp without a fire a couple of miles outside of the fort's boundaries, then settled down in the dwindling twilight to discuss their next move. Echo sighed heavily as she sat down and wiped the back of her hand across her sweating brow. She was accustomed to excessive riding. Why, she had practically been born on the back of a horse while en route to a new site for their tribe's *ranchería*. Still, she couldn't remember feeling so fatigued and sore from a day in the saddle. Determined not to allow this exhaustion to interfere with her plan to see her husband, she was careful to hide her condition from her father and the other two men, even though she'd caught Chateo eying her suspiciously on several occasions in the last few days.

"Somebody has to sneak into the fort, and it should be tonight so we can be gone by tomorrow, before anyone suspects we were here." Chateo was confident his idea was the only logical thing to do.

Nachae drew his dark brows together as he thought over the other man's words. "I'm afraid Chateo is right. It would not be feasible for me to dress as a Mexican and walk around the fort without arousing someone's attention. So, the only other alternative is for one of us to sneak in while it's dark."

"I'll go," Echo said. She had not traveled all this way so that she could return to Mexico without at least making an effort to see her husband.

Nachae huffed with annoyance at his daughter's suggestion. "I think one of us should go in alone," he said to the other men, ignoring his daughter's impulsive suggestion.

"I'm not afraid to go alone," Echo insisted. Her determination drew the aggravated stares of all three men. Their patronizing expressions enraged her. "I will not leave here until I speak with, or at least see, my husband."

"It's too dangerous," Nachae retorted as his face grew angry. "I will not permit it!" His lips drew into a firm line, but his gray gaze began to soften the longer he glared at his daughter. Her large eyes emitted the same defiant glow he had seen in her mother's violet gaze at least a hundred times. He knew he was about to be overcome by this wisp of a woman, and he was powerless to do anything about it. "I'll go with you," he said sheepishly. The Apache chief avoided looking at the other two men, although he could feel their shock, sense their gazes upon him.

A victorious smile started to claim Echo's lips, but she immediately suppressed the impulsive gesture. Her father might change his mind if she gloated over her victory. "I'll do whatever you say," she said in a humble voice.

"We'll wait until the hour is past midnight, then sneak into the fort as close to the guardhouse as possible. Each cell has a small window with bars. If the lieutenant is there, we should be able to get a glimpse of him." He leveled his gaze at his daughter and drew his expression into a fierce frown. "If we are able to find him, it is important for you to remember that we must be quiet. There can be no tearful reunions or long

341

drawn-out conversations. If we can talk to him, we will. If not, we leave." Echo opened her mouth to speak, but the chief waved his arm through the air in a gesture that always signaled silence. "I will not allow you to take any chances that might place you in greater danger than you will already be facing. You told me you only wanted to know whether he was still alive. If we see him, we will know this."

Echo knew better than to disagree with her father so she remained silent. If her husband was in the guardhouse, and within hearing distance, however, she did intend to talk to him, at least long enough to tell him how much she loved him.

None of the group slept while they waited for the moon to be high enough in the Arizona sky so that the chief and his daughter could begin their perilous task. To Chateo and the warrior, Hako, this mission seemed far too dangerous and unnecessary. They felt their chief had allowed his daughter to overrule his common sense; yet neither of the two men dared to tell him this. Instead, the two accomplices positioned themselves in a heather-hued swale of prairie grass not far from the spot where Nachae and Echo entered the grounds of the fort.

Since this was no longer such dangerous country, the fort was quiet and not heavily guarded. The Apache chief and his young daughter walked onto the grounds without encountering anyone. Even the two guards who were supposed to be on duty were snoring loudly at their posts. Nonetheless, neither Echo nor her father was able to relax within the confines of the white man's domain. They hunkered along in the deep shadows provided by the barracks, proceeding cautiously until they were outside the back of the guardhouse.

Echo glanced toward Nachae expectantly, wondering what they would do now that they had made it this far.

342

He also appeared to be at a loss, and was silently reprimanding himself for giving in to his daughter's foolishness and thereby placing them in this precarious position. He leaned forward and whispered through clenched teeth, "This is entirely too dangerous." He glanced at the row of barred windows lining the back of the guardhouse.

Echo's gaze traveled along the same wall her father had scanned, and she feared he was correct. Still, she would not turn back until she knew she had looked in every one of those tiny windows. Without replying to her father's statement, Echo crept up to the first window and raised up on tiptoe to peer inside. The little cubicle was pitch-dark, and she had to stare inside for several minutes until her sight adjusted to the blackness. The little room was empty, and a bolt of relief, entangled with disappointment, raced through her. She backed away, but avoided looking at her father again as she moved to the next window. As dozens of fluttering wings floated around in her stomach, Echo stretched herself up to look between the bars.

Without warning, a loud gasp flew from her mouth when she glimpsed the blond head of Travis Wade in the far corner of the cell. Her father immediately pulled her away from the stucco building and gestured for her to be quiet. Although the night was dark, Echo could not mistake the worry his face revealed. "He's in there," she whispered, almost frantic.

"We must go!" Nachae's gaze flickered back and forth through the dimness of the night as his tension increased.

Echo tried to pull away from him, but he held her too tightly. She knew better than to try to talk any sense into him; still, there was absolutely no way she would leave without speaking to her husband.

Nachae leaned close to her to keep his whisper low.

343

"You know he's still alive. That's all you need to know." He started to drag her from the area when a low voice halted their footsteps and filled them both with terror until they recognized its source.

"I must be dreaming," Travis said as his eyes reached through the dark night beyond his cell window. He had not been asleep, for he rarely slept since he had turned himself in; and when he thought he'd glimpsed his young wife through the barred window, he'd been sure it was only his imagination. Even now, as he looked upon her shadowy form, he doubted his own eyes. For the past couple of months, since the beginning of his incarceration, he had been thinking of nothing other than his beautiful wife. Now he feared this sight of her was just an illusion, an extension of his constant musings.

Echo and Nachae stared, wordlessly, at the pale face in the window. Travis' sudden appearance had shocked them into paralyzed states. When Nachae's senses returned, he glanced around to see if the commotion had caught anyone else's attention. Echo felt his grip grow lax, and she took advantage of the opportunity to escape from her father and run up to the window. Travis' hands were holding onto the bars; she reached up to them. The feel of his warm skin was like a jolt of lightning to her slender form. A loving smile curved her lips as their eyes met through the bars, and her blue gaze glistened with unshed tears in the darkness.

Although her gentle touch was proof he was not dreaming, Travis still found it hard to believe she was really before him. He pressed his face against the cold metal of the bars so he might be as close to her as the barrier permitted. "Why have you come here?" he whispered, letting go of the bars and wrapping his fingers around her small hands. "It's too dangerous."

"I had to know what happened to you. I couldn't go

another day without knowing."

Love for this young Apache woman exploded within Travis as he gazed into her eyes. Her devotion to him had put her in terrible danger, but they were together, able to confirm their love for one another, even though that entailed incredible risk. "Oh, love, I can't tell you what it means to me to see you again, but I would die if something happened to you as a result." He released one of her hands and tenderly stroked her cheek through the narrow opening. "Please, go!" His pleading whisper almost became too loud, but he caught himself.

Echo retaliated by imitating his gesture and reaching out to caress his stubbly face. She had never thought love could be so painful; to be separated from him again would be devastating. "When will you return to Pa-Gotzin-Kay?"

Face pressed against the bars, he spoke. "I was lucky. I was only tried on the charge of desertion. Sergeant Roberts declined to press charges against me for hitting him with the rifle butt because several of the other men threatened to testify on my behalf."

"I-I don't understand?" Echo asked, trying to recall the events on the night the lieutenant had come to her rescue.

"The men who were under the sergeant's command when you were being taken to Fort Sill didn't go for his dragging you off and attempting to rape you. They were prepared to testify at my court-martial about his despicable actions."

Echo's surprise was evident as his words filtered into her mind. Knowing the way most white men felt toward Indian women, she would have thought the *soldados* would have applauded the sergeant's actions. Then she looked at the handsome face of her blond husband, and she understood. Because she knew her husband was such a fair and kind man, it was only natural his men would not turn their backs on him if they knew the truth. She, too, would do anything for this man.

"In that case, how long do you have to stay here?" she repeated as she balanced herself on tiptoe so their faces were almost touching through the bars.

"Only six months! But Sergeant Roberts is hellbent on revenge, and he's always trying to find fault with everything I do." His hand fondled her face, while his mouth burned to feel the touch of her soft lips. Having her this close yet not being able to hold her in his arms was the greatest torture he had ever known. "But don't worry. I don't let him get to me, and I won't be here that much longer. I've already served nearly two months of my six-month sentence."

His words were filled with hope, and his feelings of optimism slowly began to rub off on Echo. There was more she wanted to tell him, though, so much more. She glanced toward her father, who was standing at the corner of the building, his rifle drawn, in case their presence was discovered. Her gaze returned to the handsome face of her husband. He would be back to her in little more than four months, and until then he had enough to worry about without her adding more to his burden. Still, she debated whether or not her news would be a burden or something that would make his imprisonment a little bit easier.

"Somebody's coming!" her father said in a voice that was almost too loud to be considered a whisper. He fell back against the wall and held his breath as he listened to approaching footsteps clicking against the wooden planks of the walkway in front of the guardhouse. The steps paused. Then the sound of the guardhouse door opening froze Nachae and the young couple in their tracks. The footsteps echoed down the corridor as they

346

approached the cell. Travis had barely turned from his wife before the door at the end of the hallway opened. He swung around, but did not make an attempt to flee back to the narrow cot he had been allotted for sleeping. There was not time, and such a rash action would be all the more suspicious.

Echo's terrified gaze flew to her father. He was frantically motioning for her to duck away from the window, but she had only enough time to crouch down on her knees before she heard the sound of another man's voice.

"Lieutenant?" the soldier held his lantern up and peered into the dark cell. Flickering light shimmered across the narrow space and hit the prisoner in the eyes.

Travis threw a hand over his eyes and moved away from the window. "I can't sleep." He clutched the tall bars that served as the doorway to his cell. "Don't suppose I could talk you into getting me something to drink?"

The soldier hesitated a moment as he pondered over whether or not he was allowed to do this for a prisoner without being ordered to do so. He held the lantern up higher and stared into the lieutenant's face. "I don't reckon it would matter if I gave you a small vial of whiskey or something. That always helps me when I can't sleep."

A look of gratitude broke out on Travis' sweating countenance. "I would be eternally grateful, and it would be just our secret."

The young soldier gave a quick nod before twirling about on the heels of his tall boots and setting off to retrieve the whiskey. Travis did not move again until he heard the front door slam shut. He then took a couple of long strides, which had him back to the window. "Echo, you must leave—now!"

The urgency in his voice caused her blood to turn to

347

ice. Leaving him was inevitable, but she did not want to go. Through the narrow space between the bars, she reached for him again. She needed to touch him just once more before her reluctant feet would allow her to leave. He grabbed her hands and pressed his face against the bars once more as Echo strained to meet his lips with her own, but he was just out of reach. Their mouths could not touch. She felt the heat of his breath against her face, and even when he released his hold on her, the feel of his touch lingered on her skin. She drew her hands against her breast as though she could preserve the feeling forever if she did not allow the night air to steal it from her.

Her father was tugging on her arm, pulling her away from him. "I love you, Travis Wade," she called out in a hoarse voice. It didn't matter that she was no longer whispering. She was sure she would die of a broken heart, even if the soldiers did not catch them before they were able to sneak back out of the fort. "I love you!"

Travis opened his mouth to tell her that he felt the same way about her, but she was already gone. He stared at the spot where she had been standing only an instant before, and reached out through the bars to touch the empty air that had just been filled with her beautiful presence. "I love you, Echo Wade," he whispered to himself.

Echo was barely aware of the rapid departure she and her father made from the fort, their feet flying across the dark desert ground. She heard the voices of Hako and Chateo when they joined them and continued to race toward the horses, but she did not pay attention to their conversation. Her thoughts were still with the man she had left behind in the fort, with her husband, whom she loved more with each frantic beat of her shattered heart. Four months sounded like an eternity to the young woman, especially since four months would make such a drastic difference when he saw her again. She swung up into her saddle and began to follow the men as they galloped their horses through the flat expanse of desert which led toward the Mexican border.

By morning the four riders had crossed the invisible barrier that divided the property of the United States from the lands of Sonora, and it was not until then that they stopped to rest. The three warriors were jubilant over the successful infiltration of the fort, and they savored the excitement of the mission by discussing it over and over, each time making it seem more dangerous than it had actually been. Life at Pa-Gotzin-Kay did become mundane at times for its occupants, and recapturing just a bit of their past glory was cause for celebration. Echo could not help but feel the edge of their excitement as she listened to them talk about past raids and victories. Their stories were a part of her legacy, and though she had taken a white man for her husband, a part of her Apache blood boiled like molten lava when her wild spirit was set free to roam through the memories of her people's savage and glorious past. Eventually, she knew, the past must merge with the future, and like the crisp leaves of autumn, memories must crumble and turn to dust. So the tales of these proud Apache warriors, stories of battles and gory victories, began to summon up memories of those who had died for a war that had led nowhere.

Echo lay back against the bedroll she had spread upon the ground and relived, in her tired mind, each of the tales the men had just related. She could look at the past now without recalling so many painful memories. Knowing Margaret had not been killed had something to do with it, though she had resigned herself to the fact that she would never regain the closeness she had once shared with her twin. But she had someone else now, someone who was closer to her than anyone had ever been. Echo's mouth curved into a grin as she thought of her green-eyed husband. Four months, only four more months. She tenderly placed her hand upon her flat abdomen where the seed of their love already blossomed with a new life. She still wondered if she had done the right thing by keeping this a secret from Travis, but he would be back at Pa-Gotzin-Kay long before the baby was born. Echo sighed as she allowed her weariness to overcome her, and as she fell off into an exhausted sleep she clasped her hands tightly over her breast in the hope of recapturing the feel of his last touch . . . a touch that stretched across the miles which separated only their physical beings. Because they would always be together, just as he had told her they would be before he had left Pa-Gotzin-Kay. With this thought in mind, Echo's hand rested over her heart, where he dwelled at all times. She closed her dark blue eyes in contentment as visions of their promising future welcomed her to dreamland.

Chapter Twenty-Four

The Apaches referred to the month of April as T'aa'-nachil, meaning the leaf buds are swelling. The high country had paid its dues during the winter months of snow and cold, and now the land was reborn in vibrant shades of green and in blossoms of every shade of the rainbow to dazzle the senses and eyes of those who gazed upon them. Echo sat upon a rock at the base of one of the high ridges overlooking the trail that led to Pa-Gotzin-Kay. She had started going there every day since the snow had begun to melt. On her perch she waited, watched, and prayed that one day soon she would look down the narrow path and see a lone figure moving up the mountain.

She lived for the day when her blond green-eyed husband would come back to her. It had been nearly eight months since he had been sentenced to serve only six months for desertion. So, where was he? She carefully readjusted her position on the rock and rubbed a hand across her swollen stomach. It was her greatest hope that Travis Wade would come back to her before the birth of their child, but the time was growing near, and with each day that passed, Echo grew more doubtful about his return. She could only come up with two reasons why he was not yet back, and both were causing her more distress than she could cope with at this critical time in her pregnancy. Perhaps he was not able to come back to her, even though he desperately wanted to do so. If he was hurt or ill, she couldn't bear the thought of not being with him. He could even be dead! And there was always the chance that he had decided he did not want to return to Pa-Gotzin-Kay. Maybe the six long months he'd spent in the guardhouse had caused him to rethink their impulsive marriage and the hasty plans they had made for the future. Maybe . . .

Echo gasped in surprise when the baby inside her kicked violently against her ribs as though protesting the thoughts going through its mother's head. She held onto her rounded abdomen as she rose to her feet and began to lumber back up the trail at a slow walk. Her mother had told her not to venture out of the *ranchería,* and Echo had promised her that she would not come down the trail anymore, since the weight of her child did not allow her the mobility she had once possessed. But this morning everyone had gone out into the fields to work on the spring crops, leaving Echo to tend to the menial chores around the wickiup. It was impossible for her to concentrate on anything other than her husband, and watching the trail for any sign of him was the only thing she wanted to do.

When she'd come down the trail she'd felt fine, in spite of her awkward condition and the treachery of the narrow path. Now, however, she felt flushed and tired. The idea of climbing back up the mountainside seemed overwhelming, and she began to wish she had followed her mother's strict orders to stay at the *ranchería* where she belonged. She placed a hand over her eyes to shield them from the bright rays of the sun and glanced up toward the crest of the high ridge. Why did I come down so far? she asked herself with aggravation. Since she had no choice other than to go back up the same way she had descended, she knew she had better get started. She had no intention of telling anyone she had been foolish enough to come down here again today, and the quicker she got back to the *ranchería* and rested up, the easier it would be to convince the others that she had not left the wickiup all day.

After only a couple of steps, though, Echo knew her return trip would not be as easy as she had hoped. The trail was steep, and the winter snows had left it littered with loose rocks and gravel that had not yet been beaten down by constant use. With her balance so unsteady, Echo had to move at a slow pace, stopping every few steps to catch her breath and regain her balance. The baby felt heavier than usual and seemed to be pressing down in her pelvic area with more weight than she remembered feeling before. She squinted in the sunlight as she looked up to see how much farther she still had to climb. To her dismay it seemed as though she had not progressed at all.

Not far above her, a section of the pathway ran along a stone escarpment with a scattering of small trees sprouting from its sides. To the other side was a drop-off to several shelves of rock, the ledges layered like stone steps before they ended above a fall of a couple thousand feet into a deep rock quarry. Echo drew in a sigh of relief when she reached this area because she was able to grab onto the little trees protruding from the embankment on the one side and pull herself up, with the help of the branches. She clutched onto one of the skinny trees and heaved herself up a couple more steps, then reached out to take hold of the next branch. That, however, was not as sturdy as the first one. The newly sprouted tree was barely more than a twig, and its fragile roots were pulled free the instant Echo tugged on it.

Ordinarily, the young woman would have had no trouble regaining her balance on the rocky trail, but due to her protruding midsection, her feet did not respond with the quickness they once had. Echo stumbled backward, and even as she tried to regain a firm footing, she felt herself going backward over the cliff. Everything that happened next seemed to be occurring in slow motion. She began to tumble down the stone embankment. Somewhere off in the distance, she thought she heard a shrill scream, but she was not aware that the sound tore from her own throat. She tumbled downward, her heavy stomach slamming against rocks and gravel, until she came to rest on the flat area of the first stone ledge.

Echo landed on her stomach, and the tremendous pain that seared through her rendered her almost incoherent. Dirt and rocks blocked her mouth when she tried to cry out for help, and the pain in her abdomen was so intense it nearly stole away the energy she needed to get her mouth clear. She managed to cough to rid herself of the dust which threatened to choke her; still, nothing but a horrified cry came from her throat. Thinking straight was not possible because of the terrible pain she was experiencing, and because she was more frightened than she had ever been.

Lying on her stomach was unbearable, and she knew she had to get the pressure off her unborn baby. At first, she feared her arms or legs might have been broken in the fall, because not one inch of her wasn't screaming with horrendous pain. Slowly she raised her quivering arms to support herself and, with an agonizing movement, managed to roll over onto her back. The midday sun hit her in the eyes, although her gaze would not focus on the burning glow of the rays because the pains shooting through her blinded her

354

from seeing anything clearly.

Echo began to cry, though she was unaware of her sobs, for she was consumed with terror at the idea of injuring her baby. For a time, which seemed an eternity to her confused mind, Echo lay on the narrow strip of rock and tried to make her spinning senses clear so that she could decide how badly she was hurt. She forced herself to take a series of deep breaths so her mind would function again and she could concentrate on the source of her pain and on her surroundings. Since she was able to move her arms and legs, she determined that none of her limbs had been broken as she had first thought. But the crushing pain had localized itself solely in her abdomen, and it was so great that if she was hurt anywhere else, she did not think she would even be aware of it.

Echo's breath caught in her throat as she attempted to overcome her increasing fear. She was certain the fall down the cliff had done great damage to her unborn baby; still, she did not understand why she was in so much pain. She only knew that somehow she had to get back up to the *ranchería* and seek help before the baby was hurt any worse. Through glazed eyes, she tried to see the edge of the trail she had fallen from, and when she realized how far down she had rolled, another knot of terror rose up in her chest. With the pain she was experiencing, she knew she could never hope to climb the sheer wall of rock that towered at least ten feet over her head.

She also knew she could not just lie where she was. With all her energy she attempted to push herself up from the hard ground, but just as her shaky arms had managed to raise her heavy body to a sitting position, pain cut through her with such intensity that Echo was paralyzed for the length of time it lasted. She wanted to scream for help, but the sound was stolen from her

355

throat when her insides felt as though they were being ripped apart. She fell back against the ledge in a heap of agony. She knew she could not crawl out of there, and she now understood why the pain was so strong.

Echo's mind was finally able to grasp what was happening, although the awareness only increased her horror. The fall had induced an early labor, and when she felt the hot, sticky blood gushing out of her, she realized her baby was about to be born on this mattress of stone. Then another powerful pain sliced through her. She knew very little about the birthing process, because there were not many babies born on Pa-Gotzin-Kay, but she knew enough to understand that because of the brutal fall this birth was not progressing in a natural manner.

Everything was happening too fast, and there was entirely too much blood. Her skirt and the ground beneath her were soaked with the dark red substance, and the pains were excruciating, beyond anything she could tolerate. A tortured scream tore from her lips, for release from the pain and because she desperately needed help. As though Usen had suddenly noticed her grave need, the pain began to subside, until she was able to think coherently. She told herself that she must try to control her fear or else her baby would never have a chance of survival. For the brief time when the pains released her from their horrible grip, she began to pray for her child, and for the courage to face this trial which her own foolishness had brought upon them.

A calm began to settle over the young woman as a short time passed without the unbearable pain. She was able to think about the impending birth of her child without the panic that had previously consumed all her her energy. That the baby was going to be born on this ledge, and that she was going to have to get through this on her own, was inevitable, but she did not want her baby to die because she was too frightened to do anything to help herself. Nor did she want to die. As she felt the onslaught of another pain, she summoned up all the courage she possessed, and forced herself not to fight against the jagged pain, which felt as though it was intent on destroying her.

Echo's fear quickly returned, however, when the pain did not go away. She tried to scream again, but the sound only lodged in her throat once more and was lost to the depths of the canyon below. She clutched the hard ball of her stomach and drew her knees up when an excruciating pressure began to swell within her. Nature had taken control of her senses and was prodding her to push this child from within her, but Echo was overcome by such terror of being ripped in two that she began to fight against the downward pressure with every ounce of her strength. Her battle only caused the agony to grow, until she could not cope with it, and a blackness so deep engulfed her that for the instant when she fought to retain consciousness, Echo was certain she was taking her final breath.

"Will you go back to the *ranchería* and check on your sister?"

Margaret gave her mother a dark frown, but she did not voice her reluctance to do as Sky Dreamer asked. With a bored sigh, she rose from the ground where she had been pushing little seeds into little holes in the dark red earth. Every day it seemed they did the same things, and none of them seemed to mind that there was a whole other world below this stupid mountaintop! Margaret gathered up the hem of her tiered skirt and started back through the grove of blossoming orange trees. Their sweet scent filled the air with a soft citrus smell, and she drew in a heavy breath of the heady odor.

As she stomped back toward the village, she began to formulate a plan. She had been here throughout the whole winter, and had actually managed to pretend that she accepted her life here. But, in truth, her desire to find some other way to live had only increased as the cold months passed. Despite her family, who went to great lengths to try to make her happy, Margaret hated being here. She felt isolated from life. Here, nothing ever changed, because to these people, nothing existed outside this *ranchería*. She knew she would never achieve the contentment everyone else found at Pa-Gotzin-Kay, and this left her with only one option . . . to go somewhere else.

"Echo?" Margaret switched her thoughts away from leaving for a moment as she searched the empty wickiup for her pregnant sister. Coming to terms with losing Travis Wade had been easy as she'd watched her twin grow fat with his child. The same thing might have happened to her if she had pursued him. He probably would have left the Army and wanted to live on some farm or something, while she had one baby after another. Margaret wrinkled up her face in disgust at the idea of looking as swollen and ugly as Echo.

Then she set her hands upon her hips in an aggravated gesture and glanced around the *ranchería*. Where was she? Certainly, Echo had not gone too far, not the way she waddled around these days. Margaret sat down in a narrow strip of shade that bordered one outside wall of the wickiup and sipped some tea left over from the morning meal. Her thoughts returned to the day she would be able to go back to the world of the living, which was anywhere besides here. She made up her mind that the first person going down the mountain would have company. Regardless of where the Apache was going, she was going, too. Once she was off this forsaken shelf, she would find a way to make a living and continue with her original plan of living a life of freedom—free from her Indian bloodline.

Margaret smoothed back her long, ebony hair and contemplated her uncertain future once again. She could still pull it off, once she figured out where she would go. Staying in Mexico was not feasible, she decided. She did not know enough of the Spanish language, and she did not care to learn it. Across the border was where her heart still remained, in the cities of the white man's world. She'd thought a great deal about Adam and Dona during the long winter months, and although she hated to admit it, she missed them more than she'd ever thought possible. Eight years of constant companionship was not easy to dismiss, and though Margaret balked every time the idea passed through her head, she found herself wishing she could see them again.

"Where are you?" she said out loud in an irritated tone. How far could Echo waddle? she asked herself as she finished up her tea and rose to her feet. All at once she was struck by a strange feeling that washed over her like a flooding river. Her feet froze to the ground as she waited for the sensation to go away. But it did not leave, the intensity faded somewhat, then slowly inched through her body like a heavy blanket covering her with a sense of foreboding. She had not experienced this sensation for a long time, but she could recall how it would come over her when she had been a child, before she had gone to live at Carlisle and had been told to dismiss her foresight as nonsense. The affinity of being a twin hit Margaret like a cannonball. For the first time in many years, she felt reunited with her sister, and as close to Echo as she had been in their mother's womb.

Margaret's mind snapped into action once she no

longer had to wonder where Echo had gone—she knew exactly where her twin was, and she also knew her sister was in terrible trouble. In a blind panic, Margaret started to run toward the edge of the cliff, to the top of the trail that led from the mountain *ranchería*. Her feet moved as though they had a will of their own, although she had to slow her rapid descent because the trail was slick with loose gravel. Half-sliding and half-running, Margaret made her way down the pathway. With reluctant eyes, she forced herself to look over the edge as she moved along, because she knew that she would see Echo somewhere below.

As she continued down the trail the fear in her breast ballooned. How far had Echo gone, and how far over the cliff had she fallen? Margaret's entire body felt tingly and strange, as if sharp little needles were pricking at her skin. But not once did she hesitate or wonder if she was going the right way. A powerful force was leading her down the trail and telling her of her twin's desperate situation. An increase in the adrenaline which pulsed through her signaled that Echo was near, but it wasn't until Margaret leaned over the jutting edge of the trail that she was able to get a glimpse of her sister.

Without thinking about her next actions, Margaret turned in the direction of the *ranchería* and began to scream for help. She quickly realized, however, that no one would hear her because they were all too far away. In confusion, she spun around on the narrow path as she tried to think of what she should do. Her mind told her she should climb back up the trail and go out into the fields to seek help, yet a sixth sense told her there wasn't time. From the top of the ledge, she could see that Echo's body was badly mangled from the fall, and it seemed that she was unconscious. It was the sight of all the blood soaking through Echo's torn skirt, though, that kept Margaret from deserting her sister.

In the next instant, Echo's head began to move slightly, and as Margaret watched in horror, her twin regained consciousness within the clutches of a pain that even Margaret felt within her loins. Echo was about to give birth, and Margaret realized she was the only one who could help. Frantically, she glanced around the small area on the trail. There was no way to reach Echo other than to slide down the face of the stone wall. Margaret leaned forward and peered down into the vast canyon that stretched out below the steplike ridges where Echo lay. Margaret thought it a miracle the girl had not continued to roll on down the ledges and into the deep chasm below.

In another bolt of pain, Echo was yanked back from the darkness into which she had tried to retreat, and her pain-racked scream forced Margaret to spring into action. Taking a deep breath, she fell down onto her knees and eased herself backward, over the side of the ledge. She held her body stiff and rigid to prevent all of her weight from hurtling her downward. Her fingers dug into the dirt and rocks at the edge of the trail as she squeezed her eyes shut and prepared to turn loose. She could only hope that she would fall to the first ledge gently and not tumble back over to the next. With determination, she braced herself for the fall and let her hands slide over the edge.

The ledge was less than a dozen feet below her, but to Margaret, it felt as though she fell forever before the bottoms of her feet struck solid rock. She slumped down to her knees to keep from swaying backward, then held her breath for a moment longer until her spinning head caught up to the rest of her trembling body. Echo was close enough to be touched, so

Margaret reached out a hand and laid it upon her sister's forehead, an overwhelming feeling of love washing over her. Even in the clutches of her horrendous pain, Echo sensed her sister's presence. She tried to focus on the face hovering over her until her foggy gaze was able to make out the features of her twin.

Echo did not have the energy or the time to tell her sister the fleeting thoughts rushing through her mind, because another pain knifed through her and rendered her speechless. The knowledge that she was no longer alone made the pain more tolerable, however, and it helped Echo to concentrate on getting this unbelievable agony over, rather than fighting against it. She permitted herself to bear down with every fiber of her being, in the hope that she could expel the pain from her body.

Margaret screamed in response to her sister's pain when she realized the baby was about to be born. She scooted around Echo until she was in position to raise her sister's tattered skirt. Margaret was not prepared, though, for the sight that greeted her horrified eyes. Nor did she have time to think about her next act because there was only enough time to catch the slippery body of the baby that tore from inside her sister in the next instant. For a moment, no one made a sound, even the child seemed to be stunned by its rude entrance into this world.

Margaret was the first one to snap back from the shocked trance that kept her staring in horror at the infant in her palms. She had no idea that a child was born with a coating of its mother's blood, and all she could think of was that the baby was dead and so was Echo. When the baby moved slightly in her hands, it startled her so badly she almost dropped him. Her gaze flew up to her sister's face, and she was amazed to see that Echo had survived this incredible ordeal, too. Echo even managed to speak in a raspy voice.

"Is . . . is the baby all right?"

Margaret directed her attention back to the child, now beginning to squirm and cough slightly. Except for the blood, he seemed perfect in every way. But, in the following second, she realized he was choking on the phlegm in his mouth. In panic, she used her fingertips to clean mucus from the baby's tiny mouth until the infant was able to let out a robust cry that echoed over the deep walls of the barranca. That cry was the sweetest music either of the two sisters had ever heard.

"Your son is perfect, Echo," Margaret said in a tearful voice as she cradled her new nephew in her arms, being careful not to injure the umbilical cord that still connected him to his mother. "He's just perfect!"

Relief flooded over Echo, and a rush of tears followed it. Never had she imagined so much pain as that which she had just survived, yet the words Margaret had spoken erased all but the lingering pain, which was nothing when compared to what Echo had previously experienced during her child's actual birth. She had a son . . . Travis' son, and he didn't even know of the baby.

Margaret had no idea what she should do for her sister or for the little boy, so she joined Echo in a bout of tears that lasted until their eyes met through tear-filled gazes. A smile began to break across Margaret's face as she realized how unnecessary all their crying was now that the baby appeared to be healthy and even Echo's condition did not seem so grave. She glanced down and was relieved to see that the enormous amount of blood, which previously had been pouring out of her sister, was reduced to just a trickle.

"You saved our lives," Echo said in a whisper.

363

Margaret shrugged as she glanced at her sister again. "Everything was almost finished when I got here."

Echo winced as she tried to shake her head in disagreement. "I was so filled with fear, I was sure my heart would not complete another beat. But once I realized you were here, I knew everything would be all right." She reached out to her sister, adding, "You were my courage. I know, without a doubt, I would have died in the final seconds of this child's birth if you had not appeared as you did."

Since Margaret was too choked up with emotion to reply, she remained silent. She certainly did not feel as though she had done anything other than catch the baby as he emerged from his mother's body, and she was only grateful to have gotten to her sister in time for that small accomplishment. She placed the little boy in his mother's outstretched arms and attempted to hold back the new rush of tears provoked by the tender sight of Echo's first glimpse of her newborn son. Margaret had forgotten how miracles were created, but in this joyous moment she felt as though she were reborn.

Chapter Twenty-Five

"I don't suppose saying I'm sorry about everything that happened would make you feel much better, would it?"

"No, sir," Travis Wade repeated as Captain Bailey handed him his gunbelt and the same set of release papers he had handed him two months earlier. He stuffed the papers in his shirt pocket, exactly as he had done once before, then placed his gunbelt around his hips and buckled the front.

"Are you sure you're able to ride?" the captain asked when he noticed Wade grimace as he bent over to pick up his hat from the bed.

Travis' pale face grew flushed as he straightened up and placed the hat on his head. His actions were agonizingly slow as he positioned the crutch under his arm. "I can ride," he answered with determination. Two months of lying in an Army infirmary was enough wasted time. Using the help of the crutch, he limped to the door and paused before he departed from the fort hospital. He glanced back over his shoulder at the captain. "I don't mean to act as though I'm angry with you. I appreciate what you did for me."

The captain cleared his throat. "I understand." He

followed the other man out onto the veranda and watched as the ex-lieutenant struggled with his stiff leg to mount his horse. The cavalry was losing a good man in Lieutenant Wade, the commanding officer repeated to himself. Although the captain did not understand the lieutenant's love for an Apache squaw, he still wished things had turned out differently. He raised his hand and waved when Travis balanced himself in the saddle and then kicked his horse in the side with his one good leg.

Travis Wade returned the man's gesture as he turned his mount around and began the same journey he had started eight months earlier. As he left the boundaries of Fort Huachuca, he finally exhaled the breath he had been holding ever since he had mounted his horse. Maybe this time he would make it all the way to Pa-Gotzin-Kay, and back to his beautiful young wife. A shooting pain in the leg which dangled uselessly at his horse's side reminded him of the reason for his delay and caused a shiver to race down his spine . . .

"Squaw Man!" He could still hear Sergeant Roberts' greeting as he exited from the guardhouse on the first day of his release. "Hey, Squaw Man, where you goin' now? Bet you're headed back to that hot little Apache gal, that is if she hasn't found herself some—" Travis still filled with rage as he recalled how he'd rushed at the sergeant to put an end to the man's scathing remarks about his wife. He'd shoved Roberts up against the wall of the guardhouse, then remembered that he was a free man now, and if he allowed his temper to get the best of him, he would end up right back in jail—this time for murder. He released his grip on the smirking sergeant and backed away.

"What's the matter, Squaw Man? Are you afraid to hit me again?"

Travis finally understood why Roberts was so

anxious to provoke him. He was still hankering for revenge over not being able to charge the lieutenant for striking him with the rifle butt. If the sergeant could make Travis hit him again, he could seek justification. Travis Wade did not intend to allow that to happen, however. He had a wife waiting for him, and he told himself nothing was going to prevent him from going back to her. He turned and started to walk off, but he had not counted on the extent of the sergeant's wrath. Nor was he prepared for the next challenge Roberts presented.

"I won't let you walk away from me, Squaw Man," the sergeant spat out in a voice that signaled he was about to do something drastic.

Travis Wade whirled around in time to see Captain Bailey emerge from the doorway of the guardhouse and hit the sergeant's arm just as the man drew his gun. The interference by the captain sent the sergeant's bullet astray, but it still managed to strike the target. Travis felt his knee shatter from the force of the bullet, but that was the last thing he remembered when he awoke in the infirmary, where he would spend the next couple of months in agony—not only from his destroyed knee cap, but because the time necessary for recovering from this injury prevented him from being reunited with his wife. His only consolation was that Sergeant Roberts was now occupying the same cell he had vacated. The charge of trying to shoot a man in the back was more severe than the lieutenant's charge of desertion. However, Travis Wade had no desire to linger at the fort until the execution was held.

With the military post out of sight, he finally had his first sense of total freedom in a long time. His injured leg hindered his riding ability, however, and he knew it would take him longer to reach the *ranchería,* but by this time next week he would be with Echo. He worried about the thoughts that must be going through her mind, but he knew she would not be angry once she saw him. He envisioned the first night they would spend together, the passionate ways he would reaffirm his love for her. A useless leg would not get in his way, he told himself once again.

The horrible dreams had not plagued Margaret since she had discovered her family was still alive. But on this first night following the birth of her sister's son, and the rescue of the two sisters and the child from the ledge, Margaret's slumber was once again intruded upon by the fiery fingers of her worst nightmare. The details had not changed; Margaret's terror held her immobile as she watched her village burn to the ground. Her ears still filled with the bloodcurdling screams of the dying, and heavy black smoke suffocated her when she tried to cry out for help.

As Margaret fought to awaken from this latest nighttime horror, however, her body filled with an unusual sense of calm. She stopped tossing and turning on the furs on which she slept, overcome with a strange urge to remain in dreamland for a few seconds longer. Her misted gaze strained through the heavy veil of choking fog as the smoke slowly began to part. In a stupor, Margaret watched, wide-eyed, as the burnt ground began to turn into a carpet of lush green grass. Beyond the walls of smoke and destruction she could see a small stucco building. Her mind grew confused. Why would a white man's structure appear at the edge of the destroyed Apache *ranchería?*

The calm atmosphere prevailed as Margaret continued to watch the smoke ease away, leaving no traces of the brutal ambush upon her village. The force which had rooted her to the spot began to move her feet forward, through the gentle waves of deep green grass. She stopped before the building, a sense of excitement coming over her. Was this the home she had been searching for . . . her home in the white man's world?

She watched in growing anxiety as the front door began to open, but her confusion returned when she did not see the beautiful furnishings she had expected to find in its interior. Instead, the room was filled with rows of school desks and the walls were lined with chalkboards rather than rare paintings and exquisite wall hangings. Margaret started to turn away in disappointment, but the doorway was shadowed by the figure of a young Apache man. He stepped into view, and when his gaze met Margaret's, his raven eyes glistened like fiery black diamonds. He held out his hand to her, but Margaret did not make a move as she stared at his outstretched palm. She sensed her future would be decided by the choice she made in this new dreamland.

She was afraid to make this final decision. Accepting Adam's hand would mean leaving behind her dreams of living as a white woman. Margaret began to thrash about under the furs in agony. A feverish sweat coated her smooth skin when she bolted awake and sat up to focus on her surroundings. She was still in her parents' wickiup, not standing before the school on the Indian reservation, but her dream had been so vivid, she had to rub her eyes and glance around one more time. Why would her nightmares take such a dramatic turn? she wondered. She then reminded herself it was only a dream and nothing more.

Through the doorway of the wickiup, she noticed that the sun was already up. Her parents were undoubtedly with Echo, in the wickiup used for the sick or injured. Echo certainly fell under both of those categories after her ordeal yesterday, Margaret decided as she dragged herself out of bed and prepared to pay a visit to her twin and her new nephew. She tried to shake off the lingering images of her strange dream, but they clung to her even after she had left her wickiup and headed toward the sweat lodge to see Echo and the baby. She stopped short when she met Chateo coming out of the wickiup.

"You did a good job," he said as he strode up to Margaret. She was an overnight hero among the villagers for sliding down the face of the cliff to come to her sister's aid.

She shrugged and kicked at the ground with the toe of a tall moccasin. It was still difficult for her to be in Chateo's presence, because she had not yet forgiven herself for making love to a man she did not feel anything for, other than a physical attraction. Even now, she still had to admit she was strongly drawn to him. But she did not love him, and that made her past behavior seem wrong. "The baby is awfully small," she said, hoping to sound nonchalant. "But he wasn't due for several more weeks," she added as she glanced up at him.

Chateo nodded and looked down at the round hole she was digging in the dirt with her foot. He did not know how to dismiss the uneasiness that prevailed whenever they were in one another's presence. "Both Echo and the boy are doing well this morning, though." He sighed, not knowing what else to say. "I suppose I'd better get back to Kaytee since I will be gone for a while."

His comment filled Margaret with panic. "Are you leaving?" she asked.

He shrugged his shoulders. "I'm going away for a short time. I can't seem to get this restless spirit out of my soul." His dark gaze flew up to Margaret's startled face as he quickly added, "But I'm not going away for good. I will never desert Kaytee again. The village is in need of supplies, and I volunteered to go after them."

A strange sensation inched through Margaret's being as images from her recent dream sprang into her mind. Chateo saw the odd expression on her face and grew concerned. "Is something the matter?" he asked with genuine concern.

Margaret's turquoise eyes rose to take in his handsome face, a silent plea written in their jeweled depths. "Will you take me with you?" she blurted out without thinking her decision through.

For an instant, Chateo's hope flared. He thought perhaps she was asking the question because she wanted to be with him. Almost as quickly, though, he realized she was still trying to escape from herself and this life she was trapped in. For no logical reason, his thoughts drifted back to the conversation he had overheard on the hillside above Fort Sill. Rather than wishing Margaret truly did want to be with him, Chateo found himself thinking of the young man called Adam. "I'll take you back where you belong," he replied as he continued to gaze into her eyes.

"I-I don't know where that is?"

He sighed heavily, while trying to ignore the violent pounding of his heart. She was so beautiful to gaze upon. How sad that she was so empty inside. "I think you know." His voice, filled with emotion, was barely articulate. He could not bear to look at her any longer, so he turned and began to walk away. He did not know if she understood him, but since she did not offer a retort, he assumed she comprehended the meaning of his words. If she didn't, he would not explain it to her, because this was something she had to discover for herself.

*   *   *

371

Travis Wade knew the dangers of traveling up the trail which clung to the mountain side above the Bavispe Barranca in the darkness of night. But he was not about to allow one more obstacle to prevent him from being reunited with his wife. He had to put his faith in his horse, because he knew his mangled knee would never allow him to climb the steep trail on foot. He told himself that once he reached the top and set foot on the flat ground of Pa-Gotzin-Kay, he would never leave again. He realized as he clung to his saddle horn, letting his horse pick its own pace, that the animal would do much better on the trail at night since the horse would not be afraid of the heights it could not see. Their pace was slow, but each time his mount put down another hoof, Travis' anxiety increased because his beautiful young bride was one step closer.

The horse ascended the last ridge as the sky was just beginning to fill with the hazy gray color that precedes dawn. Travis had stopped only once during the night and that was to talk to Hako, who was once again standing guard on the trail that led to the mountain paradise. Already, several campfires burned throughout the *rancheria* as the women prepared the morning meal. Life for these Indians was almost identical to the existence of their ancestors, and as long as the Apaches stayed at Pa-Gotzin-Kay, it would never change. Travis slid down from his horse's back and positioned his crutch under his arm. He intended to be walking when his wife saw him again. With slow steps he finally reached his destination without causing much commotion in the awakening village. Those who were standing outside their wickiups only gave him a curious stare as he limped past them. A dog barked at him, but its owner threw a rock at the animal and silenced it at once.

His mother-in-law was the first person he encountered as he approached their wickiup. He recalled the custom of mother-in-law avoidance, but at this moment he was too relieved to be back to care. His gaze fell upon Sky Dreamer's startled face as a grin broke across his weary face. The shaman gasped when she first saw him, but at once her expression grew calm.

"I did not expect you to arrive so early this morning, Travis Wade."

Travis opened his mouth to ask her how she knew he was coming, but her deep look of wisdom answered the question for him. He merely gave his head a slow nod as his admiration for this woman expanded. "My wife, is she still asleep?"

A broad smile came to Sky Dreamer's mouth as she realized she would be the one to reveal the surprise—his new son. She motioned for him to follow her, then paused when she noticed the crutch he was leaning on. Her visions had not told her why his return to Pa-Gotzin-Kay had been delayed, but now she understood. She would ask him about his leg later, though. Now she was too anxious to show him the baby he did not know existed.

Travis stumbled along beside the shaman, though he had no idea where they were going. Her face was glowing like that of a blushing young girl, so he did not sense she was about to show him something bad. As they approached another wickiup, he decided this was probably going to be the home he would share with Echo and that was why the shaman had led him to it. Sky Dreamer pulled back the animal hide from the doorway and stood back to allow Travis to enter. He hesitated as he bent down and caught the beaming expression upon his mother-in-law's face, wondering why her behavior was so odd.

In the center of the hut a small fire burned in a rock enclosure. Margaret Sinclair was just adding another handful of twigs to the tiny blaze when she was surprised by the appearance of a man in the doorway. She met Travis' shocked eyes for only a second, then glanced toward the sleeping form of her sister.

His green gaze followed her lead. For a moment, Travis was consumed with fear as he thought his wife was ill. Then he saw the infant swaddled in blankets at her side. He dragged his stiff leg through the opening, letting the crutch fall from his side. Dropping to the ground beside his slumbering wife, he slowly reached out and pulled the blanket away from the baby's face. Realization of his fatherhood hit him full force as he gazed down at the miniature copy of himself.

"It's a boy," Margaret said in a hoarse voice.

A nervous laugh broke from Travis. "But how . . . I mean . . . when?"

"Two days ago, but he was born a few weeks early. That's why he is so small." Margaret fought against the urge to cry. It seemed all she wanted to do lately was weep like a baby. But the birth of her nephew had summoned up emotions she had not felt for a long time. "I'll leave you alone with your family," she managed to get out before the threatening tears broke loose from the rims of her eyes.

Travis did not even glance up as she departed. He was too busy looking at his new son and falling in love with his wife again. His arms longed to hold both wife and child, but he was not sure if he should wake them. He carefully touched the downy thatch of blond hair which topped the baby's tiny round head, tenderly held one of his wife's hands in his trembling palm.

Echo was aware of his presence, even before she groggily managed to pry her eyelids apart. His touch was like an extension of her own being, and when her gaze rose to take in his face, the love she felt for Travis glistened in her blue eyes like stardust in the vast heavens.

"I'm home, Echo," Travis Wade whispered while their eyes caressed one another through the soft hazy glow of the firelight.

"You were never gone," she answered as she reached up and placed her hand over his rapidly pounding heart.

Chapter Twenty-Six

Margaret bent over in the waist-high water and let the gentle flow of the stream rinse the soapweed out of her long hair. The aloe lather floated away until the water ran pure and clear again. She gave a quick glance toward the bank before she emerged from the creek, though she was not overly concerned about an intrusion since she had followed the brook a long distance from the *ranchería* before disrobing and entering the cool stream. Picking up a woven blanket from the rock on which she had placed it earlier, she wrapped her damp body in its comforting warmth. Then, using a brush made of stiff grass bristles, she began to work the tangles from her thick hair as her thoughts wandered back to the village, then farther, beyond the rugged ledges of Pa-Gotzin-Kay.

Chateo's words would not be erased from her mind. He would take her back where she belonged, but she still was not able to figure out what he had meant by his remark. As dusk began to steal away the last rays of sunlight, her turquoise gaze traveled out over the shadowed grandeur of this high Sierra Madre stronghold. If only she could be as content here as the rest of her people. Her people! She had resisted this fact for so

377

long, but now she realized that no matter how far she ran, she could never run away from her Apache heritage. But did she really want to now?

She snuggled deeper into the cocoon of the blanket and smoothed her ebony tresses away from her face. Daylight was nearly gone, but she was in no rush to return to the *ranchería*. Even in the fading light a feeling of security reigned over this land. It was no wonder that her family and the rest of the villagers guarded their secret paradise with such devotion. As long as they could remain hidden atop of this mountain, they would never live in fear again. Margaret felt safe here, too. But then, she had also felt safe at the Carlisle School. It had been the white men who had decided she no longer belonged in Pennsylvania, but only she could determine if she belonged here at Pa-Gotzin-Kay.

She discarded the blanket and rose up from the rock. Against the elusive glow of dusk her smooth skin glistened like bronzed silk. For a moment she stood motionless and listened to the peaceful sound of the water running over rocks. There were so many things to consider before she made a final choice about her future; yet each time she tried to make a decision her strange dream intruded into her thoughts. Why would she have such beautiful dreams about Adam Washington and the schoolhouse on the reservation at Fort Sill? Undoubtedly, Adam would never forgive her, and the Indian reservation was the one place she dreaded most of all.

Margaret wrapped her arms around her midsection, completely oblivious to the breathtaking picture she presented, and to how she seemed to blend into the natural beauty of the land. During the months she had been at Pa-Gotzin-Kay a visible change had come over the young woman. Working in the fields and doing the chores necessary to survive in the wilderness had honed her body to perfection. Her raven tresses had grown almost as long as Echo's, and were now reaching below the curve of her slender waist. Her complexion, now a rich golden brown, accented her turquoise eyes and made them appear all the more vibrant. Margaret Sinclair possessed the exquisite beauty a man would worship. Sadly, there was not a man she loved enough to grant this privilege. Inside her was an overwhelming emptiness, and it continued to grow more intense with every breath she took. Not even the closeness she now shared with her family since the birth of Echo's son helped to ease the deep loneliness.

Chateo was traveling down the mountain in the morning, and he still had not talked to her about her own plans to leave Pa-Gotzin-Kay. But then, it was not easy for them to be in one another's presence, so perhaps it would be better if she didn't go with him. Margaret glanced around and noticed it had grown completely dark—so dark she could not even see where she had left her clothes. While reprimanding herself for being careless, she began to grope through weeds and brush for her skirt and tunic. When she located the garments lying in a heap upon the ground, she quickly donned them and began to make her way back to the *ranchería*. Though the trail was wide and well worn, she still had to move cautiously to avoid falling over a protruding rock or an overhanging branch.

A sense of surprise overcame Margaret when she realized she had not felt any panic because of the late hour, or at the thought of being alone in the woods. She had always harbored such a crippling fear of the dark, for it usually reminded her of the horror that occurred in her childhood. Many years had passed since the last time she had wandered this far away from her family and the *ranchería*. Now Margaret knew she would not find destruction and death when she returned to the village. Still, when she reached the edge of the quiet *rancheria* she stopped and looked toward the core of the village, just as she had done all those years ago. Gazing at the peaceful encampment before her made it difficult to remember the tragedy from the past. Again, Margaret was surprised to discover that her recollections of those horrible times seemed foggy and distant. Was it possible they were finally becoming just memories—a part of the past which would not continue to rule Margaret's entire life? Could it be true that she would be able to stop running away from the hideous nightmares at last? A startled revelation bolted through her, then was replaced by a feeling of awareness so strong she could never deny this new knowledge. There was a place where she belonged. She had been too selfish and blind to realize it until now, but Chateo had known all along.

Margaret lifted the hem of her long skirt and began to hurry into the circle of the wickiups. She had so much to do, and so many things to discuss with her family. Oh, if only she had not been so stubborn and had not wasted all this time! As she reached the front of her parents' dwelling she stopped to take a deep breath. For an instant lingering fears returned to haunt her. What if it was too late to start over? She turned and glanced in the direction of the wickiup Chateo shared with his daughter. No, she told herself firmly, the mistakes she had made in the past would not prevent her from fulfilling her true destiny.

It seemed as though Margaret had come full circle. She stood on the hillside overlooking Fort Sill; off in the distance she could see the wickiups that occupied the Apache section of the reservation. And farther on, she could see the small building that housed the Indian school. This was the structure she had glimpsed in her dream. Inside, she knew Adam would be waiting.

Almost a year had passed since she had left the Carlisle School in Pennsylvania, but she felt as if it had been a lifetime. She trembled with uncertainty as her gaze wandered over the Oklahoma territory. She could not help but wonder if she had made the right decision, but she would never know until she faced the last of her fears. Fleetingly she wondered if Travis Wade had experienced similar feelings when he had realized he could no longer run away from his desertion.

Being reunited with her family was Margaret's greatest joy. But living on a plateau high in the mountains of the Sierra Madre was not the destiny Usen had proposed for her. Absently, she ran a hand over the thin cotton material of her long tunic. A tiny pang of pain rippled through her breast as she gave up the last of her childish fantasies. She would never be clothed in velvet and silk; living as a white woman had merely been the dream of a young girl who had not yet faced reality.

"Are you sure you can go through with this?" Chateo asked quietly as he stood by her side.

Margaret nodded her head because she was afraid of bursting into tears again if she tried to speak.

"I will check on you every once in a while, and if you change your mind—"

"I won't," she said in a shaky voice. Her mind filled with the words Dona had spoken on the train—words about how they would be able to help their people with the knowledge they had gotten from the white man's school. Margaret was aware of how she had tried to use that knowledge for her own selfish purposes, in doing so hurting herself and those who cared about her the most. Once she walked down that hill, she knew there would be no turning back. Never again would she allow herself to disappoint Adam and Dona, nor would she inflict any more pain on Chateo by drifting in and out of his life. Her family understood her decision, and they had supported her wholeheartedly when she had departed from Pa-Gotzin-Kay.

Chateo bowed his head and prolonged his leaving for a few minutes longer. From the side of one eye he watched the young woman who stood motionless beside him. Her long dark hair was floating softly around her shoulders, lifted by the gentle breeze that was blowing along the top of the knoll. In a determined manner, Margaret stood, straight and tall with her head held high. But Chateo could see the slight trembling of her smooth chin, in spite of her brave act. Though he tried, he could not block off memories of their passionate rendezvous by the river in the comanchero hideout. He would always carry with him the vision of the beautiful young girl who had held him in her arms among the tall blades of grass as he transformed her into a woman. And now this same woman filled him with more pride than he had ever felt for another person.

"Adios, Margaret Sinclair," he said with a poignant smile. He resisted the urge to reach out to hug her as he backed away, and his movements hesitant, climbed into his saddle.

With actions as reluctant as Chateo's, Margaret turned to watch him wheel his horse about and head toward home. Her eyes filled with a glistening sheen of tears, but they did not fall when she raised her hand and called out, "Goodbye, my friend!"

His gaze met hers for a final time before he turned in the saddle and rode toward the opposite side of the crest of the hill. For a long time Margaret stared at the spot where he had disappeared from her view. Then, with a deep breath, she squared her shoulders and turned around to gaze down at the Indian reservation sprawled out below for as far as the eye could see. There was an endless amount of work to do down there, and she had already wasted enough time. She picked up her horse's reins and started to lead the animal down the slope, but something made her pause as she looked back over her shoulder one more time. Shimmering sunlight outlined the distant ridge of the hill, and within its golden glow Margaret's mind framed an image of the Apache renegade who would always cause the blood in her veins to race like wildfire on the tangled landscapes of her dreams.

Contemporary Fiction From
Robin St. Thomas

Fortune's Sisters   (2616, $3.95)

It was Pia's destiny to be a Hollywood star. She had complete self-confidence, breathtaking beauty, and the help of her domineering mother. But her younger sister Jeanne began to steal the spotlight meant for Pia, diverting attention away from the ruthlessly ambitious star. When her mother Mathilde started to return the advances of dashing director Wes Guest, Pia's jealousy surfaced. Her passion for Guest and desire to be the brightest star in Hollywood pitted Pia against her own family—sister against sister, mother against daughter. Pia was determined to be the only survivor in the arenas of love and fame. But neither Mathilde nor Jeanne would surrender without a fight. . . .

Lover's Masquerade   (2886, $4.50)

New Orleans. A city of secrets, shrouded in mystery and magic. A city where dreams become obsessions and memories once again become reality. A city where even one trip, like a stop on Claudia Gage's book promotion tour, can lead to a perilous fall. For New Orleans is also the home of Armand Dantine, who knows the secrets that Claudia would conceal and the past she cannot remember. And he will stop at nothing to make her love him, and will not let her go again . . .

Available wherever paperbacks are sold, or order direct from the Publisher. Send cover price plus 50¢ per copy for mailing and handling to Zebra Books, Dept. 3084, 475 Park Avenue South, New York, N.Y. 10016. Residents of New York, New Jersey and Pennsylvania must include sales tax. DO NOT SEND CASH.